Publish or Perish

by

Kerry Blaisdell

This is a work of fiction. Names, characters, places, and incidents are either the product of the author's wildly creative imagination or are used fictitiously, and any resemblance to actual persons living or dead, business establishments, events, or locales, is entirely coincidental. Swearsies!

Publish or Perish

Cover Art & Book Design by Kerry Blaisdell

Gun photo credit: Mika Järvinen (https://commons.wiki media.org/wiki/File:Walther_P38.jpg), „Walther P38", https://creativecommons.org/licenses/by/2.0/legalcode

Lello Ball Enterprises
P.O. Box 331
Beaverton, OR 97075

Publishing History: First Edition, 2019
Print ISBN 978-1-951141-00-4
Digital ISBN 978-1-951141-01-1

Published in the United States of America

"You scared me half to death."

"Sorry," Emma said. "When I saw the broken glass—"

"And I really don't like you staying here tonight, with or without Bethanne."

"What do you want me to do? Besides, it's not likely they'd come back tonight."

"I still don't like it." Vin shrugged, as though shaking something off, then said for no apparent reason, "I'm not a knight in shining armor."

"I didn't think you were."

He stared at her, then blew out a breath. "Have you considered becoming a nun?"

"Uh—"

"Never mind, don't answer that." He sighed, looked put-upon, then picked up her hand and pressed his thumbs into her palm. Emma fought back a moan.

"Here's the thing, Mike. Azi didn't exactly *tell* me you were a boy. But he implied it."

His eyes were dark, lids half-lowered, and she said, "Yes?"

He tugged her closer, pulling her against his side, and continued to work his magic on her muscles. "For weeks, in my mind, you've been Azi's buddy Mike. Then I found out who you were, met your kids, and the adjustment was…weird." He put the first hand down and reached for the other, bringing it to his lips and blowing gently on it.

"And now…?" she managed.

Vin's face hovered over hers. He was going to kiss her. God, he'd *better* kiss her. His voice was low, and he murmured, "Now I'm over it…Mike."

Dedication

This book is dedicated to all the research scientists out there who work doggedly, day after day, trying to make our lives, our health, and our world better. Most of you spend your days hidden in the background, in labs, or hospitals, or research institutes, doing work that isn't sexy or publicized, or sometimes even credited to you. But *I* know you're there, really at the forefront of everything that matters. So…

Thank you for all you do!

Chapter One

Nicholas, Patron Saint of:
Maidens, Murderers, Newlyweds and Thieves

On Valentine's Day, a Friday, Emma O'Manny woke up with two kids, a minivan, a house in the Portland suburbs, and a husband with a sick sense of humor. Three days later, she woke up with a headache, a bottle of Tums, no Kleenex—and a purpose.

"God *damn* him!" she said into her cell's speakerphone as she turned left onto Terwilliger. "I *am* going back for my master's, no matter what he and his *girlfriend* say. If that son-of-a-bitch thinks I'll lie down and take this, or that he'll get the kids or the house—"

Emma hit the steering wheel, her sweaty palm sliding off, and the car swerved toward the nearby jogging path. Tall firs loomed in the gray pre-dawn, dark and menacing, and she jerked the wheel, over-compensating, before settling back into the rain-slicked lane.

"Emma!" Karen James, best friend extraordinaire, sounded worried. "Be careful! Hang up and call me from the lab!"

Emma inhaled the musty heat of the defroster. Counted to ten, blew the breath out, and took another one. "I'm fine—don't hang up—please."

"Okay. But you have to calm down—it won't help if you…get in an *accident.*"

Shit—her kids were up. Karen couldn't say "if you go over the edge and die," because then they'd ask what the hell Mommy was doing—when they should be asking, what was *Daddy* doing?

As though reading her thoughts, Karen repeated, "I really didn't know. Honest—if I'd had any idea, I never would've taken the kids for the weekend. Screw him."

"I know. It's not your fault."

"I'm really sorry, Em."

Deep breath. Blow it out. Focus on the taillights of the car ahead.

Her hands on the wheel felt foreign. They didn't belong to her any more than did the white face and purple-shadowed eyes she'd seen in the mirror this morning. *She* was not-quite forty, blonde with brown eyes, a mother, a wife, about to go back to school and get her M.S. in Computer Science. The woman in the mirror was middle-aged, haggard from two days of lying in bed, nursing ginger ale and crackers, and about to be a divorcée.

A *Catholic* divorcée.

Karen's voice was hesitant. "Do you want to talk about it?"

Emma laughed—a sound that was also foreign. Brittle. But then, she was brittle.

"What's to talk about? He brought me flowers, a box of candy, and—" *Deep breath. Hold. Don't cry. Don't cry.* "—seduced me and then shoved the divorce papers at me and left."

Except that was a lie. He hadn't seduced her; she'd been more than willing. Which was the truly humiliating part.

"Bast—what a fu—" Karen choked. "I can't even say how pissed I am, because, well…"

"Kids are there."

"Yes."

"And you can't call him a bastard because that's a 'bad' word, and he's their father."

The father of her children—*her husband of fifteen years.* And she'd had no clue. None.

Bored with his life? Girlfriend? Taking her to *Hawaii?*

She tried to relax, to un-grip the wheel, just a tiny bit, but her hands weren't hers, and wouldn't do what she wanted.

In ten minutes, they'd have to.

Get in. Get her stuff. Get out.

"Emma—are you sure you want to go to the lab today?"

"I have to. You're taking the kids to school, but I have to pick them up. This is hard enough. I need to do it before I see them."

"I'll call in sick. If you wait a couple hours, I'll come with you."

"Thanks. But if I wait, Oscar and the other lab rats will be there, and I can't face them. It's too much—they *know*. I'm sure they've known all along."

"I understand, honey. Do you want me to come over tonight?"

The tears threatened, and she swallowed hard. "No—really. I have to tell the kids myself."

Tell them Daddy had dumped Mommy, gone to Hawaii with another woman, and was moving out when he—*they*—came back in ten days. How exactly could she explain all that? To an eleven-year-old boy and a six-year-old girl?

"If you're sure. But tomorrow, I make lemon drops and we burn his boxers."

Emma laughed in spite of herself. "Thanks, Kar. You're the best."

"Hey, you did it for me. Although even Rob looks better next to Dan. At least our dumping was mutual." Karen hesitated. "Have you…told your mom?"

Emma's fingers were so tight on the steering wheel, she'd never uncurl them. "Look," she said finally, "I'm almost to the hospital. I'd better hang up now."

Silence. Then Karen said, "You're *sure* I can't help?"

"I'm sure. I have a plan."

"That can't be good. You won't do anything dumb, will you?"

"Define dumb. Would that be marrying a low-life, cheating, scum-sucking bastard? 'Cause I already did that."

"Just be careful, okay?"

"Always. I'll call you later. Tell the kids I love them."

Emma hung up and turned left at the sign for St.

Elizabeth's, taking the back way on the narrow, one lane street lined with evergreens and small post-World War II houses. Old habits died hard. Five months since she'd been up to the lab—since Dan-the-bastard O'Manny had, oh so magnanimously, said he didn't need her as an admin assistant anymore.

Take some time off, honey. It's too late to apply for grad schools this year, but Juney's in first grade, Justin's in fifth. You can prep for next year. Oh—and the real *reason is so I can put that skank I'm screwing in your place. In your bed, at your desk, in your role.*

Shit. She was going to vomit again.

She turned right, right again toward the tiny church, left up the hill, past the odd mix of patient clinics and administrative buildings, then into the lot serving the tightly clustered research buildings that comprised the upper-hill portion of the Oregon Scientific Health University campus. Another old habit. She still had her parking pass, in case Dan's car was ever out of commission. With a five-year wait on the permit list, it seemed prudent not to cancel. Plus, you never knew when you'd have to come back.

Ha.

She rolled into a spot and killed the engine, and the sudden stillness slammed into her.

Since Friday, she'd done little more than run to the bathroom every few hours to throw up. Her whole body had been in turmoil, her mind whipping from utter denial to wondering what she'd done wrong—*why didn't Dan love her anymore?*

She shoved the door open, yanked herself up and out, and slammed it shut. Then she stomped across the courtyard to the Sion Institute for Advanced Biomedical Research.

Sion. "Idealized, harmonious community," her ass.

There wasn't a single Principal Research Investigator who wouldn't stab a fellow PI in the back if it moved his grant app to the top of the pile, or his research into publication faster. Discoveries were great, but if another PI published first, it was career homicide. They were like spiders, hiding in their lab-webs, coming out long enough to sabotage each other's work before scuttling back into the dark.

Except Dan. Loyal, honest, above-the-muck Dan.

Breathe.

Get in. Get her stuff. Get out.

She made it to the heavy glass doors just as the auto-locks clicked open at six-fifteen. Two elevator doors, nine floors, and one card key swipe later, she emerged into the beaker-, vial- and paper-strewn lab that had been her second home for ten years. She flipped on the fluorescents, saw the orange light on the alarm pad, and punched in the code before it notified security of her presence. Then she faced the room.

Everything looked the same.

If nothing changed in ten years, why would five months make a difference?

Except something had changed. She'd stopped coming in—*take a break, sweetheart*—Mollie McBride had started— *she can be my admin* and *a postdoc*—and Emma's desk had been rearranged.

Bitch.

Get in. Get her stuff. Get out.

But her stuff wasn't there. Laptop, file boxes, photos of her kids—all replaced by a new desktop system, metal wall files, and pics of Mollie's friends. What had she expected? God—she could *not* vomit again—or cry. Not now. Her stuff. Where the hell was her stuff?

She checked once more on the crowded desk, shoved into a corner outside Dan's office. The space was so tight that with his door open, the desk disappeared. She'd always hated it, put there as an afterthought—just like her marriage.

The anger boiled, and she shoved it down. This was so unlike her. She had to get a grip—for her kids' sake, if nothing else.

Her gaze roamed the lab. Long rows of metal-topped

counters crammed with machinery, books, papers, and research paraphernalia of all descriptions—but not her stuff. The food fridge, where lunches were kept. The bio-sample fridge, for anything *not* food, that should never, *ever*, be anywhere near food. But not her stuff.

And then her gaze landed on Dan's office. Of course. She tried the door. Locked, and her key didn't work.

Good for him. He'd changed the locks.

Bad for him. She was handy with a coat hanger.

Emma grabbed Mollie's lab coat off the nearby stand, pulled it off the metal hanger, and threw it on the floor, stepping on it for good measure. Then she untwisted the hanger, hooking an end between the door and the jamb, around the simple knob lock. All she had to do was jimmy it up and down and—

Pop! The latch was forced open and the hanger jerked free, throwing her back. The door hung open for an instant before starting to swing shut and—*she'd got it!*

Pulling herself up and into the office, she flipped on the light. Sure enough, a cardboard box under the desk held a jumble of her personal effects, topped by her precious laptop.

Asshole.

The rest of the room was as unchanged as the lab. Big corner office with picture windows.

Okay, it was scientist-big, not CEO-big, but it was still more impressive than her tiny desk behind the door. Which was now *Mollie's* desk behind the door, so maybe there was some justice after all.

She grabbed the box and one of the portable files. She'd have to make two trips. Maybe on the second, she'd find a Sharpie and scribble all over Dr. Dan's big freaking windows.

Vandalism could be your friend, if you knew how to use it.

****

Day One, Hour Two on the Job, stuck in a cruiser,

staring at a gas station while they drank their coffee and waited for something—anything—to come across the scanner. And so far, Vin Bronislovas was unimpressed with the kid they'd given him as a partner.

Except it was the other way around. He might be twenty years older than Joey Zitface, and have come from a precinct in South Deering, Chicago—Area 51, for cripe's sake—to l'il ole Portland, Oregon, but *he* was the new guy. *He* was the rube.

Damn it. Bad enough the state-to-state move meant he'd had to go through the Academy a second time—the *Advanced* Academy, but still—did he have to start at the bottom when he got out? If only the detective position he'd coveted hadn't vanished in a puff of bureaucratic smoke. If he hadn't promised Azi they'd be here for Thanksgiving, and Tony hadn't kicked his renters out to give them a place to live.

If, if, if.

He'd *had* to leave Chicago. Even now, six months later, he would've taken a desk job, anything, to get away—from the Deering Darling—the Long Island Lolita of the Midwest.

Isadora Higuera.

Vin shuddered.

At least the uniform spot had materialized. And the low-key northwest lifestyle was *exactly* what he wanted. Quiet. Simple. Not complicated and messy, like Chicago.

If only his partner wasn't a twelve-year-old.

Right on cue, the kid piped up again. "So, what does Vytautas Bronislovas mean, anyway? It's Polish, right?"

Vin deliberately unclenched his jaw, reminding himself most people would've guessed Russian, which was worse. "*Lithuanian.* From *Lithuania.*"

"Lithuania? Where's that?"

Vin closed his eyes, waited a beat, then said, "Next to Poland."

"Oh. So they're, like, the same?"

"Not really." *Shut up. Just shut up while you can.*

"So what does it mean?"

Vin sighed. Shrugged his shoulders, working the kinks out, his duty belt creaking. Drank from the paper cup he held. The station coffee was better here. Northwesterners knew how to do coffee—and beer. He took another sip. Joey looked at him expectantly. Ah, fuck it.

"Vytautas means 'chasing the people.' Bronislovas means 'protection and glory.'"

Joey's jaw dropped. "You're kidding, right?"

"Unfortunately, no."

"'Cause that's as bad as my phys ed teacher, Mr. Court. I'm not making this up. Your dad's a cop, too, right?"

Another sigh. "Was. Yes. He's dead."

"Funny sense of humor. How'd he know you'd go on the Job?"

"I have no idea." Vin should have picked another profession on purpose. But this was what he wanted to do—always had, and nothing else mattered.

"Hey—what about Tony? That's *Italian*."

The kid actually sounded suspicious and for the first time in a long while, a smile sneaked onto Vin's face. Joey was persistent, he'd give him that. In less than an hour he'd weaseled out most of Vin's vitals, including that he had four brothers, three sisters, and a dozen nieces and nephews; that Tony was the only sibling not still in Chicago; and that Vin and his Uncle Azi had moved here last fall, were crashing at Tony's rental house, and were neither of them encumbered by anyone of the female persuasion.

Thank God. The last thing Vin wanted was a woman needling her way between him and Azi. Az was a handful all on his own.

Vin scowled out the window, then realized Zitface still waited for an answer. Cripes. "Tony's short for Antanas— Lithuanian for Anthony."

"Like Vin for Vytautas?"

"Sort of."

"Does Vytautas mean Vincent?"

"No. Look—"

The radio crackled on. Joey zeroed in on it—more points for him—and when the dispatcher finished, he yanked his seatbelt on. "That's us!"

"Relax, kid. It's just a tripped alarm. Probably the owner punched his code in wrong. Happens all the time."

The look Joey shot him was expressive and explicit. "You're shitting me, right?"

The look Vin shot back was equally so. "What?"

Rolled eyes. You're-a-dumbass shake of the head. You-don't-know-how-stupid-you-are twitch of the lips.

"Not just *any* alarm." Joey shoved the car in gear and screeched right onto Sam Jackson Park Road. "The *only* alarm on the Hill that bypasses campus security and goes straight to us. OSHU authorized it last month. Big dealy bop PI, researching vaccines or something."

"PI?" Vin had only learned today that the OSHU campus, or the Hill as it was called, would be his beat, and while he knew it was a teaching and research hospital, he had no clue how it worked. South Chicago hadn't been a hotbed of biomedical science. More like of drug and gang violence.

"Principal Investigator," Joey explained, as he veered back and forth up the twisting, two-lane road carved onto the hillside, knocking Vin hard against the door.

"Jeez. Whose bright idea was it to put a hospital up on a hill with lousy street access? Slow down, will you? I'm telling you—I've got a feeling about this. We'll get up there and find the monkeys got out of the cage or something. This isn't a career-breaker call."

"No. But it could be a career-*making* one."

Vin just shook his head. Kids. Who the hell let kids become cops anyway? He'd never been that young, had he?

Surreptitiously he gripped the oh-shit handle and hoped they weren't about to careen off the edge into the canyon. Oh for the unending flat of the Midwest. At least when you floored it, you went in a straight line. None of this hairpin curve crap.

Then he grinned for real. Ah, fuck it. At least they were moving.

****

Emma sat back to check her handiwork. This was so far out of character, it was like admiring someone else's artistry. It'd taken longer than expected, but was still faster than a pen. Thank heaven the minivan still had junk in it from December—a.k.a., Holiday Craft Month.

Yes. Dr. Dan and *Mollie* would get quite the shock when they returned from *Hawaii*. Maybe they'd come in to catch the sunrise while sipping their coffee. Thanks to the angle of the building, both Mt. St. Helens and Mt. Hood were visible through the windows.

Emphasis on the *were*. Now the only thing visible was yards and yards of Smith's Pink Spray Tree Flocking-in-a-Can. She'd run out or she would've done the desk, too—but white was almost as good. And gold and silver added nice touches to the filing cabinets and shelves.

But the *pièce de résistance* was Dan's monitor. He'd *needed* it to complete his research—*had* to have a bigger screen, so he could finish his vaccine paper and rush it to publication, before someone else got there first, and he lost a decade of work. Or worse—his position at the university, or even his lab. But back then, the Sion was in start-up mode, bleeding money left and right, and none of his early grants covered equipment. So he'd been *forced* to dip into the kids' college funds to pay for it.

Now, thanks to his soon-to-be-pubbed research, the National Vaccine Research Endowment had funded him to the tune of one million dollars—which was lucky for him, because his five grand, flat-panel, goddamn huge display was now solid fuzzy green, front and back, except right in the middle where she'd sprayed a huge red, furry "FUCK YOU."

Merry Christmas—and Happy Valentine's Day.

So what if her blouse was a rainbow of pink-gold-silver-red-green? Or that she'd mis-aimed one can and half her head was crusted white? It was all worth it.

Get in. Get her stuff. And vandalize the flock out of the place.

Queasy panic jolted through her, but she shoved it down. Wrecking Dan's office was juvenile, petty, and wouldn't help in the long run. But he deserved it. Jesus—he'd dumped her on *Valentine's Day*. She would *not* feel remorse for giving in to her anger, just this once.

Emma set down the last can. Drew in a deep breath. Counted to ten. Exhaled.

And felt as free as it was possible to feel, when the whole rock-solid foundation of your life had just exploded.

She rose and flipped off the lights, bending to retrieve her keys from the floor. Started backing out of the office, still stooping, through the door she'd propped open earlier. Glanced to the right of the doorframe, just above floor level—and noticed the red blinking light of the new, additional security pad a fraction of a second before her rear bumped into something very large, very muscular, and very not-messing-around.

"Shit."

"Yep," a deep male voice said. "That's about the size of it."

Chapter Two

St. Mark the Evangelist:
Captives, Lawyers, and Scrofulous Disease

Emma jerked upright, then froze, though her surging adrenaline screamed *run*! Without looking, she knew it was a cop. He had that feeling—a bedrock of Authority, his tone gravel-with-a-purpose. Much as her ex-military father had sounded before he got sick.

What should she do? What *could* she do? She was breaking and entering—not to mention vandalizing— caught with the evidence all over her.

And she still stood against the cop, her back to his massive chest, her head bumping his chin. His power radiated over her and she tried to step away, but his hands clamped onto her shoulders like iron.

"Whoa, there. Easy, lady."

"I'm not going anywhere." Oh God—her heart hammered its way to an out-of-body experience—nausea churned up her throat, and she dug her nails into her sweaty palms.

"Nevertheless. Hands up where I can see them."

Breathe—in—out. In… Out…

It wasn't working—*oh God*—she was going to throw up on a cop.

"I'm *warning* you, lady."

Her face-hands-neck were icy hot. *In. Out. Don't faint. Don't faint. Clench your fists to raise your blood pressure.*

"Hands up—*now!*"

Breathe. Oh—God—her stomach muscles tightened—

"Uh, Vin?" a new, higher male voice said. "I, uh, think

you should let her go."

With an audible *pop!* the dam burst, panic flooded, driving out rational thought.

"Shut up, kid. Lady, I said *get your hands up.*"

The ache roiled—wave after wave—she had nothing left—

"Seriously, Vin. I think she's about to—"

Emma brought a hand up to cover her mouth at the same moment the cop named Vin yanked her toward the wall. She stumbled, fell into him—and retched six crackers and half a can of ginger ale all over his crisply starched dark blue chest.

"—hurl," the other man finished on an aggrieved sigh.

"Ah, fuck." Officer Vin backed away but she clung to him, smears of flocking relocating from her shirt to his, mingling grotesquely with the contents of her stomach.

"Sorry," she managed weakly, looking up at him. Then wished she hadn't.

If he'd *sounded* mad, it was nothing to how he *looked.* His blue eyes scowled into slits, topped by auburn brows, so fiercely lowered, they connected above his large, angled nose. His lips were flattened, his chin jutting so far out, it rivaled her dad's.

But what really got her was the hair. Short, neat, and *red.* Lighter than his brows, it *glowed,* backlit by the ceiling fluorescents, and she had the insane urge to ruffle it.

"You all right, lady?" The other man, also a cop, was at her side. With his help, she righted herself, letting go of Vin, who transferred the scowl to his soggy, smelly shirt.

"Fuck."

Inexplicably, she missed the feel of him supporting her. Sure, he was mad as hell, and probably wanted nothing more than to arrest her ass. But the human contact had grounded her.

Oh shit—*Damn it. Breathe.*

"I'm—I'll be fine." She turned blindly to one of the lab sinks, using the cool water to rinse her mouth and face. Too late, she recalled the flocking, which now oozed south in a gooey mudflow. Paper towels only made it worse, and she gave up.

"You wanna start by telling us your name?"

The second cop, whose clip-on tag read *Officer Joe Freeman*, was younger than his partner, in his twenties at most. He also wasn't looking at her like she was a slug he'd like to salt, so she took a breath and squared her shoulders.

"Emma O—" What the hell—the divorce wouldn't be final for months. "—O'Manny."

At her hesitation, he quirked an eyebrow, proving himself more observant than he looked. He probably got that a lot.

"Got any ID?" Vin growled, and Emma's gaze snapped back to him.

He'd given up on his shirt, and instead lounged against a metal counter like he hadn't a care. She wasn't fooled. He meant business, and right now, she was it.

"Over there." She nodded toward Mollie's desk, where she'd set her badge and the second file box, while she went on her crime spree. At least the laptop was safely in the car.

Officer Freeman retrieved the badge and glanced at it, then at her, and frowned. He handed it to Vin, who repeated the actions, in order. While he was occupied, she peeked at his nametag, briefly registered an indecipherable jumble of letters, and decided "Vin" was okay for now.

"Look, lady," he said, "I don't know who you are or what you're doing here. But unless you can produce valid picture ID, you're coming with us."

"My purse is in the car. But that *is* my ID."

"Sure it is."

He shoved the badge at her, and she got it. Of course they'd be suspicious of an ID, with *her* photo, above the name "Michael A. O'Manny."

"I can explain."

"Uh-huh."

"No, really." She looked from him to Officer Freeman,

who appeared to be reconsidering his slug-salting position. Turning back to Vin, she found he'd moved closer, invading her space, a vein in his neck twitching ominously. She stepped back and bumped the counter. "That *is* my badge, and my name *is* Emma—*M*—*A*—short for *Michael Anne*. My parents' names."

"Yeah?"

She nodded, relieved. "Yes."

"Tell me another one."

He took a black zip-tie off a clip on his belt, then shoved her against the sink, forcing the tie over her wrists behind her back, and cinching it tight.

"Ouch! What the—"

He yanked her around and thrust her ahead of him in a bad replay of every cop show she'd ever watched. She stumbled and looked down, barely maintaining her balance.

Officer Freeman cleared his throat. "Uh, Vin?"

"Shut up, kid."

"No, really, Vin—you might wanna watch where you're going."

Emma's head whipped up and she stopped dead. "Oh, no…"

Vin, a little slow on the uptake, slammed into her, knocking her flat after all—right at the feet of OSHU President-and-CEO Parker Allan James, imposing as usual in an impeccably tailored gray suit. Behind him crowded half the O'Manny Lab, arriving for work. The dark brown mane of Parker's hair and the silver sparks of his eyes made him look like a lion, defending his pride—a.k.a. Dan's post-doctoral research assistants—who murmured or tittered, depending on whether they'd recognized her or not.

"What is going on here?" he demanded.

This *couldn't* be happening. She had to hide before Parker realized—but it was too late.

"*Emma?*" He pulled her up, then glared at Vin. "Why are you arresting this woman?"

Vin glanced from Parker's furious face to her no-doubt

mortified one, and for the first time, looked uncertain. He cleared his throat. "The alarm in Dr. O'Manny's office went off."

"I know that! I am automatically notified of *any* security breech."

Vin's Adam's apple bobbed. "We, uh, found *her* coming out of the office. She…" He looked at the badge, slid his thumb over her picture, then held it out to Parker. "I don't suppose this really *is* her ID?"

Parker didn't even glance at it. He fixed his steely gaze on Vin, and Emma immediately rescinded every complaint she'd ever made about him, the way he ran the university, his distribution of funds, or anything else.

"*Michael Anne O'Manny* is Dr. O'Manny's *wife*. She worked here for *ten years*. Of course she has a legitimate reason to be here now."

"Then why didn't she disarm the security panel?"

Emma swallowed. Probably not a good time to mention the divorce. "I, uh, haven't been here much recently—it's a new system."

"Told you they just installed it," Officer Freeman piped up.

Vin looked at him with distaste, then at Parker, and Emma discovered that another thing she suddenly liked about Parker was his air of authority. Vin hadn't even asked who he was, Parker was *that* self-confident.

Parker sent her an encouraging nod, and she continued. "I came to pick up my things. Dan put them in his office for safekeeping, and when I, uh, unlocked the door, I forgot the second alarm."

A few of the postdocs regarded her curiously—likely wondering if she knew about Mollie—and she turned away from their cautious pity. So far, no one had questioned her Flocky-the-Clown fashion choices. If she could just escape, she'd 'fess up later and pay any damages. She should have known getting mad would only hurt *her*, not Dan.

Then she looked at Vin and felt better. *She* was only

covered in flocking, whereas *he* was covered in flocking and vomit. Of course, she was still zip-tied—a fact he noticed at the same time she did. He released her, then stepped as far away as possible in the small space.

"My apologies for the misunderstanding," he said, not meeting her gaze.

Parker broke in smoothly, "Quite all right." Then to Emma, "Would you like any help with your things?"

Holy Hannah—she was getting away. She chafed her wrists where the plastic had rubbed them, and saw Vin look away. *You should feel guilty, you overbearing brute.*

To Parker she said, "No, thanks. I'm fine. Just this one box. I can manage."

Officer Freeman obligingly handed it to her and Parker guided her toward the lab's exit. "You should come back soon. The Sion isn't the same without you."

"Thanks, Parker. I'll do that."

"I'll never understand why Dan didn't want your help finishing the paper. I was afraid—well, never mind. He's first to publish, and that's what counts."

Oh God—did *he* know about Mollie?

Vin was watching her again, and she forced a smile. "Officers. Thank you, and, uh, no hard feelings."

Bored with the show, the lab rats dispersed to their stations. A few nodded as she walked by, and some greeted her warmly. Oscar Dellinger, Dan's chief research assistant professor-slash-computer guru, frowned at the office door, then at the box she carried.

Please don't make a stink.

It was just her old notes. What possible use were they to him? He opened his mouth, then looked down at one of the several MP3 players he carried everywhere, into which he was currently plugged. Evidently she wasn't worth stopping his entertainment.

She'd almost made it past him when the lab doors burst open, admitting Dan's partner Nick Forte, who was also the Sion's Director. His face was slack and white, and his whole body shook.

"Emma! Thank God I've found you—your mom's frantic. Karen called, but you're not answering your cell, and Dan's desk phone is going straight to voicemail."

"Karen!" She dropped the box and her knees buckled. "The kids—are they—"

The room spun, whirled, *Jesus—no—*

Suddenly a pair of muscular arms caught her from behind. "Easy, lady."

Vin. She sagged against him, clutching his forearms, trying to make sense of Nick's words.

"No—the kids are fine—it's not them. It's Dan."

He drew up short, seeming to realize the situation called for more finesse. He sucked in a ragged breath, and she saw the tears he hadn't wiped away. And she *knew*. But he said it anyway.

"Emma—I'm so sorry. There was an accident. They—he—was flying. Island-hopping."

He broke. The floor tilted. His voice echoed from a long way away.

"I'm sorry, Emma. He—Dan died."

And then the room spun in earnest, whirling, flying, out of control. She managed a "What...?", thankful Vin still supported her. Her legs were useless, numb. She couldn't think, couldn't see, couldn't feel. Her vision tunneled, silver, then gray, then black at the edges.

"Dan's dead?" Parker demanded just as Officer Freeman said from the door of Dan's office, "Uh, Vin? I think you better come see this..."

And the black wasn't at the edges anymore. It was everywhere—in her eyes, her ears, her heart. Numb fingers dug into Vin's arms. He was still there. He hadn't let go.

"I'm going to faint," she said.

And heard him say, just before she did, "I know..."

****

"God damn day." Vin shoved out of the station and stalked to his car. "Fucking ten hours of hell." He got in,

slammed the door, and pounded the steering wheel.

His *first* day on the job, and it was the Deering Darling all over again. When Emma—*Mrs.* Goddamn *O'Manny*—had backed out of her husband's office, bent over just enough that he caught one tantalizing glimpse of creamy flesh and the lacy red of her panties above her jeans—well, as Azi would say, he might be sadder and wiser, but he sure as hell wasn't dead.

Then there was the glimpse of cleavage when she'd straightened, the whiff of her scent. She'd been right under his nose—he couldn't *help* inhaling her. Under all that acrid craft product, she'd smelled…natural. Warm, spicy, and sexy as hell.

Damn it—get a grip.

Then she'd moved to step away. A normal female response when pressed full-body against a complete stranger. But she'd been pressed into him *just* long enough that irrational fear spiked through him—that Zitface would notice, and that he, Vin, really was that dumb.

Then came the anger—at her, the easy target. At Zitface, for witnessing the debacle. But mostly at himself, for doing a shitty job. Instead of staying focused, he'd been a Class A jackass, first shoving his weight around, then jumping in to save her.

Or maybe it was simple human empathy. He must have some left, somewhere. She'd been so vulnerable, and based on their limited acquaintance—and the quantity of flocking in her husband's office—she didn't do vulnerable often.

He shook his head. Even covered in gunk, she was pretty. Honey blonde hair, eyes that were half brown, half golden—and a lush mouth that had spewed chunks all over him.

Fuck.

He rammed the car into gear and fled the station, the perpetual damp gray overhead only darkening his mood. At least Chicago was *sunny.* According to some people, Portland was, too; just not from November to March. What he wouldn't give for the clouds to lift, even for a day.

Fifteen minutes later, when he reached the rental house and pulled onto the cracked concrete drive, things were more in perspective. The chance of seeing Emma—*Mrs. O'Ma*—ah, screw it—*Emma* again were zilch. Nada. Never gonna happen. It wasn't the Deering Darling—it was one goddamn day.

The front door of Tony's craftsman banged open, and Uncle Azi barreled down the steps, his awkward gate nearly tripping him in his excitement. "Hey, Vinny! How was your first day! Didja shoot anyone? I betcha shot someone. Did he die?"

Vin grinned. "Feeling bloodthirsty, Az?"

"Youbetcha." Azi grinned, too, his joy a balm to Vin's soul.

No matter what else was wrong, Azi loved him. Wholeheartedly. Unquestioningly. Just for being Vin. And because of *that*, Vin would never, ever regret moving here. Portland was much better for someone with Azi's needs. Not that Chicago was exactly bad. It was just big. And busy. And easier for Azi to get lost in, literally and figuratively.

Vin got out of the car, barely prepping himself in time to receive Azi's bear hug tackle. The same one he did whenever Vin came home, whether he was gone minutes or hours.

"Hey, Az! You getting stronger?" Vin made a show of examining Azi's biceps. "I think you are—you work out today or something?"

Azi's grin went ear-wide, his upturned green eyes crinkling with delight. "Nah, Vin. You know I din't. Soozee's here. I helped in the yard!"

On cue, Vin's sister-in-law Susan appeared on the porch just as Tony's station wagon pulled in behind Vin's sedan. All the doors opened at once and various nieces and nephews spewed out, hurling themselves at Vin's legs.

"Watch out for Uncle Vin's bad knee!" Tony called.

The pipsqueaks obligingly focused on Vin's right leg,

avoiding his still-healing left one, as their dad came up the walk. Tony was older, taller, and broader than Vin, with his dark auburn hair tinged gray, his eyes a lighter blue. Thank God for Tony. Some brothers pounded the shit out of you growing up, then ignored you as an adult. Tony'd pounded the shit out of him, then been there through every stupid phase of Vin's life. Including this one.

"Hey, bro, how'd it go?" Tony's tone was a little too casual, and Vin noted Susan's sharp interest. And suddenly, none of it mattered.

"About as well as could be expected."

"What happened?" Susan's face and voice were filled with concern.

The pipsqueaks let go of Vin and shifted their focus to Azi, who giggled helplessly under the assault. Vin walked up the steps to the porch, took the beer Susan handed him, and sat next to Tony while she went back for two more. Then he told them. Most of it. Some things were too personal, and God damn it, he *would* get past this.

Susan was laughing outright, and Tony sipped his beer, his gaze carefully on the kids and Azi, now rolling on the grass, shrieking. Vin tried to look fierce and failed.

Susan swiped at her eyes, the corners of her mouth twitching up. "Mrs. O'Manny really threw up on you?"

"Yep."

"A lot?"

"Nah. I don't think she'd eaten much."

He frowned, thinking about everything. Like Emma's soft weight when she'd fainted in his arms, the way he'd lowered her to the floor. His relief when she came to moments later, her despair that her world had shattered. The way she'd sobbed the whole God-awful divorce story into his chest, his arms tightening around her, unable to deny her simple human comfort in her hour of need, even though she had just hurled all over him.

Christ, he was messed up.

Tony shot him a sideways glance. "Flocking?"

"The lady has style."

"What's the lab do?"

"Immunizations. Supposedly, O'Manny proved a DTaP vaccine doesn't cause autism."

"DTaP?"

Susan rolled her eyes. "Diphtheria, tetanus, and pertussis. Gee, Tony, think you could come to *any* of the kids' doctor visits?"

"Women's work," Tony deadpanned, then ducked when she pretended to thwack him.

"Caveman." But she grinned, and they exchanged one of those married-forever kisses Vin's grandparents used to do.

Susan pulled back first, leaning comfortably in Tony's arms. "Vaccine safety, huh? I don't remember reading that anything was proved conclusively."

Vin said, "The good doc's paper isn't published yet. The research is done, but now the partner, Nick Forte, has to polish and submit. It'll come out in a few months."

"Wow—it'll make waves when it does."

"You up on all that?"

"Of course. Any good parent is."

"Hey!" Tony said, but she ignored him.

"Big hotbed issue. Something like one in forty kids is diagnosed with an autism spectrum disorder now, way up from even ten years ago. Parents want someone to blame. There was a big flap about the mercury in vaccines, but they outlawed it, and autism's still on the rise. Some people are so freaked, they aren't vaccinating their kids, and now possibly deadly diseases like whooping cough are becoming more common again, too. If Dr. O'Manny proved a vaccine is safe—one hundred percent *proved* it—it would mean *big* money for the manufacturer."

Vin leaned forward, considering. "And the lab, too, I bet."

"Sure. That kind of science brings prestige to the researcher, money for his lab, fame and fortune for the Institute, *and* for the university. It's a trickle up effect." At

Tony's evident surprise, Susan looked smug. "I read. That and Ben's mom. She works somewhere up there."

"Ben?"

"Zoë's boyfriend."

Tony's gaze cut to his oldest daughter, laughing and running across the yard, looking like a nice, wholesome sixteen-year-old. "Zoë has a new boyfriend? Did I okay this?"

"You okayed the last one. I assumed the contract was self-perpetuating."

Tony looked at Vin. "Don't have daughters. They'll take years off your life."

"That's clichéd. I'm not having kids period. Why single out girls?"

"You don't want kids? Ever?" Susan sounded genuinely shocked.

"I have a kid." Vin gestured with his beer toward the yard, where Azi had turned on the hose, aiming it at the pipsqueaks and Zoë just as they screeched and dove out of range.

Susan wasn't convinced. "Don't you want a wife? A family?"

"I have a family—Azi, you, Tony, the kids. And several hundred relatives scattered across Chicago and the old country."

"It's not the same. You're over forty—" Susan began, but Tony came to his rescue.

"Leave him alone, Suze. We're getting off the subject."

Susan turned to punch him and Vin mouthed *thank you* over the back of her head.

Tony nodded. "Right. Anything funny about O'Manny's death?"

Susan groaned. "Once a cop, always a cop. Didn't you hear? The creep died in Hawaii with his *girlfriend*. Crashed his plane. The wife wasn't anywhere near him."

"Just because I'm privatized don't mean I can't ask."

"You design bank security systems. Unless he was killed

by a falling surveillance camera, it's probably out of your sphere."

"But you love me anyway."

She gave an exaggerated sigh, winked at Vin, and went inside. Tony admired his wife's rear as it disappeared from view, then looked at Vin again. "She did vandalize his office."

"Wouldn't you?" He'd kept his tone light, but Tony narrowed his gaze, and Vin looked away. "Ah, come on, man. Guy dumps her—on Valentine's Day—*after* a little nookie. Talk about scum. 'Sides, she only went in to get her stuff."

"You're saying it wasn't premeditated?"

"OSHU and the Sion opted not to press charges in light of the whole death thing, and me and Joe went on our merry way."

"That's not an answer."

Vin downed the last of his beer, keeping his gaze on the debauchery in the yard, where neither the kids nor Azi were tiring out. "Do I think she flocked his office with malice aforethought? No. Do I think something else was going on? Maybe."

"With her? Or the lab?"

"Honestly—I don't know. Something just felt…off. For one, I didn't like the way Parker James hustled Emma out the door."

"Emma?"

"I figure after she barfed on me, we're past the formalities."

"Uh-huh."

"What?"

"You tell me. What're you leaving out?"

Vin stretched his arms until his shoulders popped. "Nothing. I'm just a boy in blue. Gotta leave all that *in-vest-uh-gatin'* to them *hi-powered dee-tect-uvs*. Not my problem."

Tony shot him a look, then said slowly, "It does seem odd. Dr. O'Manny is about to publish the biggest research of his career, maybe of his life—and he crashes his plane and dies. On the *same* day his soon-to-be-widow breaks into his office. Talk about timing."

Vin stood. "Want another beer?"

Tony studied him, but Vin kept his face blank. Tony might be his closest brother, but there were some things he could still hide. Even from himself.

Finally, Tony said, "Have it your way. You usually do. And yeah, I'll take another."

A while later, dusk had set in, Tony *et al* had departed, and Vin and Azi sat on the porch swing. It was cold, but not like February in Chicago, and Vin pushed the swing back and forth, Azi's seemingly jointless legs dangling above the floorboards.

"Hey, Vin." Azi's eyes shone. "It makes me glad to be here."

"Yeah? Me, too."

"Just us. Bachelors." He warbled off-key, "'You, you got me; Me, I got you, you!'"

Vin grinned. "'The great big Brotherhood of Man.'"

"'Lifelong membership is free.'" Azi examined Vin with great concentration. "Tough day, Vinny?"

"You could say that. I…might've overreacted. A little."

"Pretty lady?"

"Yep."

"Didja like her?"

Vin stopped pushing the swing. "Yeah. I kinda did, even though I barely met her. And I guess that's what made me overreact. I didn't want a repeat performance."

Azi gave the matter due consideration. "You worry too much, Vinny."

"That right?"

"Uh-huh. Was her name Isadora?"

Vin froze. "No. It wasn't."

"Then no repeat."

Vin stared for a long moment at Azi, who stared back, unblinking, like a wise old owl.

"Thanks, buddy."

Azi nodded. "It's all good."

"That's right, Az." Vin started pushing the swing again. "It's all good."

Chapter Three

St. Radegunde de Poitiers:
Weavers, Leprosy, Parents Lost, and Scabs

Six and a half months later, Emma sat in her oak breakfast nook, eating a turkey sandwich and staring in dismay at her laptop. How had it gotten so messed up? She'd barely used it in the last year—since before Dan's death, when she was in charge of the lab's administration. Now it was Labor Day weekend, barely a month until her Computer Sci master's program would start, and the damn thing was painfully slow. Plus, it had hundreds of folders on it, most of which she didn't recognize. Dan must have used it as backup for his research. She couldn't bring herself to erase everything without looking at it first, but if it took five minutes to open a text file, it'd be next quarter before she got through them all.

The screen door banged open and Justin came in. "Mom?"

She turned to greet him, and her breath caught. He couldn't possibly be turning *twelve* in three weeks—starting middle school—and looking so much like Dan, she wanted to cry. His light-brown hair was ruffled from the breeze, green flecks in his dark hazel eyes making them alive with energy. So alive—and she thanked God every day that he and Juney were with her, coping as best they could with the loss of their father, and that they'd never learned of the planned divorce.

God willing, they never would.

"What is it, sweetheart?" she managed past the lump in her throat, then laughed at his mutinous expression. "Sorry.

I forgot. What do you want, oh Great Big Mature Sixth Grader?"

"That's better." He shifted the basketball in his hands back and forth. "Can Juney and I go play with Zorro?"

"Zorro's here? I didn't know he knew which house is ours."

"He doesn't. He's at the tennis courts. The ball rolled into the park and I saw him. His nephew went to get their gear, and he asked if Juney and I could play, too. Please, Mom?"

"I don't know. I've never met his nephew."

"Aw, c'mon, we'll just be in the park. You can practically see us from here."

"You have a point. Still…"

Justin sensed victory. "Zorro's talked about his nephew forever—he sounds really cool. Besides, we won't see Zorro as much when school starts next week. Please, Mom?"

Juney burst in then, waving various paper items in her seven-year-old fists. "Mommy! The mail's here!" She tossed it on the table, her brown eyes sparkling, curls quirking around her head like wavy golden butterflies, her cutoffs and t-shirt stained with dirt and grass.

After her came Emma's mother, who commented dryly, "Do you remember when bills and junk mail were so exciting? Because I sure as hell don't."

Bethanne von Heinrich was as cool and self-possessed as ever, like there wasn't a breeze that would dare mess with her perfect platinum bob or her crisp pink silk pantsuit. She regarded Juney's grunge with mild distaste before planting a dry kiss on Emma's cheek.

"Hello." Her tone was a notch above sultry, though there wasn't an eligible male in sight. If there was one thing she believed in, it was never stepping out of character.

Emma said, "I didn't hear you pull up."

"I had to park two houses down, since you won't make room for my car in the drive."

"We've been over this. The driveway's only big enough

for the minivan—you knew that when you moved in."

"And the sacrifice is *well* worth it." Bethanne beamed at Juney and Justin. "Living with my two best grandchildren is worth any price, even making these tired old legs work so hard."

"We're your *only* grandchildren," Juney said, while Emma thought, *Tired old legs, my ass.*

Bethanne didn't look a day over fifty, and probably never would. Whether it was good genes or all the advice her makeup artists had offered when she was an actress, Emma didn't know. She wasn't even certain of her mother's real age—Bethanne wouldn't say, and Emma's father had died before she thought to ask him.

Bethanne poured herself an iced tea from the fridge, and Justin dribbled the basketball once.

"Don't do that. You'll break something."

Justin looked about to say something very almost-twelve, so Emma broke in, "Don't you want to go play with Zorro?"

Juney squealed. "Zorro's here? Can we, Mommy? Can we? Please?"

Bethanne said, "Why you let your children play with him is a mystery. He's so much older. They can't have anything in common."

"We like him!" Juney said. "He tells us jokes."

"And he brings us free hot dogs," Justin added, sticking to the essentials.

Emma's breath caught again. Six months ago, they'd had a father. Now all they had was her, Bethanne, Karen and Nick. No cousins, aunts or uncles—neither she nor Dan had siblings, and Dan's parents had died years ago. Was it any wonder they pieced together a crazy-quilt family of their own? And Zorro *was* sweet.

Emma said to Bethanne, "It's not because of the Down syndrome, is it?"

Bethanne gave her a rare scowl. "Don't be absurd."

"Good. Because I would be really disappointed if *that's*

what you objected to."

Bethanne's expression smoothed. "But he *is* over forty."

"So? He works every morning at the hot dog stand, and I get the feeling the nephew doesn't have much time to play." She bit her lip. The kids looked so hopeful. The thought popped into her head that Dan would have let them go, and suddenly the tears were back, lurking below the surface. She swallowed. "I really wouldn't mind, but I'd like to meet the nephew first."

Bethanne saw the unshed tears and softened. "They'll be fine. I let you go to the park by yourself when you were younger than they are now."

"Different times."

"*And* it was farther away. You had to walk four blocks, but they just have to step outside the yard." When Emma still hesitated, Bethanne added, "If Zorro can go by himself…"

"All right. But I'm coming, too, after I figure out what's wrong with this laptop."

Justin whooped. "Thanks, Mom!"

He banged out the screen, followed by a squealing Juney, and Emma called, "Keep an eye on your sister! And don't forget your rackets!"

Bethanne watched them go, then joined Emma at the table to sort the mail. Emma leaned across the wood surface to kiss her mother's papery cheek. "Thanks."

Bethanne raised startled violet eyes. "For what?"

Emma gestured at the door. "For that. For them. For helping us out these last months."

"Oh, please. I'm not doing it for you. It's all about me, remember? You're going to care for me in my old age. Besides, who'd pass up a chance to live with the two most beautiful grandchildren in the world?"

Emma smiled and took her plate to the sink. "Fine, be that way. But I do appreciate it."

"Hmm. You can repay me by fixing up your disgraceful yard."

Emma sighed. "I know. I just don't have time to deal with it."

"Time? Or inclination?"

"Time," she said firmly.

"Dan took great pride in the yard, and it's shameful the way you've let it go."

Emma turned her back on Bethanne's pursed lips. "Yes. He spent all his spare time out there. I don't have time to spare."

"Then let Justin do it. It'll be good for him, and he wants to."

Emma turned back. "You talked with him about it?"

"Yes. Why not?"

"Because he's my son, and it's my yard."

"And I live here, too, and it reflects poorly on me if you let the weeds take over."

"I'll get to it…"

"And Juney wants to help, too."

"She's too young. And I don't want to talk about this now." Emma turned to the sink again and Bethanne let it drop.

A little while later, Bethanne said, "Something for you from the financial aid office."

Emma dried her hands and took the letter, opening it and scanning quickly. "Oh, no."

"Don't frown. You'll get wrinkles. What is it?"

Emma sat down. "My application was denied. They say I have too much debt."

Bethanne's own forehead crinkled in puzzlement before she caught herself and smoothed her features. "It has to be a mistake. What about Dan's life insurance?"

"I paid off our credit cards, and what he borrowed from the kids' college funds when he started the lab. I've been living off the rest. The car's paid, but there's still the mortgage."

"That shouldn't be enough to deny your aid."

Emma's heart pounded and she set the letter down

carefully. "I can't go to school without it."

"I know. You'll think of something."

"I wish I could call Dan's accountant. Damn it—why couldn't the letter have come on Friday?" She glanced up at the clock, down at the letter, and then at her laptop. "Well, maybe I can get one thing done." She reached for her cell as the doorbell rang.

Bethanne rose, transforming miraculously from mildly concerned parent to movie-star glam. "I forgot—I invited Charley for dinner. You don't mind, do you?"

Would it matter if I did?

But Bethanne had drifted into the hall. Moments later, Emma heard fawning noises as her longtime groupie Charley Addison was admitted.

Pushing down her irritation, Emma dialed, and a moment later Oscar picked up. "Forty Lab."

Of course he knew Forte was Italian, and correctly pronounced "For*tay.*" So he had to be mispronouncing it on purpose to irritate Nick—typical Oscar. Or maybe it just bugged her that it *was* the Forte Lab now, not the O'Manny lab. But Dan was dead, and Nick was PI. And Dan had still been a bastard, no matter how unresolved her feelings were about his death.

She drew a deep breath. "Oscar? It's Emma. Is Nick there?"

"It's *Saturday.*"

She wanted to point out, *You're there*, but refrained. No sense antagonizing him—it only gave him an excuse to antagonize back.

"Never mind. I need to talk to you, too—does the lab have a spare firewire cable?"

"Why?"

"There's a bunch of old data on my laptop I'd like to transfer off."

"So use a thumb drive, or burn a CD."

"It's an old laptop. The CD drive is dead, no wifi, and only a USB-1 port. It would take days. But with a firewire, I can move them to my desktop, which is faster."

"Why not delete them?" He sounded annoyed, and she pictured him cradling the phone on his shoulder, fiddling with an experiment, probably with an earbud in his other ear, listening to an MP3. He'd never liked smartphones, feeling they did many things poorly, instead of one thing well. That and he'd always been paranoid about being spied on by "the man," who he was convinced had access to any and all internet-connected personal devices.

"Are you sure? With the vaccine paper coming out, you might need them."

"Even if Dan put them there, they're at least a year old."

"Close. The most recent are from February. I'd feel better backing them up first."

There was a pause while he considered. "Yeah, okay. Hold on a sec." A minute later he came back. "I found an old cable. I'll set it aside for you. Or if you want, just bring the laptop in and I'll look at the files. Save you the trouble, if we don't need them."

"I'll think about it. Thanks for the offer."

They hung up, and Emma stared at nothing. Between the yard, her computer and the financial aid, the afternoon had gone down the tubes. Then she heard Bethanne giggle coquettishly from the front of the house, and shuddered. Escape. It was her only recourse.

She peeked into the living room. "I'm going to the park. Hi, Charley. Bye, Charley."

Charley rose, pushing his plump, yellow-suited form laboriously off the sofa. He looked every inch the peacock, his brown-dyed hair slicked back, his gold watch and rings too bright on his tanned-leather skin.

"Did you say the park?" He offered Bethanne his hand, pulling her up. "It's a beautiful day. Shall we go for a stroll?"

Bethanne batted her eyelashes. "If you say 'once more around the park,' I'll scream."

"Really," Emma began, "you don't have to come. I don't mind going alone. At all."

Charley winked at her. "'You want to make a federal case of it?'"

"Hey!" Bethanne swatted him. "'Pull in your reel—you're barking up the wrong fish!'"

Please don't, Emma thought even as Charley transferred the wink to Bethanne. "'Look, chief, I better blow 'cause if Columbo sees me, it's gonna be *Goodbye Charlie!*'"

"'Goodbye, Charlie,'" Bethanne said.

Emma suppressed a groan. Silence. Peace. Solitude.

If she couldn't have those, at least seeing Zorro might improve her day. It couldn't get any worse.

****

Vin slung his tennis bag over his shoulder and turned the key in the lock, pausing to savor the thrill. He *owned* that door. So what if the bank owned the rest of the place—the door, at least, was his. After only a few weeks, he already loved everything about the house—a craftsman, like Tony's rental, only bigger. More of a fixer-upper, too, but that was fine. He and Azi loved pouring over online catalogs, visiting Restoration Hardware, planning to bring the house back to its former glory, one crown molding at a time.

As though his thoughts had conjured him, Azi came barreling up the walk. "Vin! Hey Vin! Whatcha doin'? What's takin' you so long?"

"Relax, buddy. I had to get our stuff. We can't play tennis without our gear."

"But *Mikey's* there! You gotta meet Mikey! C'mon, Vin, hurry up!" Azi danced back down the steps and onto the walk.

Vin had been working long hours after finally making detective again, and Azi spent nearly every afternoon at the park. Now that Vin had wrapped his first official case, he hoped he'd have some time off. But if not, it was a relief to know Azi wasn't lonely. Back in Chicago, they'd had a plethora of relatives. Here, there was only Tony, Susan, and their brood. Which was sometimes a good thing, considering how *much* family they had in the Midwest.

But it also meant fewer people to occupy Azi. When Vin had become his caregiver ten years ago, it was instant parenthood. He still didn't know how his siblings did it, with so many kids each. Azi was enough for him. Not that he was complaining—he wouldn't trade Azi for anybody, not in a million years.

Ahead of him, Azi skipped down the sidewalk, eager to finally introduce Vin to his new "best" friend. With Azi, everyone was a "best" friend, but he did jabber on about this Mike kid more than average. By the time they neared the park, he was a good half block ahead.

"Wait up!" Vin called, but he was too far behind. When Azi spied a threesome tossing a basketball around the grassy area near the courts, he took off at a dead run. "Azi—wait!"

The kid off to the left must be Mike, as the other two were a petite blonde with her hair twisted up and a little girl with riotous curls. Then Vin realized it wasn't toward the *left* that Azi ran. The woman had her back turned, moving from side-to-side as she blocked the girl from making a pass to the boy. The girl, giggling and making damn fine feints left and right, also didn't see Azi. With sick certainty, Vin knew what was about to happen. *Why* Azi was hurtling himself at the blonde, Vin had no idea, but hurtling he was—and she was about to be knocked flat.

"Azi!" he yelled, then took off after him, glad of his running shoes, his knee stiff, but not too painful. "Azi— wait—Ma'am! *Ma'am*!" Azi was a yard away. "*Look out*!"

The woman finally heard him. She intercepted the girl's pass and twisted away, then looked up. Too late—Azi slammed into her. Vin was nearly there and heard her gasp as she went down. The girl jumped aside, squealing something that sounded like "Zorro strikes again!", then watched in fascinated horror as they rolled down the slope and *plopped!* into a puddle at the bottom. Vin and the other kid reached them at the same time.

"Mom—are you okay?" The kid tugged her arm while Vin hauled his uncle up.

"Azi! What do you think you're doing?"

Vin turned to offer the woman his hand and froze. It couldn't be. She lifted laughing gold-brown eyes to his and froze also, mirroring his no doubt deer-in-the-headlights look. The gunk covering her face this time was green and slimy, and her white blouse was covered in grass, not flocking, but he'd recognize those flashing eyes, that chunk-spewing mouth anywhere.

"Em—" He cleared his throat. Cripes—how old *was* he? "Mrs. O'Manny?" At least his voice hadn't cracked.

She opened her mouth, then blushed. "Officer…"

"Detective," he corrected inanely. "I mean—"

Before he dug himself any deeper, Azi tugged his sleeve. "Vin! Hey, Vin—this is Mikey! Do you know her?"

Vin stared. "*This* is Mike? I thought he was a *boy*."

"I know!" Azi grinned, and Vin realized he'd been had. He turned to Emma—Michael Anne, if he remembered right. From her face, she was having a few realizations of her own.

She looked at Azi, aghast. "*This* is your *nephew*?"

"Yep." More grinning. "Favorite one!"

The boy and the girl gazed from the woman to him with open curiosity. They had to be her kids. The boy had called her *Mom*, and the little girl was the spitting image of her. Vin tried not to fidget.

Emma looked uncertainly at him, still looming over her, because he'd forgotten his plan to help her up. "But—he's so—so big!" She went a pretty shade of pink. "I—that is—"

Vin dropped to the damp grass beside her and held out a hand. "Let's start over. Hi, I'm Detective Bronislovas of the Portland Police Bureau, but you can call me Vin."

She swiped her muddy right hand on her muddier jeans, then gave up and offered her left instead. He noted she still wore her wedding ring. Interesting. He glanced at her kids and thought about why she might do that. When he turned back, she was looking at him pleadingly, and he nodded.

She smiled then, full lips curving, eyes *glowing*, and his blood roared and he felt a little stunned. Cautiously, he assessed his own face, and determined that, no, his chin had not *actually* dropped to his chest, then noticed she was speaking and forced himself to pay attention.

"…Emma, please. Is Zorro really your uncle?"

"Zorro?"

"Juney calls me that," Azi explained, and the girl's curls bobbed in vigorous assent.

"My kids," Emma supplied. "Juney and Justin."

Juney smiled, one of those killer little girl smiles that would drive the boys wild in five-to-ten—not unlike her mother's—while Justin regarded him more cautiously.

Good for you, kid. I'd watch out for me, too.

Vin jerked back a little. Where had *that* come from? True, she was widowed, no longer a "perp," and he was obviously attracted to her. Or, he hoped, *un*obviously. But he barely knew her, and he'd done the "damsel in distress" thing with Izzy. Just look where that got him.

Vin gave a mental shake and held out a hand. Justin regarded it silently, then shook it, *hard*. Strong kid, though he couldn't be more than eleven. "Nice to meet you, Justin."

"Detective Bronislovas."

"Impressive. Most people can't get it right on the first try."

Justin's look turned to one of scorn, but before he could respond, Emma said, "Justin's very good with languages. Juney has more trouble. That's where Zorro came from."

"She was trying to say *Azuolas*," Justin said, "but she kept getting an 'R' in there. She switched to Zorro, and it stuck."

Juney nodded again. "It's true."

Vin leaned toward her, lowering his voice. "I'll tell you a secret." He hooked a thumb at his uncle. "I call him Uncle Azi, because when I was your age, I couldn't say *Azuolas*, either."

Her eyes grew big and her mouth made a pretty "O", but Justin scowled. "How come he's your uncle? You're *way* older than him."

Thanks, kid.

"Justin!"

"It's okay. We get it all the time. Azi's older, but only a couple years. My mom was the oldest of ten; Azi was the youngest. We grew up like brothers."

"Favorite nephew," Azi repeated, grinning like the Cheshire cat. He nodded at Emma. "Toldya she was nice."

"You forgot the *she* part." Vin looked at Emma. "I kind of like Mike. That's how I've been trained to think of you."

Emma blushed again. "Oh. That. It's a grade school nickname."

Azi broke in. "C'mon, Justin! Wanna play tennis? Vinny brought our rackets an' everythin'."

Justin's narrowed gaze still rested on Vin. "How come you know my mom?"

"We, uh, met at Dad's lab," Emma interjected quickly, struggling to stand.

Vin rose and helped her up, giving her the once over. "You need a change of clothes."

"I suppose I do." She looked down at herself, then back up with a rueful smile. Cripes—if she didn't stop doing that, he'd never make it through an entire conversation with her. Then she bit her lower lip, and all the blood left his brain. Luckily the effect was spoiled when she tasted mud and made a face, and he shook himself and reached for his bag.

"Here." He pulled a towel out and tossed it to her.

"Thanks." She scrubbed, smearing mud everywhere, but at least getting it off her mouth, which Vin was still staring at. Oh the things that mouth could do. Cripes. Get a grip.

"Who's your friend?"

Emma's startled gaze swung over Vin's shoulder, and he turned to see the oddest couple strolling up, looking totally out of place in the park. The woman, tall and thin, wore pink from her pearl earrings and lipstick down to her high-heeled sandals. With her platinum bob and dark-lashed violet eyes, she could have stepped out of a magazine. Vin put her in her sixties, maybe older, though he couldn't see a wrinkle on her. He would have guessed younger, but she was a little too perfect, too coiffed. Beautiful, aging well, but working too hard at it.

He watched Emma brush self-consciously at the mud and grass, and considered telling her how hot she was. In her hip-hugging jeans, shirt plastered to her soft, round breasts, her hair coming loose in an I've-just-been-laid kind of way, she had nothing to worry about. Then again, telling her that might make her feel worse, and would probably be a dumb move in any case.

No damsels in distress…

The couple reached them, and Vin watched a look of utter horror cross the man's face. "Emma, darling! *What* happened to you?"

He wore yellow linen that had wrinkled, but not in the carefree way linen was supposed to—it had wrinkled all over. And while the woman's suit seemed to repel grass stains and plant matter, the man's attracted both. His skin was sun-damaged, his hair dyed, and he'd had a facelift. Or two. Even so, there were laugh lines around his eyes, and his concern for Emma seemed genuine.

"A puddle," she answered. "And Zorro."

"Ah. 'Next time I want some *idiot* to guard a prisoner, I shall do it myself!'"

"Oh, Charley!" Blondie touched his arm, drawing his attention back. "Stop!"

Vin said to Emma, "Did I miss something?"

"You don't want to know. Bethanne von Heinrich, Charley Addison. This is Detective Bronislovas. I met him at Dan's lab—he's Zorro's nephew."

Blondie gave him a surprised look, followed by quick assessment. She held out a hand which he took. It was fine-boned and dry. "Mrs. von Heinrich."

She laughed, low and sultry. "Oh, please. Call me Bethanne, Detective."

"Vin," he said, then nodded at Charley, who regarded

him curiously.

"Grandma?" Justin said to Bethanne, and Vin regrouped.

"You're Emma's mother?"

"How sweet. People say we look like sisters, but I'm sure they're just flattering me."

"Grandma," Justin said again, saving Vin from having to come up with a blatant lie.

"Yes, Justin?"

"Can you show me and Zorro and Juney how you walked across the tightrope in stilettoes and saved the baby from the fire?"

Vin looked at Emma again. "Now I'm *sure* I missed something."

"Bethanne was an actress."

"Oh, stop," Bethanne said, not meaning it.

Charley said, "Not just any actress. *The* Anne Clarice. Did you ever see *Mafia Queen*?"

"Don't think so."

"*Mafia Princess*?"

"Sorry," Vin said cautiously. "Azi and I watch mainly musicals."

Charley made a face, but Emma said, "Don't worry. They're from the seventies. They might be out on DVD, but I don't think they made it to streaming."

"Seventies?" Vin did the math. How old was Bethanne, anyway?

Bethanne herself broke in. "Oh, but I was just a baby then."

Justin said impatiently, "Grandma! Please?"

Vin thought for sure she'd tell him not to call her "Grandma," but instead she turned to him affectionately. "Oh, very well, Justin. We can use the balance beam for the rope. Charley, come. You're our production manager, in charge of special effects."

"I live to serve," Charley said, following as they headed for the playground.

Emma called after them, "I'm going home to change. Be back in time for dinner!"

"We *will!*" Juney yelled.

Emma sighed and looked at Vin, then noticed they were alone and cleared her throat. "Well. I'd better go. It was nice seeing you again."

"No, it wasn't."

"What?" Her gaze snapped to his, uncertainty replaced with another smile when she understood he was teasing. Even though it wasn't full-watt, he still lost himself and had to refocus.

"I'm pretty sure the last time we met, it wasn't a good experience for you." Her face went small and vulnerable, and Vin could have kicked himself. "I'm sorry. That came out wrong. I didn't mean to make you sad. I—Ah, screw it. I'm making it worse, aren't I?"

"It's okay. Really."

"Hey." He touched her arm, startling her. "Don't be embarrassed. You had a lot dumped on you, and I happened to be nearby. People help each other out in crises."

"Is that why you're a cop?"

"Detective," he corrected, and she actually laughed, a real laugh that also flashed in those strange gold-brown eyes. It sent warmth straight to his gut. She should definitely laugh more.

"Is that why you're a *detective*, then?"

He still held her arm, becoming aware of it at the same moment she did. She stilled, and his blood pounded and he said softly, "I became a detective because I like a challenge. I like taking things apart, seeing how they tick. Finding out what's under the surface."

She swallowed. "Things?"

"Puzzles. People."

Christ. He couldn't make himself let go. She was so close, so warm, smelled so good. Then she pulled gently away, and he let her go, the feel of her still warming his skin.

"Do you ever put them back together?"

His brain still lacked blood and he drew a blank. "What?"

"Things. Puzzles. People. After you tear them apart—do you put them back together?"

Interesting. What about that scared her? The thought of what someone might find, or that they might leave her in pieces?

"I said take, not tear."

"What's the difference?"

"Tear is violent."

"So is take."

"But tear implies lack of consent. Take works best with *give*."

"Are you saying you ask permission first?"

"Always," he said, watching as her breath caught and her eyes darkened. *Jesus H. Christ.* He had to get away, before he did something really asinine, like try to save her from herself. "Gotta go. See you around, Mike."

He grabbed his tennis bag and turned, leaving her flushed and flustered and looking like six kinds of trouble he didn't need. Didn't want. Had to escape.

At the edge of the park, he risked a glance back, then couldn't decide if he was relieved or disappointed that she'd gone.

Stay the hell away, Vin's brain said.

Unfortunately, the rest of him wasn't listening.

Chapter Four

St. Albert the Expert:
Med Techs, Scientists, Philosophers, and Labs

By Tuesday evening, a number of things had become apparent to Emma. First, no matter what she did, Vin and his puzzle theory of life *would* keep popping into her head, distracting her. The minute she'd looked up and seen that red-auburn hair, those fierce blue eyes, her heart skipped a beat—then a few more. What on earth must he think of her? Not that she cared. But he *had* been kind when Dan died— after uncuffing her and apologizing, anyway.

That he was disposed to be nice, despite her crime spree and the fact that both times they'd met, she wasn't exactly "primped," made her even more uncomfortable. What was a widowed mother of two, who'd slept with a grand total of one man in the last fifteen years—and not many more previously—supposed to do with a hunk who was nice to her? Jump him—or run?

She pictured throwing herself at that football-field of a chest, wrapping her legs around his hips, and feeling his iron-strong arms cradling her, his chiseled mouth on hers, and immediately thought, *Run away! Run away!*

The second thing she noticed was that her laptop was still bent on driving her crazy. She *had* to get it fixed, because she couldn't afford a new one. Which segued nicely into the third thing—the one that was the real kicker, and that she least wanted to think about.

Namely, that Dan really *was* a bastard, and her feelings about his death shouldn't be the least bit confused.

"The problem isn't so much that Dan bought the stock,"

Emma said to Karen as they worked in the kitchen, pre-making the kids' lunches for the week. "It's that he bought *bad* stock."

Karen's unruly orange curls bounced crazily as she shook her head. "No. The problem is that he took out a three hundred grand, interest-only second mortgage on your house *without telling you*, and *used it to buy bad stock*." She whacked a chef's knife into a carrot, castrating it into neat little slices.

Emma stepped back. "Maybe I should do the chopping and you can mix the tuna salad."

"I'm fine. I *like* chopping vegetables."

"I can see that. It's just that the tuna's a little less, er, angry."

Karen wiped sweat off her brow, then whacked some more. "As for mad, be glad Dan's already dead. I'd kill him myself if he was here now."

"Karen!"

"I mean it. What kind of a dumbass was he, anyway?" She reached for a hapless stalk of celery. "He borrows three hundred *thousand* dollars against your house"—*whack!*—"which you think is almost paid off"—*whack, whack!*—"and uses the loan to buy stock in some start-up that tanks?"

Whack, whack, whack!

"Could you keep it down a little?"

The kids and Bethanne were watching old movies in the living room, hopefully out of earshot. Emma hooked a can of tuna onto the electric opener, keeping an eye on Karen's fingers just in case.

"Sorry. I just don't understand why Dan would sink money into a start-up. They *always* tank."

Emma bit her lip. "It wasn't a start-up. It was Prospect-Gage."

Karen stopped, knife raised, green eyes blazing. "*Prospect-Gage?* After the insider trading scandal, aren't they bankrupt? Why the hell would Dan buy Prospect-Gage?"

"I don't know. His accountant says it dropped to eleven

per share, and Dan thought it was a good investment." Emma stirred the tuna into a bowl with mayo and pickle relish.

Karen's freckles stood out on her white face. "But their high last year was fifty!"

"I know."

"Which means they were *already* tanking when Dan bought."

"I know," Emma repeated helplessly.

"What's it at now?"

Emma stared at the unappetizing mess of tuna and shoved the bowl away, then reached for the bread. "Do you have to be a financial analyst every minute of the day?"

"Yes. If Dan had talked with me, he wouldn't have gotten into this mess. What's it at?"

Emma sighed. "Four and a half."

Karen gaped, then snapped her mouth shut and thought for a moment. "Which means if you sell, you'll still have a hundred and fifty grand to pay off."

"A hundred and seventy-nine, but who's counting?"

"And if you *don't* sell, it might tank more, and you'll be even worse off."

"Gee, thanks. I hadn't thought of that."

"What about your financial aid?"

Emma winced as Karen julienned a bell pepper into oblivion. "I have to reapply. Because I didn't disclose the debt—"

"Which you knew nothing about!"

"—I was automatically denied."

"But if you reapply, you'll get approved." When Emma didn't respond, Karen narrowed her eyes. "Right?"

"Honestly—I don't know."

"What are you talking about? *What* did Dan do?"

Emma took a deep breath and pushed it out again. "The loan's no payments for twelve months, which is why I didn't find out about it sooner. But now I'm looking at nine hundred a month. My aid app could be turned down for the debt alone, or for the high payments. Even if it's approved, it might not be enough. I'll probably have to get a job and forget about school."

"No. That's just wrong. Dan can't do this to you!"

"He already has. Even if I reapply for the aid, it will take weeks to process. I'll have to pay my tuition now, out of pocket, or else OSHU will drop me from my classes."

The whole thing was even more depressing when she had to spell it out. She picked up a sandwich and a plastic bag, but Karen grabbed her arm, fingers digging into Emma's skin.

"No, you listen to me. Talk to Parker—there's *got* to be something he can do. He was freakin' VP of Finance before OSHU tagged him for President."

"And what? Ask him to put a gold star on my application?"

"Of course not. But maybe he can expedite the process—get it looked at sooner."

"I hadn't thought of that."

Karen let go of her arm. "If he won't do it for you, or out of loyalty to Dan—for which I wouldn't blame him—he'd better do it for me. After what his bottom-feeding baby brother put me through in divorce court, that family owes me. Big time."

"But—"

"Just talk to him, will you? It can't hurt."

Emma sighed. "All right. I'll do it."

"Do what?" Bethanne drifted into the kitchen, looking cool in lemon Chanel.

"Talk to Parker about her financial aid," Karen said before Emma could stop her. From her expression, Karen realized her mistake immediately.

"What a lovely idea." Bethanne pulled the iced tea from the fridge and reached for a glass. "The James boys are so nice. I never understood why you divorced poor Rob."

Karen smiled, saccharin sweet. "Maybe because *poor Rob* cheated on me two weeks after our honeymoon, didn't stop for the next seven years, and then tried to weasel out of our prenup. But that pales next to Dan the Son-of-a-Bitch. At least Rob and I didn't have kids to screw up."

"So. What *are* the kids doing?" Emma asked, but Bethanne rounded on Karen.

"That is no way to talk about the father of my grandchildren."

Emma winced. "Bethanne—"

Karen folded her arms over her chest. "No, let's hear what she has to say."

"Dan was a good man. He made mistakes—who hasn't?—and he died before he could fix them. But he would *never* hurt his children, and I know if he'd had the chance he would have come back to Emma. He wouldn't leave her like that—he *loved* her."

"Is that why he screwed around, then screwed *her*, right before he screwed her over?"

Emma closed her eyes, wishing hell would swallow her up and get it over with. "Karen…"

"As for his kids, sure, I'll buy he loved them. I'm sure they were who he thought of first when he was diddling that little *bi*—"

"Mom?"

Emma's lids popped open and Bethanne and Karen twisted toward the doorway, expressions abruptly neutral. Justin looked uncertainly at each of them.

"What is it, sweetheart?" *Oh God—please don't let him have heard.*

He cleared his throat, but she couldn't tell if he was upset or not.

"Can I bring your laptop to school tomorrow? Mr. Price wants us to share about our summer, and last week I downloaded all the pictures and videos off the digital camera onto it."

Emma closed her eyes again and counted to five before opening them. "Justin. How much did you download?"

"Counting the expansion cards? Maybe…two gigs?"

"Is *that* why it's been running so slowly?"

His cheeks turned pink. "I also changed the virtual memory and repartitioned the drive. I would've asked first, but the desktop doesn't have the right software, and the cards were full."

Emma suppressed a groan and leaned her head on the counter. "It's okay, honey. I just never thought to look in the pictures folder."

"So can I?"

He looked so hopeful that her heart twinged. It had been a rough few months—for all of them. It was nice to see him interested in something.

"I suppose, if your teacher locks it up for the rest of the day."

He grinned. "Thanks, Mom. Mr. Price is going to hook it up to the projector. It'll be the coolest of all the presentations!" He bussed her cheek, then ran back to the living room.

Karen turned back to the vegetables. "I'll just put these away."

Bethanne's lips pursed. "Just because your divorce was bitter doesn't make all men bad."

Karen looked up. "Hey—I *love* men. I even think Emma should date one again. Like this Vin guy."

Bethanne frowned. "Vin?"

"I hear he's tall, auburn, and has a habit of bumping into Emma when she's at her worst—and then sticking around anyway."

Forget swallowing—hell had marched right into her kitchen and taken over. Why couldn't Karen ever shut up? Emma tamped down her frustration. Karen didn't *mean* to make things worse—it just worked out that way.

"The *cop*?" Bethanne whipped around to face Emma. "Are you thinking of dating again *already*? Dan's barely been dead six months!"

Emma pushed off the counter. "Not that it's *anybody's* business, but I have no intention of dating Vin. Even *if* he was interested—which he's not—I'm not ready yet."

Karen said, "Of course he's interested!" at the same time Bethanne said, "I should hope not. And when you *are* ready, I'm sure you'll find someone better, who will fit in with our family. More like Dan. What about Nick? His wife has been dead for three years, he's godfather to your children. They adore him, and you've known each other since high school."

Karen went white and her fists clenched. Fortunately not around the knife, which Emma surreptitiously moved into the sink on her way to putting the sandwiches in the fridge.

Karen said, "Why stop there? We've known Parker and Rob since grammar school." She turned to Emma. "Why don't I marry Parker this time, and you can have the fun of Rob? After a month, you can divorce him, too, and *then* go after Nick."

Emma slammed the fridge shut. "*Enough.*" She gave Karen and Bethanne equal-opportunity glares. "Janice was the love of Nick's life. The breast cancer nearly killed him, too—I don't know if he'll ever be the same. And now his best friend—*my husband*—is dead. Even if I wanted to, which I *don't*, I wouldn't date him. His friendship is too important. And I've barely even absorbed that Dan is gone, let alone what he did to me. Is *still doing*. Every day, the kids wake up, missing their father, not understanding why he's gone, and I have no idea what to say to them. Any man would be crazy to date me right now—and I'd be even crazier to date him."

Bethanne started to smile triumphantly, when Emma added, "But just so we're clear: Dan *was* a bastard, and what he did was unforgivable. I won't have anyone saying it in front of the kids—but I won't have *you* praising him all the time either. Do we all understand each other?"

Karen nodded, and Bethanne followed suit a moment later. Emma exhaled. "Good. I'm going to watch TV with the kids. If the two of you are done, you're welcome to join us."

Without waiting for an answer, she fled to the living

room.

****

On Wednesday morning, Vin came downstairs to discover that Azi had made coffee.

Really *good* coffee.

"Wow. I'm impressed. What'd you do?"

Azi beamed, delighted to share his secret to success. "Terry showed me!"

Terry was the new afternoon operator at the hot dog stand downtown, where Azi worked mornings. She'd started last week, and according to Azi, knew everything anyone could possibly know about manning—or womanning—a food cart.

She certainly knew her way around a coffee filter. Vin savored another sip, and patently did not miss the swill they'd been drinking. Funny. In Chicago, neither of them had cared what they drank in the morning, so long as it was dark brown. After a year in the Northwest, they possessed the finest stainless-steel coffeemaker around, their own *grinder* for cripe's sake, and a place of honor in the corner coffee shop's Best Customers photo album. But they still hadn't been able to make truly excellent coffee at home.

Until now.

"So what's different?"

"Scoops!" Azi announced proudly.

"Scoops?"

"We used too much. Terry says even if we want strong coffee, we have to use *exactly* the right amount. Too much makes it bitter and it *tastes* thin, even if it's not."

Vin lifted an eyebrow. "Okay. I'll buy that. But what's the magic amount? We've used more, less, whatever, and never got it right. Damn." He drank again, then topped off his pre-warmed stainless-steel travel mug and twisted on the spill-proof top.

Azi's grin deepened. "B-cups."

"Say…what now?"

"B-cups," Azi repeated gleefully. "Like a bra."

50

"I heard you. But—I mean—what the hell do bra sizes have to do with coffee?"

Azi pulled out the coffee canister and dipped the scoop in. He made it slightly rounded, and said, "A-cup." Then he made one very rounded. "C-cup." He poured a little off, until the scoop was—Vin had to admit—a perfect B-cup, saying, "Just right."

"I see. Okay. Well." He cleared his throat. "Great job. Now we know."

Azi nodded. "Nothing wrong with A-cups. Or C-cups."

"Right," Vin said, because Azi clearly expected a response. "Room in the world for all sizes of cups." *And thank God for it.*

"But for coffee, B-cup is best."

"Right. B-cups are best." Abruptly, an image of Emma's perfect B-cup breasts, encased in a wet t-shirt, popped into his head. He took another swig of coffee to cover his confusion. When the hell had Azi learned about cup sizes? Not that Azi wasn't interested in girls. Women. Sometimes, it was hard to remember Azi was nearing fifty. But cup sizes were just so…specific.

Vin grabbed his bag. "Ready? We better leave or you'll be late."

Azi grabbed his own travel mug and followed Vin to the car. The drive downtown was quiet. Vin left the radio off, lost in his own thoughts, and Azi seemed preoccupied as well.

When they arrived at the cart, Azi turned to Vin and announced, "I take the bus home."

It was the last thing Vin expected. "It's no trouble. I've got time on my lunch break."

Azi nodded, happy. "It's all good. I always take the bus now. Save you time and gas."

"Always…?"

"Mornings, too." Azi nodded again, decisive.

Vin looked at him, but his expression was open and guileless as ever. Ignoring the sharp stab of doubt, Vin cleared his throat. "Okay. Sure. Do you want me to buy you a bus pass?"

"I can get one."

"Okay. Sure." He had to quit saying that. "You know how to get to the transit blocks?"

"Yep. See you at home!"

Azi opened the door and hopped out. Several of his regular customers clustered near the cart, jonesing for their morning caffeine. Azi returned their greetings joyfully, and Vin shoved the car in gear and peeled off, feeling inexplicably put out.

Azi's version of Down syndrome certainly didn't preclude public transit. But why the sudden change? Every lunch hour for six months, Vin had picked him up. If Vin ran late, Azi waited at the library. And Vin looked forward to his smiling face, and to discussing work or sports or nothing special with him.

Now, suddenly, the day stretched out, empty of Azi's companionship until dinnertime.

And it all went downhill from there.

As soon as he got to his desk, his lieutenant called him to her office, to give him his next case. He'd cleared his plate the previous week, and had taken Tuesday off for the holiday weekend. He was ready for the next thing—just not for what it turned out to be.

Lieutenant Mary Kay Barton was short, in decent physical shape, with clipped gray hair and dark eyes, and was not known for her sense of humor. Or for liking Vin, or any of her other detectives.

Vin gave it one more shot. "You're joking, right?"

She shook her head. "Honolulu PD called. They've got new information on the investigation into the deaths of Daniel O'Manny and his assistant, Mollie McBride."

"*What* investigation? It was ruled an accident."

Barton looked through her bifocals at him. "McBride's family thinks different. They live in the islands, must have some clout or something. Guy from HPD said to call when you can, but not today. Whole department's out at some retirement luau or something."

"Must not be urgent."

"That was my take. I get the feeling HPD's checking it out as a courtesy. Probably think they should check in here so they can cross their T's and dot their I's. But the McBrides say a parachute was missing from the wreckage, so they're insisting a third person was on the plane."

"How can they tell it was missing?"

"Plane was relatively intact, and the other 'chute was still in place." She pushed a case file across the desk. It didn't look full, and he probably knew most of the details anyway, since he'd heard the story firsthand. Hell, he was probably listed as a witness to the whereabouts of the first decedent's widow at the time of death. Or at least, shortly thereafter, when she'd had her soft, round ass pressed against his billy club.

Since thinking about Emma's ass was a bad idea, Vin looked back at the lieutenant, who watched him intently. It crossed his mind that maybe she'd chosen him on purpose for this, *because* he was the officer on the scene. Or—

No. If she knew about Chicago, she'd deliberately *not* assign him. Wouldn't she?

Asking her point-blank would get him nowhere, so he said, "A luau, huh?"

She flashed her patented piranha grin. *Ah, hell.*

"Yes. Must be nice. Whole department eating roast pig and getting drunk. I bet Hawaii would make even li'l ole podunk Portland look like a hub of criminal activity."

"Funny. That joke hasn't gotten old in the whole time I've been here."

"Poor Vin. Stuck in the boonies. Tell me again, why'd you give up the glam for this?"

Fuck. She *had* wheedled his "sealed" personnel records out of Jimmy, who hated Vin's guts and always would, even from two thousand miles away. No doubt he'd spilled the whole tale, and Barton had lapped it up.

Vin managed not to glower. She was his boss, after all. But he knew what was coming, and a year of working to forget made it suck all the more now it was out.

"Let's see…" She pretended to consult her notes. "You infiltrated an organized crime branch, screwed the Capo's *daughter*, then fell for her big time. What did the press call her? Oh yes—the Deering Darling. How sweet. Isadora really had you by the balls, huh? All that crime going on right under your nose. But then, you had it buried elsewhere, didn't you?"

"Are you done?" How he managed to keep his voice level, Vin had no idea. If he gave her an inch, she'd have him where she wanted, and he wasn't about to let that happen. Hell. He should sue for harassment—except she was only stating the facts.

"Then there was that little scuffle when your fiancée's Mafioso relatives found out you were an undercover cop. Didn't she shoot you with a pop gun or something?"

Vin fought back a growl, then gave up and gave her what she wanted—his control. "It wasn't her, and it was a damn .45."

Hell if he knew why she bothered, when his colossal screw-up made him such an easy target. But now that this was out, he'd be on everyone's hit list, not just hers. At least until the novelty wore off and the next grunt did something this dumb.

"How's the knee?" she asked as he stood to go.

"Screw you," Vin said and shoved out the door.

Chapter Five

St. Angela di Foligno:
Widows, Temptation, Piety, and Gibes

When Parker sat across from Emma at the Synapse, the best of OSHU's on-campus eateries, he looked as impeccable as ever. She'd chosen an outside table in hopes of enjoying the September sun—one of the Northwest's best kept secrets—and also of feeling less "intimate" while pleading her case. Asking for favors was the worst, but desperation did wonders for her tolerance. Still, as she sweated in the ninety-plus heat, and Parker managed to look cool even in a gray wool suit, she wished she'd chosen AC over space.

She watched as he ordered, searching out the boy she'd known so long ago. He was just going gray at the temples, though he was somewhere near fifty. She never could remember how much older than Rob he was, and Rob was three years older than she and Karen. Parker was long graduated from Central Catholic by the time the rest of them were done with middle school, but she remembered his visits home from college. Now, still trim and fit, rich, powerful, and president of Oregon's only med school, she wondered idly why he'd never married.

Then the waitress left and he opened his mouth, and it all came crashing back. Literally.

"How have you been?" he boomed in his presidential baritone, and Emma winced and resisted the urge to *shush* him as she would the kids, as if they were in church or at the library.

"Fine." Maybe if she spoke low, he'd follow suit. They

exchanged chitchat about the kids, and he asked after Bethanne, apparently remembering her as fondly as she did him.

Then he said, "So. You're here about your financial aid app."

Emma looked up, startled out of any pretense at denial. "How did you know that?"

"Karen humbled herself. She didn't think you'd come."

Heat flooded her face and she made herself hold his gaze. Groveling was bad enough; she would *not* look weak doing it. She took a breath, but he raised a hand.

"I'll see what I can do. I can't promise you'll be approved—"

"I'm not asking you to!" Heads turned their way, and she lowered her voice. "Did Karen—"

"No. But you do have extenuating circumstances. Someone will look at it right away. You should find out in a week, well before the term starts."

That drew her up short. "Really?"

He grinned, that same smile he probably used prior to decapitating Research Directors or neurosurgeons who refused his bidding. It *looked* friendly, but then, so did a lion on occasion.

"Thank you," she managed, and meant it. She gave him the envelope containing her revised application, and he tucked it into his briefcase, still smiling.

"I meant what I said, Emma—you should come around more. The labs weren't the same after you left, and now that Dan's dead—"

He stopped abruptly to exchange a word with a man in a black suit who passed by, leaving Emma to wonder why Parker missed her so much. And she *really* didn't want to discuss Dan right now. Maybe he'd forget he raised the subject, but it didn't seem likely.

Black Suit left and Parker said, "Sorry. Head of Campus Strategies and Solutions—we're pushing a new research facility through and the City's having fits about the parking.

More parking, more traffic, more congestion. And the only ones who care are the millionaires on Terwilliger who don't want their damn street widened. Where was I? Oh, yes. Now that Dan's gone, the whole Institute's lost its spark."

"I'm sure that's an exaggeration." She glanced around, hoping no other PIs were nearby.

"Not at all. The O'Manny lab made the Sion. In fact, Dan was at the top of my list to run the whole Institute, but he wanted to focus on research. I'll never admit this again, but he was right. Stuck in an office, he would've washed out in a year, and the Sion with him."

"But Nick—"

"Is a fine administrator. Not great, but good enough. You know as well as I that he was Dan's partner in name only. Dan was loyal, I'll grant you that, helping Nick use his GI Bill to get into a good college, and insisting Nick have his own lab. But the only solid research came from Dan. Thank God he finished the vaccine stuff before he died, or we'd all be screwed. Finished it—*and* first to publish." He stared at his glass, then looked up. "Speaking of which, the journal's out next week. I'll make sure you get an advance copy on Friday."

Emma was touched in spite of herself. "Thanks. It would mean a lot to the kids to have a copy of Dan's magnum opus. And to me."

Parker's expression softened and he took her hand, his touch surprisingly gentle, for such a volatile man. "We all miss Dan. His personal judgment was crap, and I'll never forgive him for what he did to you—but he was the finest scientist in the whole university. His article will put us on the map, and I'd bet my penthouse office he'll get a posthumous election to the National Academy of Sciences." He squeezed her hand, then let go. "Not to mention the good news for the drug manufacturer, PharmFam. All those parents, afraid to vaccinate their kids. Forget autism—it's a wonder we don't have a damn measles epidemic."

They finished the meal with more small talk, and Parker

insisted on paying the bill.

"You really don't have to," she began, rising, then stopped, staring.

Parker twisted to follow her gaze and uttered an expletive, then plastered a genial expression on his face. He rose and, cupping her elbow firmly, guided her toward a shaded table in the corner of the fenced courtyard.

"Nick—Oscar!"

Emma plastered on a smile of her own, wondering desperately how much they might have heard. Was that table open when she arrived? No—if shade was available, she would've taken it. Plus, the men were only half-done with their food. As usual, Oscar was plugged into a tiny MP3 player clipped to his pocket, but had Nick overheard anything?

He seemed preoccupied as he rose to greet her, but not upset, and she relaxed.

"Well, well." Oscar looked at the three of them while tipping his chair farther back into the shadows. "All the usual suspects, together again."

With his shock of unruly dark hair—too long to be tidy, too short to be hip—and poorly-shaven black stubble, he looked like nothing so much as the negative of blond-haired, blue-eyed Nick. Whereas Nick's tan physique suggested surfboards and breakers, Oscar's sallow complexion made it clear he preferred the indoors. And though in his late twenties—younger than Nick by a dozen years—something in Oscar's sulky demeanor made him seem older.

"Parker—I'm surprised to see you here," Nick said.

"Emma needed my help and thought she had to make nice to get it."

Nick frowned and turned to her. "What's he talking about?"

She sighed. "I suppose there's no hiding it. Yet another episode in the saga of Dr. Dan."

"Do tell." Oscar tipped forward again, perking up at the

news of someone else's misery.

As she explained about the loan and her financial aid, Nick's face went white, then darkened. Sometimes, it seemed like he took Dan's betrayal even harder than she did.

"Emma, I'm so sorry. If there's anything I can do—" He snapped his fingers and turned to Oscar. "Did Bernie fill that admin job she had advertised?"

"How should I know what happens on the first floor? That's nine floors too low for me."

Nick scowled. "You're hopeless."

"But too good to fire," Oscar said with what passed for cheerfulness on his part.

Or he could simply have been stating the facts. As Dan's chief researcher, the lab could ill-afford to lose him, especially now, when the vaccine paper was about to come out. A good portion of the research credit was his; if he left the Institute, he'd take it with him, and his next lab would benefit instead. With Dan gone, the Sion needed the original research team to stick together, presenting a united front for the ultimate fame and glory of the university.

No wonder Nick and Parker both looked like they wanted to punch him.

"Well, I'd better get going," Emma cut in, before the testosterone level rose any higher.

The thought that two career scientists and a chief mucky-muck administrator might have alpha-male issues struck her as incongruous. Then an image of Vin, broad-chested and well-muscled, suddenly loomed before her—*him* she could picture having a surplus of male hormones—and she fought down a nervous giggle.

Nick said, "Wait—Bernie's looking for an admin. Part-time, flexible hours. I know if you're interested, she'd hire you in a minute."

"What a wonderful idea," Parker said.

"Thanks, really."

Nick quirked a blond eyebrow. "But...?"

"I'm grateful for the offer. Really. But...I'd rather do

school without a job if I can."

"Of course," he said, and she thought about how considerate he was, and how lonely he'd been since Janice died. He *should* date again—just not her. This time, it was Vin's laughing blue eyes that flashed before her, until she ruthlessly pushed the image away.

"It's hard enough going back to school after so long," she continued. "Plus there's the kids. Speaking of which, I have to pick them up, run some errands, and get them to Karen's."

"Hot date?" Parker asked.

"Hardly. It's my workout day, and Bethanne has her poker game, so Karen offered to do dinner and a video. That way I can go for a nice long run. But I need new running shoes first, and if I don't leave now, I'll never fit everything in."

Oscar unfolded from the chair, saying to Nick, "We're done here." Then he turned to her. "Ready?"

Emma drew a blank, then got it. "The laptop! I completely forgot—Justin loaded it down with two gigs of photos. I think it'll be fine when he moves them off."

Oscar scowled. "Have it your way. But I bet your system's still whacked." He shoved out from behind the table, then stopped. "What about the cable? You still need *that*, for the transfer."

"Oh." He'd tried to be nice, in his own way, and she had been kind of rude. "I'll come get it now. Thanks—I appreciate it."

"No problem," he muttered, not meeting her gaze.

Emma glanced helplessly at Parker and Nick, then followed him out of the courtyard and onto the path toward the Sion.

****

Nick watched Emma walk away and felt a pang he would have been hard-pressed to define, even had he wanted to. He turned to find Parker regarding him with those strange silver eyes, and knew most of his confused emotions were probably writ clear on his face. Instead of denying them, he lifted a shoulder.

"Guilt. One of the perks of being Catholic."

Parker's heavy eyebrows rose. "Over…?"

"I introduced them. Remember?"

They turned to leave, and Parker said, "Who—Emma and Dan? Or Dan and Mollie?"

Nick froze, then frowned. "I never realized it before. Both, I suppose."

He resumed walking, staring at the scuffed toes of his brown loafers, which Janice had bought him more than ten years ago. It was past time to replace them, but he couldn't seem to let go.

So much guilt, so little time.

Thanks, Parker. Now I have even more reason to hate myself.

****

By the time Vin got home, it was past six. He'd had to stop at the store, and their video department was selling off their old DVDs. He'd picked up some of Azi's favorite musicals, and while he was browsing, found a copy of *Mafia Queen*, dated 1975. Unless Bethanne was even older than he'd thought, she really was a baby when she made it. Or at least, a teenybopper. Maybe he and Azi would watch it tonight.

After the day he'd had, and the ribbings from the other detectives, Vin needed to kick back with his "best" uncle and forget all about the O'Manny case. If there even *was* one. Stupidity had to be the leading cause of death in the US. And while his opinion of Dr. Dan was admittedly low after what the jerk did to Emma, he still thought anyone with sense would've checked the plane's fuel gauge before take-off.

He'd read the case notes. The private airport out of which O'Manny and McBride flew kept meticulous records. Onsite mechanics recorded every service performed, on all their planes, including times and amount of fuel added. But they weren't proactive. Which was to say, they might know a plane was low on fuel, but it was the pilot's job to ask for a fill. No sense having a fully fueled plane around before anyone was ready to fly it.

The plane itself—a Cessna Skyhawk—belonged to the McBrides. Mollie was a licensed pilot, but on the day in question, Dan was at the controls. Airport records showed it had a full tank a week before the accident, and had been taken out once in that time. O'Manny should have refueled, but hadn't. End of story.

Except…there were unanswered questions. Like, how experienced a pilot *was* Dan? Emma'd said he flew for the military, but in what capacity? And why wouldn't Mollie have checked the gauge herself, since it was her family's plane?

Plus, there was that missing parachute….

Damn.

It seemed he'd have to question Emma after all, just to get a clearer picture. But not until he'd spoken with HPD. He'd probably see her before then anyway. Azi counted the O'Mannys among his numerous Best Friends, and kept bugging Vin to invite them over.

So much for avoiding her.

He got out of the car with the groceries and the DVDs, imagining Azi's face lighting up when he saw them. It wasn't until he unlocked the door and stepped into the unlit hall that he remembered it was Wednesday, and Azi was at Tony's.

The injustice of it all was too much. First Azi ditched his ride, now he wasn't home to boost Vin's spirits after his lousy-ass day. Never mind that Azi always went to Tony's on Wednesdays. The damn holiday weekend had screwed up Vin's sense of time. He threw the DVDs on the couch, shoved the groceries in the fridge, yanked out a beer, stomped back to the living room, and prepared to sulk.

Then he realized he was being a dumbass. He set the beer on an end table and ran a hand through his hair. It was too late to go out—not that he had anywhere to go—and too early for bed. Watching TV alone would be depressing. He could go over to Tony's, but half the point was so Azi could play with the kids while Susan and Tony did stuff around the house. And the other half was so Vin could have alone time.

Except he was a pathetic loser who couldn't think of anything to do by himself.

Well, that was bullshit.

He stomped upstairs to change. *How's your knee?* Fuck that. He'd show Barton how his knee was. It'd been mostly functional for some time, and the docs had given him the official green light weeks ago. The multiple surgeries and months of physical therapy had paid off; it was finally good as new. But he'd been too busy to test it out.

The sun was just set. It was mild, but not hot, with a light breeze. Perfect for a run.

At least, it was until he rounded a curve in the park's jogging path and tripped over a woman tying her shoe. He landed on her first and his knee second. She yelped "Ouch!", he said "Fuck!", and pain exploded up his leg.

Vin rolled off her, clutching his knee, eyes screwed shut in agony. "Christ!"

She lay next to him, breathing hard, then he heard her push herself up. When she didn't say anything, he thought, jeez, would it kill her to ask if he was okay?

Then she blew out a breath. "Fine. I'll say it. We *have* to stop meeting like this."

He opened his eyes to see a pair of gold-brown ones laughing down at him. "Perfect."

"Oh, come on, you big wuss. It can't be that bad. *You* landed on *me*, remember?"

Vin deliberately glowered. "If you had the day I've had, you'd know it *is* that bad."

"I had that day. It was yesterday. But some of it spilled over to today, so I think we're even."

Emma moved closer and abruptly he realized he was seeing her for the first time with only a few smudges on her face, instead of her habitual glop. It was too dark to see well, but he thought she cleaned up as expected. Better. She wore black running spandex and a tank that barely concealed a hot-pink jog bra, which in turn barely concealed *her*. Her honey hair was pulled into a ponytail just the right length for pulling, and he resisted the urge to tug it.

Then she knelt beside him and touched his thigh and a jolt of sexual heat surged through him so fast he jerked away.

"Sorry," she said, looking concerned.

"It's fine."

No damsels in distress. Except, *he* was the one in agony, on so many levels. Plus there was the whole O'Manny non-case. *Damn it.* Not like she was a suspect, because so far, there was nothing to suspect.

"At least let me look at it."

Her hand slid down his leg to his knee, and what started as a jolt grew to megawatt proportions. "It's *fine*," he repeated, not caring that he sounded like the world's worst grouch.

She noticed the fading constellation of scars on his skin and traced one with her finger. Her touch was gentle, tender. Agonizing. Her heat practically scorched him, her scent filled his nostrils, and the images crowding his brain were anything but gentle. *Rough, hard, slick, fast*—that's how he wanted her. And God did he want her—potential case, or not.

Vin snatched his leg away, ignoring her startled exclamation, and prayed his shorts were loose enough to maintain propriety. He rolled away and examined the knee himself, silently reciting as much of the *Oregon Revised Statutes* as he could from memory, to take his mind off the woman sitting behind him. A small scrape grazed his skin, and he'd probably have a bruise, but a little probing assured him no lasting damage had been done.

"What happened to it?" Emma asked.

"I was shot last year. Surgery to remove the bullet and

fragments of bone, then more to rebuild the joint. At this point, most of the scars are from surgery, not the wound itself."

"Ouch."

He grinned in spite of himself. "I think I picked a stronger word. Or ten. But that works."

"And you can run on it now?"

"I don't know about *now*. But yeah, fifteen minutes ago the docs thought it was as good as new." Vin tried to glower again but he was suddenly having too much fun.

Emma clearly hadn't realized he was teasing and looked stricken. "I'm sorry! My shoe came untied. I should have moved off the path."

Which reminded Vin where they were. "Never mind about that. What the hell were you doing out here, running by yourself in the dark?"

Even with the low light he saw her eyes flash. "It wasn't late when I started. Besides, my house is right over there."

"Even better. A rapist can lurk in the bushes, wait for you to leave your house, then follow you in here to attack."

"Oh, please."

He stood and offered her his hand. "Sorry. Cops can't help thinking about these things. But you really shouldn't run at night by yourself. Unless you *want* to get attacked, in which case, feel free."

Emma rolled her eyes, but she let him pull her up, then brushed the leaves and dirt off her legs. And *damn* she had nice legs. *Great* legs. Legs that went on for miles, even though she wasn't exactly tall.

Then she bent over to finish tying her shoe and Vin's brain shorted out.

Hell.

...Under ORS 40.225, there is no privilege for, uh, communications, if the declarant has a—a clear and serious intent to subsequently commit a crime...

She faced him, and he cleared his throat. "I'd better walk you home."

"That's not necessary—"

"It's my civic duty."

He watched with amusement while her exasperation rose and she tried to figure out how to get rid of him. "But I'm not done with my run."

Vin glanced at her obviously new running shoes, thought, *how bad could it be*, and heard himself say, "I'll go with you, *then* walk you home."

"But—your knee—"

"It's fine."

"Are you sure? What if you reinjure it—"

"Shut up." He took her arm, turned her around and gave her a little push.

She blew out a breath. "Fine. Don't say I didn't warn you."

"Big talk. Let's see what you've got."

She shot him a look, then jogged gracefully down the path, and he followed.

Fifteen minutes later, Vin's lungs ached, his knee burned in fiery torture, and he was having the time of his life. Watching Emma's spandex-covered rear moving in front of him, he wondered what she'd think if she knew he was having one of the oldest cop fantasies in the book, involving her, a four-poster, and several pairs of velvet-covered handcuffs.

Shit. This was nuts.

He shook his head, then quickened his steps until he was beside her, her rear safely out of view. Except now her chest was *in* view, the thin pink of her bra not doing a damn thing to stop her breasts from bouncing as she ran. He fought back a groan—*…to subsequently commit a crime involving physical, uh, injury, a threat to the physical safety of any person, or death…*—then forced his gaze up as they neared the edge of the park and she finally slowed to a walk.

He adjusted his own stride and cleared his throat. "So…dumb question, but—how have you been?"

Emma was silent. He'd asked mainly as a distraction, but

also out of curiosity. How did one recover from something like what she'd been through?

At last she said, "I'm okay. It's been…tough."

"Yeah?" He waited for her to elaborate, and when she didn't, stole a glance at her profile. Something in her expression—betrayal, lost innocence, humiliation—twisted his gut.

"I imagine it would be. After what your husband did, you must be angry. And then he goes and dies, and you can't even have it out with him. I'd be damn confused, to put it mildly." Her gaze jerked up, and he smiled. "What? Because I'm a cop, I can't understand feelings? I'm a sensitive guy."

She laughed. "Real sensitive. Tonight, you flattened me, and if I remember right, the first time we met, you handcuffed me and threw me on the floor."

Her description, while accurate, was too close to the fantasy he'd been having. He tried to come up with more of the ORS—*anything*—then gave up and hoped the darkness covered him.

"Sorry about that," he said as they stepped into a small cul-de-sac. "Just doing my job."

"I know. No hard feelings. Here we are."

Whatever he'd expected, it wasn't the dull gray, rectangular two-story right at the edge of the park, into whose drive they now turned. Emma had a casual-classic look about her, but this was one of those boring late-seventies boxes, without even a dormer window to break its façade. It had an uncovered wood deck for a porch, perfectly square, with a lone wrought-iron bench on it. Custom landscape lights shone on flower beds that were either bare or scattered with weeds, and the lawn, though neatly mowed, had more dandelions and clover than grass. Next to the deck, the porch light illuminated at least ten dirty, upturned planters.

Vin gestured at them. "What gives?"

Emma looked where he'd indicated. "Oh. After Dan died, people sent me plants. Some floral arrangements, but lots more were live ones I could transplant to the yard.”

He took in the utter lack of live shrubbery on the property and lifted an eyebrow.

She grimaced. “Bethanne said I over-watered some, under-watered others, and didn’t feed them right.”

He touched her arm. “It wasn’t your fault.”

“It’s all right. I used to love plants, too.”

She withdrew her arm, clearly not wanting to talk about it, and walked the rest of the way up the drive. She had a dark green minivan, a much older model than he would have expected, and the fence separating her property from the park was old and in need of repair. Her husband had only been dead six months, but then, probably brilliant scientists didn’t have much brain power leftover for home repairs.

Emma stepped onto the porch, repeating, “Here we are.”

“‘On the street where you live.’” She seemed confused. “Never mind—not your genre.” He stopped, unable to think of anything to say, yet unwilling to leave. Damn.

Cul-de-sac. Minivan. Case.

Damsels in distress…

There—better.

“I’ll wait ’til you get inside.”

She looked like she wanted to object, then gave in. She unlocked the door and pushed it open. “Home safe and sound. You may go now, Officer.”

“Detective.”

She pretended to glare. At least her melancholy was lifting.

“Good-bye, *Detective*. And—thank you.”

“No problem, Mike.”

This time, the glare was real. Cripes but she was fun to tease. She stepped into the house, waved cheerily, then shut the door and clicked the lock. A light went on inside and he turned to leave.

And then she screamed.

He was on the porch and hammering at the door without

knowing how he got there. He rattled the knob, heart thundering, and pounded harder. "*Emma!* Are you all right? *Open up!*"

He drew back, preparing to kick the damn thing in when she finally opened it.

Vin grabbed her shoulders, raking his gaze over her, assessing, looking for damage. "What is it? What happened?"

"I'm okay," she said, and he wanted to yell at her for scaring the crap out of him. To wrap his arms around her and thank God she was safe, and tell her he'd keep her that way.

Then she added, "But someone broke into my house."

And all he could come up with was, "*Fuck.*"

Chapter Six

St. Zita the Domestic:
Housemaids, Waitpersons, Missing Keys, and Wives

"You're sure nothing's missing?" Vin asked Emma for the fifth time, and she scrunched herself farther into the couch.

"Not even Bethanne's costume jewelry, or her classic movie collection. I *wish* someone would steal that."

Instead of pulling her close and murmuring assurances into her hair—not that she *wanted* him to—Vin leaned forward, elbows on knees, frowning. "They had to be looking for something. Your purse was in plain sight, and they didn't touch it. You're sure they didn't touch it?"

"Positive. It's exactly where I left it, right next to my keys. They could've stolen the van, not that it's worth much. It needs some work. Half the time it won't even start."

She couldn't seem to stop babbling. Probably due to shock—not that Vin even noticed.

He scrubbed a hand over his face, then sat back, his sprawl taking up more than half the couch, but not bringing him nearly close enough. Emma fought back a sigh, and reminded herself that she only wanted him to hold her because she was scared and tired. And because she'd pretty much wanted to touch him all evening. But that was beside the point.

Little worry-creases in his forehead and around his eyes softened when he looked at her, and he reached for her hand, caressing it gently and making her feel instantly better. "And you have no idea what they might have been looking for?"

"No."

After she'd turned on the light, it took a few seconds for her brain to register what her eyes saw. The room felt odd, too cold, and she'd looked through to the dining room, with its sliding doors onto the back deck. Except one of the doors was…*gone*…broken glass everywhere, a gaping hole in place of safety.

She started shaking again, and then Vin did pull her to him, and she buried her face in his chest and tried not to cry.

"Hey, it's all right."

He shifted so that more of her was pressed to his side, caressing her back, and even though it didn't mean anything, she pretended it did and relaxed into him.

"The detectives are almost done. They'll take the print they found, and anything else, to the station. We'll find out who did this."

And why.

He didn't say it, but she knew he thought it, because it's what she'd wondered ever since rational thought returned. *Why* would someone do this? Why break in, and take nothing of value? Whoever it was searched—thoroughly— and then left, apparently empty-handed. Drawers, cabinets, closets—all opened, most emptied. The roll-top secretary in the dining room was upended—fortunately not damaged— and even the kids' rooms were searched.

Her babies. How would they ever feel safe again? Fortunately, Karen had kept them at her house for a sleepover, sparing them from coming home to *this*. It would be bad enough dealing with Bethanne's reaction. Thank God Vin was outside when she screamed. He'd given the house a once-over, helped her call the police and Bethanne, and stayed while the detectives worked.

He moved his cheek over her hair, and Emma gave up and sighed into him. "Mmm…And you thought the danger was in the park."

He stilled. "You sure you'll be all right here?"

His heart thumped beneath her cheek and she thought *stay with me.* But she only said, "I'm fine. Bethanne will be back by eleven."

"She's not on her way?"

The implied question—*isn't she worried about her daughter?*—didn't have an easy answer, so Emma said, "It's her weekly poker game. They never finish early."

He was quiet, and because he'd be leaving soon, she let her fingers wander a little over his impressive chest. He gave no sign of objecting, or even noticing, but then he turned his head and she thought his lips brushed her hair. He smelled of spice and clean male sweat and something uniquely *him*, and she couldn't help it—she nuzzled.

And…an image of Dan popped into her head. He was smaller and thinner than Vin—most men were. But Emma had loved cuddling with him just the same, on this very couch. Vin was big, strong, capable. Dan was tender and funny. At least, before he screwed around on her.

Actually, even after.

She had to stop doing this.

"I'll be fine," she repeated, sitting up. Her eyes burned, and she looked away so Vin wouldn't see, but he was still preoccupied anyway.

There. Not so bad.

"I'll stay until Bethanne gets here. And I'll board up the door. You have any plywood?"

"I think so. In the shed."

One of the detectives came into the living room. "We're done here."

Vin went into cop mode. "Find anything else?"

"Maybe. This look familiar?"

Emma examined the round silver pin, bagged and resting on the woman's palm. It was about three quarters of an inch in diameter, with a tiny caduceus on it, flanked by a one and a zero. The border read, "OSHU: Teach—Discover—Heal."

"That's a university ten-year pin, for ten years of

employment. I hate to disappoint you, but it's probably Dan's."

"Where do you keep it?"

"It must have been in my jewelry box. Dan wore it a lot—he was proud of how long he'd been at the university, and how he, Nick, and Parker founded the Sion. I assumed he took it to Hawaii, but I guess not. Where did you find it?"

"Outside, on the back deck."

Vin got the implications quicker than she. "So…either Dan's ghost left it, or the perp took it and dropped it while leaving. Or—it isn't Dan's."

The detective asked, "Was your jewelry box messed with?"

"I don't think so—just big stuff, like dressers. It might not even have been in there. It could have been in the secretary—maybe it fell out and got stuck on the guy's shoe."

"Maybe. Any way to confirm if Dr. O'Manny had his in Hawaii?"

"He went down in a pretty wild area. The plane was intact, but the luggage scattered all over. They didn't find many personal effects."

"How many people have worked at OSHU that long?"

"Tons."

"Off the top of your head?"

Emma laughed. "Seriously? A quarter of the Sion alone. Same with the hospital, the med school. Other research facilities."

The detective seemed surprised. "I had no idea OSHU was such a great place to work."

"They're the only game around. Loyalty's a given."

The woman's partner appeared, and Vin saw them out. Emma was too antsy to sit, so she started straightening up. By ten, Vin had covered the broken door with plywood, and she had the house mostly restored. She'd just finished righting the secretary when Vin appeared, bearing two wine glasses and an open bottle of merlot.

"I found this in your pantry. You look like you could use a drink."

"Oh, God, yes." Emma took the glass he offered, pausing to savor the first sip.

Vin watched her, then frowned and steered her to the couch. "And you need to sit."

"I'm fine."

"No, you're not. You've been cleaning for two hours, and before that, you ran. God knows what you did earlier. Now sit."

He pushed her onto a corner section, then sat on the middle seat. One of the floor lamps had been knocked over and she hadn't replaced the bulb, so the room was half dark. Vin's profile was unyielding, and she couldn't decide if he was mad or just thinking. They drank in silence, until he abruptly took her glass and set it with his on the coffee table.

"Hey! I wasn't done with that."

He spread his arms over the sofa back. His mouth was a tight line, and his body took up more space than one person had a right to. He looked determined—about what, she couldn't fathom.

"You scared me half to death."

"Sorry," Emma said. "When I saw the broken glass—"

"And I really don't like you staying here tonight, with or without Bethanne."

"What do you want me to do? Besides, it's not likely they'd come back tonight."

"I still don't like it." He shrugged, as though shaking something off, then said for no apparent reason, "I'm not a knight in shining armor."

"I didn't think you were."

He stared at her, then blew out a breath. "Have you considered becoming a nun?"

"Uh—"

"Never mind, don't answer that."

He sighed, looked put-upon, then picked up her hand

and pressed his thumbs into her palm. Emma fought back a moan.

"Here's the thing, Mike. Azi didn't exactly *tell* me you were a boy. But he implied it."

His eyes were dark, lids half-lowered, and she said, "Yes?"

He tugged her closer, pulling her against his side, and continued to work his magic on her muscles. "For weeks, in my mind, you've been Azi's buddy Mike. Then I found out who you were, met your kids, and the adjustment was…weird." He put the first hand down and reached for the other, bringing it to his lips and blowing gently on it.

"And now…?" she managed.

Vin's face hovered over hers. He was going to kiss her. God, he'd *better* kiss her. His voice was low, and he murmured, "Now I'm over it…Mike."

He waited, giving her a chance to pull back. When she didn't, he bent and she lifted her mouth, meeting him halfway. Their lips connected, lightly, and little jolts of desire shot through Emma to all the right places. Vin pulled her tight, deepening the kiss. She slid her hands up his chest and around his neck, and suddenly, urgently, his tongue ran along her lips. She opened to him, then gasped as wet heat flooded through her.

****

Vin groaned. Emma tasted sweeter and sexier than—hell, anything. From the minute he'd tripped over her in the park, he'd known this was inevitable. Maybe even since Azi tackled her, or when they'd met at the lab. Everything about kissing her was inevitable.

His tongue thrust deeper, and then hers brushed against his and he almost lost it. He pulled her onto his lap, then slid a hand up her side, needing to touch her, to cup those full B breasts. He waited a heartbeat—what if she pushed him away?—but then she straddled him, urging him on, and he explored her sweet curves. Her breasts were perfect, their soft weight just right in his hand. He ran a thumb over her

75

nipple, the bud hardening, and she jerked and moaned, "Bethanne…?"

Through a haze of urgent hot lust, Vin murmured "What?", then moved her down onto the couch beneath him.

"Oomph!" Emma said, urgent, but not with hot lust. She shoved his chest, but for the life of him, he couldn't figure out why. Surely she was as turned on as he was—he couldn't have misread her that much.

She finally pulled her mouth away and gasped, "*Bethanne.*"

Vin blinked. Emma's eyes were dark with desire, her nipples taut against him, her mouth swollen and rosy from their kiss. Why the hell was she talking about her mother?

"She's trying to tell you I'm home," Bethanne's voice said dryly from behind him.

Vin shot off the couch and pretended she wouldn't notice his raging erection if she looked down. She didn't. Her violet eyes glittered, and he didn't think it was from amusement.

"Are we interrupting something?" the man behind her asked archly.

Great. Charley, too. His eyes *were* twinkling. He glanced at the boarded door, then at Emma. "I see where the breaking part happened. Was this the entering?"

Emma's face was pink, and she lurched off the couch and straightened her clothes.

"No, not at all. Vin was just—we were—Oh, never mind." She looked at him. "I'll walk you out."

"You do that," Bethanne interjected. "Then come back and tell us all about the break-in. I do hope nothing of Dan's was taken."

Now wasn't *that* the biggest, fattest double-entendre Vin had ever heard?

"Yes," Charley said. "Dan's things are *so* important around here."

Emma ignored them both, and Vin followed her to the

porch.

"Thanks." Her tone was forced, her expression closed. "For helping me. It was…"

He had the panicky sense that she was about to brush him off. He couldn't let the evening end like this. Not after the most amazing make-out session he'd had since he was a teenager, when they were *all* amazing.

"Shut up," he said and drew her close. He kissed her, not rough, but not gentle either. Possessive. She stood rigid for a moment, then sighed and kissed him back.

"That's better," he murmured and she laughed.

"Sorry. It's just—Bethanne—and—Dan—"

"I know. It's okay. But we're not done here." Vin kissed her again, enjoying the feel of her. Then he reluctantly let her go. "I'll call you tomorrow."

She nodded, and he left.

****

On Thursday, Barton put Vin in charge of the investigation into the O'Manny break-in, which he should have expected, but somehow hadn't. A possible murder *and* a robbery at the widow's house, would be an awfully big coincidence. However, when he explained he had a prior acquaintance with the victim, Barton merely said no other detective was available, and told him to mind his p's and q's.

Which he did.

First, he called Honolulu PD, but the detective wasn't in, so he left a message. Then he set about determining how many of OSHU's eleven thousand employees had received ten-year pins, and if any of them were connected to Emma or Dan—or Bethanne, since she lived at the house, too. As predicted, it was a needle in a haystack operation from the get-go.

He did catch one lucky break. The nice OSHU Personnel Director told him the round pin they'd found was only in use from 2007 to 2014. Before and after that, OSHU gave out square pins. So whoever owned it had likely been hired between 1997 and 2004, which narrowed the field considerably. The Personnel Director also emailed him the list of Sion employees right away, sorted by hire date. Not surprisingly, Nick and Parker—who retained his Co-Director title despite little day-to-day involvement in the Institute—were at the top. Vin left messages for them, then began working his way down the list.

Meanwhile, Azi rode the bus again, which put Vin in an encore of a bad mood; not that he wouldn't have been in one anyway. He hated making phone calls, and after several hours of tracking down pin recipients, his head ached, and he desperately needed to see Emma to—hopefully—finish what they'd started last night. Or at least further it.

Then HPD called him back.

"God damn it," Vin said after he hung up.

Of course Barton just *happened* to be lurking nearby. "Having fun yet?"

"No. But you may have to send me to Hawaii before all this is done."

That shut her up. When five o'clock came, he was worn down, beat up, and in no mood to be polite. He called Azi and told him to be ready at six. Then he called Emma, told her they were coming over to cook dinner, and hung up before she could object. And for the first time since last night, he felt cheerful again.

****

Karen's office phone rang at five-fifteen, just as she was leaving. Caller ID showed an OSHU prefix, so she pretty much knew who it was, but she answered anyway.

"James here."

"What do you know," Parker boomed. "James here, too."

Karen gritted her teeth and set down her briefcase. "I knew I should've gone back to my maiden name."

"So why didn't you?"

"Oh, come on. After a lifetime spelling Wiczniewski, would you?"

"I like it. Wiz-*nyew*-ski. Not difficult at all."

"Only because I married your dumbass brother, and you can already spell it."

"No, really. Has a nice ring to it. Karen…Alexis… Wiczniewski."

Wasn't there a Native American belief that uttering someone's true name gave you power over them? A shiver ran down Karen's spine. "What do you want?"

He laughed, obviously enjoying her discomfort. "Emma told you she stopped by?"

"Yes…"

"I said I'd help, make sure her app landed on the right desk."

"Uh-huh…" *Here it comes.*

"And you owe me a dinner."

Damn. It'd seemed like a good idea, a way to get him to help Emma, and from what Rob said, Parker wasn't dating much. In a moment of desperation, the offer to buy him dinner had popped out. What the hell was she thinking? An entire evening…with *him?*

But she'd promised. "Fine. Pick a restaurant."

"Too easy."

"It's okay, really. Sky's the limit."

"No. *Too easy.*" The way Parker lowered his huge voice, like a hunter on the prowl, sent the dread back *up* her spine. "I can't think how long it's been since I had a home-cooked meal. Shall we say tonight at eight?"

"Me—cook for you? *Tonight?* Are you *insane?*"

"My apologies. Of course you need time to make it special."

"*Special?* If you think I'm wasting my energy on my ex-husband's older brother—"

"Tonight it is."

She might have promised, but she wouldn't be a doormat. "Look, jerk, someone broke into Emma's house last night. I'm going over to keep her company."

The line was silent. Finally he said, "I'm sorry," and for once, sounded like he meant it.

"It's okay. You didn't know."

"Tomorrow, then. Eight, your place. I like salmon."

He hung up before she'd finished spluttering.

It was only after she'd gotten in her car that she realized he hadn't been surprised by, or even interested in, the break-in. Which just went to show how self-absorbed *both* the James boys were. What the hell had she gotten herself into?

****

"You're a glutton for punishment," Emma said forty-five minutes later as they sipped wine on her porch.

"I guess." Karen tamped down her queasiness.

Inside, the kids were setting the table and arguing about something catastrophic, like who got the red plate and who got the blue. Now and then Bethanne tried reasoning with them. It never worked, but she hadn't figured that out yet.

"Why do I *do* this?" Karen said, and Emma's expression went thoughtful. "What?"

"Do you think…*maybe*…you have trust issues?"

"Well, duh. My mother abandoned me and my dad when I was eight. And, let's see, Rob couldn't even stay faithful for *three weeks*."

"Fine. I just think Parker's not *so* bad, and maybe you're overreacting. Maybe you could let him be nice to you. It's only one dinner."

"But *why* does he want it?"

"As to that, you're on your own." Emma took a sip and Karen followed suit, thinking it through, using her analytical skills to seek a solution.

Finally she said, "I think he wants to punish me for dumping Rob."

"You think Parker loves his baby brother that much?"

"Sure. He's über loyal—he's been pissed since the day Rob brought me home. Every family dinner, Parker avoided me like death. He never thought I was good enough. He should be *glad* Rob and I divorced. Today he suggested I stop using James and go back to Wiczniewski—like I'm too low even to share his *name*. The nerve."

80

Two men emerged from the park into the cul-de-sac. The first was Zorro. The second was six feet tall, muscular, with a purposeful stride and fierce red hair. He carried a sack of groceries and frowned when he saw her next to Emma.

"*Hel-lo*. Is that who I think it is?"

Emma turned pink when she caught the hunk's eye. "If you think it's Vin, then yes."

"What's he doing here?"

"Cooking dinner."

Karen stared. "Did I miss something?"

Emma's blush deepened. "We sort of…made out."

Karen screeched, then clapped a hand over her mouth at Emma's panicked look. "Sorry. But what does 'sort of' mean?"

The men were in the drive and Emma whispered, "He kissed me."

"And you…?"

"Kissed back."

"Tongue?"

"Karen!"

She opened her mouth and Emma said in a strangled voice, "*Yes*. Tongue. Happy?"

"Groping?"

"Groping what?" Fierce Hunk said from the steps.

Emma looked mortified, and Karen felt a pang of guilt, but Fierce Hunk didn't notice—too busy devouring Emma with his eyes, like she was dessert and he'd been on a lifelong diet.

Inside the house, Justin and Juney reached a crescendo, and Bethanne angrily cut them off. "Damn it! Give me those *right now*. Tomorrow, I'm going to Meier & Frank and buy a whole *set* of red plates."

"Hi, Zo—I mean, Azi." Karen turned to Fierce Hunk. "You must be Vin. I'm Karen." She glanced back at Emma. "Does Bethanne know?"

Thank God looks couldn't kill. Emma ground out, "Know *what*?"

"That you and Mr. Hunk here—"

"*Karen!*"

Fierce Hunk's gaze bored into Karen, and she coughed. "What I meant was, does Bethanne know Mr. Hunk and Hunk Junior—" She winked at Azi who grinned and gave her a thumb's up. "—are coming to dinner?"

"Who's coming to dinner?" Bethanne said pleasantly as she walked onto the porch. "I invited Charley, if that's who you mean." Then she saw Vin and her expression went flat. "Well, hello, Detective."

"Bethanne." Fierce Hunk's tone was equally flat.

Emma looked at Bethanne. "Sorry. I forgot to tell you."

"It's your house. Of course you can invite whomever you want."

Vin frowned and Karen smiled. The evening had just gotten a *lot* more interesting.

****

Two hours later, Vin's cheerfulness had evaporated, and he wasn't sure if he was about to explode more from needing to throttle Emma's so-called friends, or from his inability to touch her. Probably the latter. The minute he arrived, he'd needed to kiss her. And not just a peck. No, what he needed was more along the lines of when-can-I-drive-myself-deep-inside-you. Since he hadn't trusted himself *not* to kiss her that way—avid audience be damned—he'd grunted something clever like, "*Hi.* I'm making chicken," and escaped into the house.

While he unloaded the bags and hunted for cookware, Azi ran out back with Justin and Juney. Vin had known they wouldn't be alone, and had invited Azi with that in mind. What he hadn't bargained on was how hard it was not to jump her, in spite of the lack of privacy.

At dinner, he finagled a seat next to hers, then wished he hadn't. He felt her nearness, though they never touched. And he *ached* to touch her, to run his hand over her bare thigh, slide his fingers inside her bra and cup the curve of her breast. Hear her sharp intake of breath, push her down beneath him—

Cripes. He fought back a groan and attacked his dinner.

Meanwhile, it seemed Bethanne, Karen, and Charley were bent on embarrassing Emma, at least partly on purpose. And Emma did nothing to stop it. Bethanne repeatedly showcased the Wonder that was Dan, while Charley egged her on or baited her, both of which hurt Emma. And Karen was fiercely loyal, but oblivious, so that half her comments only made things worse.

Like now.

Emma had risen to clear the table, when Bethanne said to no one in particular, "Emma's been having such a difficult time since Dan's death. He was the love of her life, you know."

"No, he wasn't," Karen said, completely missing Emma's agonized look. "He—"

Justin and Juney turned to her, the former mutinous, the latter confused. Even Azi sensed something was up.

Vin cut in smoothly, "Dan was a brilliant man. I'm sure Emma misses him terribly."

She shot him a grateful look, and Justin transferred his glare to Vin, but that was to be expected. Justin was not dumb. Vin wished he could make it clear he just had the hots for Emma, with no desire to become New Dad. But he doubted Justin would appreciate *that*, either.

He pushed back from the table and grabbed a stack of dishes. "Here, let me help."

"Thanks," Emma said in the kitchen. "For dinner, and for what you said out there."

"Don't mention it." He set the dishes down and turned on the faucet. Discussing Dan sent a weird feeling to his gut. Partly it was personal. But it was professional, too. All evening, he'd wanted to tell her what HPD had said. It wouldn't exactly be a breach of protocol, but...

"What?" she asked, watching him curiously.

"Nothing. Just deciding which of my embarrassing relatives to tell you about first."

"That many to choose from?"

"Tons. Really. I'm not making this up. We're all Catholic, so there's that, and then we're from Lithuania, which is—"

She held up a hand. "One of the Baltic states. Near Poland. The first country to declare independence from the USSR."

He shut off the water. "Most people haven't heard of it."

"I pay attention. Sometimes."

"Yeah?" Vin couldn't keep the huskiness out of his voice. "Then you probably know what I've been wanting to do all night."

She was so close. Her lips parted and her breath caught and—

The swinging door banged open and Karen walked in. "Oops. Am I interrupting something?"

Emma backed away before he could stop her. "No, nothing." She turned to the sink and began rinsing dishes for all she was worth.

"Oh." Karen sounded as disappointed as Vin felt. Then she brightened. "I'm taking the kids and Azi out for ice cream. Azi's tired, so I'll drop him off at your place on my way back."

"Okay." Vin wasn't sure what to do with that. Azi often went to bed early. But here lately, it seemed like Azi was avoiding him.

Then Karen added, "And Charley's taking Bethanne to a movie. They're leaving now."

And Vin could have kissed her. Maybe she wasn't *totally* oblivious. A suspicion borne out when she said, "I'll help with the trash," and jerked her head at him, then toward the door.

Emma missed it, and Vin followed Karen out and dropped the trash into the can she held open, wondering how she planned to warn him off.

She didn't make him wait long. "Here's the scoop. So far, I like you—nice, respectable guy with no skeletons in his closets." If she noticed him flinch, she gave no sign. "But

Dan really hurt Emma. If you're just fooling around, great; a fling would do her good. But you better tell her up front. I won't let anyone treat her that bad again."

Vin crossed his arms. "Oh? Don't want her hurt, huh?"

"No."

"Then why sell her short? Isn't she worth more than a 'fling?'"

She regarded him curiously while he glared back. Her words made perfect, logical sense, and even fit with his own ideas of how his relationship with Emma should play out. But the way she'd put it sounded cheap.

At last she said, "Sorry. I shouldn't have spoken. Azi and the kids are waiting."

"Wait. Since you're so concerned, maybe you can help with this. She said she used to love plants, until she got a bunch after Dan died. Do you know what that was about?"

Karen bit her lip. "The plants were meant to be lasting remembrances, but they just made more work for her. She was already overwhelmed, but instead of telling people she didn't want them, she did her best to care for them."

"Even though she was stretched thin taking care of the kids, herself, Bethanne?"

"Perceptive. I knew I liked you. Yes, she went with the flow, never refused a plant, and never threw one out."

"Like you would have done?"

"Without a second thought. But Emma's not like that. She wants everyone to be happy. In the end, the plants all died, depressing her even more."

"How'd her dad die?"

He could tell the question caught her off-guard. After a minute she said, "ALS."

"Lou Gehrig's Disease?"

She nodded. "Bethanne's not very nurturing, in case you hadn't noticed. Emma took care of him when he got sick, and after he died, she arranged the funeral herself. It changed her. Then when Dan died, she had to do it all again."

"Bethanne didn't help? Either time?"

"Emma would say Bethanne did her best."

"Whatever that means." She only shrugged, so Vin asked, "How old was she when her dad died?"

Karen waited a beat. "Twelve."

Vin couldn't think of anything to say to that. Karen lifted an eyebrow, then left him on the deck, thinking about a pre-teen Emma, watching her father die by inches, then arranging his funeral. While Bethanne quoted old movies and "did her best."

Ouch.

Chapter Seven

St. Dymphna the Abused:
Martyrs, Therapists, Runaways, and Nuts

When Vin returned, Emma was ready for him. Until she saw him. She'd finished the dishes, wiped the counters, put away the leftovers and was trying to think of something else to do when he opened the back door and came inside. He paused, watching her, his expression serious, and her stomach did a few flip-flops, and she realized she'd *never* be ready for him. She turned away and reached for the first thing she saw, which happened to be the wine he'd opened last night.

Last night—they could talk about the break-in. She cleared her throat. "So. Any news about the pin?"

Vin moved to stand behind her, not touching her, but she felt his breath on her neck. Suddenly, the wine bottle was too slippery and she couldn't get the stopper out.

"Here. Let me." He reached around her and she fought the urge to lean back into his hard strength. The stopper pulled out instantly at his touch—of course it would—and he rested his hands on her shoulders, saying against her ear, "You were right. Lots of folks were hired by OSHU more than ten years ago."

If only she'd had more experience before marrying Dan—if it hadn't been so long since she'd dated *anyone*—maybe she'd know what to do now. Vin obviously did. He dug his thumbs into her shoulders, his hands so large they dipped well below her collarbones.

"Mmm. I should…"

"What?" He kissed her neck.

She gasped and instinctively moved away, but he tightened his grip, holding her in place. Much as he'd done when they first met—which he also seemed to notice just then.

Abruptly he released her and stepped back. "Emma."

His tone was serious and she faced him, suddenly, irrationally, afraid of what he might say. "Yes?"

"I need to tell you something. I spoke with the Honolulu Police Department today. McBride's family never thought the crash was an accident. They pushed for an investigation."

"And…?"

"HPD found a third set of prints inside the plane—on the control panel, and where a missing parachute should have hung."

Cold dread shivered up her spine. "Someone was on the plane with them?"

"We don't know that he was *with* them, but yeah—at some point."

"Couldn't the prints have been left during a—a maintenance check or something?"

"HPD's looking into it. But—there were a lot of prints. More than Dan's, which would be difficult if they were left *before* his. Emma, I want to be sure you understand. Dan's death is under investigation. We don't know if anything will turn up, but we have to look."

"Of course."

"And I've been assigned to the case."

Emma swallowed. "I think I'd better sit down. Outside."

Vin followed her through the newly replaced sliding glass door to the back deck and sank down next to her in the porch swing. Though it was warm out, she shivered again, and Vin wrapped an arm around her.

"It'll be okay."

She managed to nod. "I'm just—it's a shock, that's all. I thought I was coming to terms with Dan's death. But the break-in—and now this…"

"I know." He kissed her hair. "I didn't want to upset you. But, going forward, I thought you should know. I didn't want you to be blindsided by it later."

"Going forward…?"

Vin brought his free hand up to brush her cheek. She tilted her head into him—if he didn't know by now how much she wanted him, he was dumber than a rock. Luckily, he wasn't, because she also couldn't make herself do anything to speed things up. He appeared to understand.

He moved off the swing and squatted in front of her, forcing her to knee him in the abdomen or open her legs. She chose the latter, allowing—no, *inviting* him in. His arms corded on either side of her, protecting and trapping all at once. He dropped his hands to her bare legs and drew slow, lazy circles with his thumbs on the insides of her thighs. She was still fully clothed, he hadn't even touched anything good, and yet she was achingly ready.

For him.

Someone other than Dan.

She'd thought it would feel weird. But somehow, with Vin, it was the most normal thing in the world. Natural, and exciting and…wonderful.

He hooked his thumbs under her shorts, sliding his fingers around to cup her rear. Still not quite where she wanted him, but closer. Definitely closer.

He placed a kiss on one thigh, then the other. "I don't know how much more alone time we have, so I'll be brief. You're an amazingly strong person, Michael Anne."

She let her lids flutter closed, giving herself up to the sensation of his touch, the way his quiet voice rolled over her, leaving little pulses of desire in its wake.

"You take care of a lot of things around here. A lot of people. Your kids. Bethanne. Dan, when he was alive. And…your father."

Emma froze, then opened her eyes.

Vin held her gaze. "Now it's your turn. Let me take care of you tonight."

He slid her zipper down slowly, exposing the plain white of her underwear. Self-conscious, she started to close her legs, but Vin prevented her. "No."

She tore her gaze away and looked at the dark sky, embarrassed but needing him to understand. "I—" She choked, then tried again. "I haven't been with many men." He was silent and she added, "I wanted you to know, in case…I'm not what you expected."

"Emma. Look at me."

She forced her gaze down. Even in the dark, she saw the raw need in his expression, and let out a strangled half-sob, half-laugh. He slid her shorts off and tossed them aside. Then he reached for her underwear.

"I've had two kids."

He paused, and a smile crept over his face. "I know." His voice was rough, his fingers gentle as they slid under the cotton and elastic that was all that protected her.

"I mean—everything's a little more…south…than you might think."

Vin laughed—he actually *laughed*, the jerk. But somehow, she knew he wasn't laughing at her. He sounded…joyous. "I know you've had kids. I even know how babies are made, and where they come out when they're done. But I'll be honest—I don't usually date single mothers. Or any mothers, since the married ones are mostly off-limits."

She couldn't help it; she laughed.

His eyes twinkled, then he sobered. "But…you're much more than a mother. You make me laugh. You make me hornier than hell. And you're beautiful." He pulled her underwear down and tossed them onto her shorts. "*Everywhere.*"

And just like that, she was exposed. He blew against her, his hot breath chasing away the cool night air and any lingering doubts. With one hand, he tilted her hips. With his other, he slid a finger over her, parting her just enough to dip into her. He withdrew, and when he slid inside again, one finger became two. Then he dipped his head and licked…*there.*

Emma gasped, her hips rocketing off the swing. His grip tightened, holding her in place. And then she forgot everything except the heavenly pressure he built, his fingers thrusting deep inside. His tongue teased until she was mindless with need, and then he closed his mouth over her, his fingers rocked inside, and he sucked, sending her up, up, up and then finally—*finally* over the edge. Everything shattered, wave after wave pulsing from deep inside. She came so hard, her whole body vibrated, until slowly…slowly…she floated down again.

"Oh, God, *yes*," Vin said.

She looked at him, still dazed. "That turned *you* on…?"

"Hell yes." He leaned up to kiss her, then sat on the swing, shifting so her naked sex rested on his shorts. He was hard, but made no move to free himself. Instead, his hand slid beneath her t-shirt and bra, cupping her breast and teasing her nipple while he continued to make love to her mouth.

She rubbed against him, and when he didn't take the hint, broke the kiss. "What about you?"

"I'm good."

"But…" She pressed into him deliberately and he laughed.

"Okay. You caught me. I'm desperately horny right now. Unfortunately…" The sound of a car came from the street out front. "…our luck is about to run out."

She squeaked and leaped off the swing, grabbing her underwear

He gave a regretful sigh. "Besides, I didn't want to."

That stopped her. He was serious. "I don't understand. Was it…me?"

Instantly he was off the swing, pulling her close. "God, no. No—Emma—I want you so bad right now, I can't stand it."

"Then…what?"

"Tonight was about you. I wanted to give you

something—to take care of you, without you having to take care of me in return."

Suddenly she couldn't say anything. He lifted her hand and softly kissed it, then gazed down at her, eyes glittering. "But next time, I won't be this magnanimous."

"God, I hope not. I don't think I could stand not having you inside me next time."

Vin froze. Then he groaned and kissed her, hard. And Justin and Juney's voices floated over the junipers from the driveway.

"Thank you," she whispered as he let her go.

"My pleasure…Mike."

****

Early Friday morning, Tony arrived to drive Vin to the doctor for his knee, complaining loudly about having to get up at five.

"I could have taken the bus," Vin said mildly. "If Azi can do it, I can. Hell, I could probably even drive myself now." He flexed his knee. Stiff, but better. This was the last of his physical therapy appointments, and he never knew how sore he'd be until after they worked on it, so Tony'd gotten in the habit of driving him.

"Susan would never forgive me. The clinic's practically out in Gresham. Besides, what's family for if not to get up early to help each other out? Speaking of which, she wants to talk to you about Azi." He backed out of the driveway and headed up the street.

"Azi? What about him?"

"How the hell should I know? She's got some bee in her bonnet, and you're his go-to guy. So—tag, you're it, man."

"I need to spend time with Az this weekend anyway. I've barely seen him, and this appointment screwed up my morning."

"Well, whatever it is, it's important to Suze. She reminded me three times to tell you."

"I'll ask her tomorrow. Az and I will come over, after I do something about Emma's yard."

"Her *yard?*" Tony gave Vin the once over. "How was she?"

"Fuck you."

"Okay. How's she *going to be?*"

Vin laughed in spite of himself. "You're so full of shit."

"Hey, I'm not the one doing yard work to get laid." Vin opened his mouth, and Tony said, "No married jokes. Marriage is about *so* much more than gardening. Or getting laid."

"Such as?"

Tony opened his mouth, then shut it again. "Never mind. You wouldn't understand."

Vin let it drop, and for a time, the only sound came from the windshield wipers, clearing off the first rain in nearly a month. The showers weren't supposed to last, but they were a much-needed break in the drought. They would certainly be a boon to Emma's dead lawn.

Abruptly, Vin turned to Tony. "What's it like, having a bunch of kids?" The sideways glance Tony sent him was only half as bad as the knowing grin that followed. "Ah, come on, man. Just answer the damn question."

"You know what it's like. You've been at our place."

"It's not the same—they're your kids. I can give them back, no harm, no foul." Vin pushed out a breath. "Look. Azi's about the best thing that ever happened to me. I'm just wondering if it's possible to, you know, love all your kids the same."

"No."

Startled, Vin looked at him, but Tony gave every indication of being serious.

"What the hell do you mean by that? Bobu loved all her kids, and her grandkids, too."

Tony glared. "Of course Bobu loved us—she raised us, didn't she? But you asked about loving your kids the *same.*"

"I don't get it."

"A friend of Susan's has eleven kids. The first was an early riser, the second slept late, so when she had the third, she figured no problem. She knew what to do, either way."

"And the third kid…?"

"Didn't sleep at all."

"Great. What's your point?"

"Every kid is different. No matter how many you have. You can't love them the same, because they *aren't* the same."

"But…?"

"But you fall *in love* with every one of them." He looked at Vin seriously. "If you have kids of your own, or—ahem—get involved with a woman who does, I can't promise it'll be easy. But Azi's got a lot of love to toss around—look at how he loves my pain-in-the-ass kids. Maybe you're selling *both* of you short with your 'no other kids' policy."

"It's not a policy," Vin grumbled, and Tony shot him a look. "Okay, maybe it *was* a policy. But it's currently under review. And now I want you to shut up about it."

"Okey-doke. So, what's new on the job?"

"Nothing." Tony shot him another look, and Vin said, "Confidentiality of the case…"

"Yada yada. I won't tell. Spill."

"Honolulu PD found prints in McBride's plane—not Dan's or Mollie's. Looks like they came after Dan last touched the controls. And one of the 'chutes is missing."

"Nice. Killer for hire?"

"Maybe. Nothing concrete. If they find a match on the prints, we'll know more."

"Anyone want Dan dead besides Emma?"

"*She* didn't want him dead. And I still think this is a flash in the pan, and the crash was an accident."

"You better hope so. History repeats itself?"

Vin dug his fingernails into his palms. "She's not a suspect."

"We'll see." Tony's voice was noncommittal. "Tell me more about Dr. Dan and his research. Why is it so important to the Sion that this one vaccine is proven safe?"

Some of the tension eased out of Vin, and he sat back, stretching his legs out. It would be good to rehash the vaccine stuff with Tony, maybe get a new perspective.

"The Sion's relatively new, and since most research takes years to ramp up, they need to start logging successes or they'll fold. The vaccine manufacturer, PharmFam, is a big drug company, with a lot of clout in the industry. It's a control issue. If the vaccine is proven safe, PharmFam can apply to extend their patent. Whoever holds the patent controls the drug, and all the profits that stem from its sale."

"Why did all this come up now? Didn't you say the vaccine's been around a while?"

"Patents are issued during R&D—research and development—sometimes decades before a drug receives approval to be marketed and sold. By the time it's profitable, the patent expires, and can only be renewed under certain conditions."

"Such as?"

"I can't believe you're this interested. I *have* to think about it, and I'm sick of it already."

"Have to get my jollies somehow. Bank surveillance only goes so far."

"Whatever. PharmFam wants to extend their patent so they can study one component of the vaccine for other uses, which is the most common renewal loophole."

"Why can't they apply for renewal if the drug is shown to be *unsafe*?"

"They can, but the FDA probably won't approve it. If the whole thing is supposedly unsafe, why approve a patent to study it for another use?"

Tony was clearly intrigued. "So if the vaccine was proven unsafe, PharmFam can't market it as a vaccine *or* anything else. But with the patent expired, and the formula released, their competitors can use it as a base to apply for their own patent, and develop a new, presumably safer version."

"Bingo—earning millions for the competitors, and damaging PharmFam's reputation when the public discovers they sold an unsafe vaccine."

"Plus, PharmFam did all the initial research, which the

other companies capitalize on. So, renewing really is a big deal to PharmFam."

"Exactly," Vin said. "Five more years of exclusivity, and as a by-product, big accolades for the Sion and OSHU."

"Lots of pressure on Dan to produce good results."

"Even more pressure to publish them."

"How so?"

"From what I've learned, it's not enough to make a discovery. Scientists have to publish their research, continually beating out other scientists with newer, bigger, better research. If they don't, they lose their grants, tenure, even their labs."

Tony whistled. "Good thing Dan nailed it before he died."

"Yep. Journal's out next week, and everyone can heave a big sigh of relief."

"You said Nick finished the final edits. But was Emma involved in any of this?"

"Peripherally. She was the lab admin, but has no actual research background. Her thing is computers. She programmed the results database, created apps to automate experiments, stuff like that. Even if she *was* involved with the research, I don't see how it could relate to Dan's death. He proved the vaccine is safe, everyone's happy, end of story."

"Except someone killed him, and from what you've said, his research was his life."

"That and screwing Mollie."

"Point taken." Tony drummed the steering wheel, keeping his gaze on the road. "Speaking of…It's the eighth."

Shit. "Yes. It is." Vin shifted in his seat.

Tony shot him a speaking look, and Vin said, "I know Izzy gets out of the can today. What do you want me to do about it?"

"Nothing. Just checking in."

"I'm fine. It's been more than a year. It happened, I was

dumb, it's over."

"Yeah, you look like you're over it. If you really want to start something with Emma, you're gonna have to deal with this first."

Vin opened his mouth to tell Tony off, then stopped. "You're right. I know you are. Just not today, okay? I've got enough on my mind."

Tony looked at him once more, then nodded. "Fair enough. But if you don't deal with crap like this, it comes back to bite you in the butt."

"Brother Tony's Advice for Living?"

"Brother Tony's Been There, Done That."

"Care to elaborate?"

"Nope."

They rode in silence, and Vin tried not dwell on his own incompetence. The questions on the O'Manny non-case were racking up. He didn't need anything else to worry about.

****

Later that day, Nick stared out the corner windows of his top-floor office in the Sion and watched the afternoon sun glint off the buildings of downtown Portland. Behind him, on his desk, sat the advance copies of the *Journal of the American Medical Association* containing Dan's article. He couldn't face them—not knowing what a fraud he was. Bad enough his office was directly above Dan's old one—that this office should have *been* Dan's.

Now he'd been given co-credit for the research proving the DTaP vaccine was safe.

He sighed and thrust a hand through his hair. Maybe he deserved *some* of the credit. Not equal billing—but a *little* recognition…

Survivor Guilt, his therapist called it. Like naming it made it acceptable, this feeling that it should have been *him* on that plane. Not Dan, who had so much to live for: a loving wife, successful career, beautiful kids. What did Nick have? His career consisted of riding Dan's coattails, Janice had died before they'd had kids, and his only girlfriend since her death had dumped him immediately. He hardly blamed her—who'd want a washout when a rising star offered instead?

The intercom buzzed and Nick's admin, Lori, said cheerily, "Oscar's on one."

Nick glared at the phone. "Tell him I left early."

"Will do. Oh—and Parker called. He's running late, but he should be here in a few."

Nick grunted and went back to staring out the window. Maybe if he sat there long enough, everyone would forget about him and he could fade quietly away, like the dimming sunlight. He'd never wanted fame and fortune; mild, average success would have been enough. Yet here he was, the director of a soon-to-be prestigious research institute, when his personal success amounted to zilch.

Maybe having his name next to Dan's on the *JAMA* article wasn't so bad. Of course, that's probably what Oscar wanted to discuss. He didn't miss much; it was unlikely he'd miss this. The question was, would he expose Nick? Or let Nick have his moment of glory, false though it was?

You could never tell about Oscar. Brilliance combined with anti-social tendencies made him necessary but difficult. He'd worshipped Dan, but without Dan's influence, he had trouble recalling who buttered his bread. Or maybe the problem was, he had too many butterers. Dan's lab and the Sion both needed him, and Parker had *suggested* his expulsion would be frowned on by the University.

Nick needed to think about that. Oscar couldn't be fired without cause. But how much longer could they put up with him?

The intercom buzzed again. "Parker's here."

And in he barged, flinging the door open so hard it bounced.

"Parker." Nick gestured at the stack of journals. "You're here for those."

"Damn right I am. Couldn't wait to see the piece that'll

save our skins."

"Yes."

"PharmFam should be pleased, too. Their vaccine is safe—their investors are happy. And the grants we'll get—" Parker practically drooled.

Nick nodded, then turned to the window again. Lori's voice drifted in from reception, chatting on the phone. She was getting ready to leave; it was the end of the day. That's what normal people did at five. They left. Maybe Parker would take the hint and Nick could escape.

He didn't.

Instead, he flipped the pages of the journal and skimmed, then sat in front of Nick's desk to read in earnest. Several minutes later, he exhaled heavily. "Excellent! Good work." Nick turned back and forced a tight smile. Parker didn't notice; he still stared at the article like it was the Holy Grail of biomedical research. Which it basically was.

He tossed the journal onto the desk. "Thank God it's finally published. Dan's research will really save the Sion."

Something came over Nick—some inexplicable urge to *not* be a washout, for once.

"And mine," he said. Parker's head shot up and Nick cleared his throat, then said more firmly, "My research. You said Dan would save the Institute. But I deserve credit, too."

"Of course." Parker eyed him thoughtfully. "I didn't mean to exclude you."

Nick straightened his shoulders—his therapist would be proud. Whatever mistakes he'd made couldn't be changed. But from now on he would handle things differently. Starting with how he let Parker treat him.

"Last year," he said, "the Sion was so broke, Dan used his *own money* to buy equipment. We didn't know if we'd even be here this year. Well, we pulled it off—*we* did it. *We* proved the vaccine is safe, and thanks to *our* work, the University will be known as one of the top ten in the country for immunization research."

An odd look crossed Parker's face. "Your money, too.

And—mine."

Fuck. "Yes. Of course. I—I didn't mean to imply I'd forgotten."

"A hundred grand loan is hard to forget."

"Yes. I—"

"Especially after bankrupting yourself first." Parker paused, watching. "How is the new scanning electron microscope, anyway? You ordered it, what, six months ago?"

Nick took a steadying breath and reminded himself that Parker had every right to ask how his personal funds were being spent. Besides, he must know how much Nick hated this part of the job, having to justify every penny, every decision, every delay. It wouldn't stop Parker from asking, but it might help him accept Nick's answer, lame though it was.

"Apparently, the electron scanning market is still highly charged." It was a poor joke, and Parker's expression didn't change. Nick sank into his chair, rubbing the nape of his neck. "It's still on back-order. They said maybe next month."

Parker rose and braced his fists on the desk. "You're right—you deserve credit. And so do Dan and I. All *three* of us kept the Institute running when it was in the red. I for one am relieved as hell we're finally producing results sexy enough to attract big donors. But for Dan, it wasn't just a job, a way to get recognition or money. He put his heart and soul into his lab—the Sion—everything he did. *Everything.*"

Nick looked away. Parker hadn't taken the thought to its natural conclusion—*what have you put your heart into?* He didn't have to; the words hung between them nonetheless.

Parker pushed off the desk, taking one of the journals. "I have a hot date tonight. You'll bring a copy of the article to Emma?" Nick nodded, and Parker added, "Today."

"Yes," Nick managed, and Parker left.

Nick stared, unseeing, at the place where Parker had stood, before shoving his chair back. He had to get away.

Everything closed in on him—even the windows. He grabbed the stack of journals and fled the office, past Oscar, standing insolently by Lori's vacant desk. He stumbled through the lab to the tenth-floor lobby, and the elevators that would take him down, away from this personal hell he'd found himself in.

Why, oh why *did you have to die? Why* you, *not me?*

He punched the button, then waited while the doors slowly closed. *Please don't let Oscar follow me—I can't face him. Not now, not like this.*

Tears burned his throat, and he wasn't sure if they were for Dan or Janice.

Maybe for himself.

Wouldn't his therapist just do a happy-dance about that. *Let your feelings out.* What bullshit. Didn't anyone realize that when you let your feelings out, *that's* when disaster struck? If you pushed them far, far inside, you might rot from within, but at least you wouldn't hurt the people you loved.

The floor indicator light flickered, rapidly decreasing the time he had to regain control before the elevator would split open again. If he could just make it to his car, he'd have twenty minutes to push his feelings even farther down, before he'd be with the one person who absolutely *could not* be allowed to see what he was really thinking.

Why, why, why not me? Why did it have to be you...?

Chapter Eight

St. Joseph the Flying Friar:
Pilots, Paratroopers, Planes, and Astronauts

Emma opened the door to Nick, looking handsome and chipper as ever. Well, maybe not *chipper*... She wasn't fooled by his cocky grin and quirked eyebrow. But she also knew he wouldn't appreciate being called on it, so she accepted his buss on the cheek and led him in.

On the couch, Karen straightened—sort of—when she saw him. "Hey, Nick. How've you been?"

"I'm sorry. I didn't mean to intrude."

Emma smiled. "Not at all. Justin and Juney are at soccer practice, and we were enjoying the peace and quiet before dinner."

Nick's glance took in the empty bottle and lone wineglass on the coffee table, and Karen said glumly, "She means she's been fortifying me with hooch before I walk the green mile."

Nick blinked. "Sorry?"

Emma said, "Don't pay attention to her. She's moping. She has to cook for Parker."

Nick blinked again. "*You're* Parker's hot date?"

"Apparently. God knows why he wants me to be. Sorry—I don't even know why it bothers me. We ate together all the time when I was with Rob. It's just, you know, he never *talked* to me. And now we'll be *alone*—for *hours*..."

Nick glanced at the wine again, and Emma said, "Vin and I opened that bottle two nights ago. She's probably had a glass and a half at most."

"Vin?"

Heat rose in her cheeks. "Oh. Sorry. You met him, but it was so long ago. He's the cop who handcuffed me when…" Nick's face went white, and she could have kicked herself for bringing up Dan's death. "Anyway. He lives near here, and the kids are friends with his uncle."

"His…uncle?"

"Never mind. It's not important. Please, sit down. Would you like a drink?"

Nick declined, then sat next to Karen, looking self-conscious. "I won't stay long. I just came by to give you one of these."

For the first time, Emma noticed the magazine in his hand. He held it out, but she couldn't make herself take it. He understood, and set it on the coffee table.

"They put my name on it, too. I took it off, but it got lost in the final edits."

"I'm sure you deserve it," Emma managed, unable to tear her gaze from the cover. Dan's magnum opus—the culmination of his research, poised to catapult the Sion to national fame, garner him a nomination to the National Academy of Sciences, and make millions of parents feel safe vaccinating their kids. And she couldn't touch it.

She cleared her throat and said to Nick, "That reminds me—some of Dan's old data is on my laptop. I think it's the vaccine research."

Nick sucked in a sharp breath. "Jesus. I'm sorry."

"For what?"

"Nothing. I just know how hard it is to find your spouse's things after they die. You think you're safe, and then you come across a shoe that fell behind the dresser, or a note reminding you to go to the dry cleaners."

She saw his unshed tears before he looked away, and her heart broke for him. "Thanks. For understanding. Not many people do."

He nodded, then cleared his throat. "I could take a look at the data for you—I don't think it's anything we need, but

I could erase it, so you don't have to deal with it."

"Thanks. Oscar offered the same thing."

"You told Oscar about it?"

"Yes. Didn't he say anything? I thought he would at least mention it."

He scowled. "He never said a word, but that's what he's like. I swear, one of these days—" He stopped, visibly trying to collect himself. "Anyway. I could take your laptop home tonight and get it back to you by Monday."

"That would be wonderful. But I can't give it to you tonight. Justin took it to school for a presentation. He'll bring it home on Tuesday."

"How about I stop by on Tuesday evening? I have to come over this way anyway."

"Okay. Come after seven—he has soccer again."

They fell silent. She glanced at the journal. "Did you…read it?"

Nick seemed as reluctant as she to discuss it. "I couldn't. I edited it, of course, but the final copy—no. Parker did. He said it came out well, and PharmFam should be thrilled."

"PharmFam?" Karen asked, looking somewhat less hazy at the mention of a potential portfolio builder.

"The vaccine manufacturer. When the autism scare started a few years back, their stock bottomed out. Now that we proved the vaccine is safe, it should shoot up again."

"Lots?"

"Planning some insider trading?" His eyes actually twinkled, and Emma thought he looked more relaxed than he had in a while, but Karen flushed.

"No, of course not."

"She can't help it," Emma put in. At least the mood was lightening. "If there's a stock rising or falling within earshot, she has to find out all about it."

"And that's my cue to leave," Karen said in a mock huff, struggling off the sofa.

Nick looked concerned. "Are you okay to drive?"

"Yes. I've only had one glass, and we had snacks, blah,

blah. What you should be asking is, am I okay to cook? Who knows, maybe I'll poison Parker's salmon."

Emma laughed. "You wouldn't."

"Don't bet on it. 'Always I accept *la challenge.*'"

"Peter Sellers," Nick said. "A *Pink Panther*, though I couldn't say which one."

Karen's brows rose. "You're good."

"No. Just around Bethanne long enough for osmosis to kick in."

"Same here. Think there's a cure?"

"I doubt it. But let me buy you lunch sometime and we can discuss it."

He seemed as surprised by the offer as she was, and Emma tried to blend into the upholstery while they eyed each other warily. *Interesting.* All three of them in a funk was a bit much; maybe Karen and Nick could pull each other out. Then Vin's words popped into her head: *Let me take care of you.* She could use a little funk-relieving herself.

Make that a lot.

"Seriously?" Karen asked at last.

Nick squared his shoulders. "Absolutely. How about Monday?"

"Sure. I'll, uh, call you and we'll figure it out."

"Sure."

Emma saw Karen to the door, and when she returned, Nick stood by the fireplace. "I should go," he said, not moving.

"Would you like to stay for dinner?"

He gave one of his self-deprecating smiles. "No, thanks. I'm fine. But before I go, maybe we could..."

He looked so vulnerable. It would be so much easier if she *could* fall in love with him. He was such a good, caring man, and the kids adored him. But her belly didn't flip-flop when he was near the way it did with—well, it didn't, and that was that.

He laughed nervously. "I'm sorry. This is dumb. I just thought, if we sat down now, we could look at Dan's article together. Maybe it would be easier than reading it alone. I—don't think I can face it by myself."

"Me, either."

And just like that, she was crying. And then Nick was holding her, crying, too. "I'm sorry, Emma. I'm so, so sorry."

"It's not your fault."

"I—" He let her go, leaning against the fireplace, not meeting her gaze. "I introduced them. I'm so sorry. I—Mollie and I were dating. She needed a job, and I begged Dan to find her a place in his lab. The affair started right after that." He raised haunted eyes, filled with remorse. "It's because of me they got involved. My fault Dan asked you for a divorce. And…my fault Dan died in that plane crash."

"*No*—it's not. You can't blame yourself. If not Mollie, it would have been someone else. Adultery can't break up a sound marriage."

"You don't understand. Mollie's from Hawaii. We'd planned to go there together, so I could meet her family. Had already bought the tickets. But then we broke up. That was *my* trip Dan took. He shouldn't have been flying that Cessna. It should have been me. Please, Emma—can you ever forgive me? I'm sorry. I didn't know this would happen. I didn't know."

She reached for him, hugging him awkwardly while his sobs shook him. "It's okay," she whispered. "It's okay. I forgive you. Everything will be all right. I promise."

Unlike the kids, Nick was old enough to know how empty promises like that were. But he nodded, and she knew he just needed to let go for a while. And if it wasn't ever "all right," at least, after this, it might be a tiny bit better.

Tears slid down her own cheeks and she thought, *Please make it better. For both of us…*

****

Promptly at eight, in a moderately posh Southwest Portland home, the doorbell rang, and Karen took one final look in the entryway mirror. Who knew *why* she was so stressed about pulling off an evening she hadn't planned, didn't want, and couldn't wait to have over. It must be her competitive nature; Parker wanted to humiliate her for dumping his precious baby brother, and she wouldn't let him.

Now, if it was *Nick* on her doorstep, her nerves would make sense. God, she was lame.

She gave one last twitch to her clingy black dress, inhaled and exhaled, and opened the door to admit the Philistine knocking at the gate.

"Karen. Alexis. Wi—"

"Parker."

She had to admit, he looked good. Instead of a suit, he'd opted for dark gray slacks, a crisp white shirt, and a light-gray silk vest. On another man, it might look girly. On Parker, it was piratical. His dark hair was barely tinged with gray, the same tint as the silver-steel of his eyes. He was shorter than Rob, but not much; with heels on, the top of her head reached his nose. *Perfect. He can still look down on me.* In one hand, he carried a bottle of wine; in the other, a copy of the *Wall Street Journal,* which he presented with a flourish.

"If you get bored, at least you'll have something to read."

She smiled in spite of herself, and his sensual lips curved. Then he began his own slow perusal. He started at her strappy black sandals, moved up her bare legs and over the dress to the mass of wiry carrot curls she'd thrust on top of her head for lack of a better idea. The way his gaze lingered on the strands that had escaped to curve near her throat reminded her of a cat examining its prey—a big and very *deadly* cat—and she moved hastily toward the living room.

"Come in."

Parker closed the door, then looked around. He'd been here before, of course, but once the divorce was final, she'd stamped the place with her own quirky style. She found herself wondering what he thought of her choices. A man who could afford the best would surely find her thrift store art and rummage sale knick-knacks amusing, to say the least.

His expression was unreadable, and when the silence dragged on, Karen gestured at the bottle. "Should I open that?"

"I'll do it." He tossed the newspaper on the coffee table and headed for her kitchen, leaving her to trail after him like a guest in her own home.

"It's in the drawer—"

"By the fridge. I remember."

Karen suppressed her irritation and retrieved two glasses. She set them on the counter and waited in silence while he deftly uncorked the wine and poured a generous glass for her, then set the bottle down.

She raised an eyebrow at the empty second glass, then watched as another slow half-smile curved his lips.

"I'm not drinking."

"What? Tonight? Or ever?"

Instead of answering, he raised an eyebrow of his own. He stood close—so close, she could smell the spice of his cologne, feel the heat of his cool gray gaze—and she set her glass down and moved quickly to the fridge. She took out the salmon she'd prepped earlier and set it on the island, then busied herself adding a few more herbs to the pan.

Parker looked amused. "I see you follow orders."

"For your information, I *like* salmon. Plus, the farmer's market had a really good price."

"Ah. Death by bacteria. Much more creative than stabbing me with your dinner fork."

The nice glare she'd had going became a choked laugh, and then a scowl. She made herself relax, then turned her back on him. The nerve. She'd bought fish at the market *lots* of times. Still… Surreptitiously she turned up the oven. She didn't care if *he* got food poisoning, but that didn't mean *she* wanted to.

The silence stretched out. He seemed content to watch while she cooked, and after a few minutes, she wanted to crawl out of her skin. She put the salmon under the broiler, then slammed the oven door and rounded on him.

"Look, could you at least *try* to make conversation?" When the corner of his mouth turned up again, she snarled, "And stop *smiling* like that."

Parker's laugh boomed, and her face flamed. Before she could apologize for being a bitch, he handed her the wineglass, waiting while she took a large gulp. Then he took the glass, set it down, and grabbed her hand.

"How's this?" He put on his best University President face, and when he spoke, he used his thundering bass, pumping her hand up and down. "Karen! Delighted to see you! How have you been?"

He stopped, still gripping her hand, the challenge in his eyes clear: *Your turn…*

Well, she hadn't been an almost-theater-major for nothing. She said in a bright, vacuous tone, "Lovely. I've been just *lovely*, thank you."

"Excellent. How was your day?"

Why was he still holding her hand? If only he wasn't so damn *close*.

"*Fabulous*. I stopped off to see Emma, and Nick dropped by—it was a regular *Our Gang* reunion, except you and Rob weren't there."

Suddenly, Parker's face relaxed and he finally let go of her hand. It tingled from his touch, and she grabbed her wineglass again to have something else to focus on.

"Did he bring her a copy of the *JAMA* article?"

"Yes."

"Good. I wasn't sure he would."

She leaned against the counter. It was strange, talking with him this way. She couldn't recall a time when they'd just chatted. He was subdued tonight, and she wondered how much of his loudness was *him*, and how much related to his job. OSHU comprised five hospitals, dozens of research institutes, and several satellite campuses. Being in charge of such a behemoth probably necessitated a higher volume than her job did.

He said now, "Whatever mess Dan made of his personal life, his kids should know he was a brilliant scientist."

"I suppose."

"I'm sure your loyalties are with Emma. But you must admit, Dan worked his ass off on this research."

"I suppose," she repeated. "Look. He was a great scientist. I'll give you that. But he was still an asshole, who cheated and damn near wrecked Emma's life."

"She's doing all right. Going back to school, moving on. Letting go of the past."

His expression was a little too neutral. Did he mean Rob…? Or maybe *his* relationship with her?

She gave a mental shake. He didn't mean *anything*, he was just making conversation, like she'd asked. He'd always made her so uncomfortable, but maybe Emma was right. Maybe he wasn't *so* bad, and it was just her own insecurities. His style might be rough, but he wasn't a bad person. Not *exactly*, anyway.

She took a deep breath. "Thank you." *There. She'd said it.*

"For what?" His eyes twinkled at her glare. "Come on— play nice. Don't spoil it."

"For helping Emma," she ground out, and he laughed.

"My pleasure. I always enjoy helping…a friend."

Something in his slight hesitation gave her pause. His expression was ironic and suddenly she understood. "You're using me to get to her!"

Parker stilled. "Is that what I'm doing?"

"Yes. I *knew* there was a reason for this whole dinner thing."

He stared at her for a long moment, then said, sounding tired, "You caught me."

He left the kitchen, forcing her to trail after him again, back to the living room. He sat on her sofa, propping his feet on the coffee table. She perched on a funky wicker rocker by the fireplace, and realized she was starting to enjoy herself.

"You'll have to get in line, you know."

"Oh?"

His bored tone didn't fool her. She'd seen the muscle in his jaw twitch; he wasn't as relaxed as he'd have her believe.

"Yeah. In the first place, she's kind of dating a cop."

"Really. Fascinating."

"I think so. His name's Vin." He didn't say anything, so she added, "Then if that peters out, there's always Nick."

Parker closed his eyes. "Is dinner ready? I'm famished."

He so obviously didn't want to hear about Emma's love life that Karen couldn't help pushing him. "Tonight, Nick was so nice. She's having trouble with her laptop—Dan left some data or something on it. Nick's coming next week to clear it off for her."

"Not that I actually care about all this, but why couldn't he look at the laptop tonight?"

Ha! She was getting to him.

"Justin borrowed it—he's bringing it home from school on Tuesday. Besides, I think Nick wanted an excuse to see Emma again."

Parker's lips thinned in obvious displeasure. Maybe she should throw him a bone, since she was pretty sure Emma wasn't interested in Nick anyway.

"On the other hand, you probably only have to worry about Vin."

He rubbed a hand over his face. "Who?"

"The cop."

"Oh? And why don't I have to worry about Nick?"

"Because he invited me to lunch next week."

Parker's eyes flashed—she must *really* be getting to him—but he only said, "Well, except for Mollie, I can't fault his taste. Emma's taste, on the other hand…"

"What's *that* supposed to mean?"

"Nick's a mediocre scientist, an okay director."

"I didn't realize you thought so highly of him."

"Sorry. I just think *Emma* can do better."

Karen frowned. First he was cocky, then obnoxious, then *nice*—and now he'd come full circle. She'd let her guard down, fooled by his lazy, big cat demeanor. But he'd only been lying in wait, choosing the right moment to pounce, to push her down again. Well, screw that.

"What about me? I'm the one going to lunch with him. Can't *I* do better? Or is *mediocre* the best I can hope for?"

"That's up to you."

"Come *on*—I was never good enough for Rob. You made that clear from the start. So Nick and I must be a perfect fit—a bottom-feeder, scraping the bottom of the barrel."

He scowled. "Is that how you see yourself? As a bottom-feeder?"

"No, that's how *you* see me—how you've always seen me."

"Don't put this on me. Your low self-esteem is your own problem." He looked madder than hell and like he had more to say. Then abruptly he rose. "I'll go check the salmon."

And for once, Karen had no desire to follow him.

****

"Mom?"

Emma set her mug on the breakfast table and looked at Justin in the kitchen doorway, wearing a t-shirt and pajama bottoms.

"What is it, honey? Sorry," she added hastily. "I forgot again."

"Can I go out for the school play? Tryouts are Monday."

"Of course you can," Bethanne interjected, her eyes alight with more genuine pleasure than Emma had seen in them for a long while.

Emma bit back a retort and asked Justin, "Why the interest?"

He shrugged, looking a little pink around the ears. "No reason. Now that I'm in middle school, it just sounds...fun."

Bethanne said, "I think you'd make an excellent actor. What play are they doing?"

"*Macbeth*."

"Ooh." She shivered. "Tragedy. Perfect for fall. What part do you want?"

He shrugged again. "I don't know. Whatever they give me."

Emma thought he seemed antsy, like something else bothered him, but Bethanne didn't notice. "Who's directing?"

"Mrs. Edwards."

"I remember her." She turned to Emma. "Didn't you take drama from her once?"

"Yes." Emma's single attempt at becoming an actress had been a miserable failure. She could hardly blame Bethanne for looking to the next generation.

Bethanne said, "Charley can help. Be sure and tell Mrs. Edwards he did special effects in Hollywood. He knows people. Anything you need—fake blood, breakaways, collapsible knives—he can get it for you. And he can build sets."

Emma said, "You might want to *ask* him first."

"Don't be silly. He still misses it. Half the time he won't stop talking about it."

"Fair enough. You're probably right."

"So can I, Mom?" Justin asked.

"I suppose. If it doesn't interfere with your schoolwork."

"It won't." He hesitated. "I'll have to stay after school on Monday…"

"I'll pick you up. Assuming the van will start, anyway."

Bethanne frowned. "It's acting up again?"

Emma nodded. "I called the mechanic. He thinks it might be the starter, but I haven't had time to take it in yet."

"I could bike home," Justin put in, sounding hopeful.

"I don't know. It's getting dark earlier now."

"Mo-om! I'll be fine! It won't be that late—lots of kids my age bike to school."

It was obvious he'd been thinking about this for some time. Emma sighed. "All right. But be careful."

"Thanks. You're the best!" He paused, then said, a little

too casually, "Are you and Detective Bronislovas dating?"

Emma choked on her tea. "Justin—why would you ask that?"

"Are you?" His face was serious, his mouth tight, and her heart clutched.

"It's a fair question," Bethanne said.

Emma ignored her, focusing on her son. "I've always tried to be honest with you. I…like Vin. A lot. I don't know what will happen, but…even if we end up together, he would never, ever replace your father."

"I know that! *No one* can take Dad's place!"

"Sweetie—"

"Stop *calling* me that. Dad never called me that—I'm practically a teenager!"

He stormed out of the room and stomped up the stairs. Moments later, his door slammed.

"That went well," Bethanne said.

"At least it was brief. He's probably been stewing for days."

"Probably." Bethanne's own mouth was tight.

"What?"

Bethanne took her mug to the sink. "I had lunch with Gwendolyn St. John today."

"The Chief of Police's wife?"

She nodded, busying herself with the dishes.

"And…?"

Sighing, Bethanne shut off the water and turned around, her expression concerned. "Honey, are you sure you want to date a cop?"

"I'm—not sure how to answer that. Why do you ask?"

"Cops get into…situations. They have…problems. On the job. It can be tough."

"I know that. *If* it comes up, we'll deal with it."

Bethanne sighed again. "Honey, it *will* come up. I'm sorry to be the one to tell you this, but—Vin has a history of getting involved with female suspects."

Emma's pulse jumped. "What are you saying?"

"I didn't get the whole story. But apparently there was some scandal in Chicago. It's partly why he transferred out here."

"I'm sure it's nothing."

Bethanne's eyes flashed. "Don't you think you should at least ask him about it?"

"I will," Emma promised, and took her empty mug to the sink.

****

By eleven, Karen was exhausted from Parker's constant sparring. The fact that their verbal war might be of her own making only made it worse. She'd half expected him to leave after their spat about Nick and Emma. But that would've been too easy.

She'd never met anyone as stubborn as Parker; he ignored every hint, seeming determined to stay as late as possible. He ate slowly, savoring each bite of the salmon—which really *was* excellent—then gave the fruit tart she'd made for dessert the same treatment. *Then* he insisted on coffee—"I can't drive without it."—and now he'd settled on the sofa, looking like he meant to stay all night.

"Well," she tried once more. "It's late."

"So? It's Friday. I don't have to get up early."

Maybe I do. She gritted her teeth. Screw it. If he wanted her to be rude, then so be it. "Look, it's been fun, but I think we're even. I made you dinner—and dessert—*and* coffee. We're done."

"Are we?" His face wore the same cool mask he'd had on throughout dinner, but his tone held a challenge.

"I'm *tired.* I want to go to bed."

"So do I. Let's do it together."

"That's it." Karen went to the front door. "Get out—*now.* I've had it. You can look down on me all you want, treat me like a tramp even, but from now on, do it from a distance."

"As you wish."

Karen froze. "What did you say?"

"Nothing." He walked toward her, his movements slow and sure, the cat stalking its prey, and she resisted the urge to back up. Just as he reached her, her cell rang.

"I'll wait," he said pleasantly, and she fought back a growl.

It was Emma, and Karen picked up the phone with relief. "Em! What—"

Emma's voice shook. "Dan's death wasn't an accident. He was murdered."

"*What?*"

She must have looked as bad as she felt because suddenly Parker was at her side, helping her to a chair. "What is it? What's wrong? Did something happen to Emma?"

Emma said, "Vin's here. But he can't stay. Can you come over? Please?"

"I'll be right there." Karen hung up and looked at Parker, incomprehension and shock warring for supremacy in her feelings.

"Tell me," he commanded.

"Dan was…murdered."

"Damn." He turned away, but not before she saw the calculation in his eyes.

Not shock, or even surprise. Calculation. And maybe a little fear.

And suddenly *that* was what she felt uppermost. "I think you'd better go now."

He jerked a nod, then walked to the door, not meeting her gaze. He left without another word and Karen waited until she heard his car pull away. Then she went to her own car, hands shaking so hard she could barely get the key in the ignition.

And all the while, two thoughts replayed over and over in her head: Parker wasn't surprised by the break-in. And he wasn't surprised now.

Maybe Rob isn't the worst of the James brothers after all.

Chapter Nine

St. Margaret of Cortona:
Libel, Homelessness, Penitents, and Whores

"Why would anyone want to kill Dan?" Karen asked, sounding as tired as Emma felt.

It was early Saturday, and they sat on the porch, drinking coffee. Bethanne was showering, but the kids weren't up yet. Emma couldn't imagine telling them—hadn't decided if she would—and it was too much to think about. But she *had* to; this was one conflict she couldn't resolve by making everyone happy, because, well, two of the parties were dead.

She shuddered. "I have no idea."

"The police are *sure* they found a match on the fingerprints?"

Emma repeated what Vin had told her by rote. "They're sure. His name is Ramie Neakanae. He's a hitman, wanted for several murders in the Islands."

"And the crash wasn't due to pilot error—or—or a malfunction or something?"

"The FAA report finally came back. They couldn't find a single thing wrong with the engine or the fuel gauge, but it looks like the instrument panel was tampered with. Dan was an experienced pilot, but with no controls..."

She shuddered again. It had been cloudy that day, and with nothing to guide him, there was no way Dan could have kept the plane in the air. No one was *that* good.

"Plus, there's the missing parachute. It looks like the McBrides were right to push the investigation."

"And if this Ramie's a hitman, then someone *wanted* Dan dead." Karen sat back in defeat.

"Yes. And they need to find *him*, so they can find out who *hired* him."

"Vin doesn't think *you* had anything to do with it. Does he?"

"I don't know—I did vandalize Dan's office."

"After he *dumped* you." Karen paused. "Do cops usually make house calls this early?"

Emma looked up and saw Vin himself emerging from the park onto the street, and the bottom dropped out of her stomach.

"I, uh, need something," Karen said and vanished inside before Emma could stop her.

Vin was at the steps, and Emma took a sip of coffee and tried not to throw up. She'd already heaved on him once, so she knew he could take it. But it seemed like something to avoid at this stage of their relationship. If they even *had* one. Did a single round of mind-blowing oral sex count? They hadn't even been on a date, and now they probably never would.

"Hi," he said, not quite meeting her gaze. "I hope you got some sleep after I left."

"Yes." It was a lie, and they both knew it, but it was all she could manage.

He came up the steps and took Karen's seat. Across from Emma, not next to her.

She set her mug down carefully. "I know what you're thinking."

"Do you?" His gaze was serious, but not as remote as it could have been.

"To most people, Dan was pure as snow. I would've said the same. But then he dumped me and I flocked his office and he was murdered." Vin didn't say anything, so she laughed, hysteria bubbling. "I'm the logical suspect."

"What motive would you have?"

His voice was neutral, but then, he'd probably had all kinds of special detective training to keep his emotions under wraps. Except in the case of whatever happened back in Chicago. *Definitely* not the time to bring that up.

"Anger?" she offered.

Vin shook his head. "The vandalism, sure. But the hit was probably arranged before Dan dumped you."

"What if I knew about Mollie?"

"Did you?"

"No!"

She drew another breath. God, she hated arguments. And it was even worse that *she'd* broached the subject. *Better to get it out in the open. Better to get it out...*

"Life insurance."

The corner of his mouth twitched. "From what you've said, there was barely enough to cover expenses while you're in school. If your goal was financial security, you'd be better off with Dan alive and paying alimony."

"But no one else even *disliked* him."

"That you know of."

Emma shivered again. Vin hesitated, then started to reach toward her—*finally*—when the door opened and Bethanne stepped out, eyes red, with purple circles underneath. She'd showered, but she still looked more like the grieving widow than Emma.

"Detective. You're here early. Grilling us before breakfast?"

Vin dropped his arm, and Emma fought back a sob. Didn't either of them see how much she needed to be held?

"I would've come sooner, but Azi missed his bus and I had to drive him to work."

"You both seem very busy. You must hardly see each other anymore."

Something flashed in Vin's deep blue eyes, but before he spoke, Juney and Justin came out of the house, still in their jammies. Justin frowned when he saw Vin.

"What's *he* doing here?"

"Justin!"

"It's okay," Vin broke in. He still had that closed off look, and Emma's heart clutched. Juney looked from him to

Vin, and then to Emma.

"It's not okay," Emma said. "Justin, you will apologize to Vin this instant."

"No."

"*Justin.*"

"It's okay," Vin repeated. He stood. "I should go. I'm off today, but I've got paperwork to catch up on."

Emma fought the urge to reach for him, knowing she'd crumble if he jerked away. But Juney had no such qualms. She gave him her big-eyed little girl look. "I don't want you to go. Please, can you stay?"

Vin glanced at Emma, a flicker of uncertainty in his gaze.

Bethanne broke in. "I'm sure Vin has lots of important police work to do."

Vin held Emma's gaze. "Would you like me to stay?"

She looked straight at him and said, "God, yes."

****

Startled, Vin took a half-step toward her before he realized it, and the glow that lit her face sent heat to all sorts of inappropriate places in his body. "Okay, then."

As soon as he'd stepped out of the park, he'd wanted to grab her, pull her out of sight of the house, and make passionate love to her mouth. But she needed time to adjust to the news—she wouldn't appreciate being mauled right after learning Dan was murdered. And yet all Vin could think about was how he needed to hold her, to kiss her. To drive himself into her until they both forgot everything else. Jeez, he was screwed up.

Justin scowled harder, and Bethanne's cool expression didn't change. Apart from Emma, only Juney seemed happy.

"Do you want to play cards with me?" she asked, and Vin grinned.

"I think your mom wants you to eat breakfast first." Juney's face fell, and he added, "But how about later?"

Justin glared at her. "You have to help weed the yard."

"I'll do it after. Plee-ease?"

Bethanne interjected, "We have rules about chores, Juney."

"How about this?" Vin said quickly. "I'll make breakfast, then I'll help with the weeding. With all three of us, it'll go much faster. Then we can play cards after."

Justin said, "We don't need your help."

"Your mom does. She's very tired. Let's see if we can help her out a little."

Juney said carefully, like she was testing something, "What an *in-ter-est-ing* idea."

He remembered what Emma had said about Juney's pronunciation, and winked at her. "Excellent word. And you said it perfectly."

She blushed, and Justin scowled again. "Mom's not tired." But he looked suddenly unsure. Vin guessed she hadn't told them about Ramie and might not want them to know. Before Justin could ask *why* she was tired, Vin moved to the door.

"Eggs? Cereal? Toast? What does everyone want?"

"I'll help," Emma said and went into the house before he could stop her. He had no choice but to follow, knowing they were about to be alone and he'd have to resist groping her. And not a damn line of the ORS came to mind.

They passed Karen, who sat in the living room and winked as he went by. In the kitchen, Emma got out the breakfast things while Vin made more coffee. While she worked, she chewed her lip, clearly lost in thought. He recalled vividly how soft and yielding she'd been when he kissed her, and suddenly he couldn't do anything but stare.

"What?" she asked, glancing up.

"Nothing." He reached for a coffee filter.

"Something's wrong. What is it?"

"Why would you think that?"

Her frown deepened. Did she have *any* idea how cute she was when concentrating?

"It's just—I feel like I should say 'I didn't do it,' or something, but then you'd say 'Methinks she doth protest too much,' and—"

"I know you didn't do it."

Relief blossomed on her face. "You do?"

"Like I said, the timing's off, unless you knew ahead of time Dan was leaving. But that doesn't fit with the vandalism. Based on *that*, I don't see you hiring a hit man. If you wanted Dan dead, I'd believe it more if you did it yourself."

A laugh escaped, but then she sobered. "Which puts us back at who *did* hire Ramie?"

Vin paused. Emma *couldn't* be capable of murder. And yet… "Does his name mean anything to you?"

"No. Should it?"

Her face seemed open, and she met his gaze head on. Vin felt some of the tension easing out of him. *She's telling the truth. She has to be.*

"Maybe. I just don't know. How long ago was Dan in the army?"

"Marines. Like my dad. He—Dan—went in right after high school and stayed for four years. Roughly 1997 through 2001. Why?"

Vin thought for a minute. "Iraq War?"

"Yes. Is that important?"

"It might be. Ramie was in the Marines as well."

Her gaze flew to his. "You think they knew each other?"

"Not necessarily. Ramie was in the Gulf in 1989—a little before Dan's time. But it's an interesting coincidence." *And I hate coincidences.* "With luck, HPD will track Ramie down, and we'll get some answers."

None of it was new info, but it was good that Emma was willing to discuss it. If Dan and Ramie had known each other, it appeared Emma hadn't known about it.

"If they catch him, how will they get him to confess?"

"Follow the money. People think they can just transfer funds to different accounts, but there's always a trail. HPD already found one account that traces to Ramie. Cash deposits—twenty-five grand in February, another seventy-five a month later."

Emma's jaw dropped. "A *hundred thousand* dollars?"

"We don't know that it relates to Dan's death. But it might. And it's another reason I don't think you hired Ramie. You can't afford him."

She choked on another laugh. "In other words, I'm too broke to kill anyone." She paused uncertainly. "If I'm not a suspect, then…why are you so distant?"

Her expression—vulnerability mixed with hope—squeezed his chest tight and he gave up. One step brought him to her. She squeaked and backed against the counter. He planted his arms on either side of her and inhaled, her scent flooding through him. He closed his lids to savor her, then opened them to find her staring up, pupils dilated, lips parted. *God, that mouth…*

"I've been distant, because I knew if I touched you even once, I'd never stop. Look at me—I can't stay away from you."

"But—why do you want to?"

He fought down a groan. She was so fragile, and it was killing him, holding back like this. "I *don't* want to. Pay attention. But you need space, and—"

Whatever crap he'd been about to spout was cut short when she stood on tiptoe and pressed her lips to his, the soft contact jolting through him. Then her tongue slid over his mouth and with a growl he pulled her tight. He cupped her rear and pushed into her, letting her feel him, hard through their clothes.

"Christ." He thrust his tongue deeper, desperate as a teenager, reaching under her shirt and into her bra. His fingers curved over her flesh, then around her back and into the waistband of her jeans, only to discover she wore a thong. The knowledge sent him over the edge, and he slid a finger down the lacy piece that disappeared between the cleft of her cheeks.

Emma gasped and ground into him, then pulled his shirt loose and slid her hands inside, her palms burning the skin of his back. He moved his lips down her jaw, kissing the hollow of her neck. Another moment and he would have ripped her shirt off and feasted on her breasts, suckling her nipples, and pushing her down onto the floor. And it wasn't even nine o'clock.

A fact which was driven home when the front door slammed and bare feet thumped toward the kitchen—fast.

Vin pushed Emma away and developed an abiding interest in the contents of her fridge just as Justin burst in. A quick peek showed Emma splashing water on her face and pretending she'd been washing her hands. Thank God Justin was young and wouldn't guess what had almost happened. Then Vin caught Justin's eye and knew he'd underestimated him. The kid might not comprehend all the particulars, but he knew damn well the *essence* of what Vin and Emma had been doing. And he was not pleased about it—at all.

"Mom?" he said slowly. "Can we have pancakes?"

She smiled brightly. "Of course, honey."

"With fresh berries?"

"Anything you want."

"Thanks." Justin gave Vin a thoughtful look, then ran out.

Crap. Bad time to alienate the son. Especially when it was suddenly, crucially important that both Emma's kids like him.

On the plus side, the incident had pretty much killed his boner. For now. And he was good at pancakes. Very, very good.

He gave Emma a more-of-that-later grin and reached for the flour. *Let the games begin.*

****

Out on the porch, Karen enjoyed the quiet. Juney and Bethanne had followed Justin inside to see about breakfast, but Karen wasn't hungry, and it was nice to be alone. It often felt like she was at the constant beck and call of her clients—which made sense, as she'd built her reputation on being available, day or night. But she needed time to process her own crap, too.

Right on cue, her cell rang. She ignored it, and it went to voice mail, only to ring again moments later. *Damn.*

She checked the caller ID. Unavailable. Which could mean anything, given her highbrow clientele, who seemed universally paranoid about privacy. She hit the button to send the call to voicemail, but barely ten seconds later, the phone rang yet again.

"What?" she snarled into the receiver.

"My, aren't we in a bad mood today?" said a familiar baritone.

"Oh, hell."

"Good morning to you, too."

He sounded so normal, she wondered if she'd imagined his non-reaction to the news about Dan. Then again, why call so early if not to fish?

"What do you want?"

"Is it just me you hate? Or is it all the James men? You've been divorced from Rob for, what, five years? I'd think the statute of limitations is up."

"'I thought it was for life, but the nice judge gave me a full pardon.'"

Silence. Then he said softly, "'Ah. That's the old redhead. No bitterness, no recrimination, just a good swift left to the jaw.'"

That he'd seen *The Philadelphia Story* was bad enough; that he knew it well enough to quote back sent a shiver down her spine. Next, he'd be telling her to be "yar"—stealing her power, subjugating her—pushing her down as Dex had literally pushed Tracy.

Abruptly Karen sat up, glancing around to make sure she was still alone. She'd never had dominance fantasies, but just now, an image of Parker had flashed before her. He stood naked, legs wide, powerfully aroused. But even more shocking was where she'd pictured herself—tied to a bed, awaiting his pleasure. And suddenly she was wet, aching for him to touch her, enter her, do *anything*, so long as he did it *soon*. She clamped her thighs against the rush of sexual heat. When the image persisted, she forcibly put Nick, fully clothed, in Parker's place.

Better.

"Is everything all right?" Parker's voice broke through her haze, and she realized she was panting into the phone.

"I'm fine," she managed and tried to calm her rapid pulse.

What the hell was the matter with her? Sex was weird enough without giving either partner total control. And with Parker, control would be his number one turn on.

"You sure you're okay? Where are you? Are you alone?"

"No! I'm with lots of people. *Tons.*"

"Okay. Don't get your panties in a twist."

How did he *do* that? Know *exactly* what to say to make her uncomfortable?

"What the *hell* do you want from me?"

There was a pause, and then finally he said, "To apologize."

"For what?"

"Last night. I was rude, and it was uncalled for."

"Oh." For some reason, that rankled even more. Karen pinched the bridge of her nose and tried to think of a snappy comeback. "Well, uh, thanks. See you around."

"Wait—there's something else."

"How did I know there would be?"

"How is Emma?"

Her chest clenched and she had to force the words out. "Fine. She's fine. Considering."

The ensuing pause was pregnant, but she refused to fill it with empty chatter. Let him work for it.

The seconds ticked by, until he said, "Good. I'm glad. I just…wondered…if she said anything. Any details, about what happened?"

Karen hugged herself against a sudden chill. "No, not a thing. And—I've changed my mind. Stay away from her.

Please."

"I see. Why?"

Karen made her voice neutral. "No reason. She and this cop are hitting it off—I'd hate for you to mess it up."

Parker was silent a long time. Finally, he said, "Sounds like a challenge to me."

He hung up, and a moment later, the house phone rang and Emma answered it.

"Oh—hi, Parker. What's up?"

Her voice receded as she carried the phone deeper into the house, and Karen started to shake. *What the hell have I done?*

****

Several hours later, Emma hummed to herself as she stepped into the front yard to call Vin and the kids for lunch. She paused to watch while he patiently showed Juney how to remove a dandelion for the umpteenth time. Their heads were bent in convivial conversation while Justin scowled nearby and attacked every weed in his path with vicious energy.

Something in Emma's heart swelled and she gave herself a shake. *Careful.*

Still, Vin *was* being pretty amazing. He'd ignored Justin's grousing, made *the* best pancakes, laughed with Juney, and—inexplicably—made it his personal mission to clean up her yard. On top of that, he'd insisted Emma relax with Karen while he worked. Which wasn't very relaxing. Karen was agitated and upset, but when Emma pressed, she only shook her head.

"It's nothing. Just, you know, with everything going on—be careful, okay?"

Emma promised she would, and eventually, Karen left. Charley came to take Bethanne for a round of golf, and with nothing else to do, Emma made sandwiches. Which were now drying out while she drooled over Vin's muscles, straining under his t-shirt as he weeded her poor, dead yard.

He looked up and caught her staring and she felt herself

blush. "Food's on," she said quickly and turned back to the house, when something at the edge of the park caught her eye. She froze, caught between wonder and a faint, inexplicable dread.

Stepping into the cul-de-sac was a woman in her mid-twenties, if the high thrust of her breasts and her firm hips were any indication. Her Marilyn Monroe-platinum hair was at odds with her light brown skin and black eyes, but her lush curves fit the bill. She wore a neon green tube top and black skintight pedal-pushers, and her platform sandals added six inches to her already tall frame, making her look like a blonde Aztec goddess. Her bright red nails were long and expensive and she exuded a sexual confidence that Emma would have given a year's income to possess.

Behind this vision strode a giant of a man, big in every sense of the word: tall, wide, large bones, thick dark hair, the works. He wore a black suit and sunglasses, and though he wasn't touching the woman, Emma was sure his sole purpose was to protect her. Or maybe prevent her escape.

The whole scene was odd enough, but it became even odder when Emma realized that the person walking next to the giant was Azi.

"Hi, Justin! Juney!" he called. Then to her, "Mikey— look who's here!"

"I, uh, see," Emma said as they arrived at the yard en masse.

Vin looked up, then went dead white, his expression a rictus of shock.

"Look, Vinny!" Azi said, needlessly, since Vin plainly couldn't tear his gaze away. "They were on the porch. You tol' me to come here after work, so I brought them with me."

The Giant grinned at Vin, then said in a deep, cigarette-scratched voice, "Vytautas. Long time." He turned to Emma, and even with the sunglasses on, she *felt* him sizing her up. She had a sudden urge to shove the kids in the house, out of his sight, but he didn't seem interested in them. The Vision simpered at Vin, unconcerned by his lack of response, but the Giant offered Emma his hand. Refusal was not an option; refusal probably led to cement boots and a swim in the river, so she let him crush her fingers and pump her arm.

"Little John," he said. "And you are…?"

"Emma," she managed, then turned to Vin, who rose slowly to his feet. Of their own accord, Justin and Juney dropped their spades and came to stand on either side of her. She pulled them in close. "Vin? Are you going to introduce us?"

The Vision tore her gaze off Vin long enough to glance at Emma. One assessing look at Emma's baggy t-shirt and ratty jeans, and a slow, satisfied smirk crossed her dark red lips.

"Didn't he tell you, pumpkin? I'm his wife."

****

"I can't believe Bethanne was *right*," Emma said. "That's what's truly humiliating."

"What the hell does that mean?"

"Stop shouting at me."

"I'm *not* shouting," Vin bellowed, then shoved a hand through his hair. She sat on the sofa looking calmer than he was sure she felt, while he paced. The kids had disappeared upstairs, and Azi—the traitor—sat companionably on the porch with Izzy and Little John.

Vin sighed. None of this was Azi's fault. And Emma was right; he should have told her.

"I'm sorry. I fucked up. I didn't know how to tell you, and I didn't think it would matter. At least, not yet."

"You didn't think being *married* was something I should know about you?"

"We're not married. At least—not anymore."

"Go on."

He dropped to the floor and took her hands. She didn't pull away, which would've been a good sign if it wasn't so passive. Her lack of reaction terrified him more than if she'd screamed at him.

"I wanted to tell you about Izzy, but there was never a good time. I made some stupid mistakes back in Chicago. She's one of them. But it's been over for more than a year."

"Then why is she here?"

"I don't know. I haven't even spoken with her since before the trial."

Her eyes narrowed. "Trial?"

Fuck. He must look like a total idiot. He blew out a breath. "It wasn't one of my finer moments. But if you want, I'll tell you all the details. I won't hold anything back—I promise."

She looked away, and he waited for the explosion—for *her* to yell at *him*. God knew, he deserved it. Instead, when she spoke, her voice was calm as ever.

"It's just that, I thought I knew Dan. I trusted him. If we had a disagreement, I figured out how to make it work, to keep us together. And then one day, he tossed it all out. I've never been so mad in my entire life."

She raised her eyes, and the anger did spark then, brief but bright. No matter what she looked like on the surface, she was more bothered than she wanted to let on.

Thank God. It meant she cared.

"I need to know I can trust you—that if something goes wrong, or you change your mind about us, you won't just dismiss me like that."

"Jesus, Emma. Don't talk about the end. We're barely at the beginning."

"Okay. But for now…you'd better go." She stood, and waited while he rose.

"Can I call you tomorrow?"

She nodded and left the room, still calm in the midst of the storm—except he knew better—knew how much this might have cost him. Between Bethanne, her father, and Dan, it was obvious Emma'd weathered one storm after another, keeping the peace for everyone else. And just when Vin started to break through, Izzy showed up. Emma probably felt like she'd been sucker-punched.

Damn Isadora, anyway.

Izzy had no idea what she'd just stepped in. But she was about to find out.

Chapter Ten

St. Rocco the Spy:
Bachelors, Invalids, Skin Problems, and Sores

"I can't fucking *believe* you know Anne Clarice."

Little John stared at the still shrink-wrapped DVD of *Mafia Queen*, holding it carefully in his gigantic hands. Sprawled on Vin's sofa, wearing only the boxers he'd slept in, he looked like an awestruck teenager. A *gigantic*, very *badass* awestruck teenager, but still.

Vin dug a thumb into his forehead, pushing back the headache he'd had for two days. "Tell me again why you're here."

"She did her own stunts. Did you know that? Every one of them." LJ's gaze stayed riveted to the photo of a very young Bethanne, wearing a strapless evening gown and pointing a Walther P.38 at the photographer. Probably a fake, but if nothing else, Vin admired the director's taste in guns.

"And you're *dating* her daughter. I didn't even know she *had* a daughter."

"With you in my living room and Izzy upstairs, I'm not dating anyone."

LJ finally dragged his attention off the box and shot Vin a big-toothed grin. "Don't blame me. I told her to stay the fuck away from you."

"Yeah—I see how hard you tried."

"You know what Izzy's like."

"No, I don't. Everything she ever said to me was a lie. I don't know who she really is, and I don't care. I want her out of my house, and out of my life."

"Don't take it out on me. I'm just insurance."

"Meaning, you're here to make sure Federico Higuera's daughter gets back to Chicago in one piece."

Vin dropped into a chair. It was Monday. Azi was at work, and Vin had to go to the station, but he didn't relish leaving LJ and Izzy here alone. LJ had emptied the fridge already, while Izzy seemed content to lie around, looking at magazines. When Vin had suggested a hotel, LJ laughed. He seemed to derive great pleasure from Vin's discomfort, which was unfair, since Vin had never done anything to him. Mostly. Not on purpose, anyway.

"About that," Vin continued. "Explain again how Izzy can run away from home, taking one of Rico's goons with her."

"Oh, babe," Izzy said from the doorway, barefoot and braless in a t-shirt and shorts. Her bleached hair was twisted up, and she wore enough make-up to rival a hooker. "I didn't take him with me. Daddy made him come."

Vin closed his eyes and reopened them, but unfortunately, she was still there. That he'd ever found her remotely attractive or interesting was one of life's great mysteries. Now he ached for the smaller curves and incredible patience, humor and intelligence of a petite *natural* blonde, and if he didn't get Izzy out of his house, he'd never get back on track with Emma.

"Izzy, you can't stay here. You know that."

"Aw, c'mon. I don't have anywhere else to go." She gave him her patented pout and flopped onto her stomach on the sofa, putting her feet on LJ's lap. He obligingly rubbed them while she picked up one of Azi's sports magazines and thumbed through it.

"Bullshit. You have 'family' all over Chicago. Or if you really want to punish Rico, go find one of his rivals and stay with them."

Izzy looked genuinely shocked. "Jeez, Vin. I just had to get away—I'm not suicidal."

"But you don't care if my ass is grass."

"Daddy was mean when I got out of jail. He said I

should be grateful I was outta that stink hole *you* put me in. So I told him to shove it and that I'd take care of myself."

"And your version of independence is crashing at my place."

"You bein' my husband, you *have* to take care of me." She winked and returned to the magazine.

"*Ex*-husband. You were never even in love with me."

Her profile looked suddenly vulnerable, but it was gone so fast, Vin thought he must have imagined it.

She said without looking up, "Poor Vin-Vin. Did I bweak his wittle heart? I'm such a bad girl. You should punish me."

"I'll do it," LJ said and slapped Izzy's rear, making her giggle.

Vin gritted his teeth. "Rico hates my guts, and this will only make it worse. I let you stay because I value my life. But you *being here* will piss him off, which I'm sure is why you came."

"Aw, Vin. I came because I missed you. Want to see how much?" She rose from the couch and dropped to the floor, and he barely caught her before she grabbed his crotch.

"Get out of my house." He pushed her away and stood up, looking at LJ. "I want her—and you—gone before I get home."

Izzy's expression went suddenly canny, and Vin got a bad feeling.

"Well, see, the thing is, if you kick me out, I won't grant you your heart's desire."

The feeling got worse. "What are you talking about?"

She batted her eyelashes. "I mighta forgot to file the divorce papers. Oops."

And there it was. The ticking bomb he'd known was coming. Why he'd trusted her to file—but it didn't matter. He drew a deep breath before the fury made him do something more stupid than marrying her—like kill her.

Izzy watched his face, saw when she had him, and smiled triumphantly.

He grabbed his work bag and headed for the door. "This isn't over. I have to go, but when I get back, I'm calling a lawyer. We *are* getting a divorce." He shot LJ a look. "Don't tell anyone about this. If my lieutenant knew—or—" *Christ.* Emma would be hurt beyond belief if she found out he was *still* married. He *wouldn't* let that happen.

LJ grimaced at Izzy, scowling on the floor. "I ain't the problem. It's her."

"Tell me about it," Vin muttered and stalked out.

****

Bethanne not only made coffee on Monday morning, she also cooked breakfast, packed the kids' lunches, and got them off to school, all before Emma crawled out of bed.

"Why don't you just say I-told-you-so and get it over with?" Emma groused, dumping sweetener and half-and-half into her mug.

"You know I'd never do that." Bethanne set down a plate of toast and eggs and sat across from her. "Besides, I'm sure this will all blow over."

"Why are you being so nice?"

"Aren't I always?"

"As a general rule, no. Where Vin is concerned—never."

"Nick called this morning. He wondered how you were holding up, so I told him all about Vin's wife. He said if you needed anything to call him."

"She's *not* Vin's wife. They're divorced. And even if things don't work out between us, I won't date Nick. Period."

"I never said you would. But he is the nicest man. And he's in our parish. He goes to Mass every week. He even goes to confession."

Which I'd know if I ever went. Emma resisted the urge to throw her coffee across the room. "Besides, Nick and Karen might have a thing."

"Really? If he knew you were available, I'm sure he'd drop her."

"I don't *want* him to drop her."

Bethanne shrugged. "It's your life." She tapped a fingernail on the table. "Oh. I forgot. That man from Dan's lab called again. The young one—I can never recall his name."

"Oscar?"

"That's it. Nick asked him to pick up your laptop, and he wondered when he should come."

"Justin has it until tomorrow. But I thought Nick was picking it up himself."

"I told Oscar that. He was very rude and said Nick should make up his mind so Oscar could do his 'real' job. Then he hung up on me. Don't you want the nice breakfast I made?"

Emma set her plate in the sink. "I lost my appetite."

"I bet Nick is a wonderful cook. He's been on his own for three years."

Emma swallowed a scream and escaped the kitchen. When Vin called an hour later to ask if she'd have dinner with him, she said yes before she could second-guess herself. Even facing him and the Izzy situation would be better than another round with Bethanne.

****

Karen fumbled a cigarette from the pack, struck a match, and took a deep drag while lighting up. God it was good. No matter how long she quit, or how unhealthy it was, it was still the most heavenly taste on earth. It would be better if she had a shot of whiskey to go with it. But it wasn't even noon, and she hadn't sunk *that* low. The nicotine was something, anyway, and she realized she was inhaling so fast, the cigarette was half gone already.

She glanced at the dirty metal chairs on the small patio at the back of the Sion. Besides being covered with leaves and sap from the overhanging trees, they were in plain sight of the nearby buildings. It wasn't likely she'd run into anyone she knew, but she did have an image to maintain. Not that most of her clients gave a damn if she smoked. It was just that, having theoretically kicked the habit years ago, it would look bad to be sucking drags now like there was no tomorrow.

She stepped off the concrete onto the wooded hillside that formed OSHU's northeastern border, and found a relatively clean boulder beneath a large maple. She had fifteen minutes before her lunch with Nick, so she finished the smoke and lit a second. Might as well kill herself thoroughly. No more of this fucking-things-up-by-inches bullshit.

God, she was a mess. When had she started falling apart? After she'd finally accepted the humiliating truth that Rob had been cheating for *seven years*? She took another drag. The worst of it was letting Parker get to her. What right did he have to comment on her self-esteem? He'd never even been married. What did he know about it? The jerk.

It was his fault she was smoking. He was up to something—knew something about Dan's death or the break-in, or both. She still hadn't told Emma, though. What could she say? Parker's a bastard, but she didn't know what he did, or why, or how?

Behind her, she heard the back door to the Sion opening, and someone stepped outside. Karen peered around the tree, then choked on a drag when she saw Parker himself, standing with his back to her, blocking her view of his companion, who sat on one of the dirty chairs.

Shit. If *he* saw her smoking, she'd never live it down. She scrunched out of sight and stubbed the cigarette. His companion spoke too low to be heard, but Parker's "quiet" voice carried easily. She hadn't meant to eavesdrop, but when he said "Dan's article," she gave up fighting it.

"I've had enough," Parker was saying. "This stops. Now."

His companion spoke, and then Parker said, sounding pissed as hell, "I mean it. The article is out, the results are public. You got what you wanted. Now leave me the fuck alone."

Another response.

"You can't hold that over me. The results were good. I had nothing to do with it."

The man's voice rose. She heard "PharmFam," and then Parker growled, "I said *no*. Go ahead. Tell the police. It's *over*."

Karen heard footsteps crossing the patio, then silence. She waited, certain the other man hadn't gone in yet, and was rewarded a minute later when she heard metal chair legs scraping the concrete, followed by more footsteps, and then the Sion's door clicking shut.

Shut.

Hell.

The stick she'd propped it open with had been removed. The door was an emergency exit, with no handle on this side. The rule was, if the stick was in the door, you left it there. She shoved the cigarettes in her purse and ran around the tree to the patio.

The door was locked tight. She'd have to walk all the way around the Sion and its conjoined buildings to get to the front—in high heels, through the brambles.

"Damn it!" She kicked the door, then turned to go. She'd just stepped off the concrete, when the door suddenly opened behind her.

"Oh, thank God." She turned to find Oscar regarding her suspiciously. He wore a dirty lab coat and headphones, the cord of which trailed down to an MP3 player in his hand. An expensive looking one, large by MP3 standards, ultrathin, with a video screen.

"Did you knock?" he asked loudly around his music. "What are you doing down here?"

"None of your beeswax." He blocked her path, scowling, and she put her hands on her hips. "Let me in."

He looked at her, then at the trees, then back at her. "Whatever."

He turned away, leaving her to catch the door or be stranded again.

A few minutes later, as she waited for the elevator that

would take her to the top floor of the Sion, Karen froze. She'd noticed the dirt on Oscar's coat, but hadn't processed it. Closing her eyes, she pictured it. Yes. A few dark streaks above the hem. And mixed with it were little bits of leaf and sap, like that which covered the patio chairs.

And Oscar didn't smoke.

As Juney would say, *in-ter-est-ing.*

****

"You look really nice today."

Nick watched as Karen smiled, then dropped her gaze to her plate again. Damn it. Why was he acting like a kid on his first date? He even felt a little nauseous. Surreptitiously he wiped his palms on his napkin, then gulped his water, wishing it was something stronger. Karen ate her cabbage rolls in silence, and he took the opportunity to study her.

She did look good. She'd lost weight, and her fine cheekbones and delicate neck were pale against the vibrant orange of her hair. His gaze lingered on her small breasts, displayed nicely under her sleeveless white sweater, then traveled down to the swell of hip dipping below the table. What would she think if he touched her? Slid his hand up and under her skirt...?

He shook himself. Who was he kidding? What would *he* think if he did something that brash?

Karen glanced up, and Nick looked away before she saw too much. Surprisingly, he was a little hard. After Janice's death and the whole Mollie fiasco, he hadn't been able to work up much interest in real flesh and blood women. Fantasies were so much easier. They didn't die, didn't dump you, and didn't care when you didn't make them come.

An image of Karen, kneeling on a bed, flashed before him. He should have stopped it, should have thought of the national debt or sports or anything else. Instead, he pictured shoving his hands in her hair, holding her while he thrust into her luscious mouth until he came.

"Nick?" Karen's voice jolted him back. "Are you okay?"

His face burned and he coughed. "Yes. Fine. Sorry."

Where the hell had that come from? In all the years he'd known Karen, he'd never been attracted to her. But something about her pale skin and long legs had done it for him today. Maybe there was hope after all.

"All done?" he asked, needlessly, as her plate was clean.

"Yes. Are you?"

"Yes." He still had half a sandwich left, but he'd lost his appetite. For food, at least. His face must have betrayed him, because Karen flushed. He grinned, dropped a few bills on the table, and pulled her chair out for her.

"Thanks," she said. "For lunch. It was, uh, nice."

"Do you have to go right away?"

"Not exactly. I have to go back to work at some point, of course."

"Walk with me for a bit?"

Karen bit her lip, then blew out a breath. "You might as well know. I bought a pack of cigarettes this morning and I'm dying to have another one."

Something about the way she said it, confessing her deep, dark sin, warmed him. "No problem. I can show you where to smoke."

"I know about downstairs—" she began, but he cut her off.

"Too dirty." She looked startled, and he explained, "I have to know where my employees are, even when they're hiding out."

She laughed, finally relaxing. Probably because *he'd* relaxed.

"Lead on," she said and fell into step beside him. On impulse, he took her hand and kissed it. She turned pink, but didn't pull away, and they walked in silence until they reached a small park, just off of OSHU property.

"Here we are. Smoke away."

"Thanks."

He watched as she lit up. He'd never smoked, but the occasional joint in college had inured him to the idea. Besides, women sucking cylindrical objects was…*damn*…

what *was* the current national debt, anyway?

Karen blew out the smoke, looking into space. With her skimpy skirt, white sweater, and flaming hair, she looked like a virgin hooker, and suddenly he was stiff as hell.

Something came over him, an inexplicable urge. As she exhaled, he seized her and covered her mouth with his. She gasped, and he sucked the smoke from her. The sensation was incredibly erotic. Not only could he taste the smoke, rich on his tongue, he tasted *her*, hot and wet. He held the smoke in before blowing it out, off to the side. Her lips were parted, her eyes dark pools. She didn't pull away, so he moved in again.

****

Karen froze. The first time Nick kissed her, she'd been too surprised to stop him, so no wonder he tried again. Should she push him away? Oh, what the hell. He was so damn handsome, all that blond hair and blue eyes wasted, stuck in a lab all day. Since college she'd thought he had a thing for Emma, but maybe not.

He slid his tongue in, and she fought back a nervous giggle. All that big talk, teasing Emma about Vin's groping her; Emma had no idea Karen wasn't as sexually savvy as everyone thought. What a joke. With Nick clearly ready for action, Karen should've hooked a leg around him and rubbed right back. Instead, she just let him kiss her, mouth open but not really participating. Moments later, he pulled away.

"Whew. We'd better stop before someone sees us."

Karen forced a smile. Okay. She hadn't planned on kissing him, or done much to encourage him. But did he have to stop? Couldn't they work at it some more?

"I'll walk you to your car," Nick said.

When they arrived at the garage, he rode down with her in the elevator, then gave her another quick kiss, assured of his welcome. Not that he wasn't welcome. She just didn't know *how* she felt about it.

"Lunch again tomorrow?"

"Sure," she said, then wondered if she should've played harder to get.

"Okay. See you then."

He kissed her again, sliding his hand up her side, not quite to her breast. Which was good, because when he released her and disappeared into the elevator, she turned to find Parker leaning against her car.

"What do *you* want?"

His cool gray gaze flicked to the elevator, and abruptly she recalled his conversation with Oscar. They were utterly alone in the garage, and she tamped down a shiver.

"I saw your car. Your meter's up, so I figured you'd be by soon."

"Are you spying on me?"

He nodded at the elevator. "That was fast. He got over Emma in, what, a day?"

"Go to hell. And get off my car. I have to get back to work."

He didn't budge. She started to squeeze past him, when suddenly he grabbed her arm and sniffed her hair. "Are you smoking again?"

"What if I am?"

She tried to wrench free, but he held tight, using his other hand to dig in her purse until he found the cigarettes.

"Hey! What are you doing?"

He made a face, crushing the half-empty pack and tossing it aside. "You quit. Remember?"

"What the hell business is it of yours?"

"It's not. But I care about people who care about you—"

"Like Emma?"

"—and it would suck for them if I let you make such a stupid mistake."

"Do you mean the smoking—or Nick?"

His grip tightened, and she bit back a yelp. They were nose-to-nose, his breath hot on her face. "You said it. Not me."

"Nick doesn't care that I smoke. It turned him on."

"Only an idiot would be turned on by you killing yourself."

"Really? I thought power and violence were *your* turn-ons. Didn't one of your girlfriends complain you were too rough in bed? Maybe more than one. That's what Rob said." His eyes blazed and she recklessly pushed on. "I bet that's why you're still alone. You tried your little games too often and word got out—Parker has to control or he can't get it up. If the woman fights back, even better."

Parker went utterly still. Then he shoved her against the car, pinning her arms at her sides, his erection grinding into her belly. They stood like that, frozen, and Karen was acutely aware of her nipples, taut against his chest, and of the wet heat between her legs.

Who was worse—the man who dominated?

Or the woman who liked it?

He said softly, "You must be right. You're fighting, and I'm hard as hell. Maybe if you stopped, I'd leave you alone." His expression was unreadable. "Then again, maybe not."

Abruptly he let go and stepped away, and Karen tried not to think, *Come back.*

Then he said, all calm and casual, "Have you heard of Zymurgy's Law?"

"What the *hell* is that?"

"Zymurgy's First Law of Evolving Systems Dynamics: Once you open a can of worms, the only way to re-can them is to use a bigger can." His eyes were cold. "Keep seeing Nick Forte and there won't be a can big enough to hold all the worms you'll find."

"Are you *threatening* me?"

"Would you stop seeing him if I was?"

"No."

"Then take it however you want."

He walked to the stairwell, and Karen sagged against the car. Why did every encounter with him leave her sweaty and shaking—and more turned on than she'd ever been in her life?

Disgusted, she got in the car and peeled out of the garage. Maybe she'd call in sick for the afternoon. It wouldn't even be a lie, and if nothing else, she needed more smokes. A whole carton. She'd smoke them with Nick—get him all hot and bothered—see how Parker liked *that*.

God she was messed up. But not stupid. Even she recognized that an urge to rub Parker's nose in it meant he'd gotten under her skin. Thank God she'd see Nick again tomorrow. Finally, a *sensible* choice where her love life was concerned.

****

When Vin picked Emma up at seven, the butterflies in her stomach still flew crazily. He looked mad, furious even, which was ironic since *she* was the wounded party. Or maybe it wasn't related to "them." That was a comforting thought. Bethanne and the kids were watching *After the Thin Man* in the living room, and he barely let her say good-bye before dragging her to his car, where he yanked the door open and waited.

"Aren't we walking to your place?" she asked.

"Too crowded. Get in."

Obviously, she knew *why* his place was crowded, so she acquiesced as gracefully as possible. He shut the door, got in, and headed down the street. The silence should have bothered her, but didn't. Even mad, Vin made her feel more relaxed than anyone else. More herself. She stole a look at him, and her heart went *ka-thump!*

Then her brain went *crap*.

Now was *not* the time to have Big Emotional Revelations about the detective working Dan's case. There was probably never a good time for that.

He glanced over, and she looked quickly out the window while she worked her heart off her sleeve and back into her chest where it belonged. "Where are we going?"

He turned downhill toward the river. "My brother's rental in Southeast. His tenants just moved out and I have the key. I figure we can talk, then walk to a restaurant nearby for dinner."

"Okay," she said, and they fell silent again.

He crossed the Willamette and drove to a neighborhood of wide streets and mature trees, stopping near a brown craftsman with an honest-to-God veranda, complete with swing.

"Wow." Emma climbed the steps, and for the first time all evening, Vin cracked a smile.

She sat on the swing, and he sat next to her. "You like?"

"It's fantastic. Just what I'd pick if I could move." She sighed. "Maybe someday."

Vin watched her for a moment. "My place is a lot like this, though I have to admit, the trees are nicer here." He cleared his throat. "I'd like you to come over. Some time."

This was it. Emma took a deep breath. "I'd like that."

"Good." He stretched his long legs out. He was tan, skin dusted with soft gold hairs, and she had a sudden desire to pull his shirt off and run her hands through the curls on his chest.

Instead, she said, "But—you do owe me the truth."

"Yes—I do. It's pretty basic, and very dumb. I was undercover with a mob family, on a drug trafficking case. The Capo, Rico, is Izzy's father." At Emma's startled exclamation, he said, "Told you it was dumb. She fed me a line about going straight. I bought it, and eventually blew my own cover."

"What happened?"

"Izzy went right to Daddy, he put out a hit on me, Little John shot me, and then the cavalry came in before he finished me off."

"Little John was supposed to *kill* you? And you're letting him stay at your *house?*"

"*Let* is not the word I'd choose, but yeah."

"But—aren't you worried—" The thought was too horrible, and she couldn't finish it.

"That he'll kill me in my sleep? Not his style. Making me

watch is more LJ's thing."

"Vin! This isn't funny—stop joking."

"Who's joking? No—Emma—it's okay. Rico doesn't like me, but he doesn't want me dead anymore. At least, he didn't before Izzy came." She shot him her best glare and he went on quickly, "When the bust went down, I saved Izzy's life and got her a deal—minimum security prison for a year, instead of the five-plus she'd have done at Dwight."

"And this made Rico forget you betrayed him *and* married his daughter?"

"Mostly. He took me off the ghost list, anyway, so long as I behave."

"Does that include Izzy sleeping at your place?"

He scowled. "There is *nothing* going on between Izzy and me."

"I know that. But does *Rico* know it?"

"Oh. Well, LJ will vouch, so I think I'm good. When she realizes I won't play her game, she'll leave."

When he didn't elaborate, she said, "I hope so."

"She will. But Izzy's got it in her head that staying with me is the best way to piss Rico off. I figure the way to *really* piss him off would be to refuse. I can't make her leave. Not yet."

"Okay…I trust you." Something like pain flashed in his eyes, and he glanced away. She couldn't help asking, "How long were you married?"

"Three months, but she was in jail for most of that. I asked for a divorce on September eighth last year."

"Oh." Emma digested that. "Did you love her?"

"I thought I did. Men do dumb things, trying to get in a woman's pants." She moved, and he reached for her. "Hey. I was talking about Izzy. It has nothing to do with us."

His big hands were warm, his eyes dark, and she drew a ragged breath. "Vin. Let me go." She kept her voice gentle, and he reluctantly did as she asked.

Then she quickly pulled his keys from his pocket.

"What the hell?"

She went to the front door and he exhaled. "Cripes. I thought—"

"I know. I'm not. Did you bring any condoms?"

Vin froze, and Emma pretended great interest in the key ring. "Because I don't have any. And right now, I almost don't care. I want you so bad." She met his stunned gaze and added nervously, "But maybe you'd rather wait. Or, I don't know, eat dinner, or—"

"I don't." He stood and crossed to her in one stride. "Want to wait *or* eat. And condoms are in the car. Boxes of them." She laughed, and he said, "A guy can hope, can't he?"

Then he kissed her, and she kissed him back, sliding her hands under his shirt. The hairs of his chest were as crisply soft as she'd imagined, and he groaned, then set her roughly aside.

"Stay."

He sprinted to the car and back in record time, while she found the right key and unlocked the door. He pushed her into the house and kicked the door shut. She registered oak hardwoods and sparse furnishings before he kissed her again, backing her into the living room and onto the sofa.

He was hard—so hard. Her hands found his chest again, while his fumbled at her zipper and then his fingers were inside her panties, caressing her. She moaned and he said, "God, I love it when you do that."

He jerked her jeans down, then unbuttoned her shirt, going stock-still when he saw the lacy red satin bra-and-thong set she'd bought.

"Are you trying to kill me?"

"It opens in the front."

He slid his finger over the silky fabric. "Does it, now?"

He bent to lick her nipple through the bra. Heat pulsed through her and she gasped, desperate, then unbuttoned his jeans and reached inside his briefs, loving the way he groaned when she found him. His skin was silken, encasing a very flattering erection. He drew back to finish dragging his clothes off, and she got her first really good look at him.

He was magnificent. There was no other way to describe him. His chest was even more impressive naked. His flat stomach tapered to narrow hips, where his penis stood proud from a nest of red-gold curls. He waited while she finished her perusal, then closed his eyes as she gripped him and swirled her hands up his length.

"Oh, God." He threw his head back, but after only a few strokes, he abruptly removed her hands. Hooking his thumbs under the thong, he pulled it down, then made quick work of the bra as well. And suddenly, she was naked.

"You're incredible," he said and kissed her.

His fingers stroked her, sliding up, over, in, out. With his other hand he cupped her breast, teasing until she really wouldn't have cared if they skipped the condom. Thankfully, Vin had a few brain cells left. He tore the box in half, ripped a packet open and sheathed himself. Then his mouth was back on hers, his fingers inside. Just when she couldn't take any more, he spread her and pressed his erection into her. She moaned, urging him on, and he took the hint and slid in, filling her up, stretching her with aching slowness until she was half-demented.

"God, Vin. Please. Just—*please*."

He groaned and thrust and then he was *there*—stroking her with his full, thick length. His mouth bent to hers, her nipples rubbed against his chest, and his hands closed over her hips, holding her in place while he pushed the base of his erection against her. It was beyond anything she'd ever experienced, and when she came, it was so hard and it went on and on. She only realized she'd cried out when Vin also shouted, reaching his own climax, pulsing deep inside with everything he had. When they came back to earth, he collapsed, his slick body on hers while she still cradled him inside her.

Her heart went *ka-thump!* Her brain went *crap*. And her body sang with life.

Well, one out of three wasn't bad.

Chapter Eleven

St. Elisabeth of Hungary:
Toothache, Countesses, Death of a Child, and Tramps

"Hey, Vinny?"

Azi's voice interrupted Vin's thoughts, which was probably good as they involved Emma, naked. He'd been in a near-constant state of arousal since meeting her that day at the park, and half hoped sleeping with her would provide relief. Instead, he was now *constantly* aroused, tempted to stop by her place on his way to work. Five minutes was all he needed, probably less. But if their three times last night was any indication, relief wouldn't last. It was a vicious cycle—one he hoped never stopped.

Which made it all the more crucial he fix this damn Izzy situation. Fast.

Izzy and LJ hadn't appeared yet, but Azi was dressed and ready for work.

"What is it, buddy?"

He sat across from Vin, looking troubled. "How do you know if someone likes you?"

"Ooh. That's a toughie. Is this a new friend?"

"Terry."

"Coffee Terry?"

"Yep."

Vin thought for a minute. "Does she talk to you?"

"Every day."

"About work?"

"An' other stuff. She tol' me about her place. She has her own apartment."

"Then I'd say she likes you. When a woman doesn't like

a guy, she usually won't talk to him." Or scream his name when—

Jeez.

He shifted and tried to focus on Azi's problem, not his own.

Azi's face brightened. "You really think so, Vinny?"

"Sure. I bet she thinks you're a really neat guy."

"Thanks, Vinny! Hey, Vin—can I invite her to the movies with us?"

Vin had forgotten it was movie day. The lawyer still hadn't called back, and work was piling up. But then, Azi was more important than either of those. "Sure. I'll invite Emma."

Azi's grin widened. "Double date!"

"Something like that." He hesitated. "You know, Terry might want to come to the movies, but…she might not see it as a *date*."

Azi grabbed his backpack. "It's a date. You said she likes me, so I'm gonna ask her."

He was already out the door, and Vin squelched the urge to call after him. He was being over-protective—Azi had to make his own mistakes. But Az was so exuberant, and sometimes his "friends" didn't reciprocate. Terry had better decline politely, or accept and be a gracious "date," or Vin would have something to say about it.

Which reminded him he hadn't called Susan yet. He'd been so busy with the case—and Izzy—and now Emma. Maybe he could catch her after work this week.

Just then, Izzy sauntered in, wearing a pink silk teddy…and nothing else.

"No dice, Izzy."

"What?" she asked innocently.

He gestured at her ensemble. "That. I'm not interested."

"Aw, Vin-Vin. You sure?"

She cupped her breasts and licked her lips, but all he felt was pity.

"Izzy. I'm trying to be nice, so I don't piss Rico off again

and wake up dead someday. But get it through your head—
I don't want you. Now, or ever."

She looked like he'd slapped her. "It's *her*, isn't it? You
fucked her, didn't you?" When he didn't deny it, her eyes
blazed and her face went red. "Goddamn it, Vin—you're
mine until I say you're not!"

"Bullshit. You don't want me. You just want to make
Rico mad." He moved to the door.

"You're gonna pay for this—I swear to *God* you will.
Or…maybe I'll make *her* pay, instead."

Vin turned slowly back. "If you even *look* at Emma
funny, you'll regret it, no matter *who* your daddy is."

"Did I miss something?" LJ asked from the dining room
door.

"No." Vin kept his gaze on Izzy's furious face. "Izzy said
something dumb, that's all."

"Huh." LJ moved to the fridge. "Nothin' new there."

"Fuck you," Izzy said, including both of them in her
scowl, before flouncing out.

"Hey, Vin." LJ cleared his throat, looking embarrassed.
"Been wanting to ask—think maybe you could, um, intro
me to Anne Clarice? Prior to me and Izzy splitting, of
course."

Vin said cautiously, "I suppose. Let me figure out a
time."

"Thanks, man. I owe you."

"That'll be the day," Vin muttered and left.

When he got in the car, he dialed Emma's number on
his cell. Bethanne picked up, and he wondered if Emma was
still in bed, exhausted by their lovemaking. He grinned in
spite of everything, and even Bethanne's sour greeting
couldn't ruin it.

"Is Emma up? I'd like to speak with her."

"*No*, she doesn't—oh. Here she is."

Moments later, Emma's sleepy voice said, "What's up?"

"Tired?"

She laughed, voice husky. "Definitely. You?"

"Yes, but I'm up. Very up. So up, I can hardly stand it."

"Already? I'm flattered."

"You should be. Look, I'm in my car. Bad cop—driving while on my cell. But I wondered if you'd like to go to a movie with Azi and me today. Azi might bring a friend."

"A *girl* friend?"

"I think Az sees it that way. Not sure about the girl."

"Oh. Sure. What time?"

"Two-thirty."

"In the afternoon? Don't you have to work?"

"My schedule's flexible, and Azi's off early. We go to matinees to avoid the crowds."

"That should work. Bethanne takes Juney to gymnastics Tuesdays, and Justin has soccer until six."

"We'll be home by then, if you need to pick him up."

"Well, I used to. But he informed me he wants to bike home now—he's too big to be driven everywhere."

"Him and Azi," Vin muttered, turning onto the freeway.

Emma laughed. "I never thought I'd be a cautious parent. Not with how I was raised."

"And how was that?"

"Very few limits. Mostly I made my own structure. But Justin has a point. Practice isn't far away, and it won't even be dark. I just worry."

Vin thought about Azi. "Give him some space. He'll be fine. I'll pick you up at two and we'll get Azi and Terry and make a date of it. Our first real one."

"Yes." The word sent heat all through Vin, knowing Emma also thought about why they hadn't made it to the restaurant last night. Unfortunately, it also reminded him of why they'd had to go to Tony's in the first place. *Damn Izzy, anyway.*

"While I've got you—can I bring LJ by sometime? He has a thing for your mother."

"You're kidding."

"Nope. He's seen all her movies. Collects them."

"But—isn't he a—a—" She was clearly floundering.

"If it makes you uncomfortable, I won't. But when he's off the job, he's not a bad guy."

"You're kidding," she repeated and Vin sighed.

"It's hard to explain. LJ's honorable. Anything he does for Rico is just business."

"I thought he, you know—" She lowered her voice. "—*killed people*."

"Actually, I was supposed to be his first. White collar's more his thing."

"But—you said he'd make you watch yourself die."

"Oh. That. He can be plenty vicious—but I don't think he ever actually killed anyone."

"But he *tried* to kill you."

"And I tried to kill him back. It was business, and we're past it. What's your point?"

"Men," Emma muttered. "Well, if you trust him, I guess it's okay."

"Thanks. One more thing."

"What *now*?" She sounded exasperated, and Vin wished he could see her face.

"Do you have any more of those lace thongs?"

The heat crackled through the phone, until she finally said, "I bought a black set, too."

Vin suppressed a groan. "Wear it. Even if I can't get in your pants, I'll picture you in it. And what I'd like to do when I get you *out* of it."

Emma sounded breathless. "If it's *that* important to you..."

Vin did groan then. "I have to go now or I'll cause an accident. See you, Mike."

They hung up, and Vin thought about the most boring Cubs games he'd ever seen, so that when he pulled into the parking lot, he had himself back under control. Mostly.

****

Karen stared at her computer, not sure what to make of the info on the screen. According to the PharmFam website, their stock wasn't doing as well as Nick had predicted,

153

hovering at four dollars, where it'd been for three years, ever since the autism rumors began. Logic dictated that now the results were public, their stock should rise. But so far, nada.

She scrolled through their recent press releases, searching out why they might still be a bad investment. There was some employee turnaround, but nothing major—a VP of Public Relations had gone to another drug company, and a Marketing Exec had left "to pursue other interests," both within the last two months. But that was it. She went down the archives until she found the oldest release still on the site, from a year ago, and started working her way forward.

She'd just gotten to a release from December, mentioning that PharmFam was entertaining takeover bids from Western Pharmaceuticals, presumably to save them from ruin should the vaccine have proved unsafe, when the intercom buzzed.

"Mr. Forte is here," her assistant announced.

"Thanks."

She turned off her monitor as Nick came in. Handsome as ever, he looked a little less sad, and she wondered if she'd done that. She rose and he kissed her, softly at first, then more urgently. Karen hesitated, then put her arms around him. He pulled her close and she felt a frisson of heat. His tongue pushed against her mouth and she opened it, only a little surprised when his hand slid up to cup her breast.

"Hi." He pulled her against his erection. "You make me crazy. Did you know that?"

"Really?"

Nick laughed. "Can't you tell?"

He picked her up and set her on the desk. Her skirt rode up, but when she tried to close her legs, it only brought him closer, until he pressed into her underwear.

"Nick!" She pushed at him as he kissed her neck. "Stop! My assistant could walk in."

He moved his hands out of the danger zones, but kept her close. "Sorry. I got carried away. I—I'm not normally like this."

"Me, either." Karen hugged him awkwardly back.

"Maybe we can change together. I'll save you, if you save me."

Karen laughed and leaned back. "Deal. I'm not great at picking the right men—in case you couldn't tell."

"Rob?"

"That's the one."

His arms were hard around her, his gaze warm. "And now?"

She opened her mouth to say things were looking up, but what came out was, "The jury's still out."

Nick's eyes cooled, and Karen's heart thudded, her palms suddenly slick.

"Sorry. That didn't come out right. I meant—" He looked at her warily and she kicked herself. Of course he was nervous. So was she. And they were both terrified of rejection.

"Oh, hell."

She pulled his head down and lifted her lips. He hesitated, then kissed her, hard, desperate, and she kissed him back the same. Desperate to finally connect with someone, to make this work.

I'll save you, if you save me.

But who went first, when they both needed saving?

****

Nick returned after lunch to find Vin Bronislovas waiting in the upstairs lobby. *What now?*

"Detective," he said in what he hoped was a pleasant voice. "What can I do for you?"

"Maybe we should talk in your office."

"That bad?" The detective didn't crack a smile, and Nick sighed. "Lead on, Macduff."

Bronislovas glanced around as they entered. "It's lay."

"Pardon? Have a seat."

"The quote." Bronislovas took a chair. "It's 'Lay on, Macduff.' As in, do your worst. Macbeth throws down his shield and prepares to fight to the death. Macduff obliges and kills him.”

“Oh.” Nick cleared his throat. “Theater buff?”

Bronislovas did smile then. It wasn’t warm. “Justin’s school is doing Macbeth. I helped him prep his audition while we did yard work.”

Something sharp clenched in Nick’s chest. “Emma mentioned you were spending time together. I didn’t realize that extended to babysitting and chores.”

“I do what I can.”

Nick opened his mouth, then shut it and cleared his throat again. “Sorry—why did you want to see me, Detective?”

“Call me Vin. As you say, I’m spending time with Emma. We’re practically family.”

Nick choked. Was Vin baiting him? Laying claim to Emma just to piss him off? He forced himself to relax, concentrating until his pulse slowed and his heart calmed.

“Vin,” he managed carefully. “What do you want?”

“I’ve left you a couple of messages.”

“Sorry. With the paper coming out, it’s been busy.”

“You know about the break-in?” When Nick nodded, Vin continued. “We found an OSHU ten-year pin at the scene. Your name came up as having one.”

“So? Lots of people get those.” Nick began straightening the papers and books on his desk, then stopped when he caught Vin watching him. “Sorry. The mess…”

“Dante fan?”

Nick glanced down, surprised to discover his copy of the *Inferno* in front of him, probably left on the desk, unnoticed, weeks ago. He cleared his throat. “Brushing up on my Italian. I have relatives in the old country.”

“You and me both. Back to who had a pin. It’s not as many as you’d think, when you factor in whether they’re connected to Emma or Dan—or the vaccine research. I can’t help thinking the break-in, the murder, Dan’s paper— that they’re related somehow. The timing is awfully close.”

He paused and Nick forced himself not to fidget. When the silence dragged on, he said, "Again, I'm not the only person at the Sion who got a ten-year pin."

Vin inclined his head. "Still. I'm following up. Got yours?"

Nick swallowed. "I'm sure it'll turn up. Probably at home."

"But you can lay your hands on it?"

Nick nodded decisively. "No problem."

"Call me when you do."

"Sure."

"Out of curiosity, who else do you know who got a pin?"

"At the Sion? I'm sure you know it's thirty or forty people."

"Let's say connected to Dan's lab."

Nick pretended to think, wondering why Vin was fishing for info he already had access to. "Well, there's Parker, of course. But I'm sure you knew that. Then there's—" He felt the blood drain from his face and paused, then coughed. "You know, I never realized it, but I suppose you're right. Parker and I are the only ones connected to Dan's lab who got those pins. But as I said, mine's at home, so…" He let his voice trail off and waited.

Vin studied him. Finally, the detective said, "Well, thanks for your help. Enjoy your book." He stood. "The lipstick on your collar looks like Karen's. Tell her hi from me."

He turned and left, and Nick fought the desire to hurl something at the door. It shouldn't bother him if Emma dated Vin—he knew her feelings for himself were not romantic.

Besides, he was seeing Karen now. He thought about her, about how they'd kissed and she'd slid up and down his painful hardness. Pictured the way her small breasts fit entirely in his hand, her slender thighs wrapped around his waist. But for once, he wasn't getting hard thinking about her. Maybe because for one horrible second, he'd thought she was rejecting him, and it would be Mollie all over again.

Hot humiliation bubbled and he ruthlessly pushed it away. Karen wasn't Mollie, and she *hadn't* rejected him. She'd *thrown* herself at him. Not that he minded. Maybe he'd even tell his therapist about her at their next session, just to prove he was making progress.

He scrubbed at the smear of pink on his collar that Vin had noticed. Observant son-of-a-bitch. Not all detectives were. How fortunate Vin had been assigned to Dan's case. Nick froze, struck by the thought. Yes. Fortunate indeed. Especially considering what Bethanne had told him, about Vin and his ex—jailbait from a case in Chicago, who was now *living* with him.

He pressed the intercom, and Lori's voice sang out, "Yes?"

"Get Oscar in here—now."

"He went home sick."

Nick swore. "Leave him a message, then. I need to see him first thing tomorrow."

"Sure."

"Oh, and get me the number for Portland Police. The complaints department."

"Will do!"

She clicked off and Nick sat back, thinking. Vin was distracted by personal matters, not objectively performing his job. Somebody in the Bureau should hear about that.

****

Emma took a deep breath and opened the door to Vin, looking sexy and strong in his habitual off-duty jeans, spruced up with a button-down shirt, open at the neck. She tried not to drool, and also not to tug at her short-short skirt. She'd wanted to drive him at least a little wild, and from his drop-jawed expression, she'd succeeded.

Belatedly, she noticed Little John hovering behind him, wearing his black suit, and shifting from one foot to the other. He was so obviously nervous that Emma relaxed and opened the door wider.

"Come on in. Bethanne's in the living room. She has to

leave soon to pick Juney up, but I told her you were coming, and she's delighted."

"She is?"

"Yes."

Little John tugged at his tie and stepped inside, peering anxiously around the entry. When he saw Bethanne, his face lit. Emma caught Vin's eye and he shrugged, then made the introductions.

Bethanne held a hand out to LJ. "Charmed, I'm sure."

LJ glanced at Vin uncertainly, then gingerly took Bethanne's slim hand in his gigantic one and kissed it. "The honor's all mine, Miss Clarice."

"Please—just Bethanne, now."

"Bethanne." He savored the name, still holding her hand. "I have all your movies."

"Oh, how flattering. All two of them." She smiled coyly, inviting more of the same, and wasn't disappointed.

"I also have the TV spin-offs. And a DVD of the commercials you did in the seventies."

Emma said, "I didn't know you did commercials."

"There's a lot you don't know about me," Bethanne said, low and husky, gaze still on LJ, who was at least twenty-five years her junior, but seemed as oblivious to the fact as she.

Charley, who'd been sitting forgotten on the sofa, now stood, and Emma said, "Bethanne's friend, Charley Addison."

LJ looked up. "Not *the* Charley Addison?"

"The one and only. Do you know my work?"

"*Know* it? You were in charge of all Miss—*Bethanne's* special effects. It's because of you the audience believes she's trapped in the burning warehouse, with no way out. I'm honored—truly—to meet both of you."

Charley beamed. Bethanne exuded sultry, and Emma escaped with Vin. With luck, Bethanne would remember to pick Juney up at school. With even more luck, LJ wouldn't go with her. The last thing Emma needed was her daughter being escorted home by the Mob.

****

By the end of the afternoon, Vin realized he'd made a number of miscalculations about this whole double-date thing. The first and most obvious was that it *was*, in fact, a double-date, in every sense of the word. Vin could have kicked himself. Clearly he hadn't been paying attention, or he would have realized. Instead, he'd been so hung up on Emma, he'd barely listened when Azi tried to talk about Terry.

Coffee Terry. Who was a few years younger than Az, very pretty, and had approximately the same level of Down syndrome as Az did. Not only did she "like" Az, Vin was pretty sure she worshipped him. With good reason. When Vin and Emma picked them up at the stand, Vin had been so flustered he'd hardly known what to do or say. Azi had stepped smoothly into the breech, opened Terry's car door, and reminded Vin where to go. At the theater, Azi bought Terry's popcorn and soda with his own money, held all necessary doors for her, and escorted her to the "perfect seat to see the movie."

Vin could learn a few things, he thought dazedly, as they filed out of the theater after the show. Azi and Terry walked ahead, shyly holding hands, and Vin reached for Emma's.

She said in a low voice, "Remember how you asked me to wear the thong set?"

Vin nodded and thought about another miscalculation he'd made. When he'd asked her to wear it, he'd pictured her in jeans. But the skirt she wore was so barely there, all he could think about was how if she bent over, he'd see that thin strip of black lace, disappearing into—

Cripes.

He swallowed. "I can't think about anything else. It's driving me wild."

"Oh." She sounded worried.

"What's wrong?"

Her cheeks went pink, and she glanced at Azi and Terry as though making sure they were out of earshot. "I hope you won't be too upset that I only wore half of it."

Vin tried to hide his disappointment. Of course cotton was more comfortable than a thong. He cleared his throat. "Any underwear you put on will drive me wild."

Her face fell even further and he stopped. "What is it, Mikey? Tell me—what's wrong."

She looked down. Vin was about to get seriously concerned when she lifted her gaze again, suddenly alight with mischief. "So you like my underwear?" Confused, he nodded, then thought he'd misheard when she said, "Well, damn. Because I'm not wearing any."

His heart started again, blood roaring to all the right places, and his gaze dropped to her hem, scant inches below the slope of her rear and the hollow between her legs. A hollow that was *not quite* completely exposed, but would be if a faint breeze happened by.

She watched him with obvious amusement. "I think Karen calls it 'going commando.'"

She followed Azi and Terry to the car, and Vin watched her hips swaying. Thought about what he would *actually* see if she bent over—hypothetically—to, say, adjust her sandal. She'd widen her legs. Then she'd bend slightly, her skirt would ride up and—

Jesus Christ.

When they were in the car, he kept his hands firmly on the wheel, *not* sliding up her bare thigh. In the rearview mirror, he noted Azi and Terry making eyes at each other. Damn. He'd hoped they'd want to end the date early, so he could grab a minute with Emma. Hadn't she said Bethanne and Juney would be at gymnastics, and Justin at soccer? That meant her house would be empty. But they couldn't just ditch Azi and Terry.

He cleared his throat. "Where to next?"

Azi piped up. "Ice cream."

"Yes, please!" Terry chimed in. Pretty much any suggestion Az made, Terry seconded. Vin hadn't figured out yet if they had all the same tastes, or if Terry was just trying to impress Az. He suspected the latter, though Azi was impressed enough already.

"That sounds nice." Emma deliberately crossed her legs, causing the non-skirt to inch further up her thigh.

Sudden desperate inspiration struck. "Ice cream it is." But when they pulled up in front of the B&R near his house, he said, "Well, shoot. I just remembered—I left my cell at home. I'd better go check my messages. Right away."

Azi's face fell, then he brightened. "Terry an' I can stay here. Emma can go with you."

Vin heaved a mental sigh of gratitude. "Great, buddy. Thanks. Unless Emma would rather wait here…?" He looked at her extremely blank expression, like she hadn't a dirty thought in her head, and barely waited for Azi to close the door before putting the car in gear.

"Back in a few!" he called out the window.

"All good!" Az said, and Vin could have sworn he winked.

Vin turned to Emma. "Quick—is your house empty?"

Her eyes widened and she nodded. "Empty. No one's there. We don't even have a cat."

"Good," he said, and meant it.

Minutes later, they'd parked, hurried up the drive, and were in her house. "Bedroom," he ordered. She laughed, and he followed her up. He barely ascertained that the bed was made and available—this was good—before he pulled her against him. Her purse fell on the floor, the contents spilling everywhere, but he wouldn't let her pick it up.

"It can wait. I can't," he said, kissing her.

He maneuvered her backwards, and then she did two things that made him see stars. First, she put one of his hands on her breast. Then she put the other under her skirt. He groaned. She was slippery, her heat encompassing him as he pushed into her, his other hand massaging her nipple. She gasped and pulled his shirt loose, then unbuttoned his jeans.

He trailed kisses down her neck. "There's something I've

wanted to do all afternoon."

"What?" she asked, lids half-closed.

"This." Vin turned her quickly around and bent her over the bed, then raked her skirt up. "Christ. You're even sexier than I pictured."

He stroked her, and Emma moaned, then kicked her shoes off and pulled her top and bra over her head. Vin's mouth went dry, even though all he could see was her bare back. "I'll be right back."

He pulled a condom out of his pocket, then shoved his pants down. He sheathed himself while kicking his feet free of the jeans, which had somehow gotten tangled up with her purse. Her head was turned to the side on the mattress, eyes heavy with desire, and he could see one rosy nipple. Her legs were spread, just like his fantasy, and wearing only the skirt, bunched around her waist, she was the sexiest, most incredible woman he'd ever seen.

Vin used his knees to widen her legs. And then he was blissfully sinking in, sliding deep.

"Jesus," he groaned. Beneath him Emma moved against the bed, and he leaned over to cup her breast. With his other hand, he reached between her legs and felt her contractions begin instantly, her moans rising to cries of fulfillment.

Vin kissed her neck, loving the feel of her, the way she climaxed with her entire body. He held himself rigid until she'd finished, then withdrew slowly and thrust back in. It wouldn't take much—hell, he probably would have come standing still, but by some miracle he'd held back. Not now. He stroked into her, her soft cries urging him on, pulling him further, deeper, over the edge until the explosion came and he felt her clench a second time right with him.

He pulled out and disposed of the condom, then collapsed on the bed, pulling her into his arms. She lay with her head on his chest and he felt her pulse, matching the rhythm of his own.

Emma sighed. "I'm *so* glad you forgot your cell phone."

Vin laughed. "Too bad I never made it home to check

those messages."

She laughed with him, and something warm expanded in his chest. Desire, yes, and something else—something bigger, more…emotional. He froze, considering it, testing it out. And then she moved against him and her scent, of spice and musk, mingled with her sex and his, rose to him. He breathed deep and pulled her closer, wrapping himself around her.

Ah, fuck it.

Vin kissed her hair, then her mouth. She opened, meeting his tongue with hers, rolling with him as he moved on top of her, pressing his hardening shaft against her, and he gave up considering anything other than how far he'd have to reach for the second condom.

At times like this, thinking was highly overrated.

****

Emma's state of post-sex bliss lasted from the time she and Vin put their clothes on and drove to the ice cream shop, through the cones they ate while Azi and Terry had seconds, all the way through driving Terry home and dropping Azi at Vin's. By the time they reached her street, it was seven and getting dark. Sunset was thirty minutes away, but it was cloudy, and there was a definite feel of autumn in the air.

She was just contemplating how thorough a public good-bye kiss they could manage under these atmospheric conditions, when Vin suddenly swore. Emma looked up and saw three cop cars, lights flashing, in front of her house. Vin barely had time to hit the brakes before she'd jumped from the car and was flying up the steps, yanking the door open and rushing inside. The first thing she saw was Justin, with a black eye and various cuts and scrapes, crying on the sofa. The second was LJ and Bethanne, flanking him, Juney on Bethanne's lap. And the third was at least six police officers swarming around.

"Justin!" She ran to him, and he flung himself at her, sobbing.

"Where the hell have you been?" Bethanne demanded. "I called your cell phone, but you left it on the floor in your bedroom."

"What happened?" Vin pounded into the room, and still she held Justin tight, ignoring everything else, whispering, *Baby, baby, baby, mama's here,* over and over into his hair.

There was a pause. And then LJ said, "Justin was attacked, biking home through the park. A man hit him, then pulled a knife and tried to stab him."

Bethanne added, "If LJ hadn't been walking by on his way back to Vin's—" She paused, and for once, Emma didn't think it was merely for effect. "If not for LJ, Justin would be dead."

Chapter Twelve

St. Barbara the Suppressed:
Gunners, Munitions, and Military Camps

When Nick pulled up at Emma's on Tuesday evening, all the lights were on. A police cruiser was turning around in the cul-de-sac and his heart stopped. *Fuck.* Why had he waited until it was so late? He should have come earlier. If anything had happened to Emma—

He shoved out of the car and up the steps, pounding on the door. The biggest thug he'd ever seen opened it, regarding him coolly. "Yes?"

Panic overrode caution and he demanded, "Who the *hell* are you?"

"Nick?" Emma's voice came from the living room, and the thug stepped aside.

His first thought, when he caught sight of her alone on the sofa, whole and unharmed, was *Thank God.* Then he saw her expression. She'd been crying, her face stark with terror, and his pulse thundered. He hurried across the room to her, sitting and reaching for her hand.

"What in God's name happened?"

"A man attacked Justin in the park," she said, and his heart stopped all over again.

"My God—is he all right?"

She nodded. "He's in bed with Bethanne and Juney."

She reached for a tissue, and for the first time, Nick noticed Vin by the fireplace, watching him. *Clusterfuck.* He took a deep breath and made his fist unclench.

"Why would anyone attack Justin?"

"I don't know. He was biking, and a man jumped out

and tried to take his backpack. Justin kicked him in the face, then he hit Justin and pulled a knife. LJ heard Justin yelling."

"LJ?"

"Pleased to meet you," the thug said, coming into the room.

"My friend John, er, Smith," Vin supplied. "LJ, this is Emma's friend, Nick Forte."

Ah. He'd done a little recon on Izzy, but hadn't realized her "companion," as Bethanne described him, had become so cozy with the O'Manny household.

LJ sized him up, and Nick returned the favor, offering his hand. LJ's grip was firm, and Nick had the feeling he was reserving judgment. Which was better than at least one alternative.

He sat again. "What happened after that?"

LJ answered, "I was walking to Vin's when I heard Justin. The guy ran off when he saw me. I got Justin home and Bethanne called the cops."

"Did you get a look at his face?"

"Wore a mask."

"But you're sure it was a man?"

"Tall. Skinny. Coulda been a woman, I suppose."

Emma shuddered. "Either way, who'd want to harm Justin?"

"Maybe," Nick said, thinking carefully, "they didn't mean to hurt him. Maybe they wanted to scare him, or…you." He risked a glance at Vin, who looked at him sharply.

"Why—what makes you say that?"

"You said yourself the break-in and the murder seem connected. But Justin has nothing to do with that. I'd ask myself *who* might want to scare Emma, then worry about why."

Vin's eyes narrowed and he looked at LJ. "It's worth considering."

LJ stared back, impassive. "Can't rule anyone out—yet."

Vin frowned, and Nick made himself not add more. It

was enough that Vin got the point: the attack could be unrelated to the murder. "Was anything stolen?"

Emma shook her head. "Justin thought the guy was after his backpack, but he left it behind. Which fits with your theory about scaring me—or Justin."

"Was your laptop in it?"

"Yes. It's fine, though. Thank God. I can't afford another one. *If* I get to go to school at all." She looked up, stricken. "I completely forgot. That's why you're here. I'll go get it. Except—I didn't get my application transferred off it yet."

Vin cut in, "I'm sure Nick can get your laptop another time."

Interfering bastard.

"Of course," Nick made himself say. "Just let me know. Or bring it by the lab. Whenever you like."

"Thanks. I'm sorry you came over here for nothing. I just…I can't deal with it now."

Her voice trailed off, and she seemed so sad, Nick wanted—well, it didn't matter *what* he wanted. It never did. Vin's attention was on Emma, so he allowed himself a scowl. Then he noticed LJ regarding him thoughtfully, and schooled his features back to neutral.

"I'd better go. You'll tell me if you need anything?"

Emma smiled wanly. "Of course. Thank you."

Nick nodded at the two men and left. Upon reflection, the laptop was no longer important. The paper was out, the results public. Anyone who thought a bunch of old data would change anything had another think coming. Nick would make sure of that.

****

After everyone left, Emma stayed on the sofa, too exhausted to move. But the horror still lurked, making relaxation impossible. Vin had only gone after she'd insisted she was okay. She wasn't—she knew that, and most likely, so did he. But there were some things she needed to be alone for, to think them through.

168

Her down time was cut short when Bethanne came in and sat beside her. "Justin's asleep with Juney. I thought it would be better if he wasn't alone when he woke up."

Emma nodded, hoping she'd take the hint and leave. She didn't.

"I have something to say that you won't like. I think you should stop seeing Vin."

"Why on earth would you say that?"

Bethanne's jaw was set. "I heard you talking. I think Nick's right—whoever attacked Justin, did it to get at you. LJ told me a little about Izzy and Vin today. I'd bet every jewel I own that Izzy wants you out so she can have Vin. And from what LJ said, she fights dirty."

Emma swallowed, forcing her anger down. "Izzy may want Vin, but he doesn't want her."

"Are you sure? No—hear me out. Vin and Izzy were married. She's the daughter of a mafia kingpin. Even if Vin isn't in love with her, it could be dangerous to refuse her—and for you to stay involved."

"So because you played one in the movies, you know all about Mafia Princesses?" Bethanne ignored the barb, so Emma added, "What about LJ?"

"What about him?"

"He's mafia, too. Not just by blood, either—by choice. As I'm sure you know."

"LJ isn't the one who pissed off Izzy's father."

Emma tried another tack. "Assuming Izzy *does* want me gone, why attack Justin?"

"I have no idea. All I know is my grandson was hurt. He got away—this time. What if it happens again? What if it's you—or Juney?"

Emma's heart thudded painfully. Bethanne had a point. But still...

"We don't know it was Izzy. We don't know it was related to Dan's murder either. We don't *know* anything—it could be a random mugging."

Bethanne's face wore an expression of disbelief. "Who

mugs an eleven-year-old? What—they wanted his baseball cards?"

Emma shook with the effort at control. "I am *not* dumping Vin over this."

Bethanne pursed her lips. "I know you slept with him."

"So? What business is it of yours?"

"When my grandchildren are threatened, it's my business." Her voice softened. "Emma, sweetheart—Vin seems like a nice man. I mean it, though I know I haven't been very supportive. But is hot sex worth putting your family at such terrible risk?"

"I'm going to keep seeing him. Whether you or Izzy or anyone else likes it."

Bethanne clearly hadn't expected such resistance. Her eyes flashed. "I didn't think you were this stupid. He's using you for sex—just like he did with Izzy and God knows how many other hapless women he's met on the job."

Bethanne's tone was cold and hard, and the worst of it was, she might be right. Emma wanted to cry. If it was only hot sex—but it wasn't. It was much more. For her, anyway.

She forced a calming breath. *Get a grip.* Even if Vin didn't love her, he wasn't using her. She was sure of it.

"Don't ever speak about Vin that way." Bethanne opened her mouth but Emma cut her off. "I won't say it again. *Now back the hell off.*"

Bethanne's mouth closed, but her fury was clear. Emma rose and went upstairs to check on Justin, wishing Bethanne would've, just this once, held her and told her everything would be okay. But if it hadn't happened in the last thirty or forty years, it shouldn't be a shock when it didn't happen now.

All the more reason to do it for Justin. If she couldn't *have* her dream mother, she'd try to be one instead.

****

Of course when Karen walked into Nick's office on Wednesday, Parker was there. She glowered, but he looked unimpressed. Just to make sure he knew what was what, she kissed Nick thoroughly, tongue and everything. Nick seemed surprised, but not displeased, and kissed her back.

"Hi," he said when she stopped.

"Hi, yourself." She gave him her best I'm-a-seductress smile and he lifted an eyebrow.

"To what do I owe this honor?"

Parker leaned back in his chair, apparently unaffected by her performance. God, he was good-looking. Even with a small bruise on his forehead. *Maybe another woman put it there.* The thought left a weird feeling in Karen's belly, and she shoved it away.

He saw her glance and said, "Didn't know you cared—I ran into a door. Why are you here?"

"Not that you need a reason," Nick cut in, with a glare of his own in Parker's direction.

"Actually, I do have a reason for stopping by. I'm here to invite you to Emma's on Saturday. Bethanne is hosting a dinner party."

"After last night—she wants to have a party?"

Parker's gaze sharpened. "What happened last night?"

Karen smiled sweetly. "Out of the loop, huh? Well, isn't that just too bad."

Nick shot her a puzzled look, then explained, "Justin was attacked last night."

He filled in the details, and by the time he finished, Parker had risen from his seat to pace the office, scowling. "My God. I'll see if there's anything I can do. I have a few connections at the police bureau. Nick—you'll tell Oscar I need to see him?"

Nick's admin appeared in the doorway. "Oscar just emailed. He's still sick—he might take the rest of the week off. Said he'll be back on Sunday at the latest, to finish up that experiment you wanted him to do."

Nick and Parker both seemed nonplussed by this, especially Parker, who followed Lori out to reception. Karen made herself look at Nick instead of watching him leave.

"A party," Nick repeated.

"You know how Bethanne loves entertaining. Also, she and Emma had a fight about Vin, and Emma thinks the party might be her way of making amends, maybe getting to know him better."

Nick looked at her closely. "Or…?"

Karen laughed. "Or—Bethanne could try to drive the wedge further. She's inviting Vin's ex and that hulk of a 'bodyguard.' I think Bethanne hopes that with Izzy and Vin in the same room, Emma will see the error of her ways."

Nick shook his head. "Give Bethanne points for persistence."

"So. You'll come?"

"Wouldn't miss it for the world."

At his warm tone, Karen sighed in relief. This could work. They *would* make it work. But it would be easier if Parker wasn't stalking her ass. Which he absolutely *was*. A fact that was driven home a few hours later when she called Emma to say Nick would be at the party.

"Wonderful. Thanks for inviting him. Also, Parker called to ask about Justin, and Bethanne invited him, too. She hasn't seen him in ages. It should be fun."

Fun wasn't the word Karen would pick, but the smoking area on the roof of her office building was only an elevator ride away, and by now, she didn't give a damn *who* saw her. She took her pack out before the doors opened and lit up as she shoved out the fire exit. She checked to make sure the outer knob still worked, then sat on a nice *clean* plastic chair, inhaling drag after drag, while desperately *not* thinking about Parker and his control issues. Not that she *cared*. She just wanted him to leave her the hell alone. Was that so much to ask?

Nick was looking better and better. And thank God for it.

****

On Friday, Vin left work early to go to Emma's. She'd been running errands and was having car trouble, and

Bethanne was away at another store, shopping for tomorrow's party.

"I tried Karen," she said. "But she can't get away, and I don't feel comfortable leaving the kids at the house alone, after what happened to Justin."

"Of course—I'll leave now."

"Thank you," she breathed. "I'll get home as soon as Triple A comes to tow the van. I think it's the starter—sometimes it works, sometimes not."

"Do you want me to pick you up instead?"

"No. It would take too long, and I'll still have to get it towed. But if you can wait with the kids, I'll be there soon."

"Of course," he repeated, then hung up and called Azi.

"Guess what!" Azi said before Vin got past *hello*.

"What?" Vin glanced at the clock. He had to hurry or Justin would get to Emma's first.

"I got an MP3 player!"

"You did? That's great. I—"

"I got it on my way home. It has headphones an' a microphone an' everything. An it holds lots of music. I can listen on the bus!"

"Great," Vin managed, but Azi barely noticed.

"Can you help me set it up, Vinny?"

"Maybe Emma can help," Vin interjected quickly. "She's good with computers. I'll ask her—I have to stop by her house before I come home. Will you be okay for a couple hours?"

"Oh. Sure." Azi sounded a little deflated, and Vin experienced a pang of guilt. Then Azi said, "LJ got a pizza and me an' Izzy're gonna eat all of it!"

Vin pinched the bridge of his nose. Pizza again?

"Look, Az, I have to go. I'll get there as soon as I can."

He hung up, but before he could leave, Barton cornered him for an update on Dan's case. She'd been strangely nice to him of late, but today she had an odd predatory glint in her eye. However, she only asked routine questions, to which he gave routine answers—to whit, that Ramie was still unaccounted for and they had no other leads—and then she left.

Still, it delayed him enough that by the time he got to Emma's, Justin's bike was in the drive. His school got out an hour earlier than Juney's on Fridays, and Vin knew Emma was worried because Justin didn't like being alone after the attack. It was a miracle he'd gone to school at all this week.

Vin knocked twice, waited, then dug the spare key out from under its rock in the yard—he'd chewed Emma out for the stupidity of *that* earlier—and let himself in.

"Justin?" he called, but there was no answer.

He checked the downstairs and the backyard, then headed upstairs. He was about to turn toward Justin's room when he heard a noise from Bethanne's.

"Justin?"

He'd just reached her door when Justin's terrified voice called out, "Don't move! I have a gun!"

Vin froze. "Justin, it's me. Vin. I'm going to open the door slowly, okay?"

There was a moment of silence and then Justin said, "Okay."

Vin pushed the door open and came face to face with Justin in the center of the room, shaking hands holding what appeared to be a vintage Walther P.38, pointed roughly at Vin's bellybutton. With any luck, it wasn't loaded.

"Justin—please put the gun down. I'm not here to hurt you. Your mom asked me to stop by. The van broke down, but she's on her way."

Justin looked uncertain. "How'd you get in?"

"Your mom told me where the key was. I knocked, but I guess you didn't hear me."

Justin thought about that, then lowered the gun. "It's not like it's loaded."

Poor kid. He was already shook up, and when he'd heard Vin roaming around downstairs, it probably scared the crap out of him. Even if he recognized Vin's voice, he barely knew him—and by all accounts, didn't like him much.

"It's okay—no harm done." Vin sat on Bethanne's bed. "Mind if I have a look?"

Justin shrugged, a little too nonchalantly, and handed over the gun. Vin whistled. He checked the magazine—definitely empty—then turned the piece over. "Nice. This your grandmother's?"

Justin nodded and sank onto the bed. "From a movie. The director let her keep it."

"Nice," Vin repeated, then held it out to Justin, who looked surprised. He took it gingerly, then straightened his shoulders in a clear attempt to look worldly and sophisticated.

"I thought so, too."

"You have good taste. Does your mom know there's a gun in the house, not locked up?"

Justin's gaze slid away, and his ears turned pink. "Not exactly. Grandma got it out this morning, before school. She keeps it in a safe in her closet. But because of the—the attack—she was thinking of loading it and keeping it in her bedside table."

"Ah." Vin kept his voice noncommittal.

Justin said anxiously, "You won't tell, will you? Mom's kind of funny about guns."

"Funny?"

"Yeah. She, you know, doesn't like them in the house and stuff. Except on the police, of course," he added hastily, and Vin bit back a smile. This was serious business. And if nothing else, Justin wasn't actively scowling at him. Which gave Vin a sudden inspiration.

"I won't tell. But your mom's right—guns are dangerous. They should only be handled by people who know what they're doing."

Justin's gaze dropped as he obviously prepared to be lectured. "Sorry."

"As I said, no harm done. But—the best way to learn gun safety is to learn about guns. How about I don't tell your mom, if you come to the firing range with me tomorrow morning?"

Justin's face lit in a huge grin. "You mean it?"

"Sure. I haven't gone in a while. I need some target practice."

"Can I shoot?"

"Sure. But *only* under supervision, and *only* if you do everything I tell you."

"Yes, sir," Justin said, eyes bright with anticipation. Then his expression clouded again. "Do you think my mom will mind us going?"

Damn. This was tough. On the one hand, Vin *should* have asked Emma, before teaching her son about guns. On the other, he'd already promised Justin they'd go. The chance to get to know the kid—and let Justin get to know him—was too good to pass up.

"Tell you what—don't ask, don't tell works on some level. How about this time, we just go, since I already promised. But if you want to go again, we'll square it with your mom first."

Justin considered, then nodded. "Agreed."

He held out a hand, which Vin took, hiding his surprise. They shook, and then Vin reached for the gun. "In the meantime, I'd like to put this back in the safe."

"You can't, or Grandma—and Mom—will find out I was messing with it. Besides," he added when he saw Vin was about to object, "I don't know the combination."

"Oh. Da—sorry."

"No problem." The man-of-the-world was back. "Mom swears *all* the time."

"Ah. Well. I suppose we'll have to put this back in your grandmother's drawer for now. But Justin—I want you to tell her keeping a gun next to her bed is a bad idea, loaded or not." Justin nodded. Obedient kid, when he wanted something. Not unlike Vin himself. "Okay. As for tomorrow, we'll tell your mom I'm picking you up in the morning to—to—"

"Teach me about self-defense?"

Vin whistled. "Brilliant. It's even half true." He paused, frowning. "Justin—I don't want you to think I approve of lying to your mom."

"Of course not," Justin said, with a return of his earlier scorn for all things Vin.

Good. At least he was feeling better.

"But these are special circumstances," Vin added, and Justin nodded, looking contemplative. Vin hid another smile.

He wiped the gun off with his shirt, then placed it carefully in the bedside table. The thing was old, probably worth a lot. But still dangerous. It needed to go back in the safe, ASAP.

"Hey, I almost forgot," he said as they left the bedroom. "How'd the audition go?"

Justin turned pink around the ears again. "I got Macbeth."

"Yeah? Your first time out of the gate? That's amazing." Justin shrugged, and on impulse, Vin asked, "Who's your leading lady?"

The pink went red, and the shrug was *ultra*-casual. "No one. Just this girl from math class."

Ah. Vin hid a grin and followed Justin downstairs to wait for Juney. If Azi were here, he could play with Juney while Vin and Justin hung out some more. Surprisingly, Vin found he wanted to get to know the kid for his own sake, not just his mother's. He tucked that thought away for review later. They'd go to the range tomorrow, then take it day by day. But he had a feeling that, one way or another, he and Justin would be spending more time together.

As Azi would say, *It's all good.*

****

"This is not good," Emma said to Bethanne on Saturday afternoon as they surveyed the crowded dining table. "Even with two extra leaves, we'll never fit twelve."

Bethanne seemed unperturbed. "Azi and the kids can eat

in the kitchen, with Charley."

"I beg your pardon," Charley piped up from the living room. He only sounded mildly indignant, however, and Bethanne ignored him.

"That leaves eight, which should work."

"We only have six chairs," Emma pointed out. "Unless you want metal ones from the yard."

Bethanne made a face, then brightened. "Karen has chairs."

"I do?" Karen said coming into the dining room.

"Oh, drat. You're here."

"Always nice to be appreciated."

Bethanne shot her a look and left the room, and Emma said, "Don't mind her. How long would it take you to run home and get your dining room chairs?"

"Well, considering I took a cab and Nick's giving me a ride home…" At Emma's lifted eyebrow, Karen laughed nervously. "I'm drinking tonight. A lot."

"You and me both. Can you think of anyone else who might have nice chairs—and a car big enough to transport them?"

Karen got a funny look on her face, but said hopefully, "Vin? He lives so close…"

"Not nice enough."

"What? Him or the chairs?"

Emma wrinkled her nose. "For Bethanne, probably both. But I meant the chairs. His are linoleum and steel. Anyone else?"

"Nick? Janice had a nice cherry dining set, I think."

"Of course—that'll work."

But when Karen called, Nick was at the lab, planning to come to the party from there.

"Damn," Emma said.

Karen's face went from pale to actual gray. "It's that important?"

"You know how Bethanne is."

"There might be *one* other person…I'm pretty sure

Parker's set is wood."

"Perfect! Can you call him? I have to check the hors d'oeuvres." Karen's face got even grayer and Emma asked, "Are you okay?"

"No. But I can make it through one phone call. I *will* be smoking afterwards, though."

"Smoking? But—why on earth—?"

"I have *no* idea," Karen said morosely, exiting to the deck as Bethanne flitted back in.

"About what?" She went to the hutch and opened it.

"Karen's smoking again," Emma said. "I asked her why."

"Oh. Don't be such a prude, dear. It's not a mortal sin."

Emma blew out a breath and went to the kitchen. Something was bothering Karen, but she obviously didn't want to talk about it. Hopefully Nick would cheer her up. They seemed to be hitting it off, and Emma wondered why she'd never thought of them together before.

A minute later, Karen came in, white-faced. "Parker's bringing chairs." She slammed back out again, cigarettes in hand.

"O-kay," Emma said to the empty room. What was she missing? Karen was her best friend—normally cheerful and self-possessed, but when Emma thought about it, for the past few weeks she'd been getting progressively more...tense.

Bethanne wandered in, carrying a table cloth and placemats, which she set on the counter. "Is LJ here yet? I need help moving furniture, and Charley's—well, Charley."

"Vin dropped Justin off and went home to shower. He'll bring everyone over soon."

"Oh." Without missing a beat, she pushed back into the dining room. "Charley—come!"

Emma glanced at the clock and tried not to grin, thinking of Vin's arrival. It just didn't get any better. Not only was he teaching Justin self-defense, but Justin was enthusiastic about it, and actually laughed with Vin when they came back.

When asked what they'd done, Justin had said, "Nothing," a sure sign he'd had fun. When she asked Vin what they talked about, he'd said, "Girls. Women. Troubles with all of the above. The usual." Then he'd kissed her and left.

On the one hand, she was thrilled. On the other… The harder she fell, the tougher it got. Vin had Azi, but he didn't truly understand Dating Mom Syndrome. Neither had she, until she became one. Vin might not want a long-term relationship with her, but intentionally or not, he was *creating* one with her kids.

Meanwhile, she was glad Justin had confided in Vin. But she was also a little sad he *hadn't* confided in her. Which wasn't logical. He obviously wanted a man to talk with, but who knew how long Vin would be around? She didn't even know how long she *wanted* him around, but she was beginning to suspect it was "for good."

Damn. If it just didn't get any better, why did she feel worse and worse?

****

By the time Parker and Nick arrived within moments of each other, Karen was on her third glass of wine and her fifth smoke. Parker frowned and began unloading the chairs, but Nick greeted her with a kiss. She kissed back, hard, despite the fact that Nick still wore his lab coat and jeans.

"Whoa. You never know what's on these things. I'd better go change." He moved the coat away from her skin, then pulled dress clothes out of the car. He really was considerate, Karen thought, and followed him inside, passing Vin on his way out.

"Let me give you a hand with those," she heard Vin say to Parker, and minutes later, she was in the dining room, directing them in arranging the seats to Bethanne's specifications.

If anyone but her thought it was weird that Vin, the

detective investigating the O'Manny case, was at a dinner party with literally all of Dan's family and close friends in attendance, no one said anything. At least he was a buffer between her and Parker—not that she *needed* one.

Then Nick reappeared, looking handsome in a white shirt, tan blazer, and slacks.

"Nice pin." Vin lifted his chin toward the small round one Nick had affixed to his lapel.

"Think so? Told you I had it."

Parker shot him an ironic look. From his pocket, he pulled another pin, identical to the one Nick wore, and held it out to Vin. "Since we're having show and tell."

Vin dutifully looked at both pins, and Karen said, "What the hell?"

Parker ignored her, saying pointedly to Nick, "Just because we *have* pins doesn't prove they're the ones the university gave us."

Nick's face darkened. "What are you implying?"

"Lots of employees stick their pins in their cubicle walls, like thumb tacks. All I'd have to do is walk by, borrow a pin, and *voilà.*"

"*Touché*," Vin said. "Know the names of any of the folks with cubicle pins?"

Parker's smile widened. "I'm sure you know it's too many to count. But at the Sion—and with connections to Dan—the only one besides myself and Nick would be Oscar."

"Oscar? He's so young. And HR shows his hire date as eight years ago, not ten."

"That would be his re-hire date. Oscar worked at OSHU thirteen years ago, when he was in high school—internship for the department of Bio Sciences, now defunct. He stayed on part-time until he went to college, then came back after graduation. HR probably has two sets of records for him. If you want to see the originals, tell them to look in the Bio Sciences files."

"So," Vin said thoughtfully, "Oscar got a square pin."

Nick had gone pale, but neither Parker nor Vin noticed. Karen edged closer, reaching for his arm. He jerked, then relaxed when he saw it was her. He clasped her hand, seemingly grounded by her presence.

Parker said to Vin, "Good memory. Yes, Oscar should have gotten a square pin."

"Meaning he got a circular one instead. Why?"

"HR error. Someone saw his original hire date, and issued the pin on the anniversary of that, instead of waiting until he'd actually worked at OSHU for ten years. He thought it was a good joke—stupidity of the bureaucracy or something like that—and, I believe, keeps his pin stuck in the case of his MP3 player."

Vin turned to Nick. "Did you know about this?"

Nick scowled. "As I told you earlier, to the best of my knowledge, Parker and I were the only Sionites connected to Dan who received circular ten-year pins. Obviously, I was mistaken."

Parker said, "It's a good thing we're getting this cleared up. I wouldn't want the detective here getting the wrong impression from your mis-statements."

Nick glared at Parker and Vin equally, then said to Karen, "I hear the deck is nice this time of day. Care to join me?"

"I'd love to." She followed him out, thoughts churning. One thing was certain: Parker wanted Vin to know Oscar had a circular pin. Based on their conversation behind the Sion—*well*. If Oscar had something on Parker, maybe casting suspicion on him was Parker's revenge.

But…Parker had always seemed above all that. He was so damn honest and…*loyal*.

Until now.

Karen shivered on the sunny deck.

"You okay?" Nick asked.

"I'm very cold," she said and he gave her his blazer. It couldn't dispel the chill, which came from within, but she clutched it close anyway. At least it was something.

Chapter Thirteen

St. Christopher the Traveler:
Boatmen, Pestilence, Sudden Death, and Storms

The party was in full swing, dinner just ending. All things considered, it was going pretty well. Which should have tipped Vin off that another major speed bump loomed. Even when Charley turned to LJ and asked innocently, "Now, what is it you do?" it was only a minor blip.

LJ had showed those big buck teeth of his, and said calmly, "I'm in…disposal."

"Disposal?" Bethanne had asked. "As in waste management?"

"You could call it that."

Vin cut in, "LJ works with computers. He means he, ah, disposes of people's assets for them—when they have too much."

Karen was clearly intrigued by this, but after glancing at Emma, who shook her head slightly, she let it drop. While no one seemed exactly comfy-cozy, the rest of the conversation had been polite and casual. Until Izzy opened her big mouth about the firing range.

"You did *what?*" Emma shouted, and Bethanne looked smug.

Nick also appeared happy, while Parker looked disinterested—except when his gaze landed on Karen, something he'd appeared to be avoiding all evening. Karen herself seemed sympathetic, but LJ grinned unabashedly. Azi was playing upstairs with Juney and Justin, all three of whom Charley had been deployed to fetch. Too bad the kid couldn't stay upstairs, blissfully ignorant that they'd been busted.

But it was at Izzy that Vin glared. He should've known, if only because she'd been suspiciously well-behaved all night.

"What, Vinny? I thought Emma knew. What's the big deal?"

Vin vaguely recalled wanting Emma to get mad more often, and from her white face and clenched fists, it appeared he'd gotten his wish.

"I'm sorry—I know I should've asked first, but I'd already promised Justin."

"Justin is *my* son. You have no right to teach him about guns without my permission. I don't even allow guns in the house!"

Bethanne pinkened, but Emma didn't notice.

"I know," he said. "My dad was a cop, two of my brothers also, and my sister is FBI. Guns are a part of our lives. But that's no excuse. I should have spoken with you first. It just…came up."

Bethanne's gaze slid away from Vin's, probably wondering if he knew about the Walther. But he refused to be petty. She could dig her own grave.

Then Charley marched Justin in and announced, "But wait—there's more," at the same moment that everyone saw the gun in question, held credibly well in Justin's hand.

Emma gasped and jumped out of her chair, snatching it away. "Whose is this?" Before Justin could answer, she rounded on Vin. "Did *you* give it to him?"

Vin threw his napkin down and stood. "Of course not! What the hell do you take me for?"

"I don't know! You took Justin to the firing range— maybe you gave him a gun, too!"

"Perhaps you'd like a little privacy?" Parker said mildly.

"Yes, Emma, would you like us to leave?" Nick chimed in, clearly enjoying Vin's discomfort. But it was also clear he'd only leave at Emma's behest. She ignored him, which likely did *not* bode well for Vin or Justin.

"Mom," Justin began, but Emma's face darkened.

"Be quiet—you'll get your turn. I'm not done with Vin yet."

"But Mom—"

"I said be quiet!" She glowered at Vin. "How dare you take my son to the firing range? How *dare* you bring a gun into this house?"

"I'm a cop!" he said and stepped toward her. To her credit, she didn't back up, just glared harder. He couldn't decide whether he'd rather shake her or kiss her, which only made him madder. "What the hell do you expect?"

"Oh, so you're Mr. Macho, and that makes it okay?"

"No!"

Nick smiled openly, as did Izzy. LJ looked like he wanted to draw his own gun, which Vin knew he had on him—he never went anywhere without it, even to bed. Karen looked like she wanted the floor to swallow her up, and Parker, oddly, looked like he wanted to pull her back out. But the only thing Vin's brain could wrap itself around was that Emma was genuinely furious. He'd expected her wrath, but not like this.

"I'm sorry," he repeated more calmly. "You know how frightened Justin was. I—thought it might be a way for us to bond."

Justin cut in quickly, "Mom? It's not Vin's gun."

She looked at him uncertainly. "It's not?"

Bethanne was obviously contemplating escape, but then she sighed heavily. "It's mine."

Emma's jaw dropped, and Justin explained. "Grandma showed it to me yesterday morning. Then when I came home and no one was here, I got it out of her drawer. Vin found me with it. He wanted to tell you right away, but I asked him not to. I'm sorry, Mom."

"And the firing range?"

"That was me," Vin said. "I spoke before I thought, and Justin really wanted to go. I didn't want to take back the offer."

"He made me promise we'd ask you next time," Justin added, looking miserable. "And he only did it to show me how dangerous guns are, and how they aren't toys."

Emma's lips twitched. "Is that right?"

"Absolutely." Vin nodded vigorously. "I'd never let a young man play with guns." She didn't miss the *young man*, and neither did Justin, who seemed inordinately pleased. Vin added in his most cop-like voice, "I'm very sorry, ma'am."

Emma actually laughed, then noticed the gun still in her hand. She cleared her throat and looked at her mother.

Bethanne obviously couldn't figure out how to spin this, and so opted for contrition. "I'm sorry, sweetheart. It's not loaded—I just thought it might help Justin feel safe."

"Uh-huh. And how did he get a hold of it now?"

Justin dropped his gaze again. "It was in Grandma's drawer by the bed. I told Azi about it. He and LJ just watched *Mafia Queen*, and he wanted to see it." He looked up, the picture of contrition himself, and Vin wondered who was the better actor in the family. *Macbeth, indeed*. Vin should take lessons.

Parker held out his hand. "Now that we've established the chain of possession, maybe you could stop waving it around." He took it from Emma, then looked around inquisitively.

"On top of the china cabinet for now." She shot Bethanne a look. "We'll talk about this later."

Bethanne wisely kept quiet. Parker did as Emma asked, and most of the room heaved an inaudible sigh. Only Izzy seemed pissed the crisis had passed. She avoided Vin's gaze, and he decided to let her stew. He had some choice words for her, but not in front of everyone. God forbid she might spill the beans about their non-divorce, and ruin everything.

"Ready for coffee?" Emma asked.

Karen excused herself, but the rest of the party headed for the living room. Vin followed Emma to the kitchen, and when the door swung shut behind them, pulled her close.

She didn't resist and he felt the worry drain away.

"I really am sorry."

"I know. It's just that, after Dan, I need to know you won't keep things from me." His arms tightened convulsively, but she kept going. "To you, the firing range isn't a big deal. I get that. But between Izzy, and this—I'm losing my perspective."

Christ—he had to tell her. But he couldn't—not until he'd fixed it. He couldn't stand her knowing what a colossal fuck-up he'd been.

He forced himself to say, "No, you're not. I should have asked first."

"Damn right. You know, I think we've had more fights than dates now."

"Is that so? Well, if we can make it through this party, we can make it through anything."

Emma laughed. Vin felt a surge of something powerful and bent to kiss her. It was lust, yes, but it was also more. Relief, gratitude, and the need to be close to her, in whatever way she'd let him—and for however long.

She broke the kiss. "Remind me to *never* have another Nick and Nora Charles' patented All-the-Usual-Suspects party."

"Who?"

"Oh—sorry. I forgot your thing is musicals. They're the dashing married couple in the *Thin Man* movies from the thirties. Bethanne's been watching them with the kids. Someone always gets blackmailed, there's murder and mayhem, and at the end, they throw a party and reveal whodunit." She shuddered. "It works for them, but I never want us to go through this again."

"Amen to that."

She'd said *us*. The warmth inside him spread, and he suppressed a cocky grin.

Amen to that, too.

****

The way things were going, Karen wasn't surprised when

187

Parker followed her onto the deck. "Why the *hell* are you stalking me?"

"Is that what I'm doing?"

"Yes!" Her fingers shook as she tried to get a smoke from the full pack.

"Just making sure you're okay. Something's been bothering you all night. What is it?" He stepped toward her, and she backed into the deck railing.

"I'm fine. Leave me alone."

"No."

"*Why?*" It was too much. The dinner, everything, but especially *him*. With a half-sob she threw the pack down and put her head in her hands. "What did I do to you, that you're so hell bent on making me miserable?"

Parker's voice was oddly soft. "I'm not trying to, you know."

"And why *now?* You've ignored me for years—what's happened recently, so that now you won't leave me alone?"

He was silent so long, she finally looked up. His eyes glittered in the light from the kitchen window and at last he said, "Everyone has their breaking point."

"Do you mean yours—or mine?"

"Both."

He closed the distance between them, pulling her tight and lowering his mouth so fast, she'd barely raised her hands to ward him off before he was kissing her. And then all she could do was grab onto his shirt for dear life. Nothing about it was gentle—his body, tense with leashed power, his lips claiming hers, hands sliding over her neck and jaw to tangle in her hair. He groaned and her senses came roaring to life.

No. Not Parker.

Not *this*—with *him*.

He deepened the kiss, her head tilting under the pressure. She didn't remember opening her mouth, but suddenly his tongue was there, thrusting, hot and slick in its invasion. Fighting a moan, she released his shirt, lifting her hands to pull him closer, when abruptly he let go and stepped back, leaving her bereft and exposed.

"Sorry." His voice was hoarse. "I shouldn't have done that. I'm always doing or saying the wrong thing when I'm with you."

"Parker—" she managed, every inch of her body straining, seeking, needing his heat.

"No." He lifted a hand, palm out. "You've made it clear you despise me. And I keep not listening. I thought—" He paused, scrubbing a hand over his face. "Never mind. It doesn't matter. If you change your mind, you know where to find me."

He moved to the door just as Nick stepped out, scowling when he saw them. "What's going on?"

"Nothing," Parker said. "I just needed some air."

Nick watched as the door closed behind him before crossing to Karen. "You okay?"

No.

"I'm fine."

Nick hesitantly put an arm around her, tucking her against the side of his blazer. Not as cozy as she would've liked, but better than standing alone.

"Would you mind if we take off soon?" he asked.

"Not at all. Get me the hell away, and I'm yours for life."

A slow smile spread across his mouth. "Deal."

His light kiss was an igloo compared to the volcano Parker had ignited, but she kissed him back anyway. Screw Parker. *This* was real love—taking care of the people who needed you, keeping them safe—not terrifying them with needs and desires beyond their control.

She'd been out of control too many times—this *had* to be better.

She retrieved the crushed pack of smokes, and they went inside to say their goodbyes. Parker was nowhere to be seen. Which was good. Except she wished he could see the way Nick kept his hand possessively on her back as he guided her to his car. Or how he slid it down over her rear and squeezed as she climbed in. It was almost enough to bring back the urgent heat Parker himself had awakened.

Almost.

****

For most of the drive home, Nick was silent, until finally, Karen couldn't stand it. "Can you believe Parker? Putting all this off on Oscar, when he's only tried to be helpful."

Nick glanced over, obviously confused by the non sequitur. "Oscar—*nice*? How so?"

"Well, you know, calling about Emma's laptop and everything."

"He called Emma—about the laptop?"

"On Monday. Don't worry—he offered to come get it, like you asked him to, but Bethanne told him you were coming on Tuesday. He does do his job *sometimes*."

"Oh…good."

"Anyway, Parker's up to something, but I can't figure out what."

Nick didn't say anything, and she stole a glance at him. He'd tossed his blazer in the back seat, and with his sleeves rolled up, Karen was aware for the first time of the tensely corded muscles in his forearms. Poor guy. He'd been under so much strain. Probably the last thing he wanted was to hear her bitching about Oscar and Parker.

They reached her drive and he killed the engine and stared at the wheel. Then he turned to her. "Karen…"

She knew what he wanted. She took a deep breath and reminded herself that he was a good man, had been kind and considerate to her time and again. "Would you like to come in?"

"Thank you. I—don't want to be alone tonight."

They got out, and suddenly she realized he was shaking. "Are you okay? Let me get your coat."

"No, leave it." He drew a ragged breath. "I'm just nervous. It's—been awhile."

"If you're sure."

"I am—let's just go inside. Please?"

He followed her up the walk and into the house, and before she even turned on the light, he reached for her, pushing his tongue into her mouth. *This* was what she wanted—a relationship with someone kind and caring—everything simple for once, instead of over-complicating the way she always did.

But in the end, sex with him was both not as bad as she'd feared, and not as good as she'd hoped. It was awkward—he was distracted—but then, so was she. When he entered her, she wasn't ready, but he began thrusting anyway, climaxing right away, while she didn't come at all. But so what? It wasn't like she *ever* came during sex. Still, she'd expected him to take care of her after. Instead he withdrew and rolled the condom off, then padded to her bathroom. She heard him splash water on his face, and then he came and sat on the bed.

"Sorry," he said, sheepishly. "You just felt so damn good—I couldn't hold back."

"No problem. Happens all the time."

"I knew you'd understand. It'll be better next time. Promise."

"Oh. Okay."

For some reason, a next time of *this* wasn't as appealing as it could have been. Parker's face, taut with both anger and desire, flashed before her and she suppressed a shiver.

So what if this hadn't been perfect? Was first sex *ever* truly good? And Nick *wanted* a next time—wanted to stick around and work at making it better. She reached for his hand.

"I—" He cleared his throat, suddenly emotional, and Karen slid her arms around his neck.

"Hey, it's all right," she said, and he clung to her, his body shaking with dry sobs.

"I'm sorry. It's just—I've made some mistakes. After Janice died. Being with you—it just feels so much more right."

"Mistakes? You mean…Mollie?"

He stilled, then pulled back and searched her face. "You knew…?"

"Emma told me."

Nick rested his head against her chest. "Desperation makes men do stupid things. I thought she loved me. What a joke, right?"

"It's not your fault. Dan was going to cheat, with Mollie or someone else."

"I wasn't thinking clearly. The debt from Janice's medical bills, the money I put into the Sion. I just wanted something to be *right* for once." He raised his head, expression bleak. Then his face softened. "But you—you're *right*. And good. And strong. I know if we can make this work, things will be better. Please—help me make it better."

"Of course." Being needed was good. And Nick thought she was strong. That was good, too, wasn't it?

Then he sobered again. "I almost forgot. You mentioned Parker earlier—I didn't know if I should say anything, but— if we're going to do this—start seeing each other—I need to know something. I need to know that you and Parker— that you aren't—"

"We're not. I—he—well, he bothers me, somehow."

"Good. You *shouldn't* trust him. I don't know how to say this—I have no proof—but I think Parker did something that he's ashamed of, and someone blackmailed him about it."

"Oscar?"

"How—I mean, I sort of thought so, too. But why do *you* think it?"

"I overheard Parker talking with someone about Dan's paper. He mentioned PharmFam, and how this person couldn't 'hold it over him' anymore. Right after that, I ran into Oscar. I don't *know* he was the one speaking with Parker, but it was all just a little—funny."

Nick nodded. "Funny. That's a good word for it. Before now, all I knew for sure was that two PharmFam execs visited Parker several times while Dan was researching the vaccine. Each time, after they left, Parker went straight to Dan."

"Meaning…what, exactly?"

"The Sion's important to Parker. It's his baby. He founded it, and hand-picked the PIs. And—it was equally important to Dan. If it folded…"

Karen drew in a sharp breath. "You don't think PharmFam pressured Parker to make the data came out in favor of the vaccine—and that Parker pressured Dan?"

Nick lifted a shoulder helplessly. "I don't know. I don't want to think it, but…"

She said slowly, "That would fit with the conversation I heard—we have to call Vin."

"And tell him what? We have no proof."

"Don't you think he should know?"

Nick scrubbed a hand over his face. "I don't know. I'm sure you realize Parker and I don't always get along. But I'd hate to implicate him, if it's really nothing. Maybe he just made a mistake."

"But—if Dan was murdered—and the paper *and* the blackmail are connected—"

Nick shook his head. "Let's think about it some more. I'm sure we'll figure out the right thing to do. In the meantime—" His gaze dropped to her lips, and she saw that he was hard again. "I can think of better ways to occupy our time than talking about Parker James."

"Oh?"

She let him push her onto the bed, feeling oddly deflated. Her instincts were right—Parker *was* up to something. But until this moment, she hadn't realized how badly she'd wanted to be wrong.

Damn it all.

She couldn't make a fresh start with Nick, while Parker dominated her thoughts. Her breasts tightened at the memory of his kiss, of how good he'd felt, pressed hard against her. Nick reached for another condom and she forced Parker out of her head. Or at least, she tried to.

Later, when Nick rolled away and fell asleep, she lay staring at the ceiling. At a minimum, she'd have to warn Emma. Dan was already dead—Justin attacked. Karen couldn't let *more* harm come to Emma or her family, when she had the means to prevent it.

Suddenly she sat up, heart hammering. No—he couldn't have—Parker would *never* harm Justin. Would he? He'd certainly *acted* surprised when Nick mentioned the attack. Still…

Karen had told Parker when Nick would pick up Emma's laptop, and that Justin had it at school. Parker could easily have learned from Emma that Justin would be biking home with it. What if the data on it *was* important? To *Parker?*

And—there was the bruise on his face on Wednesday morning. Could it be from Justin?

Crap.

Then another piece clicked. Two PharmFam execs had visited Parker—and later, two execs had left to "pursue other interests." Coincidence? Maybe.

Or…maybe not.

Crap, crap, crap.

Her shoulders shook and her stomach clenched, and she pushed a fist onto her mouth to muffle the sobs that came anyway.

Everyone has their breaking point…

Apparently, she'd just found hers.

****

On Sunday, Nick finally made it home shortly before noon. The morning had started out well enough. Waking up in Karen's bed had been disorienting, but then memory flooded back—of sliding into her, deep against her womb, exploding, pouring everything into her. He'd felt empty afterwards, a clean slate. Better than confession.

Then he'd slept and dreamt of Emma, awaking hard, and more than a little angry. She didn't want him—never would. And Karen *did* want him. He'd rolled over and pressed against her, thrusting his fingers into her and suckling her nipple, and eventually she'd opened to him. The sex had been better this time. So good, the afterglow carried him through the morning.

Until now.

He barely made it to the bathroom before he vomited up everything in his stomach.

What the hell had he done?

Karen couldn't save him. Fucking her had been a huge mistake.

No.

His brain reeled. No. It wasn't a mistake—it *would* work. He *had* to make it work with her. After everything that happened with Mollie—and Dan—Karen *had* to be his saving grace.

He stared at his reflection in the mirror. Then he rinsed his mouth and splashed his face.

What's done is done.

The only thing left was to keep moving forward.

****

Vin walked into the station on Monday to find Barton leaning against his desk.

"What first?" she asked before he took his coat off. "The bad news—or the worse?"

"You pick."

"That lab rat at the Sion—the one who did a bunch of the vaccine research?"

"Oscar Dellinger?"

"That's the one."

"What about him?"

"Found dead in the lab this morning. Shot with a Walther P.38 dropped near the body."

Vin felt the blood drain from his face and sat down. "Fuck."

"I'm thinking you might know whose gun it is. I did my homework—that little piece of work you're seeing—Mrs. O'Manny? Her mama was in the movies, wasn't she?" Vin didn't respond, and she grinned. "Oh, yes. I believe she was in one where she used that very firearm. Gun's not too common now, and of course we'll check the registration. But the lab already got a few partials. So, anything you'd care to tell me?"

Vin pinched the bridge of his nose. "If it is Anne Clarice's gun, I'll get Emma O'Manny and Parker James to come in and get printed. Both of them handled that gun on Saturday night, so we can at least find out if anyone else left a print."

"Well, see," Barton said, obviously enjoying herself. "That's the other thing. Someone called the department and filed an anonymous complaint about you."

Vin stilled. "What are you saying?"

"Someone thinks you aren't doing your job—that you've lost your focus."

Vin started to remind her that he'd specifically asked *not* to be on this case, but stopped himself. She'd only point out that it was his job to be impartial, and if he couldn't, he should've stayed away from Emma. No sense adding to her bad opinion of him.

She handed him a sheaf of papers from a file she'd set on his desk. "Phone records, from the Forte lab. The complainant suggested we take a look—thought we might find them interesting. You'll see that several calls were made in recent weeks, from Oscar Dellinger's desk phone to the O'Manny residence. The last one came the day before the kid, Justin, was attacked."

"So…?" Vin's pulse jumped—he had a suspicion where this was heading.

"On the day of the attack, Oscar left the lab early. He called in sick the next day, and the two days after that."

"And…?"

"I sent someone to question him on Friday. You know, just to see why he needed to call Mrs. O'Manny so much. I would have sent you, but you left early. Helping Mrs. O'Manny out, weren't you?" Vin glowered and she laughed without humor. "The guy I sent reported Oscar was covered in scrapes and had a bruise on his face, consistent with a struggle a few days prior."

"Are you saying Oscar attacked Justin? Why? What motive would he have?"

"Don't know. But if he *did* attack Justin—and Mrs. O'Manny knew about it—well. Mamas will go to great lengths to defend their cubs. I'm betting her prints are all over that gun, so you better hope she has an alibi. The coroner thinks Oscar was killed early Sunday. Don't suppose you were with her then?"

"No," Vin said, and resisted the urge to kick the desk. Or Barton.

"Good. Your position in this department is shaky enough. If you start providing alibis to murder suspects, well…" Her voice trailed off, and she winked. "Happy Monday, Vin."

She left, and he rested his head in his hands. Emma *couldn't* kill anyone.

But if Oscar attacked Justin…

No.

Vin shoved the thought away, reaching for the phone. At least he wasn't off the case.

Yet.

Hell, fuck, Christ and damnation.

Happy Monday, indeed.

Chapter Fourteen

St. Drogo the Orphan:
Gall Stones, Hernias, the Sick, and the Deformed

Emma watched Karen sink onto a deck chair and, with shaking hands, light up and inhale. "I'm telling you, Parker *is* up to something."

With the kids at school, and Bethanne off somewhere with Charley, the deck was quiet. Karen's face was pale, and she looked like she hadn't slept. Plus, it was Monday morning, and she'd called in sick again. Karen was driven—two sick days in a week was unheard of.

"Okay," Emma said. "I'm listening."

Karen reached the filter and drew in a final drag, then stubbed the cigarette and leaned forward. "I—" She stopped, raising haunted eyes. "I kissed him."

"Who? Nick?"

"No. Well, him, too. But I meant Parker. Or rather, he kissed me. And I kissed back."

"And…this makes you think he's up to something? Besides trying to get in your pants?"

"No—I just can't believe I let the bastard stick his tongue down my throat." She turned pink. "What I really don't get is how much I enjoyed it."

Emma said uncertainly, "Enjoying a kiss is good. Parker's not a bad person—"

"But he *is*. That's what I'm telling you. I think he may be the one who attacked Justin."

"What? *Parker?*"

"I didn't say anything sooner because I didn't have anything concrete. But—have you looked at the files Dan left on your laptop? I mean, since the vaccine paper came out?"

Emma shook her head. "I've been too busy. I haven't even read the journal yet."

"Has anyone seemed overly interested in the files?"

"Well, Oscar is. He keeps calling. But how does that relate to Parker?"

"Oscar is blackmailing Parker."

Emma laughed, then frowned when Karen didn't join in. "I don't get it. What's the punch line?"

"Oscar wants your laptop—so he can get Dan's files. I bet he thinks they prove the data in the paper was faked. Nick says a couple of the PharmFam execs visited Parker— he thinks they pressured him to make the vaccine data come out in their favor."

"Pressured how?"

"I don't know. Offered him money?"

"Don't be absurd—Parker wouldn't take a bribe—he wouldn't *need* to. He has more money than God."

"That's what I would've said. But I heard Parker arguing with Oscar—at least, I think it was him—and Parker mentioned PharmFam and that it was 'over.' He told Oscar—or whoever—to go to the police, like now they couldn't prove he did anything wrong."

"Maybe he didn't. They could've been talking about anything."

Karen rose and began pacing, and Emma felt antsy just watching her.

"I poked around. Before the autism scare, PharmFam was doing really well. Their stock was high, and their drugs—not just the vaccine, but their other stuff, too—were in every hospital in the country. Then they tanked. Lost a lot of business to their competitors."

"So? That's capitalism for you."

"Exactly. Investors lost big time. Nick *knows* PharmFam came to Parker. It makes sense they'd offer him cash—or grants for the University—if the vaccine was proven safe."

"Even if they did, you don't know that Parker accepted."

Karen sat down again, looking troubled. "Nick thinks Parker pressured Dan, which would mean he *did* accept. If Dan complied, the files on your laptop could prove their guilt."

"No. Whatever else Dan was, he was a good scientist. He'd never let a pharmaceutical company influence his research. And I don't believe Parker would, either."

"Not even with millions—and their professional credibility—at stake? Think about it. The vaccine research is the only thing the Sion's got right now. If it *is* unsafe, then they're back to square one. It takes *years* for this kind of research—decades—you know that."

"No," Emma repeated, a little less certainly. It wasn't possible. It just wasn't. She drew a deep breath. "Parker's president of the whole university. One institute failing won't end his career. And I still don't see how any of this leads to him attacking Justin."

"Justin had your laptop at school. Parker knew Nick was picking it up on Tuesday. His only chance to get it—and stop the blackmail—was to take it from Justin on his way home."

Emma narrowed her eyes. "Just how did Parker know all this?"

Karen flushed. "I might've told him. I'm sorry. If I'd had *any* suspicion, I'd never have opened my big mouth."

"Why wouldn't he just ask me? I would've *given* him the laptop."

"But don't you see? He wasn't involved in the day-to-day research experiments. If he asked you about the files, you might realize it was an odd request, which could lead to the whole scandal coming out. Then Parker's—and Dan's—careers would be ruined."

Emma tried to calm the rapid beating of her heart. Karen had a point. The Sion failing might not ruin Parker, but if it came out he'd taken a bribe... Then a thought struck her. "Justin kicked his attacker in the face."

"I thought of that. Parker's forehead was bruised on Wednesday. He said he ran into a door. It was gone by Saturday—if I hadn't seen him in Nick's office, I would've missed it."

Emma shook her head. "I still don't believe Parker would attack Justin."

Karen lit another cigarette. "What about the break-in?"

"What about it?"

"Did you tell anyone—besides Bethanne and me—that you'd be out running that night?"

Emma shivered. "Okay. Yes, Parker knew I'd be gone. I mentioned it over lunch. But Nick and Oscar heard me, too. If Oscar was blackmailing Parker, maybe *he* committed the break-in—and attacked Justin."

"I hadn't thought of that." She frowned. "But—he *knew* Nick was coming for the laptop. Have you *ever* seen Oscar expend any more energy than he had to? He could've just waited for Nick to deliver it to the lab, and wiped it then."

"I suppose. But Parker—"

"Couldn't ask Nick for the laptop any more than he could ask you. And *certainly* not his blackmailer." Karen put out the cigarette. "There's one thing we can find out, anyway. Where's Dan's paper—and your laptop?"

Ten minutes later, Emma stared at the screen and said, "God damn son-of-a-bitch."

Karen paled and sat down. "I'm sorry—you have no idea."

Emma looked from the monitor to the charts in the published paper. There was no denying that the numbers didn't match. Yet the rest of the graphics—their titles, parameters, footnotes—were correct.

"Either these files are wrong, or the journal's are. And if *those* are the bad files…"

"Then the vaccine does cause autism. Or at least, we can't be certain it *doesn't*."

"We have to tell Vin."

"No! Like Nick says—we don't have any proof."

"But the files—"

Karen clasped her hands together. "Look, I know it's my theory and all. But what if it's a mistake? I mean, what are the files doing on *your* laptop anyway?"

Emma thought about it. "I assumed Dan put them there. Maybe his computer was down, or, who knows? There could be lots of reasons."

"Exactly. Like there could be logical reasons why the data doesn't match. Maybe these are from earlier experiments. Maybe they were all ready to go into the article and Dan noticed they were wrong, and swapped them for the right files at the last minute."

"I know! The creation dates."

"The…what now?"

"In the file properties. It gives more detailed info, like when the files were *created*, instead of last saved."

After checking several of the files, Emma sat back. "Huh. It looks like Oscar created them—but Mollie was the last one to edit them."

"So? Oscar was Dan's chief research assistant, but well, we know what *Mollie* was. Maybe Dan had her recheck them for accuracy."

"I suppose… It just seems weird. Why would Mollie work on these files, days before she and Dan left for Hawaii—and before the final article edits were due to the journal?"

"Maybe she changed the data?"

"Then why leave the files on *my* laptop?"

"OSHU laptops all look alike. Maybe she grabbed yours by mistake, opened the files, thought they were just from old experiments, and automatically hit save before closing them."

"An accident? That sounds better than thinking someone changed the data on purpose."

"Exactly. I'm pretty sure Parker and Oscar are mixed up in something. But I'd rather not think I was attracted— however briefly—to someone who'd take a bribe."

The phone rang. Emma answered it and Vin's voice greeted her across the line.

"Oh—hey." She felt an idiotic grin spreading across her face. "We were just—"

Karen shook her head, but before Emma could decide to tell him or not, he cut her off.

"Where were you yesterday morning?"

His tone was cool, and her grin faded. "I went for an early run, and then we—Bethanne and the kids and I—went to Mass. Why?"

"Can you tell me where Bethanne's gun is?"

That couldn't be good. "Give me a sec."

She checked the china cabinet in the dining room. "It's not where Parker left it. After the party, I forgot about it. Hold on—I'll check the safe."

When she picked the phone up again a minute later to say the gun wasn't there either, Vin sounded resigned. "Can you come down to the station?"

"Of course. Why—what's going on?"

"Oscar's dead. Shot with a Walther P.38 that I'm certain will turn out to be Bethanne's. We need to get your prints, and Parker's, for comparison to those we found on the gun."

"Of course," Emma said again dazedly and hung up.

"What happened?" Karen asked.

"Oscar's dead."

Karen crumpled onto a chair. "How?"

"Shot. Probably with Bethanne's gun."

Karen went white. "I didn't just kiss a bribe-taking, data-faking attempted thief. I kissed a murderer…"

****

"I assume the only prints on the gun are Emma's and Parker's," Tony said.

"Yep." Vin took another swig of beer.

They sat at Tony's dining room table while Susan cleaned up, the pipsqueaks played with Azi in the living room, and Zoë did homework upstairs. Vin had risen, plate in hand, to help Susan, but she'd ordered him back down.

"Gimme a break. You and Tony need to talk. Besides, the dishes don't like it when someone else cuts in."

Tony had lifted an eyebrow. "Should I be jealous?"

She'd laughed, kissed him, and whispered something that sounded like "warm, wet, and slippery," making Tony's gaze trail hungrily after her as she left the room.

Which reminded Vin he hadn't seen Emma alone since the party, and a fierce need stabbed through him. He shoved it away. Barton was right about one thing—this case had to be wrapped up before he could focus on Emma. It didn't matter that he'd started seeing her before there *was* a case. He couldn't let a whiff of scandal attach itself to his work on this.

And then there was Izzy. The lawyer was "working on" the new divorce papers, whatever the hell that meant. Meanwhile, she was at his house, a constant reminder of his past humiliation and a threat to his future happiness. Which he was pretty sure resided in Emma's hands, one way or another.

Cripes. What a mess.

Vin said, "The only thing on it besides their prints was latex powder."

"From surgical gloves?"

"Yep. Except hospitals don't use them any more—too many allergies. But labs still buy them. They're cheaper than nitrile, and if you don't have patient contact, it's less of a problem."

"So, the killer wore gloves to eliminate prints. Original."

"Or…the residue transferred from Parker's hands when he handled the gun at dinner."

"Thought he didn't get down and dirty in the labs anymore."

"Normally, no. But on Saturday he just *happened* to run into a colleague, who just *happened* to need help finishing an experiment. He told us this without prompting."

"Right," Tony said, sounding disgusted. "You'd think he

wouldn't want you to know."

"First, I don't think Parker gives a damn what anyone thinks—except maybe Karen, but that's a whole other issue. And second, maybe he is guilty. He figures we'll find out about the gloves eventually, so he tells us first, making himself look good."

"Which means?"

"No idea. He certainly knows how to play the game. He *wanted* us to know how easy it would be to borrow a ten-year pin, and that Oscar actually owned one." Vin paused. "You know, I think that's what's been bugging me."

"What?"

"It doesn't matter if the pin at Emma's was Oscar's or not. It only matters that someone *thought* it was—and wanted us to think so, too."

Tony looked perplexed. "You lost me, bro."

"Somebody made sure I knew Oscar called Emma several times before the break-in and the attack, so I'd see him as a suspect—and think Emma might feel threatened by him. We got skin samples from under Justin's fingernails. I'd bet good money they're from Oscar."

"And then Parker just happens to tell you that Oscar had a pin, which you didn't know previously, but which Emma might have."

"And *then* he offers the info about the gloves."

"Which makes Emma look even more guilty."

"Right. If we didn't know Parker could've left the residue, there'd be more reason to think the 'real' killer did." Vin shook his head. "This doesn't feel right, either. I just don't see Parker framing Emma, whether he's the killer or not. But *someone's* trying to. For one, I don't think she *or* Parker would be dumb enough to leave the gun behind."

Tony was silent.

"What?"

"I have to ask. You're sure she didn't do it?" Tony raised a hand. "Think carefully. Are *you*—your gut instincts— positive she'd *never*, under any conditions, kill Oscar?"

Vin gritted his teeth, then blew out a breath. "Under normal circumstances, no, it couldn't be her. But if Oscar harassed her, and she thought he attacked Justin…" He shook his head helplessly. "Who knows what a mother will do for her kids?"

"Do we know why Oscar called her?"

"Not exactly. She said he offered to help clean up her laptop."

"And…?"

"She seemed nervous when I asked about it. But she's known Oscar for years and he just showed up dead five feet from her old workstation. I'd be upset, too." He paused, not liking the look on Tony's face. "What now?"

"The gun was her mother's."

"But she acted like she'd never seen it before."

"*Acted* like? You have doubts?"

"No. I'm sure she didn't know Bethanne had it." Tony eyed him over his beer. "All right, it does seem odd. But based on body temp and rigor mortis, Oscar was killed between eight and noon yesterday morning."

"And Emma's got an alibi for that whole time?"

"As much as Parker does."

"That's not an answer."

"Fine. Fuck you—she went for a long run from eight until after nine. No one was up when she left, so it's only her word. Even if she did leave at eight, it's only a fifteen-minute drive from her place to the Sion. She'd have had *loads* of time to run upstairs, shoot Oscar, and come home. And all that activity would make her sweat, so it'd *look* like she'd been jogging."

"Bullets?" At Vin's glare, Tony shrugged. "You said the gun wasn't loaded."

"It wasn't when *I* handled it. I didn't touch it on Saturday."

"So Emma—or *whoever*—had to get bullets somewhere."

"It's a goddamn nine milimeter Luger—the most popular fucking cartridge in the world. Even an idiot could find bullets for it."

Tony's lip twitched. "Are you calling Emma an idiot?"

"Of course not." Vin tried to force his blood pressure back down. "But if your point is to make me admit she could've loaded it herself, then yes, she could. Happy?"

"No. But good to know you aren't ignoring the facts just to keep your dick happy."

Vin rubbed his face. "I'm not. In fact, at the moment, my dick is exceedingly *un*happy."

Tony choked on his beer. "I think that falls into the category of TMI."

"You asked, so you're gonna hear it. I'm not going anywhere near Emma until this case is solved. Period. Even if it kills me—which, the way things are going, it might."

"Fair enough. And afterwards?"

"I'll get as near to her as she'll let me."

Tony laughed. "You got it bad, bro. A word to the wise—you may be able to turn your feelings on and off like a faucet, but most women can't."

"What are you saying?"

"I applaud you keeping away while the case is so fucked up. But do you really think she'll sit around and wait while you stonewall her?"

"Emma's not like that. She'll understand."

"Uh-huh. What about Parker? His alibi's not tight, either?"

"Home alone. No witnesses."

"Of course not. Anyone else a suspect?"

"Half the Sion. Oscar wasn't exactly Mr. Sunshine. He and Nick especially weren't getting along."

"How so?"

"Oscar was Dan's principal research assistant first. Most of the postdocs say Oscar didn't take orders from Nick very well—that he went and did his own thing, regardless."

"So, Oscar didn't play nice, and Nick didn't like it."

"Yeah. But Nick was at Karen's when Oscar was killed."

"All morning?"

"And the night before. Karen's not sure when he left, but she thinks it was after eleven. She wasn't feeling good, and he made her breakfast in bed. After he left, she fell back asleep."

"She wasn't feeling well, but he cooked her breakfast?"

"That bugged me, too. She said he didn't know. He'd gone to so much trouble, she didn't want to make him feel bad."

Susan poked her head in. "Bedtime for the kids. Tone—you can do their baths."

"Great," muttered Tony, but Vin caught the look he flashed Susan, and her blush, and tried not to think about what they anticipated doing, after the kids were asleep.

Susan said to Vin, "I still want to talk to you about Azi."

"Can it wait? I'm beat. Unless it's urgent…?"

She bit her lip. "Just some ideas about living arrangements and stuff. It'll keep. You go home and get some sleep. And you—" She winked at Tony, then went back into the kitchen.

"Hot date?" Vin asked as they rose from the table.

"Hell yes."

"Doesn't it get a little, you know, weird, coordinating sex with a house full of kids?"

Tony glared at him. "In the first place, I never *coordinate sex*. I screw my incredibly hot wife senseless, so she'd never even *think* of ditching me for another man."

"And in the second?" Vin asked as they entered the living room, which resembled a combat zone more than a residence.

Tony looked at the mess, then at his kids, and his face softened. "The loss of privacy is well worth it."

Vin thought about Juney's smile and Justin's scowl. "Yeah. I know what you mean."

"Yeah?"

Vin shrugged, and Tony laughed and punched his arm.

"Well, bro, you better hope to hell she's innocent."

"She is," Vin said, and found that somewhere deep

inside, he believed it.

****

Nick washed his hands in the men's room near Dan's—*his*—lab, then leaned against the sink, trying to calm the erratic beat of his heart, and the nausea that bubbled with it.

Fuck.

He hadn't had an anxiety attack in months. Now he got them daily. But then, he'd just cleared Oscar's personal effects from the lab. That'd send anyone over the edge. Barely a day since the janitor had found Oscar's body, but the lab had already resumed normal activity. After the detectives left last night, Nick was given the go ahead for business as usual. And now, he was vomiting in the men's room, trying to remember that the world wasn't *actually* ending.

Except it *had* ended for Oscar.

Sweaty hands slipped off the sink and he just made it to the can before heaving again.

Such a small pile of possessions. Not like the whole house Nick had dealt with when Janice died. And yet the despair was just as bad.

Janice. Dan. Mollie. Oscar.

So much death. And Nick had to face it all and keep going. Maybe—just maybe—with Karen's help, he'd pull through to the other side.

Maybe.

****

"Parker is *not* a murderer," Emma repeated, and Karen saw the effort it took her not to shout. "I don't think he took a bribe, either, but even if he did, he wouldn't kill Oscar over it."

"But—"

Emma's eyes flashed. "Enough. You said it yourself—Parker told Oscar to go to the police. If he didn't *care* who found out, why kill Oscar? It doesn't make any sense."

Karen pushed her salad around her plate, the crowded restaurant seeming somehow cold and threatening. Then a laugh bubbled up, at her own visceral, negative reaction to the thought of Parker's innocence. "How pathetic am I? I don't even know why I want him to be guilty. Maybe it's all the stuff Rob said about him."

"Such as?"

"You know, that Parker's a domineering bastard who only cares about himself and power."

Emma raised an eyebrow. "Rob said this—the same Rob who cheated on you so well for *seven years*, you only found out when he confessed?"

Karen's face burned. "Yeah, that Rob."

"And you'd believe what he says about his older brother, who he hates, enough to think Parker could *kill* someone?"

"Well, when you put it that way…"

Everything was so mixed up. Nick was supposed to be the simple solution, yet here it was—two measly days since they'd slept together—and it wasn't *him* she dreamed of at night.

"I'm *so* glad I'm with Nick now," she said firmly, shoving the image of Parker, naked, back out of her head.

"Me, too. But—well—you did say Parker's kiss was—ah—"

"More of a turn-on than anything I've ever felt in my life."

Emma's face went blank with surprise. "Um, okay?"

"But Nick is sweet and good—*so* much better than any of the losers I've been with."

"Karen," Emma said slowly, "confession time. When I found out Dan was cheating, I was mad as hell."

"Me, too."

Emma laughed. "Fair enough. But—here's the thing. I really didn't know he was cheating. But, in all honesty— things hadn't been great with us in a while. Actually, ever."

"What are you saying?"

"We got together so young. Who the hell knows anything in their twenties? I thought Dan was everything. But we got older, grew into the people we were meant to be. Now that I've been with Vin, I know what I was missing. Does that make sense?"

"I think so." Karen shivered. "Why didn't you tell me this before?"

"You were going through your own stuff with Rob."

"But—I would've been there for you."

"I know. It doesn't matter now. We're talking about you."

Karen stared at her. Surely Emma knew she could confide in her best friend? That Karen didn't always expect to be the one needing help?

Then another thought struck her. Was she, Karen, as oblivious as Bethanne? Was she so self-absorbed, she didn't even notice when Emma needed her?

Emma leaned forward, her voice gaining in urgency. "I love Nick—you're right, he's sweet, and *nobody* could have taken better care of Janice. But—does he turn you on? Does he make your heart sing and your blood heat?" When Karen didn't answer, Emma sat back. "If nothing else—is it fair to *Nick*, if there's no zing?"

"If there was no *potential* for zing, then no. But it takes time to get to know someone. You just said it took you awhile to realize Dan might not be 'it.' Why should I give up the nicest guy ever interested in me, before I've given him half a chance?"

Emma was quiet a moment. "If you're sure."

"I am. And even if I wasn't with Nick, I couldn't date Parker. He—he scares me. I can't explain it. You're probably right—he's not a murderer. But there's something about him…"

Emma regarded her searchingly, but Karen pushed away from the table.

"So. How's Vin these days?"

"I haven't talked with him since Parker and I went to get fingerprinted." Emma stood and they headed for the cashier.

"And you're okay with this?"

"I have to be. He's the detective working Dan's—and now Oscar's—cases."

"He doesn't think *you* had anything to do with either of them, does he?"

"I don't think so. But to be fair, *I'd* suspect me. I'm sure he knew there's more about the laptop than I told him. I don't like lying to him—I think we should tell him what we found."

"No!" Karen grabbed the receipt and steered Emma outside. "We don't know *anything* for sure. And if it comes out that we know *something*, the killer might think it's more than it is. Someone attacked Justin and killed Oscar. Think of your safety—and your kids'."

"But if we give Vin the laptop, then the cops know what we know, and I'm safe."

"Not safe enough. Three people are dead. Please, don't say anything. I—I don't want to think Parker's a murderer. Or that Dan would publish bad data. But if we turn the laptop over to the police, it could ruin innocent lives. Even if, later, it turns out the published data is right, the Sion, Nick, Parker—Dan—their reputations might never recover. Please—for me…?"

Surely this was right—saying nothing, instead of announcing they had data that might be worth killing for again? Or ruining their friends' careers, over a possibly innocent mistake?

At last Emma nodded. "Okay. But I don't like it—and I may tell him soon anyway."

"Fine. But not until we know what we're dealing with."

A few hours later, Emma called Karen at work. "You were right." Her voice shook, and it sounded like she'd been crying.

"About what?"

"Oscar was blackmailing Parker—and Parker *did* take a bribe."

"You're kidding."

"Vin called an hour ago. Someone sent an unmarked

package to the station with an MP3 player in it. The note said it was Oscar's, and Vin wanted me to come in and verify."

"And…?"

"It certainly looks like it—one of those tiny, basic ones that hold tons of music. He used it all the time. The note also instructed Vin to listen to one of the files on it." Karen heard her fighting back a sob. "It's Parker, talking with someone from PharmFam. According to Vin, the guy says *we'll give you three million dollars to make sure the vaccine is declared safe*. And Parker—"

She choked, but Karen knew what was coming, even as the bile rose in her own throat.

"Parker said *yes*."

"Hell. Just—*hell*…"

Chapter Fifteen

"I'll be damned." Nick let out a low whistle, leaning back in his chair. "We were right."

Across the desk from him, Karen looked haggard. And no wonder—it must be hard, learning your former brother-in-law was a lying son-of-a-bitch who might have killed three people. He went to stand behind her, resting his hands on her shoulders, and she sagged back.

"I'll be okay. It's just a shock. I don't know what to think."

"I know. At least the police have something concrete to investigate now."

She nodded. "I told Vin what I'd overheard, and he's going to question Parker. Of course, it still doesn't give Parker a real motive."

"I'd think blackmail is an *excellent* motive."

Karen shook her head. "Remember—I heard Parker tell the guy to go to the police. If he didn't care who found out, why kill Oscar?"

Nick paused. "I forgot about that. But surely Parker's got more motive than anyone else?"

Karen twisted in her chair to look at him, her face flushed. "Well, actually, the thing is—it looks like someone's framing Emma."

He felt his jaw drop. "*Emma?* Surely Vin doesn't believe that?"

"I don't think he *believes* it. But someone *wants* him to."

"But—I mean, why—" Nick cleared his throat. This was

the last thing he'd expected, and he couldn't wrap his brain around it. "How…?"

By the time Karen had finished telling him all the reasons Emma might have killed Oscar—the most damning of which seemed to be that the gun was her mother's and had her prints on it, and that she might have thought Oscar attacked Justin—Nick's heart pounded and he had to lean against the desk and force himself to breathe normally.

"But Emma *didn't* know Oscar could have attacked Justin. Did she?"

"Not at first. But when Parker said the pin might've been Oscar's, Emma could've overheard. Maybe she figured if Oscar broke into her house, he attacked Justin, too."

Nick watched her closely. "There's something else, isn't there? Something about—" He took a wild stab. "About the break-in?"

She looked away. "It's nothing. Really. It's not important."

"Come on—you can tell me."

"I…guess. It's just that those old files Emma found on her laptop are different from the published data. We were thinking maybe the break-in was Oscar, looking for the laptop, and that's why he attacked Justin—to get it."

"Son of a bitch." Karen glanced up, and he shook his head. "Sorry. It's different when you're only guessing something. To have it confirmed… Did you tell Vin?"

"Emma wanted to, but I said no. I thought, you know, if Parker didn't know we had proof of the faked data, it might be safer for her. Or, if he's innocent—"

"You're right. If Parker *is* dangerous, or he's working with people who are, silence is safer."

"Plus, it could still be a mistake."

He gave her a speaking look, and she turned pink.

"Parker's a jerk, but I wouldn't want to ruin his career over nothing. Besides, Mollie was the last one to save the files."

"How in the world do you know that?"

"You know Emma, the über-geek. She looked in the file properties and saw who created, saved, modified them. Apparently, there's quite the digital trail, if you know where to find it."

"Is that so?" Nick sat again, thinking about what he had to say next. Something of his dilemma must have shown on his face, because Karen looked at him with concern.

"What about you? How are you holding up?"

He wiped a hand over his face. "It's been a tough week. I was just thinking—I wasn't going to tell you, because you were married to his brother, but…"

Karen paled. Maybe he shouldn't—but no, it had to be done. He steeled himself and plunged ahead.

"You overheard Parker tell someone—who you think was Oscar—that he didn't care if that person went to the police. Well, when I was here on Saturday, I *saw* Oscar and Parker arguing. In fact, I heard Parker threaten Oscar."

Karen looked faint. "Threaten him? How?"

"I don't recall his exact words. But it was something like if Oscar wouldn't leave Parker alone, Oscar would regret it. Parker looked ready to punch Oscar, but then they saw me."

"Oh, my God. Did you tell Vin this?"

"I will now. I didn't before because, well, it's my word against his. And let's face it—hardly anyone actually liked Oscar." He reached across the desk for her hand. "I'm sorry, Karen. It looks like Parker really is bad news."

Her hand was cold, and her eyes shone with unshed tears. "I already got screwed over by one of the James boys. At least now we can stop anyone else being hurt by the other one."

Nick squeezed her fingers. "That's my girl."

She offered him a watery smile, then her eyes widened. "I'd better warn Emma."

"Of course. Whatever you think is best."

****

"Thanks for coming in," Vin said as Parker sat in the chair by Vin's desk.

"Always happy to help."

If Parker was being ironic, it was subtle. Vin sized him up. The fact that Parker reciprocated should have been irritating, but instead, it increased Vin's respect. Parker had yet to crack under pressure, or defend himself against anything he considered beneath his notice.

Vin said, "Glad to hear it. Care to fill in any of the details for me?"

"About…?"

"Someone sent us Oscar's MP3 player. It contains a recording of you accepting a bribe from two PharmFam execs. The implication is that you then pressured someone—probably Dan—to make sure the data proved the vaccine was safe, and then Oscar blackmailed you."

Parker's gaze never wavered, and neither did his expression of mild amusement. "Yes. Oscar played that recording for me, and I paid him a lot of money to *not* play it for anyone else."

"You admit it?"

"Five grand a month for nine months." When Vin blinked, Parker actually laughed. "What's so surprising? That I have that much cash—or that I got off so cheap?"

"Why would you say that?"

"One's reputation doesn't always have a price tag." He leaned forward. "Tell me, Detective. How much is *your* reputation worth? Enough to uproot yourself and your uncle and move all the way out here, rather than face your mistakes?"

Vin stilled. "We're not talking about my mistakes."

Parker stood. "Of course not. If we're done talking about mine, I'll show myself out."

"Not so fast." Parker turned back, unruffled as ever, and Vin said, "I'll state the obvious. If Oscar was blackmailing you, you have an excellent motive for killing him."

"But I didn't. Check all you want—you'll never find any evidence I pressured Dan or anyone else about the data. Now that the paper's out, and the vaccine has been *objectively* proven safe—let's just say Oscar's revenue stream dried up. I told him to shove it, and I meant it. *He* may have been pissed at me, but I didn't give a damn about him."

Vin held his gaze. Damn it—he'd swear Parker was telling the truth. Except something didn't fit.

"So, your story is you took the bribe from PharmFam, but didn't do what they asked?"

Parker lifted an eyebrow. "It would appear so, wouldn't it?"

"That's not an answer."

"Actually, it is. And I have nothing further to say on the subject."

Vin sighed. "Fine. You can go—for now."

Instead, Parker placed his hands on the desk. "Think about what I said, Detective. If you focus all your energy on preserving your reputation, you may lose sight of what really matters."

"And that would be…?"

"The people you love, of course. Is alienating them worth it?"

"You tell me."

Parker drew back, for once looking like Vin had struck home. "I used to think it was. Then I found out no matter what I do, people see what they expect to see."

He gave Vin the once over, then shook his head and left.

What the hell did Parker know about it, anyway? Vin couldn't afford to lose this job—and his reputation was critical to keeping it. Besides, he wasn't "alienating" Emma, he was protecting himself. And Azi. Vin couldn't put him through the trauma of moving again. Besides, where would they go?

Vin grabbed a stack of reports off the growing pile in his inbox. His mood had already gone south—he might as well tackle paperwork. At least it would get his mind off Emma and back on the case, where it belonged.

****

When Karen got to Emma's on Thursday evening, Justin

218

and Juney were doing homework at the dining room table, and Azi hovered near the desktop computer in the corner.

"Where's Bethanne?" she asked.

Emma answered, "Movies with Charley. Double-feature—they'll be out late."

"You sound so disappointed."

Emma laughed and sat at the computer. "Let's just say living with my mother has its ups and downs."

"Hey, Karen!" Azi said excitedly. "I came over so Emma could help me."

Karen smiled, the first truly genuine one she'd felt in a while. "Hey, Zorro. What's up?"

He pointed to a stack of papers near the printer. "We're making flyers!"

Emma glanced up from the monitor. "Azi found an MP3 player on the street last week, and Vin suggested posting flyers, to give the owner a chance to claim it."

Azi handed Karen a copy, and she gave the grainy black and white image a cursory glance. "That's a good idea. Then if no one calls, it's yours, free and clear."

"You think so? I put the description in and everything. See? But I *din't* put the serial number. Vinny said not to, so if anyone says it's theirs, they hafta prove it."

"Good idea," Karen repeated.

She sat next to Emma, who said darkly, "Vin's pretty clever about these things."

"He hasn't called, has he?"

"No." Emma glanced at the table. "Hey, Az—since we're done, and Vin won't be here for a while, why don't you and the kids go play a board game or something?"

Juney's head flew up and Justin asked, "Seriously, Mom? We can stop studying?"

"Unless you have anything due tomorrow?"

"Just reading for a test next week."

"I'm done," Juney said, and held up a full page of math problems.

Emma initialed their homework notebooks and helped

them clear their stuff from the table. Then she led Karen to the kitchen where she put water on for tea.

"What gives?" Karen asked.

"I don't know. I guess Vin wants to keep his distance until the case is sorted out. But…I mean, couldn't we at least talk?"

"He hasn't called at all? Not even late at night, to breathe heavily into the phone?"

"No. Tonight, Azi invited himself over. Vin's insisting on picking him up later—he doesn't want Azi walking through the park at night, and I don't blame him. But from what I heard of their call, I don't think he was happy about it."

"Don't be ridiculous. He's just being a cop. Things will go back to normal soon."

"I hope so. After Dan, I can't be with another guy who shuts me out."

"Dan shut you out because he was a cheating asshole who may—or *may not*—have falsified important scientific data. If Vin's cooling off, it's temporary, to focus on the case."

Emma placed mugs on the table and sat, looking unconvinced. "I guess. What about you? Anything new?"

"You mean other than that Nick heard Parker threaten Oscar?"

"You're joking."

"I wish I was. He said he'd tell Vin about it today. I'm so glad you agreed to keep quiet about the data."

Emma shifted uncomfortably. "About that…"

"No. You promised."

"But I think Vin is picking up on me hiding this from him, and it's partly why he's so distant." She stiffened her shoulders. "I'm telling him—tonight."

Karen started to argue, then put her head in her hands. "You're probably right. I clearly don't have the best judgment. Tell him. Nick said we shouldn't—" At Emma's eloquent stare, the heat rose in her cheeks. "Sorry. I didn't see the harm in telling him. *He's* not a cop."

"You told Nick, who you're sleeping with, but I can't tell Vin, who I'm sleeping with?"

The heat deepened. "You're right. See? I have terrible judgment. Tell him."

Emma exhaled. "You're sure? Because, you know, my loyalty is to you. If it comes down to it, I haven't known Vin all that long. But you and me—we're for life."

"Thanks. I know I've been a little crazy. But now that Parker's off the menu—not that he was ever *on* it—things will get better. I'm sure of it."

Azi wandered into the kitchen. "Can I have a soda?"

"Of course." Emma started to rise and he glared at her. "I can do it!"

"Sorry. Of course you can. Bottom of the fridge."

He chose a can, then looked at the cupboards.

"Glasses are over there."

Very deliberately, he selected a large glass, then added ice. He poured the soda and took a swallow. He drank again without speaking, and Karen looked at Emma.

Emma raised an eyebrow, then said to Azi, "What's up?"

He frowned. "Did you ever live alone?"

"Completely? No. Karen and I roomed together in college. Then I moved in with Dan."

Azi took that in, then frowned again. "You could've, though. Right?"

"Of course. It just never came up."

He looked at Karen, and she said, "Rob and I were right behind Emma and Dan. I didn't live alone until we divorced. It's not all it's cracked up to be."

"Why?"

"For starters, I have to do everything myself. If the sink's broken or the roof leaks, I can't ignore it."

He said, "I like doing things myself."

Emma nodded. "I can understand that. It's very important But, it's good to have backup, too, if anything goes wrong."

"Yep." He set the glass on the counter, twisting it. "Vinny's my best nephew."

Emma smiled. "Is that so?"

"Uh-huh. He takes care of me all the time."

"That's nice, isn't it? But maybe sometimes, it's a bit much…?"

He sighed heavily. "You know it. But Terry lives by herself."

"Oh…?" Emma said, sounding cautious.

"Yep. It's called a Group Home. But she has her own room an' even her own kitchen. And she's number five." At Emma's blank look, he said, "Her mail. She's number five."

Karen said, "You mean she has her own address—different from other people in the house? Like an apartment?"

Azi beamed. "Yep!" Then his face clouded again. "I never had my own apartment."

Emma said gently, "Do you want one?"

"I don't know. Do you think I could?"

"I'm sure of it. You do a great job—you set up your MP3 player and helped make the flyers. You really know how to figure stuff out."

"You think so?"

"Absolutely."

"What if somethin' happened, an' I din't know what to do?"

Emma considered. "Well, I've also noticed that you know how to ask for help. That's important, too. It's good to be independent. But it's good to know when you can't do it alone."

"If I went somewhere like Terry, I could do things myself, but still get help." He blew out a breath. "An' if I move out, Vinny won't halfta take care of me."

Karen thought *oh shit*, and Emma said firmly, "I'm sure Vin loves living with you."

"You know it." Azi grinned. "He worries too much. I can take care of myself, an' he can do other stuff, like go out with you."

Emma choked on her tea. "I'm not sure—that is—"

Azi put his glass in the sink. "Thanks, Emma! You were a big help. Now I know what I gonna do!"

He went back to the living room, and Karen stared at Emma. "Did you just give him permission to dump Vin and move out?"

Emma sunk her head in her hands. "Good Lord. I hope not."

****

After Karen left and Emma got Juney to bed, she heard a knock on the kitchen door.

"Finish brushing your teeth," she said to Justin.

Then she took a deep breath and went to let Vin in. The sudden heat in his gaze would have been reassuring if it hadn't been replaced immediately with a cool professionalism.

"Emma." His voice was cool, too.

"No kiss, even off-duty?"

His throat muscles worked, but all he said was, "Where's Az?"

She took in his rod-stiff posture and iron-clenched jaw, and folded. "Watching TV."

He followed her in and closed the door, not meeting her gaze. Fine. Let him be that way. She had other things to worry about. "Speaking of Azi—"

"Are the kids in bed?"

Emma frowned, but he was staring at the black night outside the window, and missed it. "Juney's asleep, and Justin's brushing his teeth. About Azi—"

"And Bethanne?"

"Should be home any minute. How's Izzy?"

That got his attention, and he scowled at her. "This has nothing to do with her."

"I think it does. I think you're so worried about making the same mistake twice that you won't even look me in the eye."

He deliberately stared at her and she planted her hands on her hips. "*I didn't do it.* So there."

"Fine," he growled and turned to the window again.

"Now, about Azi—"

He rounded on her. "How the *hell* is Azi your business?"

Emma took an involuntary step back, then straightened. "I just spent the last two days with him. He's at least *partly* my business."

"You and Susan."

"What the hell does that mean?"

"It means you should shut up while you have the chance."

"No. Azi's going through some confusing stuff. He told me some of it, maybe Susan, too. I don't know her, but she's a woman. We *listen* when people need to talk. We don't just turn our backs and stomp away."

Vin's face had gone from red to purple and Emma almost wished she'd kept her mouth shut. She should've known he'd be sensitive about this. Azi was the closest thing he had to a son, and in some ways, it *wasn't* her business. Maybe Vin wasn't cooling off because of the case, but because he didn't want to be with her. That thought hurt, and she swallowed.

"You're working a lot, and Azi's lonely—he needs someone to talk to. He needs *you*."

"Is that a fact?" Vin's voice was quiet. And fierce.

"Yes!" *Screw it.* So what if he looked like he wanted to throttle her—she *had* to take a stand. Even if the thought made her want to hide under her bed forever.

She walked right up in front of him and took a deep breath. "*I* need you, too."

He froze, and she saw the emotions warring on his face. He took a step away from the window, and then it exploded, shards of glass flying everywhere, blinding pain bursting through her skull.

She was falling, the floor rushing up fast, and then everything was black.

****

"Emma!"

Vin threw himself over her as she fell to the floor. She didn't respond, and he listened with one ear for anything further while he checked her pulse—nice and strong, thank God. Feet thumped down the stairs and from the living room, and Az and Justin ran in.

"Get down!" Vin barked, and they dropped.

Justin saw the blood dripping from his mother's temple and went white. Vin inched up and grabbed his arm, forcing him to focus.

"She's unconscious, but she'll be fine. I won't let anything happen to her. Do you understand?" Justin nodded shakily, and Vin said, "We need an ambulance."

"I'll get the phone." Justin backed toward the door, still in a crouch.

"Vinny, what happened?" Azi asked.

Vin looked from the gaping window to the floor, where a rock the size of a baseball lay near Emma's head. It had a piece of paper on it, tied with a string, and he reached for it carefully. The rock was too rough for fingerprints, but there might be some on the paper. He started to rise—maybe the thrower was still out there—but then he saw Az's face, etched with fear. Cripes—chase the perp or stay and care for the people who needed him?

"What happened?" Azi asked again, and Vin's decision was made. He couldn't leave the kids and Az—or Emma. What if the perp came back?

"I'm not exactly sure," he began, when Emma stirred and blinked, and suddenly he could breathe again. *"Thank God.* Sweetheart—are you okay?"

"I think so. My head hurts." She touched her temple, fingers coming away red.

Justin entered, saw her, and looked faint. Vin tried to sound reassuring while gently probing her injury. "It's okay. She has a bump and a small cut. We should get her to a doctor, but I doubt it's serious." Emma tried to sit up and he pressed her back. "Not yet. Dumb question time. What day is it?"

"Thursday. September twenty-first."

"What's your name?"

"Michael Anne O'Manny. And you're Vytautas Bronislovas, the big jerk who hasn't called in three days except about Dan's case."

Relief flooded him, and he brought her hand up for a kiss. "You'll live."

The front door opened, and Bethanne's voice sang out, "Hi, honey—I'm home."

"In here," Vin called.

Bethanne walked in, saw the broken glass, the rock, and Emma, and dropped to the floor, looking at Vin, stricken. "My God! Is she okay? What happened?"

She forced Vin aside so she could touch Emma's forehead. Probably more maternal instinct than she'd displayed in her life, he thought cynically.

"Did anyone call an ambulance?"

"I will," Justin said, looking to Vin for guidance.

Emma's pupils seemed normal, and Vin considered. "I think she should go to the ER, but I don't think we need to call 911."

"Are you sure?" Bethanne demanded. "This is my baby here."

She was whiter than Vin had ever seen her, and abruptly he felt bad for doubting her love for Emma. Before he could answer, Azi spoke up.

"Terry took a first aid class an' tol' me about it. If anyone gets unconscious for more than a minute you gotta call 911."

"How long was Mom out?" Justin asked, fingers poised.

Bethanne gasped. "She was *unconscious?*"

Vin thought. "Less than a minute—I'm sure of it."

Emma cleared her throat. "Is anyone interested in my opinion?"

Four voices said "No!" and Emma glared at them.

"*Et tu*, Justin?" she tried, but he wasn't having any, and Vin hid a grin.

"You need to be super careful, Mom. I agree with Vin. You should see a doctor."

Someone knocked at the back door and Vin rose to open it. "Jeez—what now?"

LJ stood on the doorstep. "Is Izzy here? She took off an hour ago. I thought maybe…" His gaze landed on the scene in the kitchen and he stiffened. "What happened?"

"Someone threw a rock in the window, and it hit Emma on the head. Don't suppose anyone ran by when you came through the park?"

LJ assessed the scene again. "How long ago?"

"A couple minutes, tops."

"No one. I was inside the park, having a smoke, for the last ten minutes—they'd've run right past me." He raised an eyebrow at Bethanne. "Maybe they ran up the street instead?"

She looked at him, dazed, then shook herself. "It's very dark out, and the streetlights aren't very bright. I didn't see anyone."

LJ frowned, then looked at Vin. "Want me to look around?"

"If neither you or Bethanne saw anyone, they're long gone."

Emma's color had returned, and the bleeding had slowed, but her bruise was already turning purple. She struggled to sit up, and both Vin and Bethanne moved to stop her.

"I'm *fine*," she insisted, swatting them away.

"You may sit—*not* stand," Vin admonished, and she scowled at him. He stuck his tongue out at her and she laughed, then winced, and he said, "Sorry. No laughing. My bad."

Bethanne indicated the note. "Is anyone going to read that?"

LJ's frown deepened. "Who ties a note to a rock,

anyway?"

Azi said, "Like in the movies! Maybe they din't even mean to hit Emma."

"Very melodramatic," Emma agreed.

"Sure is," LJ said carefully, and Vin narrowed his eyes. "Where did you say Izzy is?"

"I misplaced her."

Vin turned back and discovered Bethanne had untied the note and was smoothing it out.

"Don't touch that!" She looked up, startled, but it was too late. "Great. You do realize you just destroyed evidence?"

"Destroyed? But—the paper's fine."

"We might've gotten prints off it. Now we'll be lucky if we get a smear."

"I'm sorry—I didn't think." She looked so distressed, he almost felt sorry for her.

Emma broke in. "Spilled milk. Do you think we could *read* the note now?"

"Of course." Vin snatched it from Bethanne, who glared at him. "It says, 'Nothing is more important than Family. If the Police find out, there will be hell to pay. Stay away!' The F in family is capitalized, as is the P in police." He looked up to find Emma's face had whitened again. "What is it, sweetheart? Does any of that mean anything to you?"

Emma shivered. "No…none of it."

Something in her response felt off. But then, she'd just been knocked unconscious by a rock. Hard to say what "normal" would be. One thing was certain—she still needed a doctor. He said to Bethanne, "Stay here. I need to take Emma to the hospital."

Justin put in quickly, "I'm coming with you."

Vin watched Bethanne struggle. It was obvious she wanted to go with her daughter, but equally obvious she knew how important this was to Justin. "Fine. I'll stay with Juney and Azi."

Justin ran out to get dressed and LJ offered Bethanne a

hand up. "Want me to stay with you? I could board up the window."

She was still pale, but she nodded gratefully. "That would be nice. Between this and the door, we're keeping the glass company in business." She cast a look at Emma, then at Vin. Her violet eyes were dark, her lips thin. She seemed on the verge of saying something, then shook her head and let LJ take her from the room, with Azi following.

Emma tried to rise and Vin shook his head. "Sit."

"I'm *fine*. I'm going to stand up now."

It was clear she'd do it anyway, so Vin slipped an arm around her, then pulled her tight. "Thank God you're okay. When I saw you go down—" His voice caught and he rubbed his cheek against her hair. "I never want to feel that way again as long as I live."

She looked up searchingly. "Really?"

"At least a thousand new gray hairs."

"I wasn't sure. I mean, I thought—"

"I know. I'm a dumbass." Cripes but it was good to hold her again. He kissed her, then leaned his forehead against hers. "Emma, you scared me shitless. But—damn it, I hate this. I—"

"It's okay. I'll wait. Just don't shut me out, okay?"

Relief washed through him. "Scout's honor."

He bent to kiss her again, and Izzy's face loomed. He shoved it away. She wouldn't ruin his life a second time. And if she *had* thrown the rock—well, even his fear of Rico wouldn't save her. This was it—where Vin belonged.

And no amateur theatrics could tear him away.

Chapter Sixteen

St. Eustachius the Cooked:
Hunters, Firefighters, Trappers, and Hard Knocks

When Karen honked from the driveway on Friday morning, Emma winced and touched her temple, and Bethanne practically fell over herself hurrying to her side.

"Are you okay, honey? Would you like another pain pill? Or more coffee?"

Emma bit back a laugh—no sense making her head worse—and managed an eyebrow raise. "The doting mother's a new role. Should I buy season tickets? Or is it a one-shot deal?"

Bethanne glared. "This is the thanks I get? I'm worried—you should be resting."

Emma carried her mug to the sink. "I'm fine. The van's still broken so I'm not even driving. But I *have* to sign one more set of papers for my financial aid, before the weekend. Even Vin thinks it's okay."

"What does he know about it?"

"Plenty. He was at the hospital with me, remember?"

"How could I forget? *I* certainly wasn't allowed to be there."

"I promise I won't be long." She opened the screen and waved to Karen.

Bethanne was still frowning. "At least let me call a tow truck for the van. If you aren't driving anyway, we may as well get it fixed."

"Already taken care of. Vin's coming at eight on Monday to take it to his mechanic."

Bethanne's surprise was comical. "But we *always* go to

Marcus."

"No, *Dan* went to Marcus. Vin's guy does all the cop cars. He's *got* to be good."

"But—how will Vin start it?"

"Nifty trick he showed me—put it in neutral and roll it down the drive, then pop it in gear. Thank God it's so ancient, it's a stick." She gave Bethanne a quick kiss and escaped.

When she got in the car, Karen looked at her bandage. "What happened to you?"

By the time Emma finished her explanation, they'd parked at OSHU, and Karen was fuming. "That bastard!"

"Excuse me?"

"I'd bet anything Parker wrote that note."

"Whatever makes you say that?"

"Don't you see? He's afraid Vin will uncover the blackmail. Nothing is more important than *family*—he's saying more harm will come to your family if you tell Vin anything."

Emma made the mistake of shaking her head. "Ouch. No. I still can't believe it's Parker. But you're right—I do think the note was meant to keep me quiet about the data."

Karen's gaze flew up. "And…?"

"I didn't tell Vin. I was about to, when the rock hit me."

"Good."

Karen got out, and Emma followed her through the garage. "But I still think if I just *tell* Vin, the data won't be an issue anymore."

They reached the elevators, and Karen pushed the button. "*Whoever* threw that rock may be responsible for everything. If you tell the cops, who's to say they won't go after you—or your *children*—for spite? *Three* people are dead already."

Emma shivered and stepped into the elevator. "Okay. I'll wait. But for the record, even if Parker *did* take a bribe, I don't think he's capable of murder."

Karen looked away. "I'd like to believe that. You have

no idea how much." When she met Emma's gaze again, she seemed more fragile than ever. "I sure can pick 'em, can't I?"

"I thought you and Nick—"

"I'm trying to make it work. I really am. But Parker..." She shrugged helplessly. "At least don't say anything until I talk with him. When everything's out in the open, Nick and I can move forward. But I *have* to know the truth, from Parker himself, before I can let go."

"Oh, honey." Emma reached for her, holding her tight as they rode to the financial aid offices ten floors up.

"Thanks," Karen whispered when the doors opened. "You're always there when I need saving from myself. But now it's my turn to save you."

She stepped out before Emma could ask what she meant, and Emma let it drop.

****

Karen spit out her Nicorette and took another piece from the pack just as the doorbell rang. Great. If only it quelled nausea, too. Dropping the pack into her purse, she squared her shoulders and opened the door to find Parker glowering on the threshold.

"I came as soon as I got your message, though God knows why. What do you want from me?"

"Happy Friday to you, too."

"Cut the crap, Karen." He pushed past her, and she reluctantly closed the door. Emma *had* to be right—he couldn't be a murderer. Could he?

Parker flung himself into a chair. "You clearly hate me. So what's so damn important that I had to come all the way over here?"

"I—" Karen cleared her throat. How in the name of anything was she supposed to begin? *Do it for Emma— anything to keep Parker away from her.*

She tried again. "Did you throw the rock that hit Emma in the head last night?"

Parker's expression was so blank with astonishment that

Karen sagged with relief. Then his eyes narrowed and he rose. "Why *do* you hate me so much? What have I ever done to you?"

He took a step toward her, then another.

When he was barely a foot away, she finally found her voice. "I—I don't hate you. I—" His gaze was penetrating, like he saw right through her. "I just want you to leave me and my friends alone. Just stay away from Emma, okay?"

She could feel the heat radiating from his body. His voice was low and she had to clench her fists to keep from reaching for him.

"You really think I'd hurt Emma, don't you?" Karen shook her head, but he didn't seem to notice. His gaze raked over her, lingering on her legs, exposed below her skirt. She resisted the urge to clamp her knees together, and he looked up. "But while you despise me, I also turn you on."

She gasped and shook her head again, but he'd seen the truth she couldn't hide. For one moment, he looked so hurt, she could actually feel his pain, slicing through her.

Then his expression hardened. "So, it's the violence that does it for you. That's too bad. Get it through your head— Rob lied. I'm actually a pretty boring guy."

He turned away and before she could stop herself, she said, "It's not the violence. It's you."

Parker froze, then turned slowly back.

Hell. She'd really done it now. Nothing for it but to keep going. "I know about the bribes and the blackmail."

"And?"

Her heart sank. "That's it? You won't defend yourself?"

"Why should I? You made up your mind about me long ago."

"What about the data on Emma's laptop?"

"What data?"

"You know. For the vaccine paper."

"Emma has vaccine data?" He seemed genuinely confused.

"I mean—that is—" For once, she couldn't think of

anything to say. If he really knew nothing about the data—didn't even recall discussing it—then maybe he hadn't thrown the rock. And if he admitted taking the bribes, why not admit he knew about the data? None of it made sense.

Parker's eyes glittered. "Why did you ask me here? To get me to admit I'm the scumbag you think I am? Or are you actually interested in the truth?"

"Of course I want the truth! I just thought—" Her face burned. *Emma,* she reminded herself. "I know you're attracted to me. If I sleep with you, will you leave Emma alone?"

Parker's jaw dropped. Then he snapped it shut. "You might think that little of yourself, but I sure as hell don't."

He reached for the door, and Karen blocked his path. "Wait, don't go."

"Get out of my way."

"Parker—please."

"Damn it, Karen! You have no idea what you're playing with."

She opened her mouth, and all at once, he shoved her against the door, raking her skirt up, sliding his hands over her bare thighs.

She gasped and batted at him. "What are you doing?"

"I can't take it anymore." His voice was hoarse. "You want cheap sex? Well, this is as cheap as it gets." He shoved one hand into her underwear and thrust his fingers inside her, then froze, raising startled eyes. "You're wet. You really do want me."

"Big deal." Maybe he wouldn't notice she was practically pressing herself onto his hand.

He didn't budge. "I think it is a big deal." With his other hand, he cupped her breast, caressing it until she moaned. His voice was low and wicked. "You like that, don't you?"

God, he felt good—better even than she'd imagined. This had to stop. "Get off."

"I plan to."

Karen choked on a laugh. It had to be hysteria—she

couldn't possibly think he was *funny*, on top of everything else. "I meant *get off of me*."

"I will if you tell me you don't want this." He pushed his fingers deeper, the rough pressure building an ache that left her breathless. "Or this." His other hand slid inside her bra, cool on her hot flesh, and he teased her nipple into a tight little bud.

"Oh…God…." Karen's head fell back and she gave up pretending to fight him.

It was all the encouragement he needed.

He dropped his head and took her mouth. He was hard against her and she undid his fly, needing to touch him, to make him as crazy as he made her, and he groaned and ground into her hand.

Ha! Take that, she wanted to say, but her own need was too great and all she could manage was another moan.

Suddenly he let go and reached for his fallen trousers. She panted, too hot and wet to be embarrassed. He pulled out a condom and rolled it on, and then he was kissing her again, pressing her against the door, lifting her hips, sliding in, up, deep, so deep, sliding out, thrusting back. It was slippery and rough, like his kiss, and then she came, *hard*, so fast and unexpected, she had to choke back the sobs while the spasms went on and on.

"That's it," he said into her mouth. "That's it, baby. Let go. Let it all go. God, you're so good." Then he thrust again, deep, deeper, out, in, until he exploded, his spasms as intense as her own. "Jesus…Karen…."

He dropped his head to her shoulder, breathing hard, and she knew he would see the tears, would know how much his "cheap sex" meant to her. It was fantastic—the best sex of her life—but it was Parker, and she couldn't give him that kind of power. She *couldn't*.

So she said, "That was quick." He looked up, and he was too smart, he wouldn't buy it, so she scowled and shoved his chest. "Fun's over. Get off—you're hurting me."

"What are you afraid of, Karen?"

She forced a bored tone. "Not a damn thing. But here's the deal. Even when sex is cheap, it usually lasts longer. I expected better from you."

He looked like she'd slapped him. "Fine. Have it your way." He pulled out and let go so fast she stumbled.

"A gentleman, too. I sure can pick 'em."

"You sure can."

He rolled the condom off and yanked his pants on, and she'd never seen him so angry. She straightened her skirt, then made herself look at him, level and cool.

"Thanks for the ride. Let's *not* do it again."

"Absolutely not."

That stung. "I mean it. Don't come back, thinking you can fuck me anytime you want."

Parker moved fast, pinning her to the door with his whole body. She barely registered that he was either *still hard*, or else *hard again*, before his mouth landed on hers. He grabbed her jaw, pushing his tongue inside, possessing her. Then just as fast, he shoved her away.

"Sorry," he grunted, not meeting her gaze. "I shouldn't have done that. You just make me so *mad* sometimes. But that's no excuse."

"I—"

He rounded on her, eyes flashing. "Shut up, Karen. For once in your life, just *shut up*. You have got to be the dumbest smart woman I ever met." Suddenly all the anger left him. "Forget it. I don't know why I bother. You got what you wanted. I'll leave Emma alone. And from now on, I'll leave you alone, too."

He walked out, leaving the door open, and Karen watched until he disappeared from view. Then she slid to the floor, and it wasn't enough. So she rolled into a ball, clutching her knees to her chest, waiting for the sobs to come. But she had nothing left, not a damn thing, so when they came, it was a terrible dry wracking, so hard, her ribs were about to break.

Better her ribs than her heart.

Only she could fall for a bribe-taking probably-not-murderer.

Dumb didn't begin to cover it.

****

Emma set her purse down and pressed the replay button on her voicemail, not sure she'd heard correctly.

"I'm very sorry, Mrs. O'Manny," the financial aid officer's voice said through the speakerphone, not sounding sorry at all. *"If you'd been honest with us, it would've saved a lot of time. I'm sure you understand, but with so much money in your accounts, we have to turn down your aid application again."*

"What's that about?" Bethanne asked, coming inside with another load of groceries.

Emma checked the clock. After five, and it was Friday. Why couldn't these things happen first thing Monday, when she could actually *do* something about them?

"Somebody," she said, voice catching, "thinks I'm too rich to qualify for financial aid."

Bethanne stared blankly, then set the bags down. "How would anyone get that idea? What about the debt?"

"I have no idea." Emma fought back a bubble of hysteria. "'Mr. Bartholomew—if I had a quarter of a million dollars, believe me, I'd know it.'"

"*Charade.* Audrey Hepburn to Walter Matthau." Bethanne frowned. "They think you have two hundred and fifty grand?"

"Actually, I don't know. They just said I have *too much*."

The kids banged in, Justin looking excited and carrying a small, brown-papered box. "Mom! This was on the porch—I think it's a birthday present. Can I open it? Please?"

Bethanne leaned over. "There's no return address."

Emma's heart clutched and she grabbed the box. "Give me that!"

"Mom!"

"What is it?" Juney asked, looking confused. They hadn't told her about the rock—the attack on her brother was bad enough; she shouldn't be worried about Mommy, too—but she obviously sensed the tension in the room.

"It's okay, sweetie." Emma carefully removed the paper by its edges and lifted the lid. A folded, typed note lay on top. "It's from Vin," she began, relief flooding through her. Then she saw what the package contained, and sank into a chair, pulse rocketing all over again.

"What is it, honey?" Bethanne demanded.

"It's a box of bullets."

"From *Vin*? How *dare* he?" At Emma's pointed look, she scowled. "I didn't *give* a gun to Justin. I just showed it to him, to help him feel safe."

Justin peered in the box. "Mom? I don't think it's from Vin."

"What makes you say that?"

"Well, when we went to the firing range, Vin barely let me touch the guns. He made me learn all kinds of safety stuff, and he said no one under twenty-one should be allowed to own a firearm. Plus, isn't it, like, a federal offense to send ammunition through the mail?"

Bethanne snatched at the paper wrapper at the same moment Emma did, and it tore in half. "No postmark," Bethanne announced, holding her half pinched between forefinger and thumb. "It must have been hand-delivered. Maybe there's prints on it."

"I'm calling Vin. Someone's sending me a message, and I intend to stop them."

****

Vin walked into the living room, followed by LJ, who set down two suitcases.

Izzy glanced up. "What the fuck are you doing, Vinny?"

"You," Vin said neutrally, "are leaving."

"The hell I am!" She flung her magazine down. "Where do you expect me to go?"

"Izzy," LJ broke in. "Where were you last night?"

She turned the force of her glare on him. "What business is it of yours?"

He crossed his arms and stared her down like the spoiled brat she was. "Know anything about a rock that hit Emma in the head?"

"*What?*" Her outrage at least *sounded* real. She turned on Vin. "What happened?"

"Thought maybe you could tell me."

"Damn it, Vinny! I don't know anything about it!"

"How about the box of bullets someone gave Justin today?"

"You think I'd give bullets to a *kid?*"

"I think you'd like nothing better than to drive a wedge between Emma and me."

She rolled her eyes. "Only a moron would throw a *rock* at her. Jeez, Vin. I told you. I just came out to tell you about the papers and piss Daddy off. I could really give a fuck about you and your little sweetheart."

LJ grabbed the suitcases and headed for the door. "C'mon. Vin's brother's gonna let us crash at his rental until you decide to go home."

Izzy stared at Vin, then shrugged. "Have it your way, babe. But for the record, Emma ain't worth my time."

She left without further comment, and Vin stared at the suddenly empty room. She'd almost sounded sincere. But if Izzy hadn't thrown the rock or sent the bullets, then who had?

And…why?

Obviously, he was missing something. Both of those acts felt amateurish—like the attack on Justin. But that was probably Oscar, and now he was dead. The bullet delivery could have been organized in advance, but not the rock. Unless he had an accomplice.

Parker, while clearly up to *something*, didn't fit the role. He'd been upfront about paying Oscar thousands of dollars, but refused to say yes *or* no about the bribes. Vin couldn't shake the feeling that something more complicated than simple blackmail was going on. Either way, Vin's gut said Parker wasn't a killer. And he was too smart to tie a note to a rock, unless he wanted to make the crime look dumb on purpose.

Of the other Sionites, the one most involved with the vaccine was Nick. But while he'd shown up at Emma's shortly after Justin's attack, Vin couldn't see him harming his own godchild. Or Emma. When Vin had questioned Nick yesterday, he'd looked downright ill at the thought that she might have been hurt. Either he was an incredible actor, or he hadn't done it.

Plus, Vin still couldn't connect him to Dan's death, or Mollie's. Nick and Mollie had dated briefly, but by all accounts, their break-up was amicable. Both labs agreed that work went on as normal, with no loud fights or obvious animosity between the exes, or between Nick and Dan, who'd been best friends for over twenty years and seemed to have weathered this just fine.

Vin glanced at the clock. When Emma had called about the bullets, she'd said she had something to tell him, but wanted to do it in person. Azi was with Terry. If Vin ran over to Emma's now, he could spend some time with Justin and Juney before bed, then talk with Emma alone. He'd promised Juney a police "badge" and coloring book, and there was Justin's Lady Macbeth to follow up on.

All in the name of public service, of course.

His text notification pinged—Barton. Great.

"What now?" he barked when she picked up the phone.

"HPD called—they found Ramie. Arrested on a DUI, but he's wanted on a bunch of other charges. His lawyer's pushing for a better deal on those cases, so we won't know everything for a day or two. But here's a juicy tidbit for you—he wasn't after Dan originally. He was after Mollie."

****

Emma's eyes were wide and she certainly seemed shocked.

Vin scrubbed a hand over his face. No—she *was* shocked. Do *not* go down that road.

Still… So far, she was the most likely suspect. Parker, as

near as he could tell, had zero reason to want Mollie dead. Nick might—killing the ex was a common scenario—but *none* of the evidence pointed to him. Which left Emma, who no doubt hated the woman who'd poached her husband, and had a direct link to the gun that killed Oscar.

No. Emma wasn't a killer. They didn't even know for sure if Oscar's death was related to the other two. The solution had to be with the whole vaccine thing.

"But," Emma said now, for the third or fourth time, "*Dan*—I mean, we all assumed—"

"Apparently we were wrong."

He couldn't keep the weariness from his voice. He sat back in the porch swing, stretching his shoulders until they popped. He hadn't even seen Justin or Juney. One look at his face and Emma'd led him out here, leaving the kids with Bethanne. They were probably in bed by now, and who knew when he'd see them again?

"I don't understand," Emma said. "If Ramie told you all that, why not the rest?"

"He'll sign a detailed statement after he dries out. But that could take a while—who knows what's in his system. Most likely it'll be Monday before we know everything." He leaned forward, watching her. "I still think all this relates to the vaccine paper somehow." Was it his imagination, or did she give a guilty start? "And you had something to tell me…?"

That was *definitely* a guilty start. She cleared her throat. Her gaze slid away again. Crap.

"Emma. What did you want to tell me?"

She blew out a breath, still avoiding eye contact. "Okay. I know this sounds bad. But we didn't know if it was intentional or not, and Karen was afraid if we were mistaken, someone would think we knew more than we did. And with Justin and the rock and everything—"

"Emma." She met his gaze at last, looking genuinely contrite. Which set off all kinds of red flags. "Just tell me whatever the hell it is that you didn't tell me before."

"It's about my laptop…"

Vin's pulse pounded, but by some miracle, he managed to keep his mouth shut until she'd spilled the whole sorry tale. Even then, he at least *sounded* calm.

"Give me the laptop."

She hesitated, then pushed off the swing and went inside. When she returned, he took the computer from her and moved to the steps.

"Vin, wait. Aren't you going to say anything?"

He stopped. Set the laptop carefully down on the deck. Turned around. Watched as she saw his face and jerked back.

"Uh—"

He kept his voice low and even. "You lied to me. You withheld evidence. You may have put yourself and your children in even *more* danger. What would you like me to say?"

She flushed. "I'm sorry, okay? I didn't know what to do, and like I said, the data may just be a mistake. How was I supposed to know if it was important or not?"

"You were supposed to *trust me* to make that decision."

He picked the laptop up again, but she didn't take the hint.

"God damn it, Vin! I screwed up. I admit it! People make mistakes. This isn't the first time, and it won't be the last. Are you going to walk out on me every time?"

"Assuming we make it past *this* time—"

"What does *that* mean?"

"I don't know!" He was shouting, and he forced the volume back down. "I can't be here right now. Let me go, so I can do my job. Unless you're keeping anything else from me…?"

She shook her head, looking miserable. "I'm sorry."

She might even mean it. But right now, he didn't care. Barton would have a field day, but it would never be as bad as what he thought of himself.

Never get involved with a suspect. Even one you didn't

suspect of anything.

Make that, *especially* one you didn't suspect.

****

Karen's face was earnest. Sincerely regretful. Much more apologetic than Mollie's had been, though her message was the same.

Nick swallowed around the hard lump in his throat. "You're…breaking up with me? *Why?*"

"It's…complicated."

She faced the windows, watching the clouds amassing over the Willamette. Corner office. Top floor. He'd worked hard for this—was even here on a Sunday. *Again.*

And she was *breaking up with him?*

"Try me." His voice sounded flat to his own ears. Good. Much better than the screaming rage inside. This couldn't be happening again. *Janice—why does everyone always leave…?*

Karen turned back, her expression bleak. "I'm sorry, Nick. You're a great guy. I thought we could make it work, but…"

She was so fragile, like she would break if he touched her. He rose and came around the desk, standing between her and the door.

"Karen. We've only been on a couple of dates. Let's give it a little longer. You're so good for me—I know you can help me through this. Please—just one more shot."

She got a funny look on her face, and glanced toward the door. They were alone, probably no one else in the building. "I'm sorry," she repeated, and moved to go around him.

He trembled with the effort at holding himself in. No. He wouldn't. He wasn't that weak—he was in control. His therapist had taught him how to take deep, calming breaths. He closed his eyes, inhaling, exhaling. She'd just gotten past him when a thought struck him and his lids popped open.

"There's someone else."

Her gaze flew to his. Damning evidence, though she shook her head in denial.

"Parker," he said flatly and watched as she went white.

Fuck. "I thought you hated him as much as I do." *Too whiny.* Nick tried again. "He's an arrogant bastard who'll walk all over you until there's nothing left." Better. Except her expression had gone inexplicably thoughtful.

"Actually, Parker treats me better than any man I've ever been with. It took me awhile to notice, because his delivery's a little unvarnished. But he calls me on my crap, and still respects me more than I do myself. I'm really, really sorry. If it helps, I'm not dating him—I doubt I ever will. I think I finally screwed that up for good."

"Then why won't you give us another chance?" *Fuck.* Whining again. Why did women do this to him? Make him act like a toddler who'd lost his toy.

Only Janice hadn't.

And Emma.

The realization washed over him, a waterfall of enlightenment, cold and clear, awakening him from the haze he'd been wrapped in.

"It's just not working out," Karen repeated, but he barely heard her. When she moved to the door, he let her go, and it clicked softly shut behind her.

Emma...

His feelings for her were so deeply buried he hardly noticed them anymore. She'd always been unattainable—partly from being with Dan, but mostly because she deserved so much better than Nick could ever offer.

But... He was her children's godfather. Maybe he *should* have tried after Dan's death. It had just seemed too soon—for both of them. And now there was the slight problem of Vin.

Nick sat down again. Emma had let slip that they'd fought. She most likely hadn't meant to tell him, the news couched in a conversation about her car—Vin was supposed to take it to a mechanic, and she was worried that now he wouldn't.

If Nick were to get her car fixed instead...

Would she be grateful? Would she finally notice what

he'd been hiding all these years?

Nick shook his head. Whatever else, Vin was honorable. He'd keep his promise, even if he never spoke to her again. But that didn't preclude Nick from insinuating himself into the process. He steepled his fingers and looked out at the gathering storm.

Perhaps Karen's breaking up with him was a blessing after all.

Yes. Maybe it was finally time to make a move on Emma.

But first, he needed a plan. For once in his screwed-up life, he'd go in with his ducks in a row. That way he could pick them off, one by one.

Bang. One down.

Another—*bang!*

And so on…

Chapter Seventeen

St. Erasmus di Formiae:
Birth Pains, Explosives, Ordnance Men, and Shells

By five-to-eight Monday morning, it was clear Vin wouldn't be coming for the car. Emma could have called him, but he'd been so mad on Friday. Which was her fault. He was right—she should have told him about the data. Who knew if the crime lab could extract anything useful from the files, but either way, she shouldn't have kept them from him.

Even so, he shouldn't have walked out. Couples *talked*—they worked things out.

It was Dan all over again.

Pushing that thought away, she slipped into Bethanne's room and kissed her mother's still-sleeping cheek. "I'm taking the car in."

Bethanne murmured something that might have been a question about the kids, so Emma said, "Sarah picked them up already, so you can sleep in. I'll see you later."

She tiptoed out, probably unnecessarily. Bethanne was *not* an early riser; it usually took several alarm clocks, spaced around the room, to get her up before ten.

The morning was cool and damp after last night's rain. Emma shivered and pulled her sweater close before climbing into the van and inserting the key. She twisted it once, but as expected, the engine didn't turn over. Vin thought it must be a loose wire somewhere, which would explain why it occasionally worked but mostly didn't. Luckily, the driveway was sloped just enough, and she'd remembered to ask the tow truck driver to back it in for her.

She put it in neutral, keeping her foot on the clutch, then lifted her other foot off the brake to start the car rolling. When it was just picking up speed, she popped it into second and quickly took her foot off the clutch. The engine turned over and she stepped on the gas, making the van lurch forward, but at least it started. And it was only a minute or two past eight—she'd have plenty of time to get to the mechanic's and catch a bus home, before Bethanne got up.

She'd just breathed a sigh of relief when there was a sudden flash of light behind her and a deafening *BOOM!* She coughed and gasped as the whole back half of the van was engulfed in smoke. Her seatbelt was stuck—*she couldn't unclasp it…*

****

"What did you just say?" Vin demanded, and across the line, Barton laughed.

"Not awake yet? It's almost eight."

"My alarm didn't go off. You said something about Mollie's laptop…?"

Barton gave up, for once. "I said we got the first part of Ramie's statement. HPD sent it over. Not only was he not supposed to kill Dan—he wasn't supposed to kill Mollie, either."

"*What?*" Vin swung his legs over the side of the bed and reached for his pants.

"He said an old army buddy hired him to steal Mollie's laptop."

Vin's shirt was stuck on his head. He yanked it down. "What was the buddy's name?"

Barton snorted. "Nice if it was that easy. He claims he can't remember. Hard to say if he's screwing with us, if he's still too whacked to think straight, or if he really doesn't know."

"What happened—why'd he kill them if he was only trying to steal the laptop?"

"He tried to get it from the hotel, but they loaded a

bunch of stuff on the plane the night before the flight. Ramie broke into the hangar, they surprised him, and he panicked."

He shoved a hand through his hair in lieu of a shower. "I'll be damned—we've been going at this all wrong, thinking someone set out to kill Dan on purpose. Wrong target—wrong motive—not finding the right clues."

"Pretty much. For all we know, Oscar's death isn't even related, since it seems no one *planned* to kill Mollie or Dan. Instead it looks like your girlfriend just wanted her laptop back."

Vin froze. "Excuse me?"

Barton's satisfaction was so obvious, it crackled through the line. "Didn't I tell you? We ran the serial numbers on Emma's laptop. It's not hers—it's Mollie's. OSHU standard issue, but they can be bought at a discount for personal use. Before she went to Hawaii, Mollie must've switched 'em. Or Emma did. So the question is, who's covering up what? And why?"

Vin glanced at the clock. Eight, straight up.

Girlfriend.

Emma.

Shit.

"I have to go. I'll be in later."

"Vin—I need you to come to the station. Now."

"I'll be there as soon as I can."

He hung up, grabbed his keys, and jogged toward the park. He should've called Emma, though he was still pissed—especially now it seemed the data *was* significant. Mollie must have known someone would look for it, or else why switch the laptops? Not only had Emma put herself *and* her family at risk, but if the laptop contained the *correct* data, then the vaccine could be harming innocent children even now.

He shook his head, disgusted. *Definitely* still mad.

He'd just reached the cul-de-sac when the bomb went off.

"*NO!*" The scream tore from him and his legs pumped him forward.

The van rolled down the street with her inside, struggling with her seatbelt.

"Emma!" He pounded on the window and she looked up, terrified. Most of the flames were in the back of the car, but they could spread fast. "Pull the brake and unlock the door!"

She yanked the handbrake and the van jerked to a stop as she popped the lock and he pulled the door open. Whipping his pocket knife out he sliced through the seatbelt, then dragged her out and a safe distance away. Several neighbors had run into the street, and he saw phones out, calling 911. Someone aimed a fire extinguisher at the car and Vin turned his attention to the woman in his arms.

"Jesus Christ!" He clutched her close and she clung to him. "Thank God—are you okay?"

"*Emma!*"

Bethanne, wearing a nightgown and robe, dropped to her knees before them. She reached for Emma but Vin wasn't letting go. Not now or ever. He didn't care what she'd done—none of it mattered. She was *his* and they'd figure it out. Period.

Bethanne glared at him. "Let me see her! Is she all right? Emma—are you hurt? I saw the explosion from my window. Sweetie, please—talk to me! Tell me you're okay!"

Emma drew back reluctantly, and looked at her mother. "I'm fine." Her voice shook, and she was covered in soot, but otherwise seemed unharmed.

"Thank God," Bethanne whispered and crossed herself. "If anything happened to you..." She turned to Vin, her expression abruptly furious. "Where the hell *were* you?"

"Excuse me?"

"You're supposed to be protecting my daughter. Why weren't you here? How is it that someone planted a bomb in her car—tried to *blow her up*—*after* hitting her with a rock—and you weren't able to prevent it?"

Tears streamed down her cheeks, but Vin didn't think she even noticed. Self-absorbed or not, Bethanne loved her daughter. No one could fake the horror on her face. Hell—his face had probably worn that exact look when the bomb went off.

"I'm okay," Emma broke in. "Really."

Bethanne stared at her, ascertaining the truth of her words, then choked on a sob. "My baby—my poor baby." She brushed a hand over Emma's hair, then her eyes widened, and she turned to Vin. "She wasn't supposed to be driving. *You* were. What if the kids were with her?"

Emma blanched and Vin's gut roiled. "Jesus."

Just then Nick's sedan turned onto the block. Well now, and wasn't *that* convenient?

When he saw the scorched, still-smoking van, he hit the brakes and got out, coming toward them at a dead run. "Emma! My God—what happened?"

"Get in line," Vin said coolly. "That's what we all want to know."

****

"You okay, Mikey?" Azi asked, concern wreathing his face. He perched on Emma's sofa, Terry next to him, both looking equally upset.

"I'm fine."

Emma tried to keep the exasperation from her voice. It was hardly Azi's fault that everyone from Bethanne on down was hovering like she was an invalid. Vin had insisted she get checked out at the hospital, then left her there to go to work. No chance for a private talk, but he'd kissed and touched her constantly, until he *had* to let go, and had promised to call later.

Then Bethanne jumped into the fray, and Emma hadn't had any peace since.

"Charley," Bethanne commanded. "Tea for Emma, and more sodas for our guests."

Charley rose obediently, but Emma waved him back down. "For God's sake—I'm *fine*."

"No, you aren't," Bethanne said. "You could have been *killed*." Her voice shook, and even Charley looked pale and distraught beneath his tan.

"It's no trouble," he began, but Emma rolled her eyes and made it to the kitchen before they stopped her.

She was just returning with the drinks when the doorbell rang.

"I'll get it!" Bethanne and Charley said simultaneously, and crowded into the entryway in truly comic form.

Azi and Terry each took a soda from her, and she sank down next to them. "How are you two doing?" she asked, though their ear-splitting grins rendered the question moot.

"It's all good." Azi put his arm around Terry. She blushed prettily, but didn't rebuff him.

"Who's watching the hot dog stand?"

Terry said shyly, "When Azi's nephew called, I asked our manager if we could close early and he said sure."

"Sounds like a nice guy," Emma said, as Bethanne and Charley reappeared with LJ.

"How you doin'?" he asked, giving Emma one of his "sizing up" looks, which no longer freaked her out.

"No damage. Let me guess—Vin sent you. Are you supposed to keep me safe—or keep an eye on me, so I don't slip up and commit a heinous crime under his nose?"

"Both. Need any help in the meantime? Not with committing a crime of course."

His tone was teasing, but Emma closed her eyes and counted to ten. Then she looked him right in the eye. "I screwed up. I should have told Vin about the files. But after the rock hit me, I was afraid if I said anything, something worse might happen."

LJ cleared his throat. "About that."

The doorbell rang again, and Charley fell over himself to get to it. Bethanne sidled over to LJ, and Emma tamped down her frustration as Karen walked in. "What's shakin'?"

"Unfortunately, not me."

Karen laughed. "It sucks to be loved, doesn't it?"

"You're awfully chipper."

"I am, aren't I?" Her gaze took in the assembled crowd. "Tell you about it later. What have I missed?"

Bethanne piped up, "LJ just offered to help Emma with anything she needs. Isn't that sweet? He's *so* nice."

LJ shot her an odd look. "Believe it or not, I try. I—"

"Of course you do!"

Azi rose and offered Terry his hand. "We gotta go."

She let him pull her up, saying shyly, "Azi's gonna show me his new MP3 player."

Karen said, "No one claimed it?"

"Nope. I gonna get it all cleaned off. 'Cept I don't know how."

"I could help you. I had one that style before I started using my phone for everything."

Azi beamed. "That'd be great! Thanks, Karen! You work downtown. I can come tomorrow after work."

"Sure. Any time."

Karen walked them out, and LJ cleared his throat, glancing at Bethanne. "I gotta split, too. But the offer still stands."

"Thanks," Bethanne said, and Emma wondered which of them he was talking to.

Charley seemed to be having the same thought. "Leaving so soon?"

LJ kept his gaze on Bethanne. "I have things to do. But maybe I'll stop by again later."

"I'd like that," she said. "Charley—will you be a dear and help me pick the kids up? You know how I *hate* to drive alone."

Mollified, Charley agreed, and the three of them left, leaving Karen and Emma alone.

"Thank God." Emma flopped back on the sofa. "Now, what's new with you?"

"What isn't?"

Karen pulled out a pack of gum, and Emma said, "You quit smoking again."

"Yeah." Karen's smile was beatific. "Isn't it wonderful? I'm finally doing something good for myself."

"This I gotta hear."

"Okay. But it probably won't *sound* very good. Just trust me—I sold myself to the devil, permanently ruined my chance at long-term happiness, and made so many dumb mistakes, they're canceling each other out." At Emma's blank look, she laughed. "Isn't it marvelous?"

She popped the gum in her mouth and sat back. "It all begins with Parker. And it kind of ends with him, too…"

****

"Let me see if I understand the score," Tony said on Monday evening as they sat on Vin's porch, eating sandwiches from the deli. "Someone hires Ramie to steal Mollie's laptop, but he winds up killing her and Dan. Then it turns out Mollie had the wrong laptop, so now everyone wants Emma's laptop instead. Meanwhile, Oscar blackmails Parker for—supposedly—taking bribes from PharmFam. Yes?"

"So far, so good."

It'd been a long day. Barton had asked to see him several times, but something always intervened. He'd finally escaped, but who knew what tomorrow would bring?

Tony took another bite, talking while he chewed. "Someone, likely Oscar, breaks into Emma's house. Then he attacks Justin. Probably after the laptop both times. Then somebody shoots him. Someone throws a rock at Emma, which she thinks is a warning not to tell you about the data. Justin gets a box of bullets, supposedly from you. And today, someone plants a bomb on Emma's car, but it's too small to do any damage other than scaring the crap out of her." He shot Vin an appraising glance. "And you, by the look of it."

Vin rubbed his eyes. "It was a simple pipe bomb—the kind anyone with internet access could make. But whoever did it either made it wrong, or kept it small on purpose."

"Big boom, low damage."

"And as you say, big scare." He shuddered. Emma was home safe now, and Karen had taken the afternoon off to stay with her while Bethanne ferried the kids around. Which was a huge relief, especially as Karen had sounded pretty good when he'd called her from the hospital. Healthier, like she'd made an important decision or a step in the right direction.

Tony swallowed. "Any leads on the army buddy?"

"Goes by Strongman. Ramie claims he's forgotten the guy's real name—that they used codenames whenever they got back in touch. Ramie's been pretty whacked out for the last twenty years, so it's possible. He says they met in boot camp, so we're trying to get ahold of his records." Vin finished his own sandwich and crumpled the wrapper. "Back to the laptop."

"Okay." Tony thought a minute. "If Oscar was looking for it, he probably knew about the data. So…was he blackmailing someone else? Or is Parker somehow involved in the fraudulent research? What do we know about the files themselves?"

"They were originally created by Oscar, then saved by Mollie. Emma noticed them a couple weeks ago, but didn't realize the data differed from the published paper until last week."

"And Emma did *not* tell you this when she discovered it."

"Yes."

"All right. You're certain she's telling the truth now?"

"What do you mean?"

"Maybe she planted the data herself. Maybe she switched the laptops, not Mollie."

"Why?"

"To set Mollie up? To get even with Dan? Maybe she planned the whole thing—was going to reveal the real data when the paper came out, discrediting Dan and ruining his career."

"And those of everyone else at the Sion, as well as

putting innocent children at risk?"

Tony shrugged. "Revenge—and love—are strange. They don't always make people think clearly."

Vin said slowly, "She had the means and opportunity. She worked in Dan's lab for ten years. Plus, she's almost as much of a computer whiz as Oscar." He bit back a growl of frustration and rose to pace the porch. He *had* to think objectively, no matter how his gut clenched when he pictured Emma guilty of anything this bad.

Izzy flashed before him again. Hell. It wasn't like *he'd* been completely honest, either.

"The problem is, we don't know *which* files are correct—the laptop's, or the paper's."

"What do Nick or Parker have to say about it?"

"Nick claims the published files are the ones Dan gave him before going to Hawaii."

"So either he's ignorant, or suggesting that Dan is the one who altered the data. What about Parker?"

Vin shook his head. "I can't figure out his game. My gut says he's not a crook. But he admits Oscar blackmailed him, and withdrawals from his bank account confirm it."

"How much did he pay out?"

"Over the last nine months, forty-five grand."

Tony whistled. "Guess when you're university pres, you've got that kind of change."

"Tell me about it. In the same time period, he also loaned the Sion a hundred grand for a fancy new electron microscope."

Tony's brow furrowed. "All at once?"

"Twenty-five down in February, the rest a month later. It hasn't even arrived yet—it's on back order. Why?"

"Didn't you say Ramie had two deposits into one of his accounts—one for twenty-five grand, another for seventy-five, spaced a month apart?"

"Holy crap."

Tony sat back, looking smug. "I still got it."

"Yeah. I'd take you down a peg, but I'm too busy beating

myself up for not noticing this sooner." He grabbed his cell and dialed, then started pacing again. When the research tech picked up, he said, "I need to find out if the Sion Institute got a pricey microscope in the last few months. Or at least, if they—or Nick Forte or Parker James—paid for one."

He hung up to wait for the call back and Tony said, "If the Sion *didn't* order the new microscope…"

"Then a hundred grand of Parker's money is unaccounted for. And Nick lied about it."

"Strange bedfellows, from what you've said of their mutual disrespect."

"Maybe, maybe not. Follow the money trail. Wherever it ends, there's your perp."

****

Nick banged a fist on the steering wheel, then inhaled deeply. From his vantage point up the block, he watched as Bethanne's car pulled back into Emma's driveway, and she, Charley, and the kids got out. Karen's car was still in the cul-de-sac, and if he wasn't mistaken, that goon from Chicago lurked in the park. How many smokes did one thug need?

It was a circus—like the damn dinner party all over again.

Clusterfuck.

He made a quick u-turn and gunned the engine. He needed to talk with Emma, but not with all these damn people around. They needed privacy. If he could just get her to focus on him for a minute, she'd listen. And she'd understand. She had to.

If she didn't, no one would.

****

The phone in the house rang and Vin rose to get it. Then his cell went off also.

"You get your cell—I'll get the other one," Tony said and went inside.

Vin's cell showed Barton's extension. "What?"

"That flag you put on the stocks Dr. O'Manny bought?

It just paid off. Turns out, since February, Prospect-Gage has been quietly taking over—you ready?—PharmFam."

"Fuck," Vin said and sat down.

"Pretty much. Just recently finalized."

"I thought they were nearly bankrupt themselves. O'Manny bought their stock because it dropped so low."

"They still have big clout. They're assuming PharmFam's debt, restructuring, reaping any new profits. O'Manny's broker had instructions to sell if the stock went above fifty."

"And since the paper supposedly proves the vaccine is safe, I'm guessing it just did."

"You got it. Late on Friday, which is why we didn't find out until now. What's more, the profits from the sale were transferred to an off-shore account, before going into Emma's personal savings. Looks like someone's trying to cover their tracks."

"Exactly how much are we talking about?"

"Oh, not much." Barton's voice was sly. "A little under two mil."

"Hell."

He started to hang up and she cut in quickly, "I still want to see you in my office first thing tomorrow. Top priority. I mean it Vin—or else."

"Yeah. Whatever."

He hung up and stared at the yard. When Tony came out, Vin said, "I just found my money trail." He looked up, hating the pity he was about to see in Tony's face. "It leads to Emma."

Tony sat down. "It gets worse. That was the tech working up the pipe bomb specs. He has fond memories of me from my days on the force, and gave me the scoop."

Vin's gut clenched. Without a doubt, he did *not* want to hear this. "What?"

And there it was. The pity. "I'm sorry, bro. The materials to make the bomb were bought online on Friday—with Emma's credit card. She had them overnighted to a PO box.

Guess now we know why the bomb was so small—she didn't want to hurt herself, just deflect suspicion and gain your sympathy."

"Jesus Christ," Vin said as the whole world ricocheted around him. "Jesus *fucking* Christ…"

****

"You think I have *how* much money?"

Emma stared at Vin, whose expression remained closed and hard, his eyes so dark they actually receded, taking him farther and farther away. Abruptly she wished she'd insisted they have this conversation in the house, not on the evening-shrouded porch. But Karen and Charley were still here, and then Vin had inexplicably refused to set foot inside.

Now she knew why.

"Your bank says you have one and three-quarter million in savings alone." His voice was cold, emotionless, and it made her want to pound her fists and howl.

"Savings *alone*? What does *that* mean?"

"Got a safe deposit box?"

"Of course! What—"

"Where's the key?"

Emma opened her mouth, then closed it. Drew in a deep breath, counted to ten. Blew the air out again. "Can we start this over?"

"How about the key to your PO box?"

"Why on earth would you want *that*?"

"Evidence."

She couldn't have heard him right. "Of *what*?"

"I know about the bomb, too."

"What about it? Vin, you aren't making any sense."

"At least be honest with me now. What's the point of lying?" His face was impassive, but he suddenly sounded tired. Defeated. "It's like I've said all along. Follow the money. Did you think we wouldn't find out? Using your own credit card." He made a tsk-ing sound. "You're smarter than that. And shipping to your own PO box. All to cover your role in the real crimes."

Emma's jaw dropped, then her pulse roared. "You think I stuck a bomb on *my own car*?" He didn't respond and fury exploded. "You arrogant—pig-headed—*blind*—" There wasn't a word strong enough. "—*jerk!*"

Vin ticked the points off on his fingers. "One, you worked in Dan's lab. You had to know all about the vaccine, and how low PharmFam stock sank last year. Two, the second mortgage is in your name as well as Dan's. At first, I thought your signature was forged, but now..." He shrugged. "Three, you have the computer smarts to fake the data. Four, you tried to hide your tracks by saving the data on Mollie's laptop instead of your own."

"I did *what?* On *Mollie's* laptop?" They had the same model. But surely she would have noticed it wasn't her machine. "You think I faked research that affects *millions* of children?"

"That bothered me, too. But then Susan's friend at OSHU gave me the answer. If the vaccine isn't safe, then after PharmFam renews their patent, they can take it off the market for 'further study.' The article shows it's safe, so there's a better chance of avoiding the bad PR. All they really wanted was the patent renewal, so you'd still have fulfilled the terms of the bribe."

"You really think I'd do all that? And then save the data on Mollie's laptop on purpose? If Dan was in on it, too, why would *he* let me do that?"

Vin narrowed his eyes, and she felt his examination like a physical probe. This was crazy—he had to know it was. But he only shook his head and resumed his narration.

"The dates line up with when you found out about the affair, so maybe you did it on your own. Who knows? Maybe the original data was a mistake, but you saw a chance to make trouble for Mollie. Which brings me to five. We got Ramie's service records back and compared them to Dan's. For a few weeks, nineteen years ago, they were at the training camp in San Diego together. Dan was on his way in, Ramie was being kicked out."

Emma's knees quit working and she sat down, hard, on the porch bench.

Vin's gaze never left hers. "The old CO remembers them. Says Ramie was fond of codenames, and called Dan 'Strongman.' CO wasn't sure, but he thought it was supposed to be a joke—the ninety-pound weakling scientist, enlisting in the Marines."

Emma couldn't breathe. "Dan *knew* his killer?"

"Yep." Vin paused. "But then, you knew him, too."

"*What?*"

"Ramie told us he visited Portland twelve years ago. Naturally, he stopped off to see his buddy, Strongman— stayed with him and *his wife*. Got to know her pretty well, in fact. Enough that if she called and asked him for a favor, he might just do it."

His words hung between them and he waited, watching, gauging her reaction.

Emma rose slowly from the bench. "I did *not* hire Ramie to kill Mollie—or Dan!"

Vin's expression was thoughtful. "I suppose that could be considered truthful. It's certainly a clever way to lie."

"*Urgh!* I didn't hire anyone *else*, either!"

Was it her imagination, or did Vin actually look disgusted?

Fine. Let him be that way.

"Get off my porch. I don't want to see you—now, or ever!"

"Ditto. Unfortunately, when we have more solid proof, you'll have to." He pushed away from the porch rail. "I haven't figured out how the rock and the note fit in with any of this—or giving the bullets to Justin—but I will. One way or another, the truth will come out."

She swallowed. She would *not* stoop to defending herself.

Vin continued. "Since your prints and Parker's are all over the gun that killed Oscar, it seems likely he's your accomplice. Maybe you staged that scene at dinner—an elaborate ruse to ensure both your prints would *already* be on the gun, *before* one of you shot Oscar. In any case, all of this should be enough for a new search warrant. Maybe an arrest warrant, too."

This time, even when Emma tried to speak, not a damn sound came out.

He turned and went down the steps quietly, the same way he'd come, making her blood boil all the more. She hadn't learned a thing from her marriage to Dan. He hadn't loved her enough to be honest with her. If he had, maybe they could have worked things out. Or at least ended on a good note. Instead, he'd cast her off without a backward glance.

And now Vin was doing the same thing.

Of all the insufferable—

Emma stormed into the house, slamming the door so hard, the molding cracked.

How could he think those things of her? *How?*

Chapter Eighteen

St. Walburga the Healer:
Mad Dogs, Mariners, Plague, and Coughing Spells

"Mornin', Karen!"

Azi bounced into the office on Tuesday, and Karen smiled. "Hey, Zorro! You're here early."

"Terry let me clock out at eleven, so I can buy you lunch after you help with my MP3."

"Oh, that's sweet. But you don't have to repay me."

His nod was emphatic. "I do. You're busy. You got an important job."

Karen hid another smile. "Okay. But for the record, I'd help you anyway. Um—how's Vin?" Azi's mouth set in a grim line that was comically reminiscent of his nephew's, and Karen sighed. "Never mind—Emma's the same. Where's the player?"

"I got it in here." He rummaged in his backpack. "There was only a couple of songs on it, an' I took 'em off, but it says it's still too full."

"I'm sure it's something we can fix."

"Here it is!" He yanked the player out and displayed it on his palm triumphantly—and Karen had to brace herself against the desk to keep from falling out of her chair.

"Where did you say you found that?"

Azi frowned. "On the street near the park, a couple weeks ago."

"Before Justin was attacked—or after?"

"I don' remember."

"Please, Azi—it might be important."

He concentrated, clearly trying to get it right. "After."

Karen blew out a breath. "May I?"

He handed it to her, and she stared in wonder. When Azi had shown her the flyer, the photo was grainy and she'd been distracted, hadn't look at it closely. Now, seeing the actual player—it *couldn't* be Oscar's, could it? Emma had said the one she ID'd for Vin was his. But this sure as hell looked like the one Karen had seen Oscar plugged into that day she'd been smoking at the Sion.

Unless he had *two* of them.

Holy mackerel.

She connected it to her computer. Her music software launched and displayed the contents of the player sorted by type, then by date. She scanned the screen. If it *was* Oscar's...

"Here's your problem. You deleted all the songs, but there are some other sound files, too. See here—" She pointed, and Azi leaned over her shoulder. "This folder is labeled *Memos*." She glanced at the MP3 itself. "Looks like this has a microphone, so you can record notes."

"Cool!" Azi beamed, but Karen directed her focus at the drama unfolding onscreen.

Right-clicking on the memo directory the way Emma had showed her, she read the username of its creator: oscard. And inside was a collection of files, including one titled *Parker_Original*. The date was late December of last year. Above that was another, dated early January of *this* year, titled *Parker_New*.

With shaking fingers she moved the mouse, hovering— which one first?—then clicked on the more recent file. She turned her speakers up, and a moment later, heard two PharmFam execs offer Parker three million dollars, to help him build a new research facility and increase parking at OSHU, if Parker could *"ensure that the vaccine results are positive."* Then Parker himself said, *"How could I refuse?"*, with a barely noticeable hitch right at the "I".

Karen's heart pounded. Anyone—*anyone*—hearing that would think Parker had just accepted a bribe. But there was that pause… Tiny. Almost imperceptible.

But there, nonetheless.

Azi, though he might not know what was at stake, had picked up on her tension. "Play the other one! Play the one that came first!"

A few seconds later they heard the same execs, making the same offer. Only this time Parker answered, with no hesitation, *"I refuse. How could you even suggest such a thing? Get out—before I call your superiors. Or the police."*

Karen was faint. She was delirious. She turned to Azi, rose, threw her arms around him. Laughing and crying all at once.

"He didn't do it! Zorro—*he didn't do it*! Oscar doctored the file. *Parker was framed."*

****

"May I speak with you?"

Nick jumped at the unexpected female voice, nearly dropping the solution he was titrating. Carefully, he squeezed out two drops of reagent, then set both the beaker and the pipette on the counter and turned to face his visitor.

"Bethanne. What are you doing here?"

"'Well that's a fine how-do-you-do.'"

He took a stab. "Abbott and Costello."

"Close. Laurel and Hardy."

But her heart clearly wasn't in it. She looked distracted, and if he wasn't mistaken, those were bona fide circles under her eyes. When had Bethanne ever greeted her public looking less than perfect?

Nick peeled off his gloves. "What can I do for you?"

The lab was quiet, most of the postdocs having moved their stations to Dan's area. It made sense, because Dan's lab was the only one producing viable research, but whenever Nick worked on his own experiments, he noticed the emptiness.

If Bethanne did, she gave no sign. She set her purse on the counter and said warmly, "I just wondered how you've been. It's ages since we spent any quality time with you."

"We being…?"

"Your godchildren, myself, and Emma, of course."

"Ah. A certain police officer might have something to do with that."

Her smile faltered, then firmed. "That's just it. Vin and Emma had another terrible fight—he said all sorts of things. Ridiculous accusations. None of them are true, of course."

"Such as…?"

"He has some crazy idea that Emma knew Dan's killer. Vin thinks she either helped Dan fake the data, or did it on her own, then saved the files to Mollie's laptop in order to frame her. Then when Mollie took the laptop to Hawaii, Vin thinks Emma hired this person to steal it."

Breathe—he had to breathe.…

"The man who killed Dan…knew *Emma?*"

"Of course not! But somehow Vin got the idea he did. He says this man even visited Emma and Dan a few years ago. Absurd." She frowned, then smoothed her expression. "But that's not why I came today. I know you have feelings for her." The shock must have been clear on his face, and she lifted a hand. "Hear me out. You're like family. Nothing would make me happier than for you and Emma to be together."

Nick opened his mouth. Closed it. Tried to think how he should respond. "Are you saying it's…over…between Emma and Vin?"

Bethanne looked down at her hands. "I believe it might be. I just want what's best for my daughter. That's all I've ever wanted." She glanced up. "Vin has hurt her so much— just like I knew he would. You're Dan's best friend. You've always tried to be there for her. If you were to talk with her, maybe tell her how you feel…"

For one brief moment, hope flared, strong and bright. *Could* he…?

Bethanne continued. "She's so mad at Vin, furious, even. She was in love with him. I think he may have hurt her worse than Dan did."

Everything went flat again. "She loves him anyway."

"She'll get over it. I know she will. But right now, she's mixed up. I thought, if you told her…" Her voice trailed off. "I'm sorry. I know I should stay out of her life. I just can't help it."

"You love your daughter. Of course you want what's best for her."

"Thank you—for understanding. If anyone can cheer her up, it's you."

She left, and Nick looked at the lab without seeing it. Bethanne was right—he was just the person to help Emma through this. He'd already determined that. But now he knew *how*. The knowledge had been a long time coming, but there it was, the plan he'd been waiting for.

I'm sorry, Janice. Can you ever forgive me?

So much guilt, so little time.

But now that the path had been chosen, there was no going back.

Emma would see that. She had to.

****

Karen practically ran down the corridor on the top floor of the OSHU executive building. The place was deserted—it was still lunch time—and she prayed over and over that Parker had decided to eat in. It occurred to her she didn't even know his daily routine, but God willing, she'd find out. She'd tried to call him before leaving her office, but he was "unavailable." On the way to taking the MP3 to the police station, she'd tried him twice more on her cell, then again on her way here. He'd refused all her calls. She didn't blame him—but he *would* hear her out.

Karen rounded the corner and saw through the plate glass walls that his admin was still there. She pushed into the presidential suite and said to the admin—a middle-aged woman whose name tag read *Marianne*—"Is Parker in? I need to see him."

"And you are…?" The woman's gaze was cool, assessing.

"Karen James." Marianne blinked, and Karen said, "I mean, Wiczniewski." When Marianne sucked in a breath, Karen's stomach dropped. "Please, you have to let me in. I'm—"

"I know who you are."

Marianne reached for the phone, probably calling security. Karen fought the tears and turned, then froze when she heard Marianne speak.

"Parker? There's someone here to see you." Her voice was crisp, professional. Not agitated. Karen turned back and caught a twinkle in Marianne's eye.

Parker obviously was refusing, but Marianne only nodded. "I understand. This is important." She gave Karen the once over. "She's a, uh, reporter. She says if you don't let her in, she'll print an editorial about how the OSHU juggernaut is polluting the neighborhood by allowing more cars to park up here every day. On purpose." Another pause. The twinkle grew. "Uh-huh."

She hung up and quirked an eyebrow. "Go right in. But if you're the Karen I think you are—well, better you than me. He's been absolute *hell* these last few weeks." She picked up her purse. "I'm going to lunch. In case you're worried about privacy."

She escaped, and Karen wondered briefly if Marianne had done her a favor—or thrown her to the lions. From the look on Parker's face when she walked in, it was the latter.

"What the *hell* are you doing here?"

She took a deep breath. "I owe you an apology."

"You don't owe me anything. Now get out."

He dropped his gaze back to the report he'd been reading, but Karen saw his hand shake, just a little, and hope flared. She sat in the chair across from him, ignoring her own nerves.

"So." She cleared her throat. "Why did you pay Oscar when you didn't take the bribes?"

The report slipped through his fingers, disappearing below the desk, and he froze. Then he slowly leaned back in his chair, his flashing eyes the only sign she'd gotten to him. "Companies settle out of court all the time. I didn't want the bad PR."

"For the university? Or…because of me?"

He flinched—as good as an admission. It was now or never.

"You never cared what anyone thought—except me. I thought so badly of you already, you were afraid if I heard about the bribes, I'd assume the worst, even if your name was eventually cleared. No matter what you did, I saw what I wanted to see. So you decided it was easier to pay Oscar and wait for the paper to come out. Because you *didn't* take the bribe, your conscience was clear—no matter what the data proved."

He stared back, expressionless, and she sighed.

"I know I'm right. If the vaccine proved unsafe, then obviously you didn't pressure Dan. And if it *was* safe, you'd also be clear, as soon as the results were public. You never even mentioned the bribes to Dan, so if Oscar tried anything further, you could go to the police after all, and Dan could testify—truthfully—that he knew nothing about any of it. You didn't take a bribe, didn't pressure Dan—and you absolutely did *not* kill anyone."

She waited, watching his impassive face, hating that she'd shut him out so well, when all he'd done from the start was try to care for her. The realization was amazing. Even more so, because she suddenly wanted to let him. *Please, God. Let us get through this. Please…*

"Interesting theory," he said at last. "Did you come up with it on your own? Or did Nick help you work it out after you screwed him?"

She hadn't seen that one coming. "How…?"

His face was hard, unbending. Furious. "Nick told me. Yesterday, he made a point of letting me know you'd slept with him. Guess you really do like the bottom-feeders after all."

"I—" Karen choked. "It was before us. And it's over. I

broke it off on Sunday, if it matters."

"It doesn't. Now get out."

Karen's heart pounded, her stomach roiled. "No. We have to talk. You can yell all you want, but I know you'd never hurt me."

"Great. Wonderful. You finally realize what a nice guy I am. Now *get the hell out* or I'll show you my violent streak after all."

His hands were fisted on the desk, the muscles in his neck corded tight. Karen shook so hard, she could barely stand, but she managed it.

"I'm sorry," she whispered, and saw the hurt flash in his face before he looked away.

"Just go."

She stumbled to the door. Her sweaty fingers fumbled and slipped on the metal handle. *Please-please-please....* Finally, the lock clicked into place and she exhaled shakily. Then she faced him.

His gaze jerked up, wide with shock. She forced her legs to take her back to the desk and planted herself in front of it.

"Parker James—I'm not done yet. And I'm not going anywhere until you hear me out."

****

"Hey, buddy, what's up?" Vin said when he came back from lunch and found Azi seated by his desk.

"Hey, Vinny! Guess what me an' Karen found!"

"I saw the clerk on the way in—great work." He knew he'd been right about Parker. Though the files wouldn't totally exonerate him of murder, they at least removed his motive.

Which left Vin back with his latest suspect. Unfortunately.

"It's all good." Azi grinned, clearly happy to be a part of the excitement, even if he didn't know what it was about. "Hey Vinny—didja call Emma yet?"

Vin felt his expression closing off. None of this was

Azi's fault—but even hearing her name was more than he could stand. "No," he said shortly, taking out a blank report and a pen.

Azi didn't take the hint. "She din't do it, Vinny. I know she din't!"

"Thanks, Az, but you don't know anything about it."

"I know one thing—her name isn't *Izzy*."

Vin's gaze flew up to find Azi glaring like Vin was a bug he'd found squished under his shoe.

"Emma din't do anything bad—even *I* know that! You're just all mixed up."

Barton came out of her office and headed their way. Great—an audience, *and* she still wanted some alone time with him.

"You're not payin' attention, Vinny! To Emma, or to me!"

Vin's gaze snapped back to Azi. "I—guess not. Did I miss something?"

"I been tryin' to talk to you, an' Sooze has, too."

"I'm sorry. I—"

Barton stopped near the desk, but Azi didn't notice her. He looked suddenly earnest. "Vinny, you're my best nephew. I love you an' all. But—I wanna move out."

Suddenly all the air was gone. "Azi—"

"Number six is open, an' I'm movin' in. Next week."

"*What?*"

"Number six. Sooze and Emma and Karen know—they been payin' attention."

The blood roared in his ears; he couldn't think. Az *couldn't* want to move out. Could he? They were bachelor buddies—the Brotherhood of Man. *Lifelong* membership.

And then Vin got it.

"You're moving in…with Terry?"

Azi nodded, miserable. "I'm sorry, Vinny. I gotta live my life, and you gotta live yours."

"But—we love living together. I love living with you." The whole thing was surreal—asinine—Barton's silent observation only making it worse.

"Sorry, Vinny. I never lived by myself before. An' Terry an' I are in love."

"You hardly know each other. Give it time—"

"I know what I want. If you been payin' attention, you'd know it, too."

He turned, and Vin watched him go.

Legally, Azi couldn't move without Vin's permission.

But even as the thought occurred, Vin sped it away. He loved Azi so much—but he couldn't hold onto him if this was what Az wanted. Vin would have to trust him, scary though that was. And if moving out didn't work—or Terry dumped him—Vin would be there when Az came home.

Home.

Vin thought of the house, empty, no Azi—and no Emma, Justin or Juney. *Cripes.*

Vin brought his gaze slowly back to Barton, who said, "There's more bad news."

"Great. What?"

"Not here. In my office. Now."

She turned and Vin had no choice but to follow. Dead man walking. But even with that premonition, he wasn't prepared for what she had to say.

✳✳✳✳

Karen paced the spacious room. Parker had risen from his chair to stand behind the desk, arms crossed, brows lowered, but he hadn't physically removed her. Yet. Still, she couldn't remember the last time she'd been so sick with nerves.

Probably the last time she'd seen *him*.

She drew a shaky breath. "Just answer me three questions."

"Only three?"

Karen ignored him—she deserved far worse than mere sarcasm. But she had to know. "First, why did you sleep with me?"

"To save Emma. Remember?"

271

Ouch.

"Parker, please. I know I don't deserve it, but—just tell me the truth."

He stared a moment longer, then relented. "I slept with you because you're smart and sexy, and I've wanted to for a long time."

"That's it?"

"Isn't that enough?"

He was starting to scowl again, so she said hastily, "Okay. Number two. Why didn't you sleep with me before? I mean, in all the years we've known each other."

"Was it only *my* choice?"

Karen blew out another breath. "Why didn't you *try to get me to* sleep with you?"

He moved then, coming around to the front of the desk, and rested against it. He was awfully close—she had to tilt her head to see his face, but she would *not* retreat.

"I didn't try to get you to sleep with me because I didn't want to."

"But you just said—"

"Yes, I wanted to sleep with you. No, I didn't want to *get you to* sleep with me."

"I don't understand. If you wanted to have sex with me—"

"Damn it! What *is* it with you and sex? Is that the only way you measure your own worth?"

"I'm only trying to understand—"

"Jesus, Karen," he ground out, clearly pushed to the limit. "I don't just want to *fuck* you. I want to spend the rest of my life with you."

She dug her nails into her palms. "What are you saying?"

"Is that the third question?"

"*Please.*"

He regarded her silently, then sighed and shoved a hand through his hair. "Fine. You want me to spell it out? When Rob brought you home after college, I was there. Remember? I looked at you, all grown up, and I knew—I *knew*. But unfortunately, you were dating my dumbass brother."

"You think Rob's a dumbass?"

"Do you want to hear this or not?"

"Sorry."

He pushed off the desk to roam the office. "I told myself I just wanted what Rob had, but it was a lie. Then I kept thinking he'd get bored, you'd break up, and I'd make my move."

"But instead, I married the dumbass. Which was really dumb. Hindsight, and all that." She paused. "And after the divorce…I made it pretty clear I despised you."

He scowled. "Yes."

"And because you're actually a *nice* guy—unlike your dumbass brother—you held back. You could have tried to railroad me into liking you, but instead, you showed me more respect. More than Rob showed me, and—more than I showed myself. All this time, I thought you felt I wasn't good enough for Rob. But really, you were just trying to keep your hands off me."

"You could look at it that way." He stopped and leaned against the desk again, restless energy barely contained beneath that cool exterior. "So. Now you know. Happy?"

"'As you wish.'"

His gaze shot to hers. "You got that? At dinner…?"

Karen nodded slowly. "*The Princess Bride*. All he ever says to her is 'as you wish,' and she finally notices he's really saying 'I love you.'" He didn't deny it, and she sank into the chair. "My God. You love me."

"As you pointed out, that's what I've been saying. Why the lightbulb moment?"

"You didn't pressure me."

"The fact that I *didn't* pursue you convinces you I'm serious?"

"Yes." Something tiny and warm went *pop!* inside. "Parker. I love you, too."

Hope warred with the pain in his eyes. "What are you

saying? That you want to have a fling, or—that you'll marry me?"

She wanted to kiss him, to hold and be held by him, and never let go. Wanted to let him make it all better, make it all go away. Let him take care of her for the rest of her life.

And therein lay the difficulty.

"I can't marry you." When he blanched, she added quickly, "Not yet, at least."

He gripped the edge of the desk, knuckles white, voice hoarse. "What are you doing to me?"

"I'm sorry." This was harder than she'd imagined. But, if she did it right, there might be a light at the end of the tunnel. A reward so precious, she could barely let herself believe it was within her grasp. She said carefully, "I'm kind of messed up."

"I noticed."

She laughed, even though he hadn't meant it to be funny. "I know. That's one of the things I…love…about you. You notice me—things I don't notice about myself."

"Then *tell me* what's wrong."

She looked away, and then he was kneeling before her, turning her gently so she had to face him. His eyes widened when he saw the tears she didn't try to hide, and he wiped them with his thumbs.

"Baby, what is it? Tell me what it is, and I'll fix it."

She gave a half laugh, half sob. "That's just it. You can't fix it—it's me. I'm the problem. When we get together, I want it to be the best it can be. Right now, I'm still pretty mixed up. I know you love me—and I love you. But…I don't love *myself* a whole lot."

"And we'll figure out how to help you with that."

"I know. I just think I should get myself together, before *we* get together. So when we—" She hesitated, amazed to find herself blushing, suddenly shy at the tenderness in his gaze. "—when we start our life together, it will be on the best possible foundation. I did the unhealthy thing with Rob, and just about every other man I've been with. With you, I want it to be *right,* from the start."

He absorbed that. Then he said, "What was the third question?"

"What?"

"You said you had three questions. What was the third?"

"Oh. It's not important anymore. Really."

"Tell me."

"It's not even a question, more of a—a statement. Kind of silly, after all this…"

"*Tell me.*" He held her gaze inexorably, and she let out an exasperated sigh.

"Fine. I'm Jewish."

He blinked. "I, uh, knew that. It's been a complete non-issue ever since I've known you."

Her face flamed again. "Yeah. Well. I was pretty young when Rob and I got married, and I wasn't thinking about, you know, starting a family. But you might want our kids baptized Catholic. And I'm okay with that. It's just—"

Parker's grip tightened. "Are you saying you want to have children with me?"

She nodded, unable to look away or speak. And the heat that flashed in his eyes—that cool, silver gaze she would wake up to for the rest of her life—sent shivers all through her. And then his next words left her breathless.

"I'll convert."

"You'd do that for me?"

"Anything you want. Judaism, Buddhism. I don't care. Just say you'll marry me. Not later, *after* you've gone through hell, 'fixing' yourself. Marry me *now,* so I can go to hell with you."

"Parker—"

He covered her mouth with his hand. "Karen…Alexis…Wiczniewski…James. Will you marry me?"

"Mmmph."

He shook his head. "The hand stays. Nod yes, and I'll take it away. Shake no, and I won't be responsible for my actions."

She tried to glare at him, but she loved him too much. Still, she wasn't ready to give in yet. Pushing her tongue out, she flicked it against his palm. Startled, he loosened his grip and she pounced, using her teeth to pull his index finger into her mouth. Then she slid her tongue along him, and relished the bob of his Adam's apple, the groan that escaped as his eyes closed.

"Jesus, Karen."

"Parker." She slid the finger out and moved her mouth to the next one. "Allan." He groaned again, shifting in obvious discomfort, and she moved to his ring finger. "James." She placed a soft kiss where a wedding band would rest. "Yes. I will marry you."

"Now?"

She couldn't stand it. She'd tried. But maybe he was right. Maybe waiting for perfection meant they'd never get anywhere, because perfection didn't exist. And who better to face her imperfections with than someone who loved her *because* of them?

"Now. Today. This minute. I know you know people who—"

And then his mouth was on hers and he pulled her down to straddle his lap, his erection pressing into her. "This minute, I have something else in mind." She moaned, grinding down on him. He fumbled with his zipper, and she pushed her panties down. Then, when he'd freed himself, she slid onto him, unable to wait a second longer.

"Condom!" he said with obvious effort.

"*Baby.*" She slid her tongue into his mouth, and felt the clutch of his arms, pulling her tight when he got her meaning.

"Christ…" He groaned and rocked deeper into her. "But as soon as we're done here—oh, *Jesus*—we're going to City Hall." He paused and looked at her. "Unless you want a big wedding—"

"You. Me. Judge."

"God, I love you."

His mouth covered hers, his tongue sweeping inside as he drove himself into her, filling her in ways she'd never imagined. And it was so good, and she loved him so much, that the tears came. Crying for all the wasted years, for the precious gift of the years to come, and for the beauty and strength of the man buried inside her.

They moved together, awkward, tender, sweet and hard. Parker really could be restrained when it suited him—or when it gave *her* pleasure. And Karen showed him, in turn, that she trusted him. When he whispered, "I love you," she whispered back, "I know…"

****

Vin hadn't heard Barton right. He *couldn't* have.

"You're *demoting* me? Back to the streets?"

"Unless something changes my mind before Monday."

"*Why?*"

"I've had concerns from the start about your objectivity on the O'Manny case."

A muscle in his jaw twitched, his teeth clenched so tight he could barely force them apart. His hands were balled into fists, and he couldn't uncurl them. "You *put* me on this case, even when I asked you not to. If this is about Emma, we have no real proof yet—but as soon as we do, I'll get a warrant. Besides—"

"Damn it, Vin." She looked disgusted. "It *is* about Mrs. O'Manny, and your lack of perspective. But it's not about a damn warrant. It's about you not doing your job."

"I *am* doing my job," he exploded, fist slamming so hard on the desk, she actually flinched. "I admit I thought Emma was innocent at first, but obviously she's not. What the fuck do you want from me?"

Barton stood and leaned her hands on the desk. "Ob-jec-tivity. *Why* do you think Emma hired Ramie to steal the laptop, then paid him off after he killed Dan and Mollie? And why go on to kill Oscar herself? Why would an otherwise upstanding citizen be driven to sink so low?"

"Well, somebody sure as hell was! And the money—"

"Exactly. *Dan* bought the stock. Even if Emma was capable of faking the data, why would she? Why kill anyone? To help her husband commit insider trading? He *left* her. If Emma was gonna do anything, she'd hire someone to kill Dan, on purpose. Which we know she *didn't* do." Barton straightened. "You're so hung up on Chicago, you aren't thinking this through. And after I put my ass on the line, giving you this case. Chief St. John wanted me to assign it to someone else."

"*What?*"

"You heard me. St. John thought it was a bad idea. But you've been on eggshells since you got to my department. I gave you a chance to prove to us *and* yourself that you're still a good detective. And you're blowing it."

"But you—the whole time—"

Her cat's grin flashed. "I never said I wouldn't have a little fun along the way. But unless you get past your past, you'll never make it in my group."

His jaw worked.

Emma. Azi. And now this.

"Are you saying," he managed, "you think Emma's innocent?"

"Could be. Or she could be guilty as hell. But you've convinced yourself she did it, and you aren't looking anywhere else." She sat down. "Take a few days off, Vin. Think about where you'd like to be—in my department or on the street. I'll see you Monday."

Chapter Nineteen

St. Pulcheria the Chaste:
Orphans, Empresses, and Victims of Betrayal

When a knock came on the back door Wednesday morning, Emma jumped. It wasn't quite seven-thirty. The kids were getting ready for school, and Bethanne wasn't up yet. Nervous energy shot through her. Maybe it was Vin. Who else would come to the back of the house at this hour? Maybe he realized what an ass he'd been, and they could talk it out.

She opened the door—and found Izzy on the stoop.

Her face was pinched and determined. "I came to say good-bye."

"Oh."

"Can I come in?" She pushed past Emma and slid into the breakfast nook, setting her purse down like she planned to be awhile.

"Okay." Emma shut the door. "Sure. You want a cup of—"

"Cream. Sweetener. Thanks." Emma brought the mug to the table, then sat while Izzy sipped. "Jeez, that's good."

"Thanks. I don't mean to be rude but—"

"You wanna know why I'm here."

"Well, yes."

Izzy watched her for a moment, then sat back. "I'm going home to Chicago, but first, I want to clear the air about something. It's about Vin. But you probably guessed that." Her manicured nails tapped the table, then her hands circled the mug, twisting it unconsciously. "Vin's a great guy. Really top-notch. He even tried to make me a better person. What a joke."

Her smile flashed, warm and genuine, and Emma found herself responding. Damn it. Liking Izzy was *not* what she wanted right now.

"Anyway, Vinny thought he could save me, from the Family, and myself. I said yes—who wouldn't like that romantic hero shit? But I was never in love with him. And he only thought he was in love with me. So I did what I always do—fucked up a good thing, 'cause I thought something better was around the corner. I ratted him out to Daddy, set him up. Even after he found out, Vin still showed at the drop."

"Vin *knew*, and he came to the ambush anyway? Why?"

"Because if he hadn't, I'da been dead meat."

"Not literally? Your father wouldn't actually *kill* you." Emma paused. "Would he?"

Izzy laughed. "No, Daddy wouldn't—he really is a loving parent, believe it or don't. But somebody woulda done it eventually, as payback."

"So Vin saves you, almost gets killed, and makes sure you get low jail time. And you repay all this by coming out here just to screw up his new life?"

Izzy frowned. "He still didn't tell you?"

"Tell me what?" Emma frowned back.

Izzy chewed her lip, then shook her head. "Sorry. For once, I gotta keep my promise. I do have *some* honor, you know."

Her grin flashed again, and Emma smiled back. "Fair enough. But you had a specific reason for stopping by?"

"Right. I wanted to tell you I didn't mean to fuck anything up for Vin. His job, or with you. I—well, I had some news I had to give him in person. Plus, I was just so mad at Daddy, I wasn't thinking straight. So I thought I'd come crash here for a while and then go home. Mind you, if he'd jumped my bones, I wouldn'ta turned him down. But he was clear right from the start. No more Izzy. Buh-*bye*."

Emma laughed. "This is crazy. Why are you telling me

this? You must know Vin's really pissed at me right now. I don't know if I'll ever see him again."

"Not my problem. I just wanted you to know he's free and clear, and to set the record straight, in case you thought I threw that rock, or sent the bullets—or set the bomb."

Emma looked at her blankly. "Well, of course you didn't. Those were all threats to me, relating to Dan's death." And then it hit, slamming so hard, it was a physical blow. "Unless…they *weren't*. They were all aimed at getting to me *through* Vin. The note—it was warning *him* that your Family would come after him if he dated me, and he'd lose his job if the *Police* found out he was involved with another suspect."

Izzy's eyes widened. "*He* was supposed to drive your car to the shop."

"And the bullets. They were meant to drive a wedge between us, because I'd think he sent them. But who would want to keep us apart, if not you? No offense."

Izzy grinned. "None taken. I told Vin the rock wasn't my style, but he wouldn't listen."

"What rock?" Juney asked as she and Justin came in from the dining room.

"The rock with the note on it," Izzy said before Emma could tell her they hadn't told Juney about it yet. "The one someone threw in your window last week, that hit your mom."

"Oh," Juney said, obviously unconcerned. "Like in *After the Thin Man*."

Emma froze, the blood in her veins suddenly needles of ice. "*What* did you say…?"

Juney opened the fridge and got out the milk. "You know. The real old movies we've been watching with Grandma. In one of them, someone throws a rock through a window, with a note on it. It's a clue, but not a real one." She finished pouring and turned to Justin. "What's that called? When it's a red hair-tie? De—del—"

"Deliberately misleading," Justin supplied. "When it's a

red *herring.* Grandma says it's a common trick in Hollywood, to make the viewer think something's important for one reason. But really, it means something else."

Emma gripped the table. "My own *mother?*"

"Well, hell," Bethanne said from the doorway.

****

Nick took another sip of coffee, watching as the light blue late-model minivan pulled into Emma's drive and honked once. A moment later, Justin and Juney tore out of the house and down the steps. Emma followed them out, waving as they got in the van, which backed out and drove away. She was too far away for him to read her expression, but she seemed agitated. Then Izzy came out, said something to her, and headed toward the park, where Nick could just see LJ lurking. Again.

Another clusterfuck day at the O'Manny residence. But today, it didn't bother him. Today, he had all the time in the world. Because he finally had a plan. It felt good, being decisive. Passivity hadn't gotten him anywhere; it was time to act. Bethanne had helped him see that—he owed it all to her. Now everything was in order, awaiting the right moment, when it would all fall into place.

Nick watched as LJ stopped Izzy at the edge of the park. She gestured toward the house, and LJ abruptly ground his cigarette out, then stalked across the cul-de-sac. He didn't even glance up the block—didn't notice Nick's car, parked near the corner. Sloppy fucker.

Nick shook his head. He hadn't done any surveillance since his flights with Dan, back in Iraq. He was rusty. But truthfully, he wouldn't have cared if LJ *had* seen him.

It didn't matter. He just needed to speak with Emma. She'd understand—she would. What a relief, to talk, and have someone listen. He'd tell her everything and she'd forgive him.

Then he'd never have to be alone, ever again.

****

Emma had barely closed the front door behind Izzy

when someone pounded on it, making her jump. She opened it to find LJ scowling on the porch.

"I knew it! Of all the stupid, *dumb*—" His massive fists clenched at his sides. "Where the hell is she?"

Emma blinked. "If you mean Bethanne, she's in the kitchen."

He shoved past her, and she followed him to the back of the house. Bethanne sat at the table, where she'd come to rest after Izzy and the kids began their mass exodus. She glanced up when LJ thundered in, then looked guiltily away.

"I don't think you should be here right now," she began, but Emma interrupted.

"That's what I thought. But upon consideration, it's probably better to have a third party around, in case I decide to throttle you."

LJ said, "No dice. I may throttle her myself."

"Huh. At least I'll have company, either way."

LJ crossed his arms and scowled some more. "What the hell were you thinking?"

Bethanne's mouth worked silently. She wore her robe, hair mussed from sleep, her only makeup a light coating of lipstick. And she still looked beautiful—fragile and helpless.

Which didn't seem to impress LJ. Good.

"Fine," Bethanne said at last. "I admit it was a dumb idea."

"*What* was a dumb idea?" Emma asked.

"I only wanted what's best for you. Surely you can see that Vin's *not* it…?"

"Get to the point," LJ said, and Bethanne seemed more upset by his censure than Emma's.

And wasn't *that* typical?

"Originally, I just thought of tossing the rock through the window with the note on it. It was supposed to make Vin think if he didn't stay away, Izzy's father would get mad."

"The implication being that Rico would hurt Vin? Or— me?"

"Either. Rico was never really going to find out—at least, not from me. So, as long as Vin was warned, that's all I cared about. As I said—it was dumb."

"What happened?"

"I threw the rock—I didn't see *anyone* at the window, I swear—then ran to the front and let myself in like I'd just arrived." She at least *appeared* to be genuinely remorseful. "I'm so sorry, honey. You can't imagine how horrible I felt when I realized I'd hit you."

"You're right. I *can't* imagine—because I can't imagine throwing a rock through a window, to ruin my own *daughter's* happiness."

"I'm sorry," Bethanne whispered again.

LJ ground out, "And the bullets?"

"I left them on the porch earlier in the day, knowing we'd leave through the back, and when we got home, it would seem like the mailman left them. Then, like the rock, I made sure I touched the paper in front of you, in case Vin dusted for prints."

"What were you thinking? That I'd dump him without even asking if he sent them?"

"Of course not! I'm not *that* stupid." At LJ's speaking look she coughed. "Well. Anyway. I guess I thought it would remind you he's a cop, that guns are a daily part of his life."

The conversation couldn't possibly get any more bizarre, so Emma asked, "What about the bomb?" Then her throat constricted. "My God—*you* used my credit card and PO box. *You're* the reason Vin thinks I did it to myself."

Bethanne nodded miserably. "By then, he knew you'd kept the laptop from him. I thought if a bomb went off on the van, it would convince him of your innocence. I knew he'd be driving, and I thought if I made it small, no one would be hurt. I never dreamed he'd accuse you of killing Dan *because* the bomb wasn't big."

"How—" Emma began, but LJ said, sounding resigned, "Charley."

Bethanne sank farther down in her seat. "You said it

yourself. Special effects are his *forte*. He helped me figure out what to buy, and how to put it together, so it would make a nice loud noise, but not really endanger Vin's life. Thank heaven it was mostly smoke, not flames. Though of course, that was bad enough." She looked defeated, worn out. Older than Emma had ever seen her. "And, you do need a new van…" Her voice trailed off and she trembled under Emma's stare.

"*Insurance fraud*, too? But *why?*"

Bethanne's violet eyes filled with tears. "I didn't want to be alone. You don't know what it's like—your father died so long ago. My parents, most of my relatives. I have no siblings, not even any cousins I'm close to. Charley's the only friend I have from my acting days, which I gave up for your father—and for you. The time I've spent here, with you and the children, is more precious than you can imagine." She looked down at her hands. "I saw how fast you and Vin were falling for each other, and it terrified me. I didn't want to lose you."

"And scaring Vin off—maybe harming him *and* me—was a way to *keep* me?"

"I don't know what I thought. No, that's not completely true. I did think that if Vin were out of the picture, you might…"

"Start seeing Nick?"

She shrugged helplessly. "I knew you'd never love *him* as much as Vin, so I could keep more of you for myself. I'm so sorry, sweetheart. At every step, I made the wrong choice—even when I was trying to protect you. Can you ever forgive me?"

"Of all the *selfish*—" Emma's nails bit into her palms. "I don't want to be with Nick. Can you understand that? Once and for all, I'm in love with *Vin*. Big jerk that he is."

Bethanne dropped her gaze. "I know. I'm sorry."

"I can't think about this now. I have to go see him." Emma glanced at LJ. "I have an appointment at the bank in an hour, to try to straighten out this whole second mortgage mess. Will you stay with her?"

"Sure thing. Anyway, Izzy took the car back to Tony's." He regarded Bethanne thoughtfully, but she didn't notice. She lowered her head to her arms, as though the confrontation had wiped her out.

Good. It had wiped Emma out, too.

And now she had to force herself through another one.

****

Vin let the bell ring three times before he thumped down and yanked the door open.

"What the—" he bellowed, then stopped when he saw Emma, white-faced and glaring. Her jeans were wet below the knee, so she must have come through the park. Alone. He was about to chew her out when he remembered he was mad at her for maybe being a murderer, or at least a white-collar criminal. He clamped his mouth shut just as she opened hers.

"I came to tell you something about the bomb and the—"

"Tell it to someone who gives a damn," he said, and started to shut the door.

"Wait!" She stuck her foot inside, and since he didn't feel like being arrested for assault—at least, not before breakfast—he stopped short of breaking her ankle.

"Go away—I'm not in the mood."

"But it's about—"

"I said *go away*. Go tell it to a *real* detective down at the station."

"What's that supposed to mean?"

"Haven't you heard? Thanks to you, Barton's demoting me."

"How is *you* getting demoted *my* fault?"

"Because I got involved with you, I'm out of a job. And now Azi's moving out, so I'm losing him, too." He hadn't meant to let that slip, and her eyes widened, then her gaze slid guiltily away. He narrowed his own gaze at her. "Did you know anything about that?"

"Maybe."

"What the hell do you mean by that?"

"Damn it, Vin—I tried to tell you, but you wouldn't listen. You're so convinced you know what's right for Azi, but you don't even know what's right for *you*. Sometimes, loving someone means having a little faith in them."

"Screw you."

He started to slam the door on her again, but this time she inserted her whole body between it and the jamb. She was close enough that he could see those crazy gold flecks in her eyes, breathe the fresh lavender scent of her hair. Feel the heat of her supple body. *Cripes.*

"Leave me alone."

"No!"

He could stand there, holding her half-trapped in the door all day, or let her in. He released the door, and she fell into the entry. To her credit, she picked herself right up and planted her hands on her hips.

"Don't worry. I have *no* desire to stay longer than necessary. But I thought *someone* should know that the rock, the bullets, and the bomb aren't related to the case."

Vin crossed his arms. "Go on."

"Bethanne did all that—to keep us apart. She threw the rock, snuck the box onto the porch, and got Charley to help with the bomb. So, now you know."

Suddenly, the fight went out of her, and he felt a twinge of pride at her courage. He knew how far out of her comfort zone she was—how much it had taken for her to face the conflict head on. But that didn't mean he had to believe whatever BS she spouted. She turned to go, and he unfolded his arms and began clapping, nice and slow.

"I see Bethanne and Justin aren't the only talented performers in the family."

She turned back, two bright spots of color high on her cheeks. "Why—you—*urgh!*"

"Now *that* was not Academy-quality. Certainly not as good as when you denied all involvement in Dan's and

Mollie's deaths."

Her face went white. "Get this straight—I did *not* pay Ramie to kill my husband *or* Mollie!"

He chose his words carefully, studying her reaction. "Technically, that's true. You didn't *mean* for them to die. You only hired Ramie to get your laptop back." Had he imagined it, or did she jerk in surprise? "It must've been a shock when Ramie told you what happened, and demanded more money. How did you pay him? With the money Nick got from Parker?"

"What on *earth* are you talking about?"

"Nick told Parker he was ordering a new microscope for the Sion. No grant money was available at the time, so Parker loaned Nick a hundred grand."

"What does any of that have to do with me?"

She looked genuinely confused. Was Barton right? Was he so afraid of repeating past mistakes, he'd convinced himself of Emma's guilt just so no one could accuse him of falling for her supposed lies?

He gave himself a mental shake. There was still the one and three quarter million. *Someone* had intended to profit from the vaccine research. And so far, besides the drug company, Emma was the only one who had.

He said, "Nick never ordered that microscope. The manufacturer says he never even inquired about it. He claims he used the money for something else, and will bring the receipts in. But…I think he gave it to you. Maybe you told him you needed it for school, or maybe you were in it together. Either way, you're the only ones left who had anything to gain from all this. With Dan and Mollie dead, you wouldn't even have to split the take with them. Or with Oscar. What made you kill him? The blackmail? Or was it when he threatened your kids?"

Emma's nostrils flared and she moved until she was inches from his face. "I did *not* fake the data. I never met Ramie, and I don't think Dan did either, no matter what that CO says. And I had *nothing* to do with killing Mollie, Dan or

Oscar. If you still think I did, then you can *go to hell.* As for Azi, whatever stupid mistakes you've made are *your* fault, not mine."

"Yeah, it is my fault—I ignored my gut, and got involved with another damn perp."

"I am *not* a perp! And frankly, after chatting with her, I don't think Izzy is, either."

Vin froze. "You spoke with Izzy?"

Her stare was icy, which could mean anything. "She came to tell me she's going back to Chicago. You're free and clear. Why she thought I'd care, I have no idea."

He should shut up; he knew he should. Instead, he heard himself say, "She…told you…?"

Now it was Emma's turn to freeze. *Fuck.*

"Told me what?" Her tone was deadly calm. "She said something similar—that there was something you needed to tell me."

His fury at her—and at himself—was so great, it suddenly didn't matter whether she knew or not. In fact, he *wanted* to hurt her—to show her how painful lies could be.

"Izzy and I were never divorced," he bit out. "She's still my wife."

Then he watched with satisfaction as Emma turned white and staggered back as though she'd been struck. *Sucker punch—God, he was an asshole.*

"You…*lied*…to me?" Her voice was barely a whisper. "You knew what I went through with Dan—and you kept this from me? I *trusted* you."

"You sure did. Enough to tell me the truth about the laptop."

Another one. Right to the jaw.

She jerked back. Then her eyes blazed and she straightened. "What I did was to protect my family, and to prevent false accusations against my loved ones. What you did was inexcusable. I can't believe I put my trust in *two* men who didn't return the favor."

She stomped out of the house and down the walk, and

Vin watched her go, two things suddenly crystal clear. The first was that he'd just driven her away on purpose—but not because he thought she'd lied to him. No, the real reason was even dumber than that. From the beginning, despite his big talk, he'd let his damn ego get in the way of learning the truth. Then, when he suspected his mistake, instead of owning up, he'd deliberately hurt her to preserve his self-image, to make himself seem competent and in charge.

Shit. What a fucking joke. All that did was make him a bully—the most *in*competent asshole ever.

A fact which was immediately supported by the second realization: Guilty people shifted, literally moving and twitching. They bent the truth, told vague half-stories, circled the issues. They did *not* look their accuser straight in the eye, stand tall, and directly refute *every* charge against them.

Emma was innocent.

He'd stake his reputation on it.

Barton and Tony were right. He might not be thinking with his dick. But apparently, he wasn't using his brain, either.

****

Emma's fury sustained her until she reached the park, and then suddenly, it was all too much. She collapsed on the curb near the entrance and buried her head in her hands, shaking.

I will not cry, I will not cry.

Beating the ground and howling was another matter.

"Emma? Are you all right?"

Startled, she glanced up to find Nick's car stopped in front of her, the window down.

"Nick." She scrubbed at the tears, rising. "What on earth are you doing here?"

He smiled sheepishly. "I stopped by the house on my way to work, and Bethanne said you'd come over here. I thought I could give you a ride home while we chat."

Emma fought down an angry sob. It wasn't Nick's fault

Bethanne hadn't learned a damn thing, even after her machinations were uncovered. Or that Vin was a big *married* jerk.

"I'm sorry. I'm really not in the mood to talk."

He held up a large paper cup. "I bring coffee. A grande sugar-free vanilla nonfat latte…" His grin was earnest, his lone dimple giving him a lopsided look.

"I can't believe you still remember that."

It wasn't even eight-thirty yet. Her anger at Bethanne had fueled the walk over, but now she felt drained. Tramp through an empty park where, as Vin was so fond of pointing out, anyone could be lurking in the bushes? Or ride home in the cozy warmth of an old friend's car, sipping her favorite hot beverage?

She walked to the passenger side and got in, taking the cup. "Thanks."

"My pleasure."

Nick put the car in gear and drove up the block.

****

"Vin?" Bethanne's voice said over the phone a while later. "Is Emma there?"

Vin set his coffee down and held the cell closer to his ear, not bothering to hide his irritation. Bethanne was the last person he wanted to talk with—except maybe Emma herself. Just because he'd realized he was an ass didn't mean he was ready to 'fess up and make nice. Assuming she'd have him, which at the moment seemed unlikely.

"She left half an hour ago. Why would she still be here?"

Bethanne was silent a moment. "After what I did, I wasn't sure she'd come home. I thought maybe, if you two made up…"

Vin suddenly felt dizzy and leaned against the counter. "It's true? The rock, the bomb—all that—was you?"

Her voice quavered. "I'm so sorry. I don't know what came over me."

"And she didn't come home yet?"

"Then she really isn't there…? I thought maybe she just

didn't want to talk to me."

"That may be, but she's not exactly speaking to me at the moment, either."

A sound came from the background, and Bethanne covered the mouthpiece, then came back. "LJ says we should try Karen's. He's right—her house isn't far from yours. Emma could have walked there. And if she's too mad to speak to either of us…"

Vin grimaced. "Great. We finally have something to bond over. Emma hates us both."

Bethanne gave a startled laugh, then sobered. "I know she's mad. But it's not like her, not to call at least. And the bank phoned—she had an appointment today, and she missed it."

"I'm sure she's fine. She was probably so upset, she forgot the bank."

"You're probably right." Bethanne hesitated. "I really am sorry."

"Save it. Call Karen, and if Emma's there, call me right back." He paused. "And if she's not with Karen…"

"You'll be the first to know, either way."

Vin hung up and stared at his coffee, which had lost its appeal. Emma had told the truth. The rock, bullets, and bomb were outside the main case, and not her fault. Neither were the murders. Period. He reached for the phone, and Tony picked up on the first ring.

"Vin! Why the fuck didn't you tell me? I had to call the damn station to find out—you're being *demoted?*"

"Hello to you, too."

"Fuck you. What are brothers for?"

Vin thought about it, then sighed. "This."

"Exactly." Tony blew out a breath. "Look—I feel partly responsible. I mean, I'm the one who made you think she was guilty."

"No. I did that all by myself. She still might be…"

"But…?"

Vin sighed again. "I don't think she is."

"Good," Tony said with startling vehemence. "Not that I wouldn't enjoy you groveling, but we don't have time. I just had an interesting chat with the tech working on Oscar's MP3."

"Is there anyone at the station who doesn't love your ass?"

"No. Now shut up and listen. Two things. One, it looks like the first recording of Parker is the original. He really did refuse the bribe."

"Great. What else?"

"They ran a recovery program on the player and extracted a bunch of deleted files. Seems Oscar was one busy blackmailer. There's a recording of Mollie and Nick from early February—Oscar must've been hiding nearby. Mollie accuses Nick of messing up the research data, and he admits it, then tells her off. She says she has the original files, and if he doesn't come clean to Dan when they get back from Hawaii, she'll expose him."

"So Mollie threatened Nick, Oscar recorded it, and—probably—blackmailed *him*, too."

"Not probably—*definitely*. Oscar was pretty anal about tracking his schemes, but not exactly brilliant in their execution. They recovered another file from earlier this month—he recorded himself, *while* he was blackmailing Nick."

"Jesus. What's on it?"

"Oscar tells Nick he's looking in the wrong place for the original data files. Oscar says he knows where they are, and he's going to get them—*from her.*"

"Meaning Emma." Vin sat down, hard. "Holy shit."

"You said it. Nick had a motive to steal the laptop, *and* to kill Oscar. A motive—more like an *invitation*—which Oscar handed to him when he threatened Emma and her children." He sounded disgusted. "No people skills whatsoever."

Vin gripped the phone. "Nick did it—all of it."

"Looks like it. Totally bottomed out. He starts out faking

data, then covers it up with theft, leading to murder by proxy—and then murder by his own hand. Deeper and deeper."

Vin's gut clenched. "*Fuck*. Step nine."

"What?"

"Dante's *Inferno*. Nick was reading it." Vin was on his feet and slamming out the door. "What happens after you reach the bottom circle of Hell, before you get into Paradise?"

"Shit. You have to go through Purgatory."

Vin broke into a run at the park. "Nick's a practicing Catholic. I can't imagine he thinks he's in a state of grace right now. But I'd bet my life he's looking for a way to get there."

"What do you think he'll do?"

"I don't know. But the ninth circle of hell is reserved for the worst kind of traitor—people who've betrayed someone they love. In Nick's case, I'd say he qualifies several times over." He'd almost made it to Emma's. "Do we have enough to bring him in?"

"Better if you link him to Ramie. But yeah, I think you could at least question him."

"Call the station for me," Vin said and hung up.

He pounded onto Emma's porch and hammered the door. Bethanne opened it, wearing her robe, and not surprised to see him.

"Where is she?" he barked.

"I don't know. I was hoping you did." When she saw his expression, her face went white. "Karen's not at home or at work, and her cell is off. LJ's in the kitchen, trying Parker's cell. He's also MIA, but his admin seems to think that wherever he is, Karen's with him."

"Good for them." He headed for the kitchen, where LJ was just hanging up the phone.

"Hey, Vin." He turned to Bethanne. "No dice. His phone is off, too. Who next?"

Vin said, "What about Nick?"

Bethanne looked hugely relieved. "Why didn't I think of that? He told me yesterday he's been wanting to talk with her." She turned pink. "I was…encouraging him."

"Call his house," Vin said to LJ. There was no answer, so LJ tried his cell, then the lab.

"No one's answering."

"Nine on a weekday, and no one's at the lab?"

Bethanne caught Vin's tone and faltered. "Please tell me. What is it?"

He said bluntly, "We think Nick is responsible for everything that's happened, including all three murders." Bethanne blanched and sat down, and Vin continued. "I haven't figured out the connection between him and the Gulf War vet who killed Dan and Mollie—"

"Gulf War?" Bethanne interrupted.

"You know something about it?"

Her hands trembled and she let out a moan. "What have I done, sending him to her?"

"*Tell me.*"

She swallowed. "A few years ago, Dan and Emma were away. I ran into Nick, and he asked me to dine with him and Janice and their houseguest, an old friend from the Marines. He'd served in the Gulf and was just getting out, when Nick met him at the start of his own training."

By some miracle, Vin managed not to shout. "What was his name?"

"I don't know—I don't remember. But I do know that this man had a nickname for Nick. He called him Strongman, because Forte means 'strong' in Italian."

"Jesus." Vin grabbed the phone. "The CO had it wrong. It wasn't Dan—it was *Nick*."

They had him. But it also seemed he had Emma. And Vin had no idea where they were or what he planned to do with her. Except that it probably involved going through Purgatory.

Jesus fucking Christ….

Chapter Twenty

St. Catherine the Purged:
Grinders, Jurists, Philosophers, and Bail

Instead of driving around the block, past Vin's place, Nick took a left after the park. He seemed preoccupied, and Emma's stomach fluttered. "Aren't you taking me home?"

The smile he turned on her was sad. "Do you mind? The journal sent a box of copies to the lab. I thought the kids might want them, to remember their father by. I'd like to swing by and get them, before I forget again."

Emma drew in a calming breath, then exhaled slowly. "Of course. No problem. I have an appointment at the bank, but we should have time, if we hurry."

What on earth was the matter with her? She was so mixed up over Vin that, apparently, she'd started believing his crazy accusations. But Nick—best man at her wedding, Dan's partner, Justin and Juney's *godfather*—couldn't be a murderer. Could he?

She watched him while he drove. No. He was Nick, for pity's sake. And besides, if he was a killer, and planned on doing her harm, then why take her to a public place, in broad daylight? She forced her fingers to loosen their grip on the coffee cup and took a sip.

As usual, the Gold Parking Lot was full, but as Director of the Sion, Nick had his own space. He pulled in and Emma hopped out, relieved to be surrounded by people again. He locked the car, then took her elbow and guided her firmly toward the Institute.

"Turning into Parker?" she joked, but he didn't seem to hear.

The day had warmed up, one of summer's final, bright attempts before giving in to the inevitable wet fall. Walking quickly as they were, Emma was sweating by the time they reached the building, and all in all, she was relieved to step into the Sion's air-conditioned lobby. It was dim and deserted, as always, but she could hear the hum of activity through the open door of the main reception office past the elevators. Nick checked his watch, then pulled out his cell.

"Hang on—I have to make a call before I forget."

He stepped just far enough away that she couldn't overhear, and abruptly she had the urge to run back out of the lobby. This was ridiculous. Vin was just mad, not thinking clearly. She forced another breath, praying Nick wouldn't see how foolish she was being.

He hung up as the elevator arrived, then guided her into the car. He pressed the button for the top floor, waiting while the doors shut, then turned to her.

"I'm sorry, Emma—I was thinking about something. Did you mention Parker a minute ago?"

There. That was better. He looked and sounded more like his old self. Not exactly cheerful, but more...calm. Less on edge than in recent months.

"It was nothing—just making a joke."

"Ah. Well, you know, Parker isn't such a bad guy."

Emma blinked. "Really?"

The corners of his mouth turned up. "Really. I thought you should know."

"Of course. But...why?"

He shrugged. "Vin is still tossing crazy theories around. If he thinks Parker—or you—hired Ramie to steal Mollie's laptop, he's wrong. He must see that by now."

She opened her mouth to say what she thought of Vin and his *crazy* theories, when the elevator stopped, its doors sliding open to reveal the top floor lobby. Emma stepped out, but Nick paused inside the car, inserting a small key into the operating panel. He twisted it and pressed a button, then withdrew the key and followed her out. The doors closed, and Emma watched the indicator panel as the car descended all the way to the ground floor again.

"What was that about?"

"Nothing," he said, not meeting her gaze. "Just a security precaution."

"You were saying, about Parker—" she began, then stopped when they stepped into the lab. Which was utterly empty—not another person in sight. She turned back just as he swiped his card key over the panel near the door—and she heard the locks click into place. Her heart pounded, but amazingly, the rest of her was calm. "What's going on here?"

And then the words he'd said in the elevator clicked also, and she gasped and stepped back. Nick raised his gaze, so weary and heavy with pain that Emma felt it washing through her.

"What tipped you off?"

She swallowed as the tears came, filling her, spilling over, running hot down her cheeks. "You said Parker and I didn't hire Ramie *to steal Mollie's laptop.* Everyone else still thinks Dan and Mollie were—" She choked and watched the tears pooling in Nick's own eyes. "—that they—oh, God—were killed on purpose." She covered her mouth. "*Why?* Just tell me—*why?*"

"Ah. I've asked myself the same thing. I could tell you that none of this was supposed to happen—that it all began with a simple mistake. But that won't bring Dan and Mollie back."

He moved to one of the long work counters and touched a beaker. "The data—everything—it was all my fault. I don't think Dan ever knew there was a problem. I was helping him with it, and I made one miscalculation. I didn't realize— I was so excited. None of my own research ever panned out like that. I went to Dan, told him the vaccine was safe, and he told Parker. By the time I realized my mistake, Dan had already taken out the second mortgage and bought the stock. Mollie knew someone at Prospect-Gage and had heard about the takeover."

Emma's stomach hurt, and she couldn't force herself to speak. He didn't seem to notice.

"The original mistake happened soon after Janice died. It felt so good—for that short while—to think I'd done something *right*, something to benefit so many people, and save the Sion. Even when I knew I was wrong, I told myself the risk was minimal. The vaccine's been used for decades, long before autism went on the rise."

He stared at the counter, but it was clear he didn't see it. Emma looked around for anything she could use as a weapon, but other than glass beakers, nothing seemed viable.

"Meanwhile, PharmFam approached Parker, which I didn't know at the time. And then Oscar found out about everything. I would have just paid him—really. But he was escalating. In the Marines, we were taught to assess the situation, determine the level of threat before acting. Oscar started out blackmailing Parker, I think, just because he could. He thought he was smarter than everyone else— especially bureaucrats like Parker. When you told him about the data, he saw a way to take the game to the next level, by blackmailing me, and Parker for longer."

He raised haunted eyes. "Even later, when he found out about Ramie, I still thought he'd get bored and stop. But when he threatened you—and then attacked Justin—I couldn't let him continue. I stole Bethanne's gun on Saturday—I'm not even sure why I did it then. Instinct, I guess. But when I woke up at Karen's on Sunday, I knew what I had to do. She wasn't feeling well, so it was easy to slip out while she dozed, then come back before she missed me. I really did make her breakfast, you know," he said, sounding almost proud of the fact.

He fell silent, and Emma became aware of distant sirens approaching. Inside the lab, a phone began to ring. Nick ignored it and walked toward his research station. Removing a box from his pocket, he took something from it, then laid it on the counter and reached for a drawer.

"If Vin tests those," he said, indicating the box, which Emma saw contained bullets, "he'll find they're a match for the one that killed Oscar."

He withdrew a small handgun from the drawer and Emma's stomach dropped.

"I'm sorry I made it look like you killed Oscar. I only meant to frame Parker. He touched the gun last. I didn't know your prints would be mixed in."

He turned away and she heard him load the gun. She couldn't see his face, and that terrified her even more. Her pulse rocketed, and she looked frantically around the lab—there had to be something she could use to stop him. The phone started ringing again—if only she could get to it. But what good would it do?

"Nick—I understand. You made a mistake, and it led to more mistakes. But I can help you—I won't abandon you. Just *please*—set that gun down and let me take you out of here."

"I'm sorry, Emma."

The sirens were so loud, they had to be in the courtyard below. The police—somehow they'd found out, were here to stop him.

"Nick," she said urgently. "Why did you bring me here?"

He faced her, his expression more bleak than anything she'd ever seen. "I wanted you to know. And—I didn't want to die alone."

Emma gasped. "No! Nick, please—don't do this. I—"

"Emma. I've made my decision. It's the only way. You *can* help me, but not in the way you thought. You can help by leading me home." He turned the gun over in his hand. "Once you've killed someone—destroyed a human life—and not in combat—" He raised his gaze again, so dark with pain. "—you can never be the same. Please, Emma—take me home."

He raised the gun. And then he aimed it…

****

"I'm on my way!" Vin slammed the phone down. "She's

at the Sion. Nick gave everyone in his and Dan's labs the day off, then took her inside to confess."

"Oh, thank God," Bethanne began, then saw his face and went gray as death. "What...?"

"He called the cops first—told them to send an ambulance. And to call the coroner."

She moaned, but Vin couldn't stay to deal with her. He was halfway to the door when he realized he hadn't driven. "Car!" he barked, and Bethanne automatically tossed her keys to him.

"Please—let me come with you."

"Too dangerous."

LJ said, "I got her—you go!"

Vin hurled himself down the steps and into Bethanne's sedan, shoving it in drive and up the street. Barton had said the uniforms were on the way—Emma *would* be safe. She had to be. Surely Nick didn't intend to hurt her. The whole reason he'd killed Oscar was to keep Emma from being harmed—why would he kill her now?

Unless, like Dante's Beatrice, Nick wanted Emma to be his guide to the afterlife.

Vin's pulse roared and his foot couldn't step on the gas hard enough. Driving up Terwilliger, he saw the lights, heard the sirens. By the time he rolled to a stop near the Sion, he couldn't tell if he was even in the parking lot, with so many cop cars crowded around.

He flashed his badge, thundering past anyone in his way. Nick had used his executive key to prevent the elevators from landing on the top two floors, so Vin followed the uniforms as they ran for the stairs. His knee was in agony— it would give out—and then he was at the top, shoving into the lobby and he heard it—the *crack!* of a gunshot, echoing inside the lab.

He heard a very female scream—*thank God*—and then it was chaos, the lab doors broken in, Emma—there she was—he ran for her, grabbed her, pulled her away so she'd have to stop staring, horrified, at the bloody mess that was all that remained of Nick Forte, sprawled on his back, gun in his mouth, brains and blood and bones splattered all over the lab.

"It's okay," Vin said over and over as Emma sobbed, safe in his arms. "It's okay…"

****

Early on Sunday, a knock came at Vin's door and he rushed to grab it. Maybe it was Emma—he hadn't seen or spoken with her since she'd gone downtown on Wednesday to give her statement after Nick's death. He'd called Bethanne from the scene, and she'd gone to meet her, but in the hustle, he couldn't tell if Emma was still mad about Izzy or not. When her sobs over Nick eased, she'd seemed to realize where she was, and who she was with. She'd pulled gently back, her habitual guards back up, and murmured an awkward "Thanks," before the uniforms whisked her away. He couldn't follow her. He'd made such a mess of things, he'd be lucky if she ever forgave him.

He had managed to convince Barton he wasn't a total dumbass, however. That plus all the groveling he did on Thursday had netted him permission to come back to work, but not until Monday. Consequently, he'd been stewing in the house, alone, since Azi'd moved into the group home already, and was ecstatically enjoying his independence.

As for Emma, he knew he should face her, but hadn't got up the nerve yet.

If this was her…

He yanked the door open, and found LJ outside, grinning, and holding a large envelope.

"Yo. Special delivery."

"Okay."

Vin gestured LJ in, then took the envelope and ripped it open. The top sheet was a letter from the divorce lawyers in Chicago. Izzy had signed the original papers and turned them in under the wire; he really was free and clear. Underneath were copies of the documents, with a note from Izzy herself. It read: *Sorry, Vinny. Daddy and I made up. Now you and Emma should, too. No hard feelings!* Typical Izzy. Flit from one thing to the next, and expect everyone else to get with the program. Vin smiled. She'd be okay.

LJ said, "Thought you'd like to know."

"Yeah. Thanks." LJ didn't move, and Vin said, "Something else you want to say?"

"Now you mention it. But I gotta have a smoke. Mind if we step outside?" On the porch, he lit up, then leaned his big frame against the railing. "Damn that's good. Bethanne won't let me smoke in the house."

"Bethanne…?"

LJ grinned. "I been staying there a couple days, since Izzy went back to Chicago."

"No accounting for taste," Vin muttered, and LJ laughed.

"You got that right. I can't figure why the hell women dig you so much."

"Apparently, they don't."

"Fuck you, man. Quit your whining and go to her."

"I would, but—"

"Shithead."

Vin opened his mouth, then shut it. LJ was right.

"I should have trusted her—should've trusted *myself*. Barton was right. She'll make me crawl for a year over this. It's nothing less than I deserve. But Emma…Dan screwed her over, and then I fucked everything up worse. It won't be easy to regain her trust."

"Who said anything about easy? But she'll come around. She still loves you. 'Sides, if you don't make your move, Bethanne's gonna drive me crazy. No nookie with Emma in the house, but Emma won't leave, and Bethanne won't do it anywhere else."

"Cripes. Did you have to put *that* image in my head?"

"If I'm suffering, you gotta, too."

"Hey! I got Barton to reduce the charges for setting off explosives in a neighborhood to a misdemeanor fine. Aren't we even yet?"

LJ stubbed out his smoke, then reached for another one. "Almost. I just did Emma a big favor. I don't think she can ever pay me back. But you can—by making nice with her, so I can make *really* nice with her mother."

Vin narrowed his eyes. "What did you do? And why?"

"I wanna take Bethanne on a cruise, but she won't leave while Emma's still so upset."

An image of LJ, extremely large and white in his swim trunks and Mafia-issue shades, sunbathing next to Bethanne—almost twice his age, but only half his size—made Vin choke. "Okay. What about Rico?"

"We're cool. Izzy told him I took care of her, and he don't need me anymore anyway—white collar's not really his thing, and I can't stomach anything else." Vin choked another laugh into a cough—anyone *looking* at LJ would never believe that violence made him queasy. "You're good, too. Rico sends his thanks for not letting Izzy fuck her life up more by staying married to you."

"Uh, thanks…?"

"Don't mention it. So anyway, think maybe after the cruise, I'll move in with Bethanne. Permanently. Charley's thinking about going back to LA, and Chicago's not my thing anymore."

"Great," Vin said, wondering where this was going. "It'll be like old times. Except not. But what the hell."

LJ laughed. "Yeah. Speaking of old times—the favor. In about ten minutes Emma's finances are gonna be a little more, ah, manageable."

"How so?"

"Did I mention I'm going straight? But twenty minutes ago, I was still the same old badass crook. I may have done a little…web surfing."

Vin groaned. "I don't want to hear this, do I?"

"Probably not. But just to warn you—next time Emma checks her bank, she may find both her mortgages have been paid off. Oh, and that whole insider trading thing Dan did? Seems it was just a, ah, computer error. No wrongdoing, no nothing."

"Are you telling me one and a half million bucks just vanished into cyberspace?"

"That's the funny thing about web surfing. While all these techno-glitches were happening, someone may have made two anonymous donations, roughly seven hundred grand each, to the Autism Society of America, and the National Down Syndrome Society."

Vin swallowed. "Cripes. Thanks."

"No problem. What're friends for?" LJ pushed off the railing and down the steps. "But you owe me now. Big time. Go get your woman, or I ain't gonna be responsible for my actions."

He disappeared down the walk, and Vin stood, staring at nothing.

LJ was right. His fear was *still* holding him back, making him avoid Emma—he had to go to her, no matter how stupid he looked. *Not* facing her would be the dumbest of all.

He headed down the steps, toward the park. Emma *had* to talk with him—now or never.

****

The park was cold and damp, and Emma considered turning back for a sweater.

No. No more delays. She had to face Vin. Bethanne might be a no-good busybody interfering mother, but she'd helped Emma realize one important thing: she *had* to tell Vin she wanted to be with him. If Bethanne hadn't understood how deep Emma's feelings ran, it was her own fault, for not making them clear. Bethanne really did want her to be happy, and Vin was it. The One. The realization made her want to shout from the rooftops, to tell the world to go stuff itself—she'd found her soul mate. Now she just had to tell *him* about it.

No more slipping quietly away, no more appeasing everyone else to keep an even keel.

She had to make a wave—and not a small one. So what

if he'd lied about Izzy? So what if he hadn't trusted her? She would *not* let him shut her out. Dan might have, but not Vin.

"Jeez," a deep male voice said, startling her out of her thoughts. She looked up to find Vin himself, scowling at her from the path. "Didn't anyone ever tell you the park isn't safe at this hour?"

Her stomach lurched, and she opened her mouth. Then he reached for her and she fell into him, his arms cradling her close. She hugged him back, rubbing her face against his chest, only half-aware of the tears rolling down her cheeks.

"Ah, Christ," he muttered, squeezing tighter. They were silent a minute, and then he said into her hair, "You know I was a total ass, right?"

A small laugh hiccupped out of her and she nodded.

He blew out a breath. "I wanted to trust you—I swear I did. But I didn't trust myself to be objective. I can't stand admitting this but—Barton was right. I was so hung up on the past, I lost perspective on the present. I fucked it up with you, didn't pay attention when Azi needed me, and was generally pretty stupid."

Emma tightened her arms. "I know you're not Dan. I'm sorry I had such a hard time letting you in. I was so afraid you'd dismiss me, I just wanted to run and hide. Then when I tried to fight back…"

"It didn't get you anywhere. I'm sorry, Emma. I promise I'll never put my reputation before you, ever again. Between me and Bethanne, it's a wonder you wouldn't rather spend the rest of your life with a tub of ice cream and a spoon."

She sighed as he caressed her back. "I'm sorry if I was out of line with Azi."

"Never. The more people Az has in his corner, the better. That goes double for me." He pulled back, looking at her searchingly. "Emma—Az moved out, and now I've got an awfully large house, with just me in it. I thought, you know, maybe you and the kids would like a change. Maybe where you are now has too many sad memories, and you'd like to make a fresh start." He cleared his throat. "With me.

I can help out with the kids and stuff, when you start school next week. That is, if—"

"Yes. We'd love to. Bethanne and LJ can have the house, the yard, all of it. I don't want any of it. I just want *you*."

"Thank God."

His mouth was warm and soft, his arms strong and tight around her.

"I love you," he whispered, and kissed her as she murmured, "Me, too…"

To make a donation or learn more about the
National Down Syndrome Society or the Autism Society
of America, see the following links:

https://www.ndss.org/

https://www.autism-society.org/

A Quick Favor Please?

Before you go, can I ask you for a quick favor? Would you please leave this book an honest review online? Reviews are very important for authors, as they help us sell more books. This will in turn enable me to write more books for you.

Please take a quick minute to go to one or two online retailers/review sites and leave this book a review. I promise it doesn't take very long, but it can help this book reach more readers just like you. This Book Riot article breaks it down into six easy steps, if you need tips: http://bit.ly/BookReviewTips.

Thank you for reading, and thank you so much for being part of this amazing journey!

~ Kerry

A word about the author...

Kerry Blaisdell is the award-winning author of The Dead Series, including *Debriefing the Dead*—2019 Royal Palm Literary Award for Best Published Fantasy, RONE Award for Best Long Paranormal, HOLT Medallion Literary Award for Best Paranormal & Best First Book, and Romance Writers of America RITA® Award finalist—and its sequel, *Waking the Dead*, a current RONE nominee, which InD'tale Magazine recommends for "fans of television shows like 'Constantine' or 'Supernatural.'" She also writes Romantic Suspense and Historical Mystery.

Kerry has a Bachelor of Arts from UC Berkeley in Comparative Literature (French/Medieval English), and a Master's in Teaching English and Advanced Mathematics from the University of Portland. She lives in the gorgeous Pacific Northwest with her family, assorted cats and dogs, and more hot pepper plants than anyone could reasonably consume.

Connect with Kerry online at https://kerryblaisdell.com, or subscribe to her Very Occasional Mailing List at http://bit.ly/KerrysVOML, to get access to free reads, giveaways, and other fun stuff.

Turn the page for a sneak peek at Kerry's multi-award-winning Urban Fantasy novel, Debriefing the Dead (Book One of The Dead Series)...

Debriefing the Dead
(Book One of The Dead Series)

©2018 by Kerry Blaisdell

Used by permission from The Wild Rose Press

Chapter One

"Be sober, be vigilant; because your adversary the devil, as a roaring lion, walketh about, seeking whom he may devour."
~The Bible, 1 Peter 5:8

I smelled Death on the two men who walked into my shop that day. I should have listened to my nose.

Of course, death is an everyday part of my life, which is probably why I ignored it. I'm a dealer in rare artifacts, particularly those that haven't been acquired through, um, *normal* channels. Okay, I'm a fence, and before that, I robbed graves. But only those already being robbed, by "professional" archaeologists. And frankly, I know as much or more as they do about the care and preservation of ancient relics.

In any case, my shop, *Hyacinth Finch's Boutique des Antiquités,* now stocks items that are either stolen, or are being stolen back, by one or another of my usual clients, members of the Marseille elite who enjoy stabbing each other in the back, art-collection-wise. They pay well, and leave me to live my life the rest of the time, so I guess you'd call it a symbiotic relationship.

But these guys weren't from my client base. Until they arrived unannounced in my office above the shop, and sat, uninvited, in the chairs in front of my desk, I'd never seen them before. Which made their interest in this *exact* batch of goods even more suspect.

"Who are you again?" I asked, more to buy time than anything else.

The one on the left smiled genially. He was larger than his companion, not exactly fat, but taller and more…spread out, for lack of a better description. His dark blue eyes were rimmed with thick lashes, and his hair was oiled into a slick black shell. His tanned skin cracked and peeled in places, like he'd had one too many sunburns, and he had a heavy French accent, but as it was late August, and we were in southern France, neither was exactly remarkable. I myself spoke fluent French, but he'd begun in Franglish, and I hadn't corrected him.

"Mademoiselle Finch." He leaned forward, the flimsy wooden chair legs groaning and spreading under his bulk, making it look as if he had six legs instead of the usual two. "*Je vous assure,* nothing would please me more than to provide our *bona fides*. But the time, it is lacking." He glanced at his companion, equally dark and oily, but not as talkative. Oily Two smiled, close-mouthed, and gave a Gallic shrug. *We're all pals here, right?*

Yeah, right.

"Look," I said, suppressing a shiver of unease, despite the heat, "even if I wanted to, I'm not sure I could find this particular lot." I pretended to check a leather-covered log book I had open on my desk. "Where did you say it originated?"

"Turkey." Oily One's smile said he knew I knew that, his yellowed teeth big and sharp behind his dry, cracked lips.

I ran a finger down a column on the page. Look at me—organized, professional, absolutely-*not*-lying business woman extraordinaire. "Nope. Nothing's come in from

Turkey."

His gaze flicked to the log, then around my office. Books filled wood-and-glass cases along the walls, and papers crowded the floor. The window stood open behind me, letting in the Mediterranean breeze and the slanted late afternoon sunlight. Also, *un fourmilion*—an antlion—a long, thin-bodied insect with lacy wings, that my seven-year-old nephew, Geordi, would have been fascinated by. He loves bugs. Me, not so much, but I'm a vegetarian, and a live-and-let-live kinda gal, and this guy wasn't doing anything besides buzzing lazily around my office, looking for ants to trap. At least, that's what Geordi says they do. I hate ants, so if there were any to chow on, more power to him.

Oily One and Two didn't seem bothered by him, but I rather wished they were, so we could hurry this along. The bell on the downstairs door had only rung once since lunch—when these two entered—and it seemed like a good day to close early. One of the perks of being an independent "art dealer" such as myself. The downside is, I can't afford to alienate potential clients. I have my regulars, but business ebbs and flows, and extra cash is always handy. Especially now.

I forced a smile of my own. "I want to help you—I do. But I have no idea where to find…something like this." Technically, this was true. I'm a big believer in technicalities.

Oily One leaned in closer, waistband straining, hands on his knees, palms up. Open. Friendly. I didn't buy it, but apparently, the antlion did. It landed on his shoulder, black body silhouetted crisply as it crawled unnoticed over the expensive white of his suit.

He smiled again. "Surely a businesswoman of your reputation…?"

"*Messieurs.* I'm not sure what you've heard"—*or from whom*— "but I am merely a dealer. I buy. I sell. I don't find."

"*Vous me surprenez.* It is said you are *très accomplie* at these things."

I tilted back in my chair. "You flatter me. I've had good

luck. And good clients. I can only sell what they bring in. Speaking of which—who did you say referred you?"

Touché. Point à moi. But he wasn't giving up. "A shipment from Colossae, in southwestern Turkey—*près de la rivière* Lycus. A region in which you specialize, *non?* Perhaps you have contacts. You will make some calls. We will, of course, reward your efforts."

He took out a business card and wrote on the back, the movement causing the antlion to take flight, hovering between him and his companion. Oily Two waved it away, then caught my eye and lifted a hand, as though asking if he should squash it. His full-lipped, sharp-toothed grin was creepier even than his friend's, and I shook my head hastily, noting that the insect—no dummy—was already out of reach.

His friend passed the card to me, and though our fingers never touched, I suddenly felt…*heat*…burning off him in sharp waves. I jerked my hand away, taking the card with me. It was as cool as paper usually is, and I gave a mental shake and glanced at the number he'd written, then had to hide my shock. This would be enough for me to take a year off—or pay for Geordi and his mother, my sister Lily, to get *really* far away from her ex. Some place where he could *never* hurt them, ever again.

I flipped the card over. *Les Rousseaux* was printed on it in plain type, with a cell number below. When I looked up, he smiled. Again.

"Claude Rousseau." He indicated Oily Two, who gave a slight bow. *"Mon frère,* Jacques. We are most pleased to make your acquaintance. If you hear of anything, you will call. Yes?"

"Yes," I said, the interview's end finally in sight. "Of course."

They rose to go, their tread surprisingly silent on the stairs, given their combined bulk. I waited until I heard the bell on the front door tinkle one last time. Then I ran down and shot the bolt. I flipped the sign in the window to read

Fermé, then pulled down the shade. Next, I went to the back door and locked it as well. Only when I was alone in the dark store, so familiar and comforting in its clutter, did I take a deep breath and blow it out.

The whole experience bothered me on a number of levels, not the least of which was the timing. You see, I wasn't exactly upfront with the Rousseaux. Not only would I be able to locate the lot they wanted, I already *had* it—in storage, where it'd been for several months. The thing is, only two people should have known its origins.

One of them was me.

And the other was dead.

****

An hour later, I'd left the shop, wandering home via my usual circuitous route, past various markets, *plein air* or otherwise, where I picked up the parts of my dinner. One of the reasons I prefer Europe to the States is the whole notion of buying your food the day you cook it. I'm not exactly a health nut, but I am a vegetarian, and a sucker for anything fresh.

Walking and shopping also gives me a chance to process my day. And today, I had a lot to process. It occurred to me the Rousseaux could be cops. La Boutique has been investigated a time or two, but I always come away clean. The thing is, if they were *les flics*, asking after *this* lot, then they already knew it was stolen. But it came from Colossae, a site which has never officially been excavated, so how could anyone know part of it was gone?

I'd "inherited" the catch from my business partner, Vadim, after he died in a boating accident. A lump rose in my throat, hot and sharp, and I swallowed it back down. Though we weren't "together" romantically, Vadim was more than a partner, he was my friend. His death was so unexpected; even half a year later, I still couldn't believe he was gone. I'd never even opened the crates he left me, just locked them up to deal with later. But…was my reluctance now because of my grief? Or were my instincts right and something was off?

Unlocking the iron gate leading to my building's interior stairwell, I saw my neighbor on his way down. Jason Jones is a little younger than me and a lot taller—at least a foot, and I'm five-five. He tends bar at one of the gay cabarets in Marseille, so he's frequently on his way out when I'm coming home. In theory, he moved here to pursue a theater career, but in practice, I think he likes the bar better. Rehearsals would mess too much with his "party all night, sleep all day" schedule.

"Hyacinth!"

He broke into a grin and finished coming down the steps, then gave a low theatrical bow and pretended to kiss my hand. He wore a black dress shirt, gray slacks, Italian leather shoes, and ridiculously large sunglasses that made him look like a very large insect hovering over my wrist. He can rock a pair of jeans, too, but today he was the perfect image of the playboy bartender, a look he cultivates with great care and uses to great advantage—and he has the tips to prove it. He's not actually gay, but he doesn't advertise the fact. However, he's never once tried to hit on me, which is not as insulting as you might think. I don't have the best track record with relationships, and with Lily and everything else, I had no desire to start one now.

As soon as I had the thought, I realized he was lingering over my wrist, turning it up and inhaling deeply. The heat of his breath tickled my skin, his fingers caressed my palm, and my knees wobbled. Apparently, I'm not immune to his charms after all.

He let go and straightened, examining my face. I couldn't read his expression behind the shiny glasses, but he must have seen something in mine that made him ask, "What's up? Something wrong at the shop?"

"It's nothing. Not really. Some new clients came in and wanted to chat. Actually…they might be a good fit for Vadim's last shipment."

He flipped the sunglasses up, blue eyes wide. He's never

asked how I acquire my goods, and I've never asked what happens when he disappears for days with some girl he's met on the metro. He's entitled to his secrets, too. But he moved in right after Lily left her creepazoid husband and just before Vadim died. I couldn't burden Lily with my grief, and our parents died more than twenty years ago. If we have other family, I've never met them. I don't trust easily, but it turns out Jason has a strong, relatively safe shoulder to cry on, for which I'm eternally grateful.

That doesn't stop him from being opinionated about what I should do with my life. He gave a low whistle. "Are you going to sell it to them?"

"I…don't know." I moved up the steps, so I could look him in the eye without needing a chiropractor.

"You *have* to sell it. It's what Vadim wanted—why he *brought* it to you, for God's sake."

"I know. You're right. It's just—do I have to sell it to *these* guys?"

He planted his hands on his hips, glaring. "Hyacinth. It. Is. Time. *Let go.*"

His face was close, his breath warm, and despite it all, I found his earnestness vaguely attractive. He filled the narrow stairwell with his long, lean body, and I resisted the urge to back up another step.

"Okay, fine. I'll call them." He stood, unmoving, and I sighed. "What? I said I'd do it. Is something wrong?"

His gaze dropped to my sandals, then moved slowly up my legs, lingering on my hips, and from there over my chest and the sleeveless blouse that was all I could tolerate in this heat. By the time his gaze travelled up my throat to linger again at my mouth, before finally meeting my eyes, I had goose bumps in several inappropriate places, and was hoping the dark stairwell hid my blush.

His eyes flashed dark for a moment—almost black— then he gave an odd little shake of his head and took a step back himself. He dropped the sunglasses over his eyes, and when he spoke, his tone was light and friendly as ever. "Just checking it's really you. You never agree with me in under five minutes."

Before I could gather my wits for a decent retort, he gave a mock salute, then buzzed the gate open and vanished up the block. I blew out a breath and finished the climb to my third-floor apartment—second, if you count European style.

Jason's only a little younger than me—late twenties or so—but I think he gets that whole *joie de vivre* thing better than I do. He's a hard worker, don't get me wrong. But he also plays hard, and flits from one activity to the next with an easy metamorphosis I admire. I didn't know what to make of his sudden inexplicable interest, but he had helped me feel better. And he was right. Holding onto Vadim's last catch wouldn't bring him back. It would only hold *me* back.

The apartment stairs lead to a short breezeway, open on both ends. There's one apartment on each corner, and mine's the first on the left. I unlocked the door and stepped in. My place is tiny, but less cluttered than the shop. In a complete reversal of the stereotypical antiques dealer, I am not a pack rat. Give me open space and tidy end tables and I'm a happy camper. Wood floors, throw rugs, small table and chairs in the dining nook. A kitchen that used to be a closet, as near as I can tell—only one person can stand in it at a time, and if the oven's open, nobody can. One window in the main room, another in the bedroom, and finally, a bathroom that's bigger than the kitchen, but not by much.

I have pretty basic needs, possibly due to growing up in foster care. But that's a whole other story, and I'm well-adjusted enough to know I can't blame all my idiosyncrasies on my parentless childhood. Some, but not all. The bottom line is I don't need a lot of junk to be happy. I do need a certain amount of cash, though. Lily's custody battle over Geordi wasn't only with her ex, Nick. It was with his entire family. And I do mean Family—as in organized, with a capital F. The Sicilian Mob. Which Lily swears she didn't know until after they were married, though how either of us were naïve enough to believe Nick was just "a" Dioguardi, and not one of *the* Dioguardis, is beyond me.

Worse, since Geordi's the first son of an *only* son, Nick's family weren't about to let him go, even if Lily found the one judge in Paris brave enough to side with her. It took serious guts for her to leave, and if I had any say in it, neither she nor Geordi would ever go back.

So, if the Oily Brothers' money could facilitate that, who was I to quibble?

****

The next day was Sunday, and not only is my shop closed, most of the other shops in my area are as well. I figured the Rousseaux could wait another day before I told them of the shipment. For one thing, it would lend credibility to my claim of needing to find it first. For another, as noted, I wasn't exactly anxious to call them.

But first thing Monday, I dragged myself out of bed, showered, and drove to the warehouse I rent at the docks, near the Bassin d'Arenc. I use it to store unsorted catches or big items I can't cram into the shop. Or, let's be honest, things I don't want out in plain sight.

Ordinarily I'd walk—it's only twenty blocks—but I had to move Vadim's stuff to the shop before calling the Rousseaux. Unfortunately, my car's a Peapod prototype, and about the size of a mini-Mini Cooper. It was a gift from a grateful client, and tops out at forty-five kilometers per hour, so no *autobahn* for me. But it's electric, costs around two cents a kilometer for gas, and is perfect for getting around town.

Not so perfect for hauling stuff.

I could've asked Claude and Jacques to meet me with a truck. Since the catch was currently in three large shipping crates, this would save tons of time and effort. But though I'd decided to unload the stuff, showing these guys where I kept my stock—or what I still had on hand—might not be the smartest idea. Besides, I was curious about the contents. Vadim had never told me what he'd found, and in our line of work, it could be anything from thousands-of-years-old "junk" to priceless relics. I was guessing at least some of the latter, or why would the Rousseaux care?

In order to find out, I'd have to move everything to smaller boxes, cart it to the store, go back to the warehouse, rinse, repeat. Part of me wondered if I should just hand it over as-is and be done.

I suppressed yet another twinge at the memory of yesterday's interview. Especially Jacques, sitting still and spider-like across from me. I had a feeling he didn't miss much and wondered what I might have unconsciously revealed while Claude distracted me.

I pulled into a parking space near my unit, and my cell rang, the cheery notes of Beethoven's *Für Élise* telling me Lily was calling for our weekly chat. For a second, I thought about answering. Lily might be Geordi's mother, but I have to say, he's pretty much the light of my life. Certainly, the best male relationship I've had, even counting Jason and Vadim. Who wouldn't love a guy who brings you dead bugs he's found in someone *else's* yard, then offers to split the last éclair because you're his "favoritest *tata* ever"? He's a smart kid, too. I'm his *only* auntie, and the flattery still works.

I sent the call to voicemail. It almost killed me, but it'd be hard enough opening the crates, knowing how excited Vadim was when he landed this catch. You can't get much fresher than an unexcavated site. If I spent even a half hour catching up with Lily and Geordi, I'd chicken out. And I had to know what was in those crates, or I'd never be able to let them, or Vadim, go.

I screwed up my courage, got out of the car, and unlocked the unit's roll door. Yep. Three large crates.

Very large.

I went back to the Peapod, opened the hatch, and extracted the paltry pile of produce boxes I'd scrounged from my favorite markets. I'd have to empty them again at the store for subsequent trips, or else go beg more boxes. This was ridiculous. But necessary.

Must let go. Must move on.

****

As is so often the case, once I got going, it wasn't so bad. Opening the first crate was tough, and I won't say I didn't cry at all. Vadim was a good partner, and a better friend. At least he'd died doing what he loved—sailing the Mediterranean, with a drink in his hand and two beautiful women at his side. He was a devout atheist, but if there's any kind of afterlife, I'd like to think he's still sailing and drinking, and looking for the next big catch.

I found a roll of paper towels on a shelf and blew my nose, then metaphorically rolled up my non-existent sleeves and dug in.

The more valuable items were wrapped in acid-free paper and sealed in airtight containers, which I didn't bother to open, because Vadim had helpfully labeled them. His clear, bold printing noted statuary and relics, both Pagan and Christian, from the ancient Phrygian city of Colossae, near what is now Denizli, in southwestern Turkey. The general period was the first century, so any Christian items were very early. While this fascinated me intellectually, and I did have some experience with artifacts from Turkey, it was mainly because Vadim brought them to me. My own interests lie more in the Egyptians, one of the reasons we'd complemented each other professionally. But it meant I had little personal experience with anything of this kind.

It took several trips to move the best items, and a few more for the midlevel stuff, plus getting more boxes. By the time I got to the third crate, the sun was well past its zenith, but I'd reached the dregs. Items down here were either unwrapped, loose in the packing straw, or else carelessly covered with rough cloth to prevent scratching.

This crate wasn't as full as the others, and it looked like I was on my final trip. Thank God. I'd had a quick lunch—veggies, hummus, cheese, and bread—but otherwise worked straight through. Lily'd called twice more, but I didn't pick up. I'd call her back over dinner, when we'd have time to chat, and I could tell her of my sudden windfall.

I plopped my last empty box on the warehouse floor, then hung over the side of the crate to excavate the bottom. I found a few more canvas bundles and pulled them out, setting them in the box, then went back once more.

I thought I'd gotten everything, until my fingers brushed against something hard, wrapped in cloth, and oddly warm to the touch. I grabbed it and heaved myself out of the crate, then examined the bundle. It felt like a rock, heavy and solid. Most of the items in this crate were broken pottery shards, from vases and the like. Hard, maybe, but not heavy. Careful not to touch the item's surface, in case it was valuable after all, I turned it over and shook the covering loose.

Sure enough, it was a rock. Plain, gray, ordinary. About half the size of an American football, shaped like an irregular pyramid, with jagged edges and flat-but-rough surfaces. The only unusual thing about it was its warmth. Like Claude Rousseau. Which is maybe why, against my better judgment, I reached out and touched the very tip of the rock's pyramid.

And then it *shrieked* at me, the agony of centuries piercing my ears till I thought my skull would burst, electric shocks searing through my fingers, hand, arm, ripping through my whole body, gripping my lungs and squeezing until I couldn't breathe. I flung the rock away, covering my ears and dropping to the floor, shaking, gasping for air, while still it screamed, on and on and on and on, until I lay huddled on the concrete, red fire burning in my head, blackness filling my soul.

Then everything went silent.

~ * ~ * ~ * ~ * ~

Read the next four chapters, also for free — sign up for
Kerry's Very Occasional Mailing List
on her website at http://kerryblaisdell.com